THE Secret ORPHAN

Glynis Peters lives in the seaside town of Dovercourt. In 2014, she was shortlisted for the Festival of Romance New Talent Award.

When Glynis is not writing, she enjoys making greetings cards, Cross Stitch, fishing and looking after her gorgeous grandchildren.

The Secret Orphan is her first WW2 historical novel.

GLYNIS PETERS

THE
Secret
ORPHAN

HarperCollins*Publishers*

HarperCollins*Publishers* Ltd.
1 London Bridge Street
London SE1 9GF

www.harpercollins.co.uk

Published by HarperCollins*Publishers* 2018

A catalogue record for this book is
available from the British Library

ISBN: 978-0-00-830883-4 (TPB)
ISBN: 978-0-00-830095-1 (B)

Typeset in Sabon LT Std by Palimpsest Book Production Ltd,
Falkirk, Stirlingshire

Printed and bound in Great Britain by
CPI Group (UK) Ltd, Croydon CR0 4YY

For my grandchildren
Finley – my handsome Canadian Bear Cub
Seren, and Palin, my beautiful English roses

CHAPTER 1

14th November 1940: Coventry, England.

Boom.

Boom.

The ground vibrated with each explosion. Unfamiliar sounds surrounded Rose Sherbourne as her body received blow after blow from displaced items of furniture. She jumped when shattering glass hit falling bricks, and everything around her crashed under their weight. *Boom.*

Another explosion, followed by the sound of metal hitting metal, echoed out around Rose's ears and her breath came thick and fast. Through the opening of what was once the front room, a sudden blast of hot air blew both her and her mother off their feet. Rose's body fell against something hard and a searing pain shot through her back. For a few seconds she could not see, and she blinked, only to feel fine dust fall on her cheeks and into her eyes yet again. She wiped it away with the back of her hand and prepared herself to scrabble upright.

Boom.

A wall fell around her and, unable to move both with fear and because something was pinning down her right leg, Rose took a moment to catch her breath. Above her an intense whistling sound screamed from the sky, followed by an eerie whooshing sound. A continuous whistle followed. Rose held her breath. The sound meant only one thing; another bomb would explode within seconds and all she could do was pray it was away from her home.

Boom.

The rest of the wall fell, and she watched helplessly as brick after brick fell to the floor and her mother's body bounced as it was forced into the air for a second time. Rose tried to move but she felt a crushing sensation, a gripping tightness across her chest. She tried to struggle free from the bricks pinning her to the ground. Her chest hurt each time she tried to cough free the dust she'd inhaled when she hit the floor.

A piercing sound screeched above and once again the planes dropped their unwelcome packages.

Thud.

Thud.

One by one.

Two by two.

Rose counted them down.

One by one.

Two by two.

She could hear return fire and engines drifting off into the distance.

The sky fell silent.

The enemy were heading back to wherever they'd come from and a stunned Rose blinked away the dust, trying to make sense of what had happened. Indescribable noises came from above and she raised her eyes skyward and saw a large bright moon taunting her with its white light. There was no roof.

Bombed. The bombs had hit her home.

Rose's ears tingled inside and with each noise she felt a strange vibration along her jawline. With focus upon her face she sensed heat. Her cheeks burned as if it was a hot summer's day.

There'd been a thick frost all day, but it did nothing to suppress the heat from the raging flames nearby. With relief, Rose noted they were not close enough to burn her, but they were fierce enough to make her skin tingle and sweat.

She set her mind to where she lay and which room she was in when the bombs had hit. She needed to work out an escape route before she suffocated. Fear raged through her tiny body, and a sense of loneliness overwhelmed her. She lay back with exhaustion and as she focused upon the light of the moon, questions raced around her mind.

Why hadn't Mummy taken her to the shelter when they heard the siren sound out its warning?

Why, instead of running to safety like they usually did, did Mummy hum Rose's favourite piano piece – Beethoven's *Moonlight Sonata* – and twirl around as if showing off a new dress? She'd acted excited – strange.

With a sob, Rose remembered how her mother had screamed at her to keep playing, and how her voice had growled it out with such a fierce urgency it had frightened Rose. When Rose pleaded for them to go to the shelter her mother cuffed her around the ears.

Rose's body started to tremble until she thought her limbs would never stop no matter how hard she tried to control them. She tried to shut out the screams she could hear around her. High pitched wails of wounded neighbours. The endless shouts and pleas from the street, the screams of other children calling for their parents. Not everyone had made it to the shelters, or if they had, the shelters had failed to protect them. Either way, Rose drew no comfort from knowing she was not alone with her struggle.

She tried to turn her head away from her mother's contorted face. Rose knew she was dead. A tear trickled down the side of Rose's face. She was alone.

Eventually, after what seemed like many lonely hours of trying, she released an arm and began clawing at bricks and rubble. Her cries for help were suffocated by the louder voices and frantic sounds of motor engines and fire-engine bells. Rose recoiled at the pain when she scraped her skin against the shards of shattered glass and cement, but after a while she ignored the pain of bruises and gashes in her skin out of sheer desperation to survive.

When she pulled at the last of the bricks, nothing prepared her for the moment she clambered free into devastation and despair.

The moonlight lit the path for a man as he staggered past calling out a woman's name. He gave Rose a glance, shook his head, and she saw pouring blood running from a gaping hole in his forehead. She turned away and looked across at what she assumed was once the other side of their street but was now nothing more than rubble heaps and bonfires. Seated on an upturned tin bath, she saw a woman screaming into what looked like a ragdoll lying limp in her arms. She pleaded for it to come back to life.

Rose started towards the woman, she wanted to tell her that ragdolls weren't real and that the woman needed to go somewhere safe, but she took no more than four steps when a noise from behind distracted her. Confused and bewildered, Rose turned around and stumbled back to the hollow she'd made for herself. She called through the opening.

'Mummy? Mummy? It's all right, I'm coming. I'll help you.'

She tugged at the obstacles in her way. Furniture and twisted pipes, hissing in the night air hampered her movements. Her hands bled and burned against hot bricks and pipes. She inhaled air which dried her mouth with ash.

And then, despite wanting to save her mother, she sighed with bittersweet relief when a fireman lifted her to safety.

'Come on love, let's get you seen to. You're safe now, little one.' His husky voice sounded tired.

'Put me down. Please, go and get Mummy. She's under the bricks. I need you to save her. Her name is Victoria.' Rose begged and squirmed in his arms.

The fireman pulled her closer to his body, running. He paid little heed to her high-pitched pleas, and after they turned a corner, Rose never saw Stephenson Road, or her mother again.

Rose called out and tried to pound the chest of the fireman but the pain in her hands brought about only more screams.

Even the violet-perfumed, comforting arms of a plump lady from the Women's Voluntary Service did nothing to stop the trembling and terrors which surged through her body. The woman crooned words of comfort as she carried Rose to a makeshift medical tent, and stroked her head before unhooking Rose's gasmask from around her neck. Rose could smell the difference between her and the nurse who dressed her wounds.

The slightest hint of perfume from violets or the smell of disinfectant could still take her back to that night, even now, after seventy-eight years.

23rd November 2018

Wartime nightmares and memories often caught up with Rose during her afternoon naps, and she jerked herself awake from this latest one. She wiped away a thin layer of sweat from her top lip, and despite feeling warm, she shivered and pulled her cardigan around her. Her knees creaked as she rose from her chair and shuffled into the kitchen to make a cup of tea. As she waited for the kettle to boil, she sat and remembered telling the woman her name and calling for Elenor.

'Elenor. I want Elenor.'

'Hush now, little one. We'll find Mummy and your sister. You rest now.'

'Elenor is not my sister. She's on the farm. Mummy's not coming back. I want Elenor.'

She remembered hearing the woman arrange for a cot-bed and blanket to be placed in the corner of the tent whilst she sought a place for Rose to stay until the rest of her family were found. Rose had tried to tell her she had no family and her daddy had died a long time ago, but the woman told her to rest. She'd lain there, clutching the wooden-framed photograph of her and her parents. The fireman who had rescued her brought it to the tent and Rose overheard him telling the nurse it was all that was left of her home and family.

The recollection of the cries of pain that had echoed around the tent, followed by the hushed voices of men taking away those who had not survived the night, never left Rose. One vivid memory was of how she had lain on the bed praying in hope she was not alone in the world. For the first time in her life, at nearly seven years old, Rose understood the pain of war and loss. She understood Elenor's fears when the war was first declared, fears her mother brushed aside as a young woman's hysterics.

A sob caught in Rose's throat. She missed Elenor, the woman who'd given up her dreams to ensure Rose had a secure future.

For the first few years of her life, Rose knew Elenor more as a big sister than as the employer of her parents; or at least the niece of her mother's employer. She'd filled Rose's life with fun and laughter, and even today – 23rd November 2018 – on Rose's eighty-fifth birthday, memories of birthday party fun were only of those which Elenor had arranged. Her parents had never bothered to celebrate her special day.

Food shortages and rationing were never obstacles for Elenor, and as Rose prepared to meet her own beloved children for a birthday feast, she smiled. Their vibrancy and love of life was passed on by her, but she'd only learned to live again thanks to the love of her adoptive parents. '

In her bedroom Rose pulled on her favourite navy dress; a classic style in wool with the zip front for easy wear. She reached into her jewellery box and pulled out the piece which was known as her birthday gem. It was not an expensive piece but Elenor had designed it, and to Rose it was invaluable. It was a Celtic knot with a small maple leaf sitting in the centre and a rosebud resting in the middle of the leaf. There was also a small inscription on the back, C to C to C. This inscription connected her to the places she was born and brought up. Coventry, the town of her birth, Cornwall, her childhood home until she was nearly nine, and Canada, the country which had embraced and nurtured her through her last stages as a child, into her teenage and adult years. Sixty-four years had passed since the day she unwrapped the pewter brooch from her adoptive parents, Elenor and Jackson, for her twenty-first birthday.

Today, Rose cursed her arthritic hands as she fumbled with the clasp, her swollen knuckles screaming old age. Once set in place, she stroked her finger over the fretwork and was transported back to the day she'd received it and of how her parents had created a treasure trail for her to follow, ending in Elenor's battered suitcase.

She glanced with affection at the case which now nestled in the corner of her bedroom; she'd refused to part with it even after Elenor had died. She remembered seeing Elenor arrive in Coventry carrying it and filling it with her papers to take back to Cornwall. It still housed paper memories of lives well lived. It also housed a letter which held the truth about Rose's past life, and why Elenor had chosen to leave Britain and move to Canada. A secret Elenor had kept for so many years. A secret that had saved Rose's life.

CHAPTER 2

'Happy birthday, Mom!'

The doors of Rose's small home burst open and her family filled the silent room with their laughter and birthday greetings. Hugs and kisses were showered upon her in abundance. Floral bouquets were thrust at her from all angles and Rose felt the love flow from each of her children and her three grandchildren who stood before her, and her heart swelled with pride.

'You guys will be the death of me! And you, you are stronger than you look, Abraham. Snowboarding suits you. Come champ, give me another hug, but be gentle this time.'

The room erupted with laughter and shouts of affectionate banter and teasing. She held open her arms for the youngest of her grandchildren. At six-foot tall he overshadowed her by several feet, and his body was that of an athlete. As he gave her the hug she'd demanded and gripped her tight, she had another pang of nostalgia. She thought of the last time her biological father had waved her goodbye. He'd given her no loving hug farewell, no warm memories for her to hold close on a dark night while Hitler's bombs fell around them. She realised with a stab to her heart that he and her mother had left behind only questions and cold memories. She could never recall their love.

Her teenage granddaughters found a corner of the sofa and began clicking away on their mobile phones, capturing the moment to share with whomever would be interested. Rose forgave them their modern ways. Any form of communication was a good one. They always remembered her and brought her joy. Her grandson perched on the window ledge quietly cursing his cousins each time they snapped his way. Rose fussed around her sons and daughter, offering an enthusiastic thank you for the presents heaped upon her. They in turn delighted in her expressions of gratitude as she opened each parcel, folding the paper and ribbon with care. A habit from a lifetime of going without, Rose kept many items to recycle.

'Thank you all. You spoil me. Now, I'm famished and could eat a . . .'

'Carrot, Mother?' Her daughter quipped. And once again laughter filled the room. The joke referred to her small appetite, and the fact she'd overeaten carrots during the war and could no longer face eating them.

The banter and laughter continued throughout the family meal in Rose's favourite restaurant.

'You don't appreciate half of what you have,' Rose said when plates were pushed aside and bellies declared full.

'You've never really told us much about your time during the war, Mom,' her eldest son responded.

Rose sipped a glass of cool water.

'There's too much to tell, and some things are so unpleasant they need to remain buried in the past. I've told you about Coventry, my home, the death of my parents. That's one lifetime of darkness and confusion, lit only by your grandma and Pops Jackson.'

'I wonder what Gran was like when she was young,' her daughter said.

Rose sighed.

'I only remember her from when I was about five, the year before the Second World War started. My memories before that are all a little foggy. I can remember her brothers died and that she returned to the farm. She loved it, but not them. They were cruel to her. She missed her boyfriend, your grandfather – Pops. I think he'd returned to Canada and left Coventry. Her Aunt Maude had died; she'd been my parents' employer, and we stayed in her house until the night it was bombed to the ground. Then I went to live in Cornwall with Elenor, who adopted me and the rest is your history.'

Everyone around the table nodded or muttered their agreement.

'Tell us more, Mom.'

Their corner of the restaurant was empty aside from their long table, and Rose's family sat back in their seats indicating interest in her tale. Rose rarely opened up about her past, but she'd caught their attention. Even her grand-daughters stopped taking selfies and pouting out their smiles to listen.

She looked at their faces, all eyes turned her way, waiting, anticipating what happened next in her story.

'One of Elenor's birthdays, I remember. My birth mother, Victoria, made a cake. She wouldn't have bothered if I hadn't worn her down and Aunt Maude hadn't insisted. My mother never expressed joy over birthdays. In fact, I don't even know when my own parents were born. How about that? Their papers disappeared in the bombings, and the only birthdays I remember are mine and your grandparents'.'

'Ah, a cake for a birthday in the war must have cheered everyone up though, Mom'.

'Oh, it did, and I'd learned to play a tune on the piano,

and your gran sang songs with me. She had a beautiful voice. It was a very low-key party, nothing like today's affairs, but oh the joy we shared. I remember for my birthday I used to love receiving a new pencil, or a notepad . . .'

'Wow, they had notepads back then?' her grandson asked.

'Not the sort you know, son. The paper ones are what Gran's referring to, not electrical.'

'Oh, right. Really? You got excited over a paper book?' he said.

'I did. We had very little back than and expected very little. Each gift was gratefully received and treasured.'

'Hence the old battered suitcase full of wrapping paper and string.' Her daughter laughed, teasing her mother with a longstanding family joke. When Elenor had passed away, they'd found wrapping paper they'd used on gifts to her for years, all neatly folded in a drawer, and Rose wouldn't allow them to throw it away, but instead put it with her private papers in Elenor's case.

Rose grinned at them all. 'You have all the gadgets, and shelves full of treats but how would you cope without them? Or what if you could no longer buy soda and chocolate?'

'I'd die,' her youngest granddaughter declared with a dramatic sigh.

Rose looked at them all and gave a slow nod.

'Many did die over shortages such as soda and chocolate. Merchant ships were sunk and the service men and women died to get any types of food to us, and we still went without.' She said. 'I was luckier than most due to the farm in Cornwall. Thank goodness for the kind heart of Elenor, or I could have been in an orphanage and not had the pleasures of limited foodstuffs and fresh air.'

A silence fell around the table, and Rose let her words linger in their thoughts. She had no intention of lecturing them, but felt it was good to remind them of how much in the way of material goods they were lucky enough to enjoy.

'Anyone for another drink? No? I'll call for the bill then.' Rose's eldest son said, and she watched him walk away from the table. The rest of the family shuffled in their seats.

'Thank you all for a wonderful day. I didn't mean to make you uncomfortable with my war talk.'

'Hey Gran, no. We mustn't forget that stuff. We learn it at school and forget you were part of it all. Besides, we love that you enjoy everything we give you, right down to the pretty ribbon on a gift. It's kinda cool.'

Rose looked to her daughter who shrugged her shoulders. 'I think it was a compliment,' she said, and Rose laughed.

Once everyone had left her apartment with promises to call and visit, Rose kicked off her shoes and placed her brooch into its box. She slipped off her dress and wrapped herself in the new fleece dressing gown, a gift from her daughter. She fetched her reading glasses and read the simple picture by picture instructions on how to use the new coffee machine – a gift from her sons – and after following each one, she eventually poured the contents of the jug into a new mug that shouted out to the world she was the best grandmother. Sitting on her favourite chair, Rose settled down for the evening. She flicked on the TV from the remote control and selected a programme about purchasing a new home. It was an imported programme from the UK. Rose loved to step inside with the presenter and listen to couples deciding whether to purchase or keep looking. Some enjoyed browsing properties abroad, making the bold step to leave all they knew behind.

Rose sipped her decaffeinated coffee and nodded her approval when one couple opted to buy a property on the coast of Cornwall. With a sigh, Rose set down her empty mug, sat back and watched the credits role as the programme came to an end. She leaned back in her chair, yawned and allowed her eyes to droop into a semi-sleep as she recalled the day they'd all left England.

The sounds rattled over her head. The large ship sitting in dock blew its horn and people shouted to one another from ship to shore. Elenor had guided her one way and then another. Jackson had hailed a porter and offloaded their bags. Rose knew they wouldn't lose their luggage because she'd been given the important task of writing their names and new address on the labels Jackson had given her. She'd used her best handwriting and when it came to writing Canada, British Columbia, she took extra care creating neat capital C's.

Her new father had looked over her shoulder and gave it an affectionate tap the afternoon she wrote out each label. His praise still made her smile.

'My word, well done little Rose. Those letters are sure proud and round.'

Her new mother gave her a hug.

'She's a clever little button, and this mummy is extremely proud of her.'

Once the porter had loaded all labelled suitcases onto his trolley and headed towards the ship, her father had lifted her high onto his shoulders. The view was incredible. Everyone looked like ants scurrying about their business.

'I can see for miles! There's hundreds of children. Do you think they will play with me?'

'I'm sure they won't want to play with a little scallywag like you,' her father had teased, earning himself a tug of the ears.

They came to a standstill near the entrance to the ship. Her father had explained the gangway might sway as they walked up it to the ship's deck, but that they were perfectly safe.

'I'll take you to a suspension bridge in Vancouver, the gangway will give you a sense of what to expect. Now stand here my little Rose while I give your mom some last minute instructions.'

Rose knew he meant kissing. They'd done a lot of that since their wedding day. She stood patiently and looked around at other couples embracing loved ones. Soldiers, sailors, airmen, women in uniform, women in everyday dress, and women in fine outfits were all squashed together in the crowd. Class separated no one when it came to saying farewell.

She took hold of her mother's hand and received a warm smile.

'Elenor. I'm scared,' she said.

'Afraid? We'll be fine. What an adventure. Canada, here we come. We will be all right, you know. Besides, we have Jackson for good luck.'

Rose nodded, and she looked to the man who gave her his love unreservedly, who made her laugh and made it easy for her to love another father. He reached out and tucked one of the little blonde curls of hair struggling to break free back into place behind Rose's ear.

'It will be fine, honey. I'll be with you all the way. Isn't it a big ship? I wonder which cabin will be ours.'

As the ship left shore with her horns blowing, Rose's legs trembled, and her bladder threatened to let her down. She knew life would never be the same again. She stood between her new parents and knew whatever their reasons for leaving Tre Lodhen and moving to Lynn Valley, they were the right ones.

ELENOR AND ROSE'S STORY
1938

CHAPTER 3

August 1938: Cornwall, England

Elenor traced her finger across the label attached to the side of her battered suitcase.

Miss Elenor Cardew.
Care of: Mrs M. Matthews,
Stevenson Road
Coventry.

As the bus trundled noisily out of the village and headed for Plymouth, Elenor thought back to when the telegram requesting her help – well, more a command to do as she was told – was placed before her when she sat down for supper.

'This came. You'd best pack and be ready to leave when the bus arrives tomorrow. You must collect your train ticket.'

Her eldest brother spoke in his usual gruff, stilted tone. At eighteen, Elenor was ten years younger than her brother James, and there was never a kind word spoken, or a soft expression of love for his youngest sibling.

'Train ticket, James?' Elenor said.

'Read it. I'm eating.'

Elenor pulled out the thick white paper and read her aunt's neat handwriting, which gave strict instructions of the date and time she was to arrive in Coventry. It also informed her a one-way train ticket would be waiting for her at Plymouth station, along with instructions of changes to be made along the way.

'We're both in agreement. It has to be done.'

Elenor looked to her other brother, Walter; he too spoke in a dull tone with no kindness. The twins resented her birth, and both treated her with no respect.

'You're both in agreement? And I have no say. Aunt Maude is a tyrant. A bore. Why me?'

She flapped the letter high in the air.

'No dramatics. Just do as you are told.'

'Oh yes, James. And who will run this place? You?'

'We'll manage.' James replied.

'But what about harvest? You need all hands available for harvest time.'

'The matter is closed. Do as you are told,' Walter said and bashed his hand on the table.

With the thought of not breaking her back gathering in the hay, and chafed hands not giving her problems, Elenor suppressed a smile. In an attempt to continue her pretence of hardship, she pushed back her chair and flounced from the room, calling over her shoulder as she stomped her way upstairs.

'I'll leave you to wash your dishes while I go pack. You'd best get used to the extra chores, idiot.'

'Enough of your insults, get back here!'

Elenor ignored her brother, he really was an idiot, and slammed shut her bedroom door. What was the worst he could do? He had no intention of keeping her on the farm. She'd be as dramatic as she wanted.

She read the letter again. Not thrilled about caring for her aunt, Elenor was nonetheless excited about leaving Tre Lodhen – not the farm itself, but the life she endured within its boundaries. She loved her home and would miss the Cornish countryside, but she would not miss her brothers and their cold manner towards her. Coventry offered a smidgen of excitement for a young woman wanting more from life. The village of Summercourt did not excite her, it only held her back. A mantra she'd repeat for anyone who cared to listen. Amateur dramatics in the village hall kept her from dying of boredom, and on the rare occasion she made her escape to a village event, Elenor loved nothing more than to sing, but it had been months since her brothers had allowed her time away from her chores.

The creative Elenor was suppressed at every opportunity. There was no shoulder for her to cry on or a listening ear when she needed to vent her frustrations.

On the day her mother died, Elenor's role became obvious: she was to step into her shoes. And she did, quite literally at times. Their Aunt Maude would send a few pounds to help her family through hardship if the farm failed to produce a good crop, but it never went far and more often than not to the London Inn, their village pub. When her mother died so did any love Elenor had ever experienced. Her father had the same attitude as her brothers. He'd worked her mother to death and Elenor was made to pick up the pieces. The males in her life never gave any thought to Elenor's needs, she never saw a penny of the money sent or earned. When it came to her birthday, she soon learnt there would be no gift and accepted it as a normal working day. The ingratitude from her family over the gifts she offered them in the past meant she no longer bothered. Christmas also came and went with the only difference being her father and brothers spent a few extra hours and coins enjoying the company of the London Inn landlord.

No amount of moaning about always having to make do with what she found in the farmhouse ever gained Elenor new clothes. Scraps of cloth filled out shoes too large and repaired handed down dungarees from her brothers. When their father died four years after her mother, the twins did nothing to change Elenor's life. Neither showed any signs of marrying. There was no other woman in her life to help with the domestic tasks. She had no escape from the humdrum of daily life. The Depression meant nothing but hardship to Elenor, so this opportunity to enjoy a different style of living appealed to a girl of her age.

With no available money and the realisation that her farm clothes were not suitable, she spent her evening altering two of her mother's old dresses. She'd kept them in a trunk in readiness for when they'd fit her properly. Their drab brown and greens did nothing to flatter her tanned complexion.

She imagined her aunt Maude's stern tut-tut when she saw the brown leather belt holding her battered suitcase together. The pathetic contents would also send her into a frenzy of tutting, a sound Elenor had heard leave her aunt's lips many times in the past. Her mother's eldest sister was a force to be reckoned with when it came to snobbery – her father's words, not Elenor's. In the past the woman had scared her with her black gowns and upper-class manner, but Elenor would never dare breathe a word against the woman. When her aunt had visited the farm to nurse her sister, she'd taught Elenor a few basic rules of grace and how to conduct herself in a better manner than some of the female farmhands. Elenor often hoped her aunt would become her key to freedom, and today, in a round-about way, she had become just that.

The following morning the bus bumped its way past fields of cattle chewing the cud in a leisurely manner. It jostled over cobbles and through narrow winding streets past small stone cottages. Clusters of women stood passing the time of day with village gossip, and men gathered around a cow on a piece of ground close to the inn. Elenor knew they'd haggle for a good price until opening time when half would be spent inside the inn sealing the deal. There was no hurry or urgency in their tasks. Slow-paced and content, the villagers laughed and frowned together. Elenor envied their ability to accept their lives. Even though she felt stifled in Summercourt, under different circumstances she might have found living there more bearable.

When the slate roof and granite walls belonging to the Methodist church came into view, Elenor shivered. The last time she'd entered those doors was to lay her father to rest. It had been a sombre affair and her brothers had been particularly obnoxious that day. Her father's will had stated the farm be left to all three children, but the boys insisted it meant male heirs, and took no notice of her request for a wage. They stated Elenor was holding onto her part of the farm by living there rent-free.

Elenor continued to stare out of the murky glass and focused upon the trees as the bus meandered towards the edge of the village. She envied the power of the oak as it stood fast against the wind blowing in from Newquay, and she was fascinated by the way the silver birch dipped and swayed much like a group of dancers together in rhythm, with elegance and poise. They reminded her of the male versus female challenges she'd encountered over the years. One standing strong and the other bending to the will of another.

'Clear your head, Elenor. Think pleasant thoughts.' She muttered the words as she refocused on children playing with a kitten. Their giggles brought a smile to her face and reminded her of when she and her mother had chased three tiny farm kittens who'd found their way into the house. They'd had such fun chasing them back out into the yard.

The bus driver slowed down for a few sheep and Elenor could see Walter lumbering along in front guiding them into a new pasture. He was identifiable by his long greasy hair flapping like bird wings in the wind.

Resentment choked her. Neither of the twins had seen her off that morning. Not one had said goodbye.

Wait 'til you get home to a cold house and no meal. You'll regret your haste to be rid of me so easily. Oh, and I've left you a parting gift in the sink after the way you treated me this morning!

Both men had risen at sunrise and ate the breakfast she had prepared, then left without a goodbye. Elenor looked around but could see no sign of a coin left out for her journey.

With a heavy heart she packed food, a bottle of water and a tin mug into a cloth bag.

She was so angry with her siblings she threw the dishes into the sink. She heard the chink and ping as they crashed against each other.

'You can do your own dishes. When you've repaired them.'

She'd shouted the words to an absent audience.

Tears fell as she'd gathered her bags and walked away. Now, watching her brother she felt nothing.

'Goodbye village. Sadly, I won't be back this way again,' Elenor whispered.

CHAPTER 4

A weary Elenor forced her tired legs the last few yards to her aunt's home. Coventry city bustled around her. She jumped at buzzing noises from the car manufacturers and inhaled the delicious aroma from a bakery. It taunted her grumbling stomach. Eight hours and counting since she ate her last meagre meal.

Her suitcase bumped against her legs as she hurried along the narrow, cobbled streets. Despite her initial excitement about leaving Cornwall, the grey of the city streets closed in around her and gave Elenor a new set of anxieties. Had she been wise in leaving the farm? Maybe she should have fought harder to stay. At least when the men were at work she was left alone in peace and silence. Would that be the case here?

As the road shortened and her aunt's home came into view, it wasn't just the case weighing her down. Elenor trudged the last few steps trying to ignore the blisters on her feet, and once she'd arrived at the house she stood back to look at her surroundings. The house was smaller than she remembered. Smaller than the farmhouse, but larger than the terraced houses running either side of the street, the detached house sat as if at the head of the table, relishing in its glory of being the only one, yet to Elenor it lacked beauty. The house was a testament to her aunt's snobbery. It was too symmetrical, too neat, square with bay windows either side – unlike the higgledy-piggledy medieval properties she'd walked past to get to Stephenson Road, with their beams and angular structure. As a child she remembered peeping into the six large bedrooms and shivering in the gloomy parlour with stuffed dead animals.

Elenor took a deep breath and lifted the brass door knocker gleaming in pride of place, a lion's head. Again, Elenor had a renewed sense of foreboding.

The woman who answered the door scuttled about like a nervous mouse.

'Welcome, Miss Cardew. I'm your aunt's housekeeper.'

Elenor stepped inside the dark hallway.

'Thank you. Please, call me Elenor.'

She handed her coat to the housekeeper who busied herself hanging it in a large cupboard.

'Mrs Matthews has given instruction you will meet in the parlour before she retires for the evening, after which you will eat.'

With a nod the woman left Elenor's side. Bemused, Elenor left her case propped against the wall, and made her way to the parlour.

After an arduous journey, the last thing Elenor wanted was to entertain her aunt with information about her brothers and the farm. She wanted to put the twins to the back of her mind.

She pushed open the door and stepped into the gloomy room. It was cold to the point of unfriendliness. She was, however, grateful to note the absence of the stuffed animal heads.

Porcelain dogs and lace cloths did nothing to brighten the drab.

Unsure as to where her aunt would sit, Elenor chose to perch on the edge of the sofa, a hard piece of furniture never designed for comfort. A mantle clock ticked and Elenor shivered. A fire in the room would not go amiss. As she debated the idea, the door swung open and her aunt entered. Elenor jumped to her feet. Far from looking frail, her aunt, dressed in her usual ill-fitting black outfit, marched straight up to Elenor and stared her in the face.

'Didn't get the good looks of your mother then. Sit down.' She banged her walking stick on the floor.

Shocked, Elenor did as she was told.

'Hello, Aunt Maude. How are you?'

'Ill. Why do you think I sent for you, girl? I'm unwell. Not that you bumpkins from the country would ever care. Not one of you has written me. Oh no, but you accept the money swift enough. It is heartening to see you do not spend it on frivolous clothing.'

Uncomfortable that her clothing had drawn scathing comments from her aunt, Elenor adjusted her dress and sat back in the seat.

'Don't get too comfortable. You are here to work. To look after me. Go and fetch me a light supper. Tell that thing I employ to keep this place that she is to air my bed. I feel fatigued with entertaining guests.'

Elenor rose from the seat and fought back the urge to curtsy on her way out. She hurried down to the kitchen and welcomed the warmth of the room. It had a light airy feel due to the floor-to-ceiling cream cabinets and windows looking out onto a small garden. The housekeeper, although far from tall, was bent over a white stone sink. Elenor gave a polite cough.

'Excuse me – oh, I'm sorry I don't know your name. My aunt would like a light supper before she retires, and her bed aired please.'

The woman turned around and Elenor could now see she was much younger than she looked when they first met in the dark hallway. Certainly, no older than thirty.

'Certainly, Miss Cardew. I'm Victoria Sherbourne. You've had a long journey, miss. You must be famished. I'll see to your aunt and you can sit here with a cup of tea while I ask if she wants you to eat with her. Her mind changes like the wind. Pour yourself a cup whilst I prepare her tray.' She pointed to the teapot.

As she sipped the strong tea, Elenor wondered over her role attending to her aunt's needs. The woman didn't look ill and appeared perfectly capable. The housekeeper interrupted her thoughts.

'My husband enjoys her company and she tolerates his.'

'Your husband?'

Victoria busied herself with the tray.

'Yes, George. He's away at the moment. As a private tutor he likes to attend various talks by other masters.'

'I look forward to meeting him.'

Elenor noted a slight flush to Victoria's face when she spoke about him. Pride? Embarrassment? She couldn't tell.

Victoria returned with the tray after seeing to Aunt Maude.

'Come, I'll show you to your room. Your aunt has gone to bed. She asked me to tell you she will breakfast with you at eight in the morning. Unpack your case and I'll bring you a light supper on a tray.'

'That's very kind of you, Victoria, but it will take me all of two minutes to unpack, and I'd rather eat downstairs in the kitchen if I'm not in your way. It's such a cosy room.'

As they reached the bedroom, Victoria pushed open the door and set down the case and bag. Elenor had no time to take a look before Victoria closed it again.

'We'll eat together,' Victoria said.

Returning to the kitchen, Victoria prepared a plate of cold meat, cheese and hard-boiled eggs and set the table for two. She carved her way through a fresh loaf of crusty bread.

'A simple supper, but one I'm sure you can manage. It's been a long day for you.'

Elenor stifled a yawn and helped herself to a plate of food.

'I will sleep well tonight. Mind you, the journey was nothing like the hard work I usually have every day. I'm not used to sitting around all day, and if my aunt wants me to read to her for hours, well, I fear for my sanity.'

Victoria burst out laughing.

'I can't imagine your aunt having the patience to sit and listen. She will probably have you writing letters. She gets violent head pains and her eyes are not as strong as they once were. My husband used to write for her, but he is not always available.'

Shaking her head, Elenor pulled a face.

'My handwriting isn't the neatest. She might ask me once, but I very much doubt I'd be asked twice.'

She looked around the kitchen and saw a skipping rope and a wooden top sitting on top of a stool by the back door.

'Do you have children, Victoria?' she asked, pointing to the toys.

'Yes. A daughter. Rose.'

'Rose. A pretty name. How old is she?'

'Five in November.'

'How wonderful, a little girl. I take it she's asleep, I look forward to meeting her tomorrow.'

'She'll be no bother. I keep her busy. I can't have the girl running around making a nuisance of herself,' Victoria said as she cleared away dishes.

Tiredness crept in and Elenor stretched out and gave a yawn.

'Thank you for supper, Victoria. I look forward to meeting your family. Goodnight.'

'Goodnight, Elenor. I'll give you a knock in the morning.' Victoria put the dirty dishes in the sink.

Elenor smiled as she recalled the dishes in the sink at Tre Lodhen. No doubt that evening the inn enjoyed a visit from two miserable brothers.

CHAPTER 5

A good night's sleep and no pre-dawn work found Elenor in good spirits. She pulled open the drab brown curtains to let in a hint of sunshine. The rays bounced into the room and offered up an orange glow but failed to fight the drab brown and black.

The view was south-facing into the avenue with a row of trees on both sides. Her surroundings in Cornwall were far more attractive and a pang of homesickness caught hold. A tap at her door interrupted her thoughts and she opened the door to Victoria who stood holding a tray bearing a pot of tea and a china cup.

'Morning, Victoria.'

'Morning. Your aunt will be ready in half an hour.' She placed the tray onto the dressing table and wiped her hands down her pale blue pinafore.

'The bathroom is free. There is plenty of hot water.'

'Thank you.'

Grateful for the warmth from the teacup on her hands, Elenor sipped it with speed. She ventured to the bathroom across the hall. Another cold room where her breath puffed into clouds. The large mirror steamed over the moment she ran the hot tap. A large bar of Pears soap sat on the pretty scalloped edged sink, so delicate compared to the stone affair of the farmhouse. The chilly air prevented her from lingering and she promised herself a treat of an uninterrupted bath another time.

Back in her room Elenor pulled out her fresh dress from the wardrobe. Realising the dress would not protect her fully from the chill of the day she wore her brown cardigan with a mismatched button at the bottom, which had seen better days but kept her warm. She pulled on thick brown stockings, darned at the heel and toe within an inch of their life and hooked them onto a thin, well-worn suspender belt. With a sigh, she slipped her feet into a lace-up pair of scuffed but polished, brown brogues, stuffed with the obligatory scraps of cloth to prevent slipping. Once upon a time they were her mother's pride and joy. Sadly, Elenor could not look upon the shoes with the same enthusiasm as her mother had; to Elenor they smacked of poverty and hardship.

She released her shoulder-length hair from its night scarf and brushed life back into her red-brown curls and scooped them into a soft drop ponytail. There was no time to spend pinning them into a crown of curls as she had seen on the front page of *Nash's Pall Mall*.

Once satisfied she could do no more to make herself presentable, she left the room and descended the large staircase. The house was quiet. Elenor pushed open the dining room door and was grateful for the small amount of sunshine glistening outside the large window adding a dash of colour to yet another dark and dreary room. The cow barn at the farm had more warmth and colour than her aunt's home. At the head of the table Elenor saw the formidable figure of her aunt, who appeared deep in thought.

'Good morning, Aunt.'

'Sit down girl. I am in no mood for small talk and the morning has proved to be far from good. Eat. We have business with my solicitor at ten o'clock precisely.'

Her aunt made no move to look up from whatever it was on her plate holding her attention and slurped a mouthful of tea from her cup. Her puffy face reminded Elenor of the farm pigs at feeding time.

Elenor lifted the lid from a small serving dish and helped herself to a generous portion of creamy porridge. She noticed her aunt sipped at her tea and ate nothing.

'Would you like me to serve you porridge, Aunt Maude? Or have you already eaten?'

Her aunt shook her head and pulled a face.

'I cannot stomach food. Doctor Menzies has prescribed me stomach powders to aid my digestion, but they are useless. Sipping warm tea is all that eases the stomach pains I endure. Eat your meal. And please do so in silence, my head pain threatens to ruin my day.'

For the next twenty minutes Elenor endured the requested silence aside from the odd slurping sounds from her aunt. She gave a smile and a small sigh of relief when Victoria entered the room and began removing the dirty dishes. Elenor stood to assist her.

'Sit down girl. Mrs Sherbourne is paid to clear the table. Go fetch my coat, hat and gloves, and dress yourself for the outdoors. We will take a short walk to Mr Andrews' office after which we will continue on with a small list of shopping I have prepared. Ah, all done?'

Elenor did as she was told, and Victoria lifted the last of the dishes from the table.

'Yes, Aunt.'

Elenor envied her aunt. Her black fur-collared coat was of good quality, a heavy wool. Her shoes of stout leather, also black, were smart and well-polished and it hadn't gone unnoticed by her aunt that Elenor's own shoes were well-worn.

'We really must address your wardrobe. You are a walking disgrace. Victoria!'

Silence fell around them as they waited for Victoria to enter the room.

'What size shoe do you take? Anything suitable for my niece? Find her something decent to wear from your wardrobe.'

A stunned Victoria looked from her employer to Elenor. The difference in size between them was obvious.

'But El . . . Miss Cardew and I are different sizes, Mrs Matthews. Look how much taller she is to me. It won't be easy finding her something comfortable to wear from my wardrobe. I . . .'

'Very well. We will attend this meeting and I will withdraw an allowance for a new outfit. This really is inconvenient. Come along girl, before my body decides to give out on me with the worries you have brought to my door.'

Elenor gave a puzzled glance at her aunt and then looked across at Victoria who edged her way out of the room.

Brought worries to her door? She called for me!

CHAPTER 6

Despite the tease of the sun, Elenor's thin coat barely fought off the chilly breeze. It felt like late September, and had she been walking alone she would have moved faster to warm her limbs.

Her aunt leaned heavily on her stick and took her time over each step, stopping at intervals to catch her breath. Elenor's legs ached with taking small narrow strides. She was also impatient for another reason. She was keen to see the town properly; she'd only rushed through a few streets from the station to her aunt's the previous day. She couldn't remember ever going into town with her parents.

Just the thought of time to browse the shops and purchase new clothes sent her mind into a spin.

One part of Elenor knew she made her aunt ashamed with her appearance, but rather than hide her niece away, she chose to help, to notice and do something about the situation.

Did her aunt understand her excitement? If she did she did not show it. She walked in silence hunched over her walking stick. It took a while for Elenor to realise the further they walked, the weaker her aunt became, and guilt overcame her for wishing the old lady would walk faster.

In her haste to buy clothes for herself she'd forgotten her aunt was unwell; after all, that was the reason Elenor was called away from the farm in the first place.

'We still have some way to go and I fear you are tired,' Elenor said, adding a sympathetic tone to her voice. 'Do you need a taxi-cab?'

'Pah. Lazy legs. It is not much farther. The young today, you have no stamina.'

With a flick of her walking stick Maude Matthews took a few more paces away from her bemused niece before stopping.

'Look around you. Get your bearings. Now I have you to run errands, my time can be best spent elsewhere.'

Elenor gave a quick glance around and by the time she had turned back to speak to her aunt, the woman had walked away and headed for the end of the road.

On the other side of the road they headed for a tall redbrick building amongst a row of grey shops and canopied stalls. A brass plaque attached to the outer wall stated it was the office of *N. M. Andrews: LLB.*

'I have papers to sign. I am tired and therefore will ask Mr Andrews to assist with my transport home. Goodness knows his fee is great enough. Take this letter to Owen's department store over there.' Maude pointed to the corner of the opposite street. 'Ask for Mrs Green and she will help you. No fripperies. Sensible clothing. You understand?'

Elenor took the letter and clutched it tight against the rising wind. It was too precious to lose.

'Thank you, Aunt Maude. I am truly grateful, I . . .'

Her aunt tapped her walking stick with impatience and peered at her through her tortoiseshell spectacles.

'Don't keep me standing in the cold. I am doing this for me, not you. I cannot be seen with you in public in that outfit for too long. It is bad enough you sound like a country farmer without looking the part. Even in the Depression people were better dressed. Return home as soon as you have finished. No dallying and daydreaming.'

Elenor gave a weak smile.

'Thank you, Aunt Maude.'

She hovered, watching her aunt enter the building, and as soon as the door closed Elenor moved to the kerb. Cars milled about and when all was clear she headed for the large department store and as Elenor approached, she could feel the excitement mounting.

With clothes to tempt, the store windows held Elenor's attention for several minutes. A gown of emerald green silk flowing to the floor begged to be purchased as did the contrasting long cream gloves with mother-of-pearl buttons. Only the very rich would be able to afford such a garment, especially during the present economic downturn. Elenor watched people, mainly women, manoeuvre their way through the rotating front doors. She had never seen doors like it and noted the art to entering and leaving at just the right time.

You can do it, you can do it.

She chanted the words in her head and stepped to the entrance. Just as she was about to push the door open, it swung past her and she jumped backwards. Aware it was not the pavement she had stepped on, she turned slowly and faced the buttons of a blue serge uniform.

'Begging your pardon, ma'am.'

The voice had an unfamiliar accent and Elenor looked up into the face of a mature man with a large moustache which lifted as he smiled.

'I'm afraid it was my fault, sir. I do hope I've not hurt your foot.'

The words rushed from Elenor's mouth. She was so embarrassed and uncomfortable with the situation.

With a loud laugh, the man lifted his foot and wiggled it from the ankle.

'No harm done. There is nothing of you to have put any pressure on these boots.'

Elenor smiled back, looked down at his large black service boots, then back up to his face – still smiling down at her.

'It was the door you see. I've never, I mean, I don't . . .'

'Like stepping into the lion's mouth these things. If you don't get it right the first time, you could be going around and around until the store closes.'

Elenor burst out laughing. Fascinated by the soft accent, she wanted to listen to the man for longer but was aware she had already held him up from entering the store.

'Well, after you sir. I won't detain you any longer.'

She went to walk away.

'But weren't you going inside miss? Or did you walk out backwards and that's how we came to meet.'

A twinkle in his eye made Elenor like the uniformed man even more, and she felt her face flush at her foolish behaviour. Her aunt was right, she was a country bumpkin.

She shook her head.

'I think it safer I stay out of the store. If I have caused this much havoc just trying to get inside, who knows what will happen when I get close to a counter or worse, one of those elegantly dressed statues.'

His laughter rang louder than before and the man bent his hands to his knees.

'Miss, it has been a long day and you are the fresh air I needed. The statue if I might be so bold, is known as a mannequin in my country, and a young woman so full of grace such as yourself could not possibly cause havoc anywhere.'

He held out his hand to shake hers and she was grateful her gloves hid her calloused hands.

'Squadron Leader, Samuel Fleming, of North Vancouver, Canada. Pleased to meet you.'

She held out her hand and took his.

'Elenor Cardew, Miss, of Summercourt, Cornwall. Pleased to meet you.'

'Cornwall? That's a fair way from Coventry. I had the pleasure of visiting an air force base for NCO pilot training only last year. Pretty place.'

Elenor nodded with such enthusiasm she felt the muscles in her neck stretch. She had no idea what NCO stood for, but she was not going to set herself up for more embarrassment by asking.

'It's beautiful. My family has a farm there, Tre Lodhen, but I am here for a while to care for my aunt. Talking of whom, I will catch the devil's tail if I don't carry out her wishes. I must get inside and hand this letter over to a Mrs Green.'

The man put his hand to the rotating door.

'Now we have been introduced, I think it is safe for us to travel onto the other side together. After you.'

When they entered the vast building, they were greeted by the smell of beautiful fragrances and leather. Elenor took a step to one side; it was everything she'd imagined.

'Well, this is where I leave you. I must hunt down a small token to take back to my wife. I hope you complete your mission with Mrs Green in good time. Good day.'

When he saluted her Elenor felt like a princess.

'Thank you, sir.' She gave a giggle. 'Thank you for helping me, I no longer fear the exit journey.'

She watched as he walked away, tall, upright and confident. A posture to mimic if she was to get through the store. She had already noticed the side glances from customers and staff alike.

With a fake air of confidence Elenor approached a member of staff and held out the envelope.

'Excuse me, I need to hand this to Mrs Green?'

The member of staff looked her up and down and held out a gloved hand.

'I'll take it to her. Thank you.'

Putting her hand back down beside her hip, Elenor straightened her back.

'I'm afraid it is for the attention of Mrs Green only. It's from Mrs Matthews, Stephenson Road.'

With an impatient sigh the sales woman pointed to a stern looking female on the other side of the shop and walked away.

CHAPTER 7

'Mrs Green?' Elenor asked the plump middle-aged woman in a smart suit casting a watchful eye over the shop floor.

'What can I do for you, young lady?'

Although her appearance came across as stern, her smile portrayed a softer side.

'A letter from my aunt, Mrs Matthews.'

She handed over the envelope and hesitated about what to do next.

'I think there is an instruction for you to help me purchase an outfit. Although, I now realise she's not given me any money to purchase anything. Perhaps I should return later.'

Mrs Green pulled out a pair of round spectacles from her pocket and opened the letter. 'Well, young lady, it appears you are to have two sensible outfits for the season. A pair of shoes. A stepping out ensemble – I do love her old-fashioned ways – and a warm coat. Sensible over fashion are her words.'

Elenor gave her a quizzical look.

'But how am I to pay you? I think I need to return home and come back with my aunt another day.' An unexpected tear dripped from the tip of Elenor's nose.

41

A guiding arm went around her shoulder when Mrs Green ushered her into a small cubicle with a chair.

'Sit there dear. I will call one of my assistants. Here, use this, it is better than the hem of your frock.' She gave a reassuring smile as she handed over a cotton handkerchief.

Elenor sat in the comfortable chair and waited.

When the curtain pulled back, Elenor jumped to her feet.

'This is Sally and she will take your measurements. I assume you will require undergarments?'

Still wondering how she was to pay for one item let alone the many suggested, Elenor gave a shy nod of her head.

'Everything. But . . .' she whispered.

'Fetch me all I need, Sally. And this is to go onto Mrs Matthews' account. Her niece is to be assisted by you personally. Miss Cardew, you are happy to have Sally help you?'

'Yes, Mrs Green. And thank you, Sally.'

The tall girl gave Elenor a smile.

'It will be my pleasure Miss Cardew.'

Never had Elenor felt so grand. This time she made no attempt to ask to be addressed by her first name. Miss Cardew was going to relish the attention bestowed upon her.

For over an hour, Sally rushed backwards and forwards with outfits. A bemused Elenor could not believe trying on clothes could be so tiring. At first, she was embarrassed by her own attire but soon learnt that Sally was not there to judge. Her professional behaviour was that of an actress on the stage. She must have been horrified by what Elenor hid beneath her ugly frock, but showed no sign of shock, she simply asked if they were to be placed in a bag or sent to the basement for removal. Never one for waste, Elenor was torn. She hesitated when Sally presented the question. In true form, Sally came to her rescue.

'I'll wrap and bag them for you Miss Cardew, and that way you can decide what to do when you are home.'

'Thank you, Sally.' Elenor touched her arm. 'I know it seems odd to want to keep clothes fit for the scrap bag, but they . . . they were my mother's. They are all I have left of her.'

'I understand. Maybe you could create something from them as a keepsake. A parcel home it is then, miss.'

She gave a wan smile. 'I bet oddball country bumpkins are a one of a kind in your store – in Coventry.'

Sally waggled her finger at Elenor.

'Never call yourself that again. I must admit though, your accent amuses me, where are you from Miss Cardew?'

'Cornwall. Your accent amuses me too. I'm a farmer's daughter, hence the rough hands and unkempt clothing.'

As she folded the clothes in readiness to pack, Sally started to hum a song.

'I know that one! It's your name! Sally. I think it should be renamed Elenor of the Alley.'

More laughter followed.

'Is everything all right in there, Miss Cardew?'

Mrs Green called through the curtain.

'Come in, I'm ready.'

Approving and advising, Mrs Green made a note of the selected purchases. Elenor stroked the velvet trim of her new Sunday best outfit, reluctant to see it removed for packing.

'I think I will wear the navy skirt with the jumper, stockings and these shoes.'

Elenor lifted a smart black lace up shoe with small thick heel from a box.

Mrs Green gave her a smile.

'A sensible choice both in outfit and shoe. I like the wine colour of the other skirt too, both will suit you fine. Talking of the cooler weather, are you ready to try on the coats I've chosen? I've strict instructions from Mrs Matthews and I do think she is right – fashion comes and goes, but a traditional woollen coat in black will be both serviceable and smart and will last several years. We can top it off with a more modern hat, neck scarf and gloves which will bring no objection, I'm sure. I have just the items in mind.'

Elenor looked at the three coats.

'They're all the same.' She said.

Sally pointed out the buttons and back pleats of one.

'I think this is the one for you. Look how it hangs. Try it on.'

In the mirror a different person looked back at Elenor. She turned and twirled, allowing the coat to rise and fall back into place.

Mrs Green placed a green hat with a down-turned brim on Elenor's head.

'This is a little old-fashioned but will satisfy your aunt. To modernise it, you can pull it at an angle over one brow and trim it with grosgrain ribbon. Try the gloves. These are a size small and should fit your petite hands.'

She handed Elenor a pair of suede gloves in the same green as the hat. She clasped her hands in front of her face when she looked in the mirror again.

'Is it really me? I can't thank you both enough.'

'It is Mrs Green with the keen eye, I just do the basic assisting.'

Mrs Green gave a small cough of acceptance.

'I don't think my aunt will object to me adding a few extras to her account. Essential ones, of course. I need a cream for my hands. They are sore and chafed.'

Mrs Green gathered a few of the items from Sally as Elenor spoke.

'We have just the thing. Sally will fetch the cream. It is

by *Yardley* and contains lavender and will help them heal. Your aunt uses the brand, but it will be nice for you to have your own pot. I think you will need help carrying these home – I'll arrange for a car to take you. I will need a signature for the account before you leave. It has been a pleasure, Miss Cardew, and I do wish you well in Coventry.'

'Thank you. You have been so kind.'

After a final twirl in the mirror, a new Elenor Cardew stepped out onto the shop floor, one with the confidence of a well-dressed young woman. At the counter she signed beneath a sum of money which would have purchased a prize bull and applied a small amount of cream to her hands before slipping on her gloves. She made her way to the front entrance where she was informed a taxi driver waited for her.

She mastered the art of the rotating door and laughed as she stepped onto the pavement.

CHAPTER 8

Victoria rushed down the pathway as the driver unloaded Elenor's bags from the car.

'Gracious me, look at all these bags. Mrs Matthews is resting but I've strict instructions to wake her when you return.'

'It has been a wonderful experience. Oh dear, I . . .'

She watched Victoria pay the driver and when he disappeared she shared her concern.

'The fool I am. I didn't think of payment. Thank you, Victoria. I will pay you back when I have my allowance.'

Victoria held the door open with the heel of her shoe to allow Elenor into the hallway, both struggling with the bulging bags.

'No need. There is always money by the door for just such an event. Your aunt insists upon it, she said your uncle used to spend so much time scrabbling around for money, it frustrated her. The dish is never empty.'

'Well, thank you for the lesson. On my farm he would have been offered eggs.'

Victoria laughed.

'He might well have given you a wide berth the next time you hailed him down.'

Still laughing, Elenor climbed the stairs behind Victoria. They tiptoed past her aunt's room and deposited the bags on the bed.

'I'll give you ten minutes and then I'll rouse your aunt,' said Victoria.

With care, Elenor lifted her precious purchases from the bags and put them away.

Not wishing to keep her aunt waiting, she ventured downstairs.

'There you are.'

Her aunt sat sipping tea, and Elenor poured herself a cup from the pot sitting on the table.

'I must say you have chosen well. Very smart. Not too flimsy, well done. Mrs Green is a wise woman.'

Her aunt's head bobbed up and down with approval when Elenor set down her cup and gave a twirl.

'I don't know how to thank you Aunt Maude. The whole experience was a little overwhelming, but Mrs Green and Sally were kind. I have the same in a wine red, and the most beautiful coat, oh, and gloves and hat in green, sensible just as you asked. I did purchase a Yardley cream for my hands, I hope you approve.'

'Under the circumstances I do not mind. And not wanting to linger on a delicate subject, I'll assume Mrs Green added undergarments to my account?'

Elenor thought it funny how she was happy to stand in a cubicle discussing underwear with a stranger but felt her face burn and flush when the items were mentioned by her relative.

'Um, yes, she did, thank you.'

'Did you enjoy browsing the store?'

Elenor giggled.

'I became rather confused by the doors and stood on a gentleman's foot as I made my escape backwards. He was kind enough to help me inside. He said he was from Canada? I pretended I knew where it was, but I don't.'

Elenor picked up her cup and quenched her thirst. Across the brim she watched her aunt smile.

'It is good to hear, Elenor. I am sorry to have not witnessed the event, or to have saved the poor gentleman from a sore foot. I will have Victoria's husband fetch an encyclopaedia for you to read up on Canada, and anything else you may find useful.'

Elenor smiled back. 'He was an elderly pilot. Can you imagine it, flying in the sky? I'm afraid my bravery stays firmly on the ground attempting rotating shop doors.'

'You are not alone, young lady. I am fearful of all things mechanical and would never put my trust in a metal bird. We do have to be grateful to the brave pilots for when they gave their lives in the Great War. Bravery, such bravery.'

Aunt Maude sat back in her seat and closed her eyes. Elenor sipped her tea in silence until the gentle snoring of her aunt indicated the afternoon's conversation had come to a close. With slight disappointment, yet with the sense a barrier had been removed between them, Elenor tiptoed from the room and went to the kitchen in search of Victoria.

A male voice and whispers from Victoria told Elenor the housekeeper was reunited with her husband. She stepped into the kitchen.

'Ah, Mr Sherbourne, you have returned I see. It is a pleasure to meet you at last.'

Elenor moved towards the man who stood beside Victoria. He was not as tall as she had expected – although she wasn't really sure what she'd expected – and had a mop of unruly brown hair, almost as if curls had never quite formed. He stared at her with narrow brown eyes, almost untrusting, curious or suspicious. His presence unnerved Elenor and she wasn't sure why.

He stepped forward to shake her hand and his grip was firm. He had a large gap between his top teeth with a slight protrusion on one side. He was not a handsome man, and she was surprised at Victoria's choice of a husband. But, one should never go by looks alone. Her brothers were not ugly on the outside.

'A pleasure to meet you, Miss Cardew. George Sherbourne. If you need anything, please ask. We are both happy to help. Your aunt appears to be weaker each time I return from my travels.'

'Thank you.' Elenor let go of his hand and sat at the table. 'She was extremely tired today. Tell me, where did your travels take you? I met a man from Canada today, and my aunt suggested I ask you to hunt out an encyclopaedia for me to read more about the country.'

George Sherbourne dragged a chair from one side of the table and sat beside her. She could smell a mix of cold tar soap and pipe tobacco lingering on his clothing, and his closeness made her uncomfortable.

She glanced up at Victoria who had no expression on her face, and as if roused from sleep she shook her body, picked up an empty tray and without speaking left the room.

Elenor then understood she had walked into a domestic argument.

'Mr Sherbourne, where did your travels take you?' she asked again. 'Your wife mentioned you are a tutor for a young boy and attend conferences related to your work.'

'London. Although, I do prefer Coventry as it houses my lovely wife.'

Elenor sensed his words were not genuine. Insincere was a word she remembered from her school days.

'I've never been to London. My aunt said it is a fascinating city. Maybe one day I'll be able to see it for myself.'

George poured himself a drink of milk from a jug on the drainer.

'Do you have hobbies, Miss Cardew? Aside from milking cows, did you do anything outside of farm work?'

'I enjoy singing when I can,' she replied.

'You must sing a little song one evening. I play the piano. Your aunt enjoys listening to me play.' George stroked a finger across one eyebrow. He reminded her of her brothers. Arrogant.

Elenor gave a slight nod of agreement and tried not to laugh at his pomposity.

'About the book my aunt mentioned, where can I find it?'

George leaned in close.

'She allows me to make use of her books, and I have stored them in our rooms.'

To Elenor's horror he patted the back of her hand as if she was a child.

'I will fetch those I think useful to you and please, ask when you need more.'

His patronising manner irritated Elenor. Well aware of her status as a poor relation, he'd taken advantage of his own as a male, forgetting his manners in the process. He was married to an employee of her aunt but treated Elenor as though she were a child. She rose to her feet and drew upon a faked confidence.

'As the books belong to my aunt I suggest they be returned to the room, then I won't have to keep asking you for them.'

George gave a grimace and down-turned his mouth.

'I will miss being surrounded by such treasures.'

Irritated, Elenor walked to the doorway, turned around and gave him a polite smile.

'I am to be here for some time – who knows, maybe always, and I do need to make use of the books. We'll attend to it tomorrow. Victoria can help me collect them from your rooms.'

George said nothing but gave her a look which sent a shiver down her spine.

Outside the door she took a deep breath. The man needed careful handling, or he would become another bully in her life.

CHAPTER 9

The following morning Elenor heard the soft singing of a child from outside the back door and it occurred to her she'd not met the Sherbournes' daughter. She squinted into the sunshine. A tiny blonde child sat on a wall swinging her legs and pulling the petals from a daisy.

'He loves me. He loves me not.'

'I'm sure he loves you,' Elenor interrupted the girl's rhyme. 'I'm Elenor. Mrs Matthews' niece. You must be Rose.'

The little girl jumped down from the wall.

'I'm nearly five. How old are you? Did you bring a cow from your farm?' Rose fired questions one after the other with great enthusiasm.

Elenor laughed. 'No, it wouldn't fit on the bus. And congratulations on being nearly five, I will be nineteen next month.'

'Will you have cake? Can I have some? Pleeease!' Rose threw aside the flower and pressed her hands together as if in prayer.

Elenor was reminded of a pretty doll with a rosebud mouth and smiling eyes.

'Rose!' Victoria's sharp voice interrupted the laughter and made Elenor jump.

Rose's facial expression moved to sombre.

'Coming,' she called.

'We'll meet later and discuss cake,' said Elenor.

'I'm to stay away from you,' Rose said. 'I'm not to be a bother.'

As she ran back inside, Elenor watched her curls bounce on her shoulders and thought the child could never be a bother to anyone. She followed her into the house just in time to see Victoria reprimand the girl.

'I told you not to disturb Miss Cardew. Stay in your room until you are told to come out. Understood?'

Rose nodded, and a single tear dripped from the end of her nose.

'She spoke to me. I was already there,' she said through gulping sniffles.

Elenor stepped inside the kitchen.

'It's true, Victoria. I distracted your daughter and we made friends,' she said in a gentle tone, attempting to calm Victoria down.

'Well, she's been told to keep out from under our feet on more than one occasion. Go to your room, Rose.'

'Victoria, what if Rose is given a useful job? She could help us carry the books from your rooms to the day room.'

Rose looked to Elenor and gave a beautiful smile which lit up her pretty blue eyes and in those few seconds Elenor, unsure why, felt an overwhelming feeling of wanting to protect her.

Victoria folded a tea towel over the back of a chair and Elenor could see she was struggling with the suggestion.

'After all, why have her sitting around doing nothing? Idle hands are of no use. On the farm she would have several jobs. Think about it, but I am keen to get started.'

Not waiting for a reply, Elenor left the kitchen and entered the day room. She set herself a writing space under the window.

'I've got four books in my arms and they are heavy,' Rose's voice called out from the doorway. She was peering above a small pile of paperbacks.

'Come and put them down here.' Elenor patted her desk.

'I'll get some more. This is fun and . . .'

Victoria entered the room and Rose ran out.

Two hours later the shelves were full.

After lemonade with Rose and Victoria, Elenor sat at the desk looking through an atlas for Canada. When she found it, she traced her way across the country until she'd found Vancouver. She rushed to her aunt sitting in the parlour.

'I found Canada. Look!'

Her startled aunt looked up from her newspaper and gave a smile.

'I do think it was founded by another keen soul, but I congratulate you Elenor.'

Elenor lifted a chair from the corner of the room and sat beside her aunt.

'I'm sorry, did I disturb you? It is fascinating, this book, and Canada looks enormous compared to England. Here it is, see?'

Her aunt peered into the atlas.

'I do see, yes. Vast lands are uninhabited, and there are others where brown bears wander free, alongside wolves.'

Elenor sat back in wonderment.

'I'd be so scared if I came across a bear on our farm,' she declared.

'The chances are minimal. I would have liked to visit Canada, but your uncle was not a traveller.'

Her aunt tapped the book. 'Where shall we visit next, Wales? It is closer to home. Your uncle's family originated from there. A place called, Blaenau Ffestiniog, now there's a name for you.'

They spent an hour travelling the world and Elenor sensed the bond between them growing.

Around midday there was a tap at the door, and Victoria entered with a lunch tray. She was closely followed by her husband who, without giving Elenor a glance, strode to her aunt's side and knelt down.

'Mrs Matthews, I understand you have been unwell whilst I was away. How are you today?'

Her aunt gave a good-humoured cough.

'I take it your conference was worth the while. Victoria will no doubt be visiting her family soon. At times I fear you two are ships who pass in the night.'

Elenor disliked his familiarity with her aunt. His voice grated her nerves. Posh school boy education no doubt. Loneliness must have made the old lady blind to his false ways.

'We moved the books, George,' Elenor said, rising to her feet. She was determined not to be ignored by him. 'Victoria and Rose helped.'

Elenor noticed Victoria slip from the room; she hadn't spoken that morning and looked pale. Her husband turned as she left, then turned back to his employer.

'I'm pleased to say I learned a lot from my professors. As for Victoria, I have told her a family visit is on the cards. Now your niece is here to assist you, maybe she will go sooner rather than later. Oh, I have arranged for the piano tuner to visit in the week. I understand Miss Cardew sings, I thought we might entertain you one evening.'

Aunt Maude dismissed him with a flick of her hand as she took a bite of a piece of bread and butter.

Try as she might Elenor still could not find anything pleasant about the man.

'What a . . .' Elenor stopped, remembering her aunt was in the room.

'Arrogant man? Is that what you were going to say?'

Elenor turned to her aunt, embarrassed by her small outburst.

'I'm sorry for being rude. It's just since his return he has upset Victoria, and tries to ignore that I exist.'

Her aunt pointed to the chair opposite.

'Sit. Victoria is a timid thing when he is around. He dominates her. We have to respect their marriage and how they conduct themselves within it. If I felt for one moment he hurt her physically, I would have something to say, but I have found no evidence.'

'But . . .'

Her aunt tutted. 'No buts. You will do as I do. I watch, I listen, and I say the right words to let him know his place. Victoria is a good housekeeper and I would hate to lose her over something I said to her husband. Rose is a well-behaved child, and of no bother. Everything works as I need it to work and I will not have it altered. I'm too old to change my ways and to have them changed for me. Understand? Keep the balance – and the peace. I look forward to our musical event, at least you will find common ground with George and music.'

Elenor understood the message her aunt communicated.

Later, a gentle snore from her aunt meant their session was over, and she headed back to the day room – a room she now referred to as the study. Victoria arrived with a tray laden with a light lunch.

'Thank you, Victoria. No Rose?'

'She's in the garden. It's best when she's at school.'

Elenor shrugged, not sure how to respond.

'I take it George has returned to work?'

'Yes. He insists on eating at home. I must confess it is easier when he is away.'

With the impression Victoria resented the presence of both

husband and daughter, Elenor said nothing, but wondered at the other woman's happiness . . . or lack of it.

When she'd finished lunch, she returned the tray to the kitchen. Rose was nowhere to be seen, and Victoria sat polishing a silver candelabra.

'Do you sew Victoria? I've a mind to make something from my mother's clothes and wondered if you would help me decide what to make. A keepsake item, maybe. Oh, and young Rose can join us. Again, we'll make use of her idle hands.' Elenor smiled gently.

Victoria set aside her cloth.

'I sew, and Rose will also benefit from a lesson, if you are sure she won't be in your way.'

'You fret too much, she's no bother. Meet me in the study when you are ready.'

An excited Rose followed her mother into the room.

'I'm good at cutting out,' she declared.

By the end of their sewing session, Elenor had trimmed her hat and Victoria had created a small flower to match. As they were clearing away, the door to the study burst open.

'There you are! I'm home and thirsty, and the pot is cold!' George shouted at his wife.

'Hello Daddy.' Rose said.

'Leave. Out,' he said in reply and pointed to the door.

Rose slipped out of the room and Elenor heard her run upstairs.

'I said, where's my tea?' George's voice was low and angry.

He ignored Elenor, and she stood in shock at the way he had spoken to his wife and child.

Victoria stopped folding fabric and went towards the door and her husband stepped to one side.

Anger rose in Elenor's gullet. The man had no respect

for women and again, Elenor decided it was her duty to remind him she was in the room. Keeping her voice calm, she spoke first to Victoria.

'Stay where you are please, Victoria, and continue clearing the things away.'

She turned to George.

'Sorry to keep you waiting, George. Victoria will be a while longer yet.'

From the corner of her eye she saw an angry man leave the room as she continued about her business.

'I do hope George won't reprimand you for doing your duty, Victoria.'

'I apologise Elenor. Sometimes he forgets he is not teaching his pupils.'

Elenor leaned on the table and spoke across it to Victoria in a clear, precise voice.

'I may be young and have a simple education, but I am not blind nor stupid, Victoria. Never apologise for George. Through you he has a roof over his head, and food in his belly. There is no place for a bully in this house. We will keep him waiting a while longer and take these things upstairs.'

CHAPTER 10

Days ticked by and Elenor walked Rose to and from school. Their friendship bloomed, and on more than one occasion, Rose, Elenor, and her aunt sat learning together from the encyclopaedia. Each time she opened the book, Elenor went to the page bookmarked with a scrap of paper on which she'd written, 'a country to visit one day'. Canada had captured her attention.

Rose was fascinated by the bears. Aunt Maude proved herself a quiet, patient tutor, and Elenor enjoyed their time together.

Elenor's nineteenth birthday was just a few days away, and Rose let it be known how disappointed she was that grownups did not celebrate. From Elenor's point of view, having never celebrated the day for many years, she had no expectations. She promised herself a walk into town and a browse around the department store.

She hoped to find the courage to go to the tearooms around the corner from the store. When Elenor had peered through the window on her first visit, she'd noted a few young women seated as if in wait for a companion. Her plan was to pretend just that and enjoy a birthday treat.

She would borrow a few coins from her aunt's emergency dish and repay the money when she had earned a wage.

The morning of her birthday arrived and with it a misty grey atmosphere, but it didn't bother Elenor, knowing she had the protection of her new coat. After enjoying a warm bath, Elenor dressed in her wine-coloured outfit.

Entering the dining room, Elenor was aware her aunt had not arrived, or eaten and left. It puzzled her as to why her aunt asked for her to live in and help but had never asked Elenor to do anything for her. After waiting a few minutes, she made a start on her porridge and was pleased to see Victoria arrive with a hot pot of tea.

'Good morning Elenor, I heard you come down. Many happy returns of the day from George, Rose and myself. Your aunt apologises, she has a severe headache today and asked me to give you this with her birthday greetings.' Victoria pulled an envelope from her apron pocket.

'Thank you, Victoria. Please, send my best wishes to my aunt, I won't disturb her. I have plans to take a walk and will borrow a coin from the dish.'

Elenor opened the envelope and stared down at its contents. A silver shilling and a note for Mrs Green to allow Elenor to select toiletry items, a gift of Elenor's choosing and a small trinket from her aunt to be chosen by Mrs Green in her absence.

She put her hands to her mouth to smother the squeal of joy.

'How kind of her,' she said, as tears of happiness filled her eyes. 'It is my first gift on my birthday since my mother died. It has been years since anyone thought of me in this way. To think, I once feared my aunt, yet she is the most generous person I know.'

*

Although the air was damp, Elenor didn't mind. She relished the idea of taking time looking at beautiful things inside the store once again and pondered over the cost of a small clutch bag.

Once in town she stopped outside the window of the department store. It housed a new outfit, a mannequin sporting a red evening gown. All thoughts of a clutch bag went from her mind as Elenor stared up at the pretty outfit.

Inside the store the mingled aromatic fragrances reminded her she was to purchase toiletries, and she sought out Mrs Green to give her the message from her aunt.

She found the woman at her station, keeping a watchful eye on the shop floor like a mother hen watching her chicks.

'Is everyone behaving, Mrs Green?'

The older woman turned and took a step backwards. A smile lit up her face.

'Miss Cardew. How lovely to see you again. You do look elegant. I take it your aunt approved?'

'Thank you, Mrs Green. Wholeheartedly, I am pleased to say. She has written to you.'

Mrs Green read the letter and gave Elenor another wide smile.

'Many happy returns. What fun you will have choosing your gift. Do you have anything in mind?'

'The dress in the window caught my eye, but I am in need of a small bag, one to compliment my hat and gloves.'

'Sally is free to assist you. Ah, here she comes now.'

'Miss Cardew, I didn't recognise you at first. How are you?'

Elenor gave Sally a smile.

'I am another year older than when we last met, Sally. Today is my birthday and my aunt has been most generous. Toiletries and a new bag are on my list.'

She removed her gloves.

'And look Mrs Green, your advice about buying the lavender cream has helped them already. They are improving each day. If ever I milk a cow again it will be with softer hands, that's for certain.'

Both Sally and Mrs Green laughed their approval.

Sally guided Elenor to the toiletry and cosmetic area.

Perfumes wafted across the shop floor, and ladies sprayed and inhaled in gay abandon.

'What items were you considering, Miss Cardew?' Sally picked up a talcum powder pot to show Elenor.

'Yes, it is the same as my cream. Oh, and soap to match, wonderful.'

They ventured through to the handbag section and the smell of leather added to the luxurious surroundings.

'These are lovely, Miss Cardew, and look far more expensive than they are,' she picked up a green leather with an embossed image of a flower on the flap. 'This one would complement your hat and is proving to be rather popular.'

Returning to Mrs Green with her packages, Elenor was handed a wrapped gift.

'This is the item from your aunt. Please enjoy the rest of your day, Miss Cardew.'

With her head held high, Elenor walked out of the shop with her gifts nestling in their bags. The mist had lifted. She walked a few steps and came to a newsagent's set back between a haberdashery and grocer's. The lure of a fashion magazine to enjoy that evening was a strong one. She spotted a women's magazine for two pennies. Its price suited Elenor, and she stepped inside to purchase a copy. She unclasped her bag and took out the shilling coin and handed it over to the newsagent. Unsure whether she would have enough to sit inside the small tea rooms, she chose to walk home and enjoy a cup of tea there instead.

A familiar figure ahead caused Elenor to change her

mind. George crossed the road and was heading in her direction. Elenor couldn't determine if he'd seen her or not, but she was not prepared to wait around and find out. With a sharp turn away from the direction of home, she walked back towards the store and past its front door. A suitable window offering a clear reflective view showed George looking into the main window of a taxidermist. She entered a side lane knowing it linked up with the main road she needed to cross and if she hurried she would make it unseen. To have George as a companion in town would ruin all the pleasures she had savoured for her birthday. He was a memory she had no desire to make.

Hereford Street was busy and Elenor moved amongst the people to keep herself hidden from view. When she came to a shop selling tempting treats she stopped, glanced behind her and noticed George turning into the end of the road. Elenor knew for definite he was following her. She rushed across the road and headed towards the Geisha Café on the corner. Upon arrival she made no effort to turn around and, giving herself no time to make up her mind whether to enter or not, she stepped inside.

CHAPTER 11

Chatter and chinking teacups echoed around the pleasant room. It was large with tables dressed with delicate white cloths, but panic set in when the waitress looked her way and Elenor turned, pulled the door open to leave and walked straight into the body of another trying to enter.

'Oooph'

'My apologies. I am so sorry.'

Her rushed words were muffled into the chest of a male. She could smell tobacco and the soap George Sherbourne used. She pulled back in horror. Her efforts of shaking him off had failed.

'Miss Cardew?'

A male voice with a distinct accent spoke but it was not the person she'd winded in the doorway. Composing herself, Elenor tried to muster up a smidgen of dignity and spent a moment readjusting her hat. It was Samuel Fleming, the Canadian whose foot she'd stepped on. Dismay hit her. Although he wasn't the victim of her unintended assault, he'd witnessed another of her clumsy acts.

'Mr Fleming. How pleasant to see you again. Allow me to introdu . . .'

The man she thought was George Sherbourne was most

definitely not. The only thing he had in common with George was the tobacco aroma. Dark hair, neatly clipped, trimmed a handsome face, dark eyes melted into hers. She admired his tanned skin and wide shoulders, the complete opposite to George. She prayed her mouth had not really drooped open with pleasant surprise.

'Ma'am, it's a pleasure.'

His voice! Smooth, heart-melting and deep, and with the same soft twang as his companion.

'Allow me to introduce my grandson, Jackson St John. He's here to train pilots. Miss Cardew is the young lady I mentioned when we sought out your mother's gift earlier in the day.'

'My pleasure, Miss Cardew.'

Jackson St John held out his hand and, with no hesitation, Elenor clutched hold.

'I am pleased to meet you and I do apologise for my clumsiness. My friend was not inside, and I rushed out without looking.'

She hoped her face didn't give away her small white lie.

'We are about to enjoy a cup of English tea. Would you care to join us, Miss Cardew? Or would you prefer to wait for your friend?'

Elenor looked around. She saw no sign of George and the draw of sitting down for afternoon tea on her birthday still held. She made a mental note of the ten pennies sitting in her new bag and again begged the question, would she have enough money? It dawned on her she didn't know the price of sitting at a pretty table, or what the rules were of sitting with strange men. Although, to be fair, Samuel Fleming was someone she had met before, and he was a respectable uniformed man.

'As much as I would love to join you both, I'm afraid

I feel I should wait. Thank you again and do enjoy your tea.'

Disappointed, she took a slow walk a few steps away from the café, and it pleased her to see a flicker of disappointment cross Jackson St John's face. Whilst in the process of telling herself off for being silly and imagining things, she heard the irritating voice of George Sherbourne slice through the air as if a smarting frost.

'Elenor!'

'George. Good afternoon.'

'Many happy returns.'

Elenor made no effort to shake his hand using the pretence her hands were full with her shopping.

'Miss Cardew. It is your birthday? Well, we really must treat you and your friend now he has arrived,' said Samuel Fleming, before Elenor could mention George was not the friend she had been waiting for.

'Happy Birthday, Miss Cardew,' said Jackson St. John.

George stood with a grin she wanted to slap away from his face and introduced himself. He then followed through with a blatant lie.

'Miss Cardew won't mind, she was to have only me as company.'

Before Elenor could object, Jackson St John pulled open the door of the café.

'Maybe you can point out a traditional English cake, we want to make the most of my grandfather's last day,' he said.

George jumped in with a reply before Elenor had the chance to open her mouth.

'You must try a Kunzle cake. Shall we?'

All three stood to one side as Elenor stepped inside. She sensed George breathing behind her, his raspy breath expelling onion vapours. He was too close. Her skin tingled with displeasure, unlike when Jackson looked into her eye

– then her tingling was due to nothing but pleasure. A new sensation.

Once seated at the table they placed their order and George set about holding a conversation which failed to include Elenor.

'I notice you are both members of the Canadian Air Force, how fascinating.'

Elenor turned to Jackson.

'Can I ask, does it take long to become a pilot?'

George cut in before the conversation developed.

'Flying a plane must be exciting. Where are you based?'

For fifteen minutes George controlled the conversation, never allowing Elenor a moment to speak. Each time one of the other men answered a question, he fired them one more. Boredom set in and she allowed her mind to absorb the qualities of the younger Canadian. She heard them mention horse riding and imagined him sitting straight-backed on the farm horse her family had once owned. They'd have made a handsome pair. Her mind then wandered into the harvest fields. Glorious sunshine, bales of hay and Jackson, with rolled up sleeves pitching and exposing his muscles. She'd only ever once admired a male doing much the same – it was last year when a traveller had stopped to earn a summer's wage. He was also young and handsome, but her brothers ensured she was so busy she never got time to speak with him, just admire from afar. This afternoon she was seated beside another hand-some man, and she could see large arms and guessed they'd be firm. Arms she'd happily snuggle into on a dark winter's night.

What was she thinking? He probably had a sweetheart in Canada. More than one. He was too good-looking to be alone.

Throwing her off-balance and distracting her from her

daydream, George patted the back of her hand and she recoiled from his touch.

'It is time for you to return home, Elenor. Victoria will need you to assist her with your aunt.'

He swung her a gap-toothed patronising smile. Smug and sure of himself, he'd managed to establish himself as the superior. He'd taken control. A man no different from the father and brothers she tried to forget. Men whom suffocated women with their superior arrogance. Didn't they know the world had moved on, and women were equal?

Horrid little man. I despise you.

Elenor's anger surfaced, and she was ready to lash out her objections, but the sudden movement of both Canadian men pulling back their chairs to stand, reminded her to remain calm. Despite her inner thoughts she gave a sweet smile. She didn't want to give Jackson the wrong impression. She was no longer a country bumpkin. Her aim was to improve herself. George must not be her downfall.

'Gentleman, George is correct. His *wife* will need assistance with my aunt. George is the husband of my aunt's housekeeper and is quite right to remind me of my duties.' She emphasised the word wife. Unsure why, she wanted Jackson to know George meant nothing to her.

'Please, enjoy the rest of your afternoon, and have a safe journey back to Canada, Squadron Leader. I do hope when you return my balance will have improved and I'm no longer a danger to the public.'

'It's been my pleasure, Miss Cardew. You brightened my visit. I leave my grandson behind should you find the need to step on his toes or knock the wind from him once again.' The man gave such a loud laugh heads turned and smiled their way. Jackson tapped his grandfather on the shoulder.

'Hey old man, behave.' He gave his grandfather a deep and loving smile.

Elenor admired their ease with each other, and of how the affection between the two men was public. Not hidden and constrained. She felt she wanted more of that in her own life.

Outside the café she drew a deep breath. George needed reining in, much like the old ram when it was first brought to the farm.

Victoria greeted her with a smile but gained nothing in return.

'Your husband caught up with me and is now enjoying the company of two Canadian airmen. Don't expect to see him for a few hours. He was in full flow when I left. How is my aunt?'

Victoria looked flummoxed by Elenor's abrupt speech.

'Ah, George, once he finds someone to listen, he'll talk for years. Canadian airmen will definitely capture his attention. Your aunt is awake, in the parlour, and I am pleased to say, pain-free. Rose spent time reading to her but is driving me mad in the kitchen. I warn you, the child is excited by your birthday. Please come and see her before you go to your aunt or we will not hear the end of it.'

When Elenor stepped inside the kitchen Rose ran to her, her pigtails flapping behind. She greeted Elenor with a hug and proceeded to bounce up and down for Elenor's attention.

'Elenor. Elenor. You're home. Happy birthday! Mummy helped me make a cake, and I licked the bowl.' She stopped to draw breath and pointed to a thin sponge sitting on the table. 'Can we eat it now? Can we?'

Victoria crossed the room and touched the top of Rose's head, chiding her in a firm voice.

'Leave Elenor to catch her breath.'

'Rose Sherbourne, I think you have grown seven foot

since I left this morning,' Elenor said and laughed at Rose still bouncing up and down.

'Let me speak to my aunt first, and then we will enjoy a slice of cake with a cup of tea. Thank you, Victoria.'

A frail Aunt Maude sat in her usual chair. The room was barely lit, and the shadows from the fire flitted around the walls. It was no longer a cold room in atmosphere or temperature, Elenor felt comforted and much calmer. She was cheered by her aunt's presence.

'I am pleased to see you are up and about, Aunt. Victoria informs me you are pain free, and young Rose has kept you company.'

'Elenor. I am sorry I could not bear the light this morning. Rose is a good girl, but I can only take her in small doses. I do hope you have enjoyed your birthday. Sit, tell me about it, did you see Mrs Green?'

Elenor lifted out the present Mrs Green had prepared on her aunt's behalf and sat down opposite her aunt.

'I have, and I did, thanks to you. It was most kind of you. Mrs Green wrapped the gift, so you could have the pleasure of seeing me unwrapping it. I quite literally bumped into the Canadian gentleman and his grandson today. They – along with George – treated me to afternoon tea. George is still with them, but I confess on being keen to see what treat awaits beneath this tissue paper. You have spoilt me once again.'

'Well, unwrap. I am as curious as you.'

From the paper Elenor lifted a long box, a round one, and a tiny black velvet bag.

Inside the long box was a fountain pen. Under a square of silk inside the round one was a strand of amber beads. Elenor held out the necklace.

'This is the first piece of jewellery I have ever owned. It is beautiful.'

Pulling open the small drawstring bag, Elenor gasped with delight. She lifted out a lipstick container.

Her aunt lifted both eyebrows.

'Well, we will leave it that Mrs Green achieved two out of three for me, and three out of three for you. Ah, at least it isn't too bright.'

Elenor looked at the soft raspberry shade. It was perfect. The past fortnight had taught her so many things and given her so much in the way of affection and material items, it overwhelmed her. She started to cry.

'Forgive me. I am such a lucky young woman, I just wished I could have showed my mother these beautiful things. I have days where I miss her terribly.'

Her aunt struggled to her feet and patted her on the shoulder.

'Dry your eyes girl. Your face brought me joy, and your mother would have had great pleasure in watching you. Enjoy your gifts. Now go and put your treasures away but leave me the magazine to browse through. I have a sneaking feeling I need to update my visions of what a young woman wears these days.'

Laughing, Elenor left the room. As she did so, George walked along the hallway. She could see his intention was to enter the parlour.

'Ah, George. Did you enjoy your time with our Canadian friends? I did. Please, do not disturb my aunt. I understand Victoria is cooking me a special meal tonight, we'll see you then.'

Without allowing him to reply she went upstairs. She listened out to hear if he defied her, but she did not hear the parlour door open; instead she heard Victoria and Rose's voices as he entered the kitchen. A small smile played on her lips. George would not win his power struggle with her.

'Elenor Cardew you are ready to evolve. Be strong,' she whispered to her reflection in the dressing table mirror as she applied a dab of lipstick.

Back downstairs she met with Rose.

'Can we eat the cake now?'

She grabbed hold of Elenor's hand and tugged her into the kitchen.

Victoria sat waiting.

Rose snatched something from behind her mother's back.

'Open your present. I made it with no help from Mummy. She told me it was wonky in places, but I said you won't mind, you are not posh like some ladies.'

'Rose!'

Rose was telling the truth and Elenor gave Victoria a smile to show she didn't mind.

'I bet it is perfect, Rose. Thank you.'

She undid the yellow ribbon and unfolded the paper. Inside sat a square of blue material. The stitching around the edges was far from perfect, but to Elenor the headscarf was beautiful.

'It's the perfect gift. Thank you. I'll treasure it always.'

Her voice cracked. The gift was given with so much affection. She looked at Rose and hoped one day she'd have a daughter with a heart as big as Rose Sherbourne's.

CHAPTER 12

Autumn cooled down and drifted towards winter with no hesitation. Rose turned five and Elenor organised a small tea party. Two school friends were invited, and an excited Rose made the effort all worthwhile.

At the end of the day Elenor handed her a gift; a simple ragdoll dressed in a blue dress. The doll had a wonky smile, neat pink nose and large blue eyes embroidered onto a cream face. With a whoop of excitement, the little girl snatched it from its wrapping into her arms.

'Thank you. She's beautiful. I'm going to call her Annie.'

'Annie. It suits her,' said Elenor.

'Thank you for my tea. Mummy said you did it all.'

'It was my pleasure and an extra present.'

Elenor didn't like to point out her parents showed no interest in her birthday, and she was thankful Annie made up for their lack of gift. Even Aunt Maude had knitted her a red cardigan.

Christmas brought with it great excitement as Elenor chose gifts for her aunt and Victoria. She brought her aunt a new woollen blanket in shades of pink, and for Victoria a new recipe book. She'd also purchased George a sheet of piano music.

Buying Rose's gift gave her the most pleasure. It was a wicker doll's pram, something Elenor had dreamed of owning as a young child. With due diligence, she'd paid into a Christmas club set up by Mrs Green.

She asked to pay a visit to her brothers and made new neckties for them. She'd also bought chocolates, and two magazines related to motorbikes.

Her aunt paid for a return ticket and the week before the festivities planned in her Coventry home, she made the journey to the farm.

The bus pushed its way through the last of the sludge which laid around the village. Nothing had changed, only the season.

Her bags weighed heavy as she walked to the end of the lane in her newly acquired wellington boots. There was a mild wind, nothing like the cold chill she'd expected, yet still she shivered. The farmhouse came into view. Fences lay in ruins around the boundary of the bottom field surrounding the house. In the two months she had been away, Elenor could see the brothers had neglected the family home. It saddened her greatly as she still loved her home, just not the residents. Maybe the old saying of absence makes the heart grow fonder would be proved today.

She didn't knock and pushed the door open.

Stale, sour aromas hit her and wafted from pails by the sink – pig swill, which had sat for days rather than hours.

'Who the hell are you lady, just walking in here?'

The gruff voice of James spoke from a chair by the unlit fire. He lifted a bottle and took a swig of its contents. Walter lay sleeping in the opposite seat, snoring the sleep of a drunkard.

'Lady? Why thank you, kind sir.'

Elenor opted for a jovial manner as her reply. Her words registered with James and he jumped to his feet but found the need to steady himself against the fireplace.

'About ruddy time you came home. This place needs a darn good clean. You can start when you've taken off that coat. Who the ruddy hell do you think you look like? Oi, Walt, see what the cat dragged in?'

James kicked his brother's foot, and the startled man swore back at him. Pointing his finger at Elenor, James spat into the fire.

'It's crawled back from Coventry.'

With slow, deliberate movements, Walter also rose to his feet. He studied Elenor through slit eyes. It made a comical sight but Elenor knew better than to laugh.

'Hello brother. I see you both have been busy,' she said with a hint of sarcasm.

'Don't bring that snobby tone round here. Get to your room before I give you a slap. Unpack and come down to cook us something.'

Not responding with words, Elenor handed them each a wrapped parcel. They stared at her, then at each other, then back at her.

'Didn't you hear me girl?' Walter yelled at her.

Elenor kept her nerve.

'Christmas greetings to you both. This is a brief visit. Much briefer than I'd anticipated in fact, as neither of you care I have returned as your sister; I will not be staying as your skivvy. The neckties are from our mother's clothes, not that you will appreciate the sentiment.'

James threw his gift onto the chair.

'Appreciate the sentiment? Who do you think you are, you la-di-da bitch? Do as you are told.'

He tottered a few steps towards her and Elenor could smell the fumes of unwashed clothing and alcohol. When drunk her brothers could become nasty, handy with their fists.

'As I said, I'll not stay. Thank you for the offer of a room though. Nice of you.'

She turned and opened the door.

'Don't wave me off. You'll let out the heat.'

Unable to resist another stab of sarcasm, she walked away. With only one bag to carry, her physical load was lighter. Her emotional one was much heavier. In her naivety, she'd hoped her brothers might have missed her and welcomed her back.

The walk back into the village was a sad one. She turned to take one last look at Tre Lodhen and her heart broke. Her tears remained in full flow until she spotted the bus on a return trip. She ran without looking back and climbed on board and burst into tears.

'What on earth is the matter gal? Come now. Where you headed?' asked the driver.

'Back to Coventry. I can't stay here.'

'I know your brothers. Pair of drunkards they've become. They owe money all over. Let's get you to Plymouth, you are best out of their clutches.' Elenor slumped into a seat and changed her boots for her city shoes.

From the moving train she watched Cornwall fade away as if curtains closing on a stage.

A young man in a uniform sat opposite and Elenor was reminded of more pleasant times. Her birthday tea with Jackson St John and his grandfather.

She wondered if she would be blessed with a man who loved her at some point in her life. So far, she'd only had negative or undesirable communications from her father and brothers. Men who were supposed to love her. She wouldn't want a man like George in her life. A man full of his own importance and no respect for women. She wanted someone who would smile when she entered a room, a man who would appreciate her gifts. Forcing back tears that seemed to threaten when least expected, she directed her thoughts on the pleasant image of Jackson in the hay field. She closed her eyes and imagined touching his muscular arms. Embarrassed by her new thoughts and the feelings they encouraged, she opened her eyes and looked out of the window just as they were pulling into Coventry station.

On the platform she could see George.

'George. How did you know I was on the train and returning home?'

A scarlet-faced George stared at her in bewilderment.

'I, um . . . err . . . I . . .'

Elenor noted he had a suitcase by his feet.

'Are you waiting for me or off on one of your trips?'

He opened the door of the carriage she'd just left.

'Another work-related lecture, Miss Cardew. Victoria is off to see her family in the morning, so your aunt will appreciate your early return.'

The whistle and scream of the train about to leave blew away some of his words. Elenor caught he would return Christmas Eve.

Confused by the fact Victoria was leaving her aunt alone and had not mentioned she had any intentions of visiting her family before Christmas, Elenor did not wait to see him off, although she had a sneaking suspicion he might have liked the attention. She took a quick walk home and went down the side entrance to the kitchen with the intention of making a hot drink before she went to bed.

To her surprise as she switched on the light, Victoria sat at the kitchen table in her nightwear. The woman never moved as Elenor walked up to her.

'Gracious Victoria, you startled me. Are you unwell?'

Victoria shrugged her shoulders but didn't give an answer. 'Why are you home so soon, Elenor?'

Her voice sounded tired and Elenor sensed a hint of sadness.

'I've just bumped into George. He said he is off on another trip, and you are to visit your family tomorrow. Is that right, you are leaving my aunt unattended? Were you taking Rose with you?'

Victoria rose from her seat. 'How come you are back so soon?'

'That's my business. I can appreciate you wanting to visit your family, but my aunt needs support.'

She waited for Victoria to explain her decision to leave her aunt, but Victoria appeared distracted by other thoughts.

'Victoria?'

'I have no choice, George insists. I must be away for two days. I explained to your aunt I would leave everything in readiness for her, and she agreed. After all, I am her house-keeper, not her nurse.'

Elenor pushed her cup to one side.

'It is not up to George when my aunt is to be left unattended. We call you housekeeper, but you know your post means caring for my aunt in all areas. Leaving her for two days is simply unacceptable. You can go because I am here, but understand I am not happy about the situation. I'm off to bed. I hope your family visit is more successful than mine. Goodnight.'

Elenor left the kitchen in a state of agitation. As she snuggled under the comfort of her eiderdown her anger towards George heightened.

CHAPTER 13

The following day, Victoria sought out Elenor.

'I apologise for last night, but I do have to return home.'

Elenor stared at her.

'It is not up to George to suggest things which threaten my aunt's well-being. I take it Rose is at school?'

Victoria nodded and stepped out into the drizzling rain.

'Yes. A friend will bring her home.'

'I'm surprised you are not taking her with you. All this to-ing and fro-ing by you and George needs to be addressed. It is happening more often than not lately.'

'Rose needs to stay here.'

Picking up a basket, Victoria walked away, not waiting to continue the conversation.

Elenor sensed a change in the woman and stared out onto the garden. She couldn't wait for spring when the flowers poked through the soil bringing promises of warmer days.

Setting up a tray for her aunt, she thought of how life might be if Victoria or George didn't live with them. Thinking ahead, Elenor pondered on an idea. As George earned his own money and appeared to only spend it on trips away, Elenor might suggest they find a place of their own and ask Victoria to become a daily help rather than a live-in housekeeper. Then she remembered Rose. The girl lit up her life, and Elenor would miss her. She tucked the thought to the back of her mind and took the tray upstairs.

'Good morning, Aunt. How are you this morning? Curtains open or closed?'

'Good morning Elenor. Open. Why are you back so early?'

Elenor set the tray on her aunt's lap.

Elenor relayed to her aunt about the upset in Summercourt. Her aunt finished eating and pushed the tray away.

'Consider this your home now. You are surprisingly better behaved than I'd been led to believe. I enjoy your company.'

Selecting clothes from the wardrobe and drawers, it unnerved Elenor that her aunt appeared to not realise they may not have many years left together and Elenor's future would need to be one of independence.

'It is reassuring Aunt, thank you. I am an independent sort, so will seek employment for the future. There will be a time . . .'

'Yes, yes. Come along, I do not want to stay in my nightgown all day.'

They spent the day talking about family members Elenor had never heard of, and Maude reminisced about when she had been the same age as Elenor.

'You are very much like me. Fierce and independent.'

'That is a compliment, Aunt.'

'Ah, but you have the traits of your mother too. Quiet and loving. You have the qualities I would have wished for in a daughter.'

Elenor remembered the affection between the Canadian relatives and walked over to her aunt. She placed her arms around her neck and gave her a kiss on the cheek.

'Thank you,' she whispered.

By four o'clock the calm of the house had disappeared. Rose burst through the door bringing with her the damp fresh air.

'Elenor. I missed you!'

She raced over and hugged Elenor's body.

'Gracious, I was only gone for a day,' Elenor said with a laugh. She wiped her floured hands on a cloth and bent down to Rose.

'Let's get this damp coat off you and we can chat about your day. Sit at the table and I'll make you a warm milk. My aunt is snoozing, so we'll stay in here.'

The easy atmosphere gave Elenor comfort.

'It is nice when Mummy and Daddy aren't here,' Rose said.

'Rose. I'm not sure you mean that. It is different. I might not be as strict when they are home, but you will not get away with things while they are away, young lady,' Elenor said but she was in silent agreement. The place had a calm feel, a natural rhythm.

'Are you looking forward to Christmas? I am,' Rose said.

'Of course, who doesn't like Christmas? This will be a special one for me,' Elenor said.

'Why?'

'Because of you and my aunt. And your parents.'

'Mine will be special 'cos of you. Can I go and read in the study?'

'Yes, but don't disturb my aunt.'

Rose scrambled down from the table and placed her cup in the sink. Elenor watched her leave and knew she loved the child. Her parents would have to stay.

Christmas Eve arrived and the smells from the kitchen wafted around the house. Elenor's mouth watered in anticipation.

'It is such an exciting time of the year, Victoria. We never celebrated after my mother died, and never with other members of the family even when she was alive.'

The pair sat at the table and snipped green foliage for decorations. Rose tied rag ribbons around the completed wreaths, and Maude applauded their efforts.

Midway through the morning, George arrived home. He instructed Rose to fetch his slippers and asked for a few moments of Victoria's time. Maude noticed Victoria hesitate and shooed her away, giving her five minutes to reunite with her husband.

When they came back downstairs the atmosphere altered to a more subdued one. Rose sat in silence pencil rubbing over leaves on paper. Her face no longer wore its cheery smile.

'I assume your lecture was an interesting one, George?' Elenor asked in an attempt to ease the tension. Her aunt made excuses and went to her room for a nap.

Elenor and Victoria prepared and chopped vegetables between them. George sat on a chair by the back door polishing his shoes.

'I *gave* the lecture. It was well received. The audience were receptive to my modern ideas when tutoring young men.'

Elenor wanted to laugh at his pomposity. His chest stood out prouder than a stuffed pigeon.

'Interesting. So, what are your modern ideas, George?'

Elenor had no real interest but needed a conversation to focus on. Shaking his head, George gave a chuckle, as if addressing a young pupil.

'Ah, I fear they are a complicated set of ideas, and there are far too many of them for me to spend the time relaying to you ladies today. Forgive me.'

With hackles now risen, Elenor was not going to let him get away with belittling both her and Victoria.

'Not at all, George. I am always interested in complicated ideas. Why, I have them myself sometimes.'

George raised an eyebrow.

'I doubt your idea of complicated and mine are the same, Miss Cardew,' he said, and Elenor heard the sneer in his tone.

She shrugged off his rudeness knowing she would find a way to knock him off his pedestal. He was sly, and underhand but she was quick thinking and far from a silly airheaded girl. George never knew her brothers and of how Elenor had to outwit them on a daily basis. They'd given her a good education in that area.

'Tomorrow will be fun. I suggest we enjoy music around the piano. A game of charades after dinner might be amusing.'

Victoria looked up from her task and smiled.

'It has been a long time since we played charades. Remember when we were children and played them, George?'

Elenor turned to George as Victoria spoke. His face held a dark look, and she wondered if he was embarrassed by Victoria's outburst. It was the most she had said all morning.

'Oh, I didn't realise you were childhood sweethearts. How wonderful!'

'Not exactly sweethearts,' George muttered.

'Oh, you tease. He's teasing you Victoria,' Elenor said, and turned to the housekeeper as the woman, bright red in the face cleared away the vegetable peelings.

'As he said, not exactly sweethearts. George and I grew up together, and this is where we are. No more, no less.'

Deciding their recent argument was still ongoing, Elenor changed the subject.

'I am making traditional Cornish pasties for supper. My aunt asked I make them for her. Instead of you both eating out here, I invite you to join us in the front room where we will decorate a tree. My aunt mentioned she used to have a Christmas tree before the Great War, but never had one since. I saw one for sale and we will surprise her with it this afternoon. The tree is outside and needs bringing in, George, if you wouldn't mind.'

She could see he did mind but ventured into the yard with no argument.

The pushing and shoving of the tree through the home brought about a light-hearted mood, with much squealing and laughter from Rose. Soon the odd atmosphere of the kitchen was forgotten. Her aunt clapped her hands as they pulled the tree into place, and all inhaled its pine perfume.

'It is a fine tree,' George said and stood back to watch the women add their decorations.

Once finished, Victoria took Rose and made her way back to the kitchen. George excused himself to completing various chores.

Elenor went to bake the pasties and decided George could distribute some to the needy in town.

'Any idea where George is, Victoria?'

'No, sorry.'

'I'll catch him at supper. My aunt sent a message, Rose, she's making paper chains and asked for your help.'

'Can I, Mummy?'

Victoria nodded in agreement.

'I'll be at my desk until you are finished here, Victoria.'

On entering the study, to Elenor's annoyance George sat at her desk. He appeared to be studying a map. Her writing items and Christmas cards were set to one side on another small table in the corner. The room was awash with his pipe smoke. Not wishing to show how angry it made her, she chose a friendlier approach.

'Caught you planning your escape from Christmas chores, have I, George?' she said and laughed.

He turned around unamused. Hastily folding the map, he placed it in his pocket and made no move to stand up.

'Important lesson preparation. Can I help you with something, Elenor?'

He spoke as if she was a member of staff, the old-fashioned master talking to his maid servant. The smoke spiralled from his pipe as he puffed at the tip. He crossed his legs and leaned back in the seat.

'Not at the moment, George, thank you. But you *will* be helping me tomorrow morning. You and I are to distribute food to the men injured in the Great War who can no longer work and feed their families. We have a responsibility to bring a little joy into their lives at Christmas.'

From his neck upwards George went pale. Elenor watched him flounder, then run his finger around his collar.

'Are you warm, George? Might I suggest as Victoria is busy preparing our meal that you might fill the coal scuttles? Let Victoria relax for the evening. We will sing carols to start off the Christmas festivities, you can play for us. What do you think?'

With amusement she watched his Adam's apple bob up and down as he swallowed. Not moving, she waited for his response. A beaded row of sweat formed across his brow and she knew he battled with his temper.

Biting into the side of her cheek and clenching her fists to stop an outburst of giggles, Elenor watched him stand up and adjust his jacket.

'Now, I really must finish writing in my aunt's card. If you would kindly return my items to my desk, thank you.'

She made a pretend fuss of moving a silver bird from one side of a cabinet to another and watched him return her desk to order.

'Oh, and please leave the door open, I need to listen out for my aunt.'

She watched him stomp from the room and hesitate, pondering whether he dared slam the door. He left it open.

The afternoon was productive on her part, and the evening turned out to be a jovial affair. Each chose a carol to sing together, and Elenor chose 'Silent Night' to sing for her solo. Rose played several tunes, all with perfect precision. Elenor noticed neither parent praised her. They expected nothing but perfection. When the singing was over, Rose fell asleep on the mat beside the fire.

'Ah, little thing looks like a contented kitten,' Aunt Maude said. Elenor scooped her up and handed her to Victoria. As she kissed the top of the Rose's head, she realised she'd never seen Rose's parents show the same affection.

When the evening drew to a close, Maude called George to her and whispered something to him. He left the room and Elenor looked to her aunt who tapped the side of her nose and grinned back at her.

He returned carrying a large object covered in a sheet.

'Set it down over there, George. Careful. Gently does it.'

Her aunt pointed to the object on the small table next to the Christmas tree.

'This belonged to your uncle and now it's yours. Tomorrow we will be able to listen to King George give his speech. We will be part of history.'

Elenor jumped to her feet and pulled away the sheet. She clapped her hands in delight.

'A wireless set. How wonderful. Oh, but how does it work?'

'Fret not. When I couldn't see it in your uncle's bedroom, I asked George to look for it and get it serviced. He's learned how to set it to the right frequencies.'

Elenor could see by George's face that was not the case and guessed he had hidden it away for his own use.

'Thank you, George. It was most thoughtful of you, and

now my aunt will be able to enjoy it on a day-to-day basis. I suggest after tomorrow you move it to the parlour. After all, that is where she spends most of her days.'

His faced flushed just as she guessed it might. Elenor sensed his intention had been to use it whenever he wanted in the room her aunt rarely entered.

'If at any time either of you wanted to listen in with us, I am sure you wouldn't object, Aunt?'

'Not at all, although it is yours, so maybe your study? That way, if I want to doze, you can still listen to your music. Talking of dozing, it's time for my bed.'

CHAPTER 14

Squeals of laughter came from Rose as she pulled out the contents of her Christmas stocking.

'Ah, Rose reminds me of you at that age, Elenor,' said Maude.

'Really? I was that noisy?' Elenor laughed.

'If she's too noisy she can go to her room,' George grumbled as he poked at the coals on the fire.

'Not at all. It is a day for her to have fun. Goodness knows, there is little joy in the world at the moment. With preparation and talk of another war, we must focus on bringing happiness into our homes. If anyone retires to a room today, it will be me. Now, you four go about your business, and I'll sit here quietly until dinner time.'

Elenor gave her aunt a wide smile.

'We won't be long. I don't think Rose will allow it.'

The trip delivering her pasties took Elenor a little longer than anticipated, but she found it worthwhile despite George's grumbles. Back home the table was soon laden with an array of tempting treats, and after they'd eaten, Christmas Day afternoon was spent discussing the King's speech.

George debated with her aunt about the horrors of the

past, and of how the invasion of Austria was having an impact upon Britain. The threat of war threatened to dampen the mood for Elenor, but she battled against it by playing with Rose. After four games of hide and seek, she caved in and declared it was Rose's bedtime. Victoria and George took the hint and went to their own rooms.

When left together for the evening, Elenor and her aunt sat nibbling at a slice of Christmas fruitcake.

'Do you think there will be a war, Aunt?'

'I did think it was all hot air and males locking horns across the waters, but confess I fear there is more to the call for us to have gas masks and be prepared to evacuate children.'

Elenor shuddered.

'Rose gagged when I took her for her mask fitting. She screamed when she saw me in mine,' she said.

'You took her?'

'Yes. George and Victoria were going on another of their visits. They asked me to take her. It was the week before I took you for your fitting.'

Her aunt put down her glass and leaned back in her chair.

'Why don't they ever take the child anywhere with them? Aren't the grandparents interested in the child?'

'Victoria says nothing, but I wonder if the families don't approve of her and George. I'm sorry, but if it was me then my child would always come first.'

Maude sighed.

'Enough of them. What about you, Elenor? What plans do you have when I'm gone?'

The question threw Elenor into a frenzy of splutters after sipping her drink. She coughed into her handkerchief and looked at her aunt.

'I think you will be here a while yet, aunt. I need you

to tame me. I'm still a country bumpkin deep down.' She giggled.

'I'm serious, Elenor. Is there anything you'd like to do, to try? I won't be around forever.'

'I'd like to travel one day. Maybe visit Wales, and some of the places we've studied together.'

'Ah yes, talking of that. The Canadian pilot's grandson is paying us a visit tomorrow. George asked if he could invite him for a light lunch and drinks. Of course, I said yes.'

Thankful she'd put down her glass, Elenor stared at her aunt in amazement.

'Pardon me? George still communicates with the pilot?'

'From what I gather, yes.'

'Kind of him to invite him,' Elenor said and hoped her voice sounded calm and steady.

Inside her feelings raged around with great excitement. Jackson St John was to visit their home!

Why does the man generate such emotion in me? Elenor wondered.

'Aunt. Can I ask? When you met my uncle, how did you know he was the man you wanted to marry? How did you know you were in love?'

Her aunt flapped her skirt away from her ankles and sat upright.

'Why did mention of a young Canadian pilot visiting for lunch bring about such a question?'

Grateful for the dimmed lights and her aunt's inability to see far, Elenor made no effort to wave away the heat in her cheeks – cheeks which were probably flaming with embarrassment.

'I . . . I meant . . .' She shifted around in her seat and gave up trying to get out of the question. She picked at the corner of her handkerchief. 'He made me feel special.

That one time when we had tea. He didn't appear to notice my flaws. My freckled face, and that my accent was different to the local people. He made me feel an adult in adult company.'

'Ah, I see. Did he flatter you excessively? Sweet talk you?'

Maude's voice had a stern, urgent tone to it and Elenor felt the need to defend Jackson's effect on her.

'No. George barely gave him the opportunity to talk to me, but when he did it was as if he was interested in my company as me, not as a flighty woman he was trying to impress. My brothers have a different way they speak to the young women on the farm. It always embarrasses me. Jackson did none of those things. Does that make sense?'

Her aunt rose from her chair and crossed over to her. Elenor stood up and her aunt took both her hands in hers. She leaned forward and kissed her cheek.

'My dear girl. If he makes you feel special and treats you with kindness, then he will be the man for you. You will know, deep inside, you will know. My only words to you are this, and it is a delicate thing, but you have no mother to guide you. Do not be flattered into his bed before marriage. I suspect that is how George and Victoria came to have Rose. Do you understand my meaning? Their anger towards the child is quite obvious to us, isn't it?'

Elenor dropped her head to look at the floor.

'It is. I do understand. I think I do.'

'Good. Now, it's been a long day and we want to be at our best for our visitor tomorrow.'

Maude gave her hands a gentle, reassuring squeeze.

'I need to meet the young man who has put my niece's heart into a flutter.'

CHAPTER 15

'Drat.' Elenor picked up the hairpin which refused to remain holding the curl behind another. The style was from a magazine spread out in front of her, and she soon realised no amount of step-by-step instructions would hold her soft hair in place. As she released the stray length of hair it fell in a flattering loop of its own beside her left ear. She shook her head and it held fast.

'Different. You'll do.'

Her dress slid over her curves, feminine curves which had appeared since leaving the farm. Her scrawny body now had a shape she appreciated. The skirt of the dress fell just below her knee, and she wore new woollen stockings and shoes. Both shoes and dress were in emerald green and sported bows. According to Sally they were all the rage and the season's new arrivals to the store.

Elenor skimmed the raspberry shade of lipstick across her lips, and mascara over her lashes. With a light puff of blush across her cheeks, she considered herself preened enough.

Each time she thought of Jackson visiting their home and her confession to her aunt the previous evening, a nausea swept over her, followed by a flicker of excitement.

She looked at her watch, a gift from her aunt's jewellery box, and saw it was time for breakfast.

Seated downstairs, she waited for her aunt to arrive. The clock ticked loudly in the room, but its hands never appeared to move. Elenor sighed, it was going to be a long day.

The room door clicked open and her aunt entered. Elenor rose to her feet and pulled out her aunt's chair.

'Good morning, Elenor. I trust you slept well? The green suits you.'

'Good morning and thank you,' Elenor said and gave her aunt a peck of a kiss on the cheek.

'Nervous?' her aunt asked and gave a wide grin.

Taken aback and enjoying the transformation in her aunt, she gave a loud laugh.

'You wicked lady. Behave.'

She gave another laugh when she realised she'd mimicked Jackson's ticking off of his grandfather the day they first met.

'Yes. I am nervous. Nervous of George boring him to death, and of you questioning him into running away never to be seen again.'

Her aunt threw back her head and laughed louder than ever, and Elenor giggled through tears of joy. This was a Boxing Day breakfast she'd never forget.

'Describe this young man to me. I'd hate to entertain some poor soul merely knocking on the door looking for work.'

'You are a wicked tease, Aunt Maude. If you must know, he is very handsome. A little older than me, taller, much taller, and he has a dark head of hair. And his eyes are the deepest brown I've seen. His skin is tanned from working outdoors. He has broad shoulders. Strong arms.'

Aunt Maude listened with patient interest and gave a fake swoon.

'He sounds like a film star. I'll assume you are guessing at how strong his arms are.'

Sitting astounded by the antics of an aunt who'd shown no sign of humour when Elenor first arrived, she watched bemused at the elderly woman draping her arm across her forehead, mimicking many an actress.

'What has got into you? Who took away my serious aunt?'

Maude sat upright in the chair.

'It's your fault. You have brought the devil out in me. All this talk of young love. It has brought back memories; some need suffocating with humour, and others need to be embraced once again. Don't try and impress your man, be yourself. If he is worthy of being in your life, he will see your beauty inside and out. I'll distract George, you concentrate on gaining a husband.' Maude chuckled and bit into her toast.

'Wise words and thank you for the advice. Oh, and please do distract George or I'll find it hard to be a lady in his presence.'

'We will listen to the news and invite Rose in for a game of snap with her new playing cards, until our guest arrives.'

After two loud games of snap, Elenor ventured into the kitchen to offer her help to Victoria. George sat at the table reading a newspaper. He peered over the top and raised an eyebrow at Elenor.

'Rather overdressed for cooking lunch?' he said and went back to reading the news.

Victoria shook her head at Elenor, a warning to say nothing; yet again the atmosphere was thick with tension.

'I'm preparing a cold lunch, Elenor. Your aunt's instructions,' she said. 'You could set the table for me, which would help, thank you.'

Elenor wandered into the dining room and busied herself

with preparing the table and seating arrangements. On small cards she wrote out each name, careful to keep Jackson close to her.

The clang of the front door knocker made her jump. Flustered she rushed across the hall into the front room and joined her aunt. Rose ran from the kitchen.

'There's somebody at the door,' she called out to anyone who'd care to listen.

George's footsteps fell heavy down the hallway and Elenor stood holding her breath, waiting for him to let Jackson into their home.

'Welcome. Merry Christmas. Do come in.' George's voice boomed out.

'Happy Boxing Day, George.'

'Mrs Matthews and her niece are waiting for us to join them in the front room. This door. Do go through.

Elenor looked to her aunt who gave her a reassuring smile.

Rose pushed open the door and ran to stand beside Elenor.

'Daddy's friend is here. He's very tall,' she announced in a loud voice.

Jackson followed and gave Elenor a smile before he strode to her aunt and handed her a box of chocolates.

'Mrs Matthews, I wish you a Merry Christmas. It is kind of you to entertain me today.'

Elenor watched her aunt as she rose from her chair and shook Jackson's hand.

'Mr St John, it is kind of you to join us. We embrace our cousins from abroad. I believe you've met my niece, Elenor.'

Jackson released her aunt's hand and Elenor held out hers as he walked towards her. He was just as handsome as she remembered.

'Miss Cardew. My pleasure.'

'I'm Rose.'

Rose peeked around from behind Elenor before she had a chance to respond to Jackson. She reached round and tugged out the smiling child.

'Yes, and this is Rose Sherbourne. Our resident trouble maker.' She tickled Rose who giggled.

'Hello Rose. Trouble, eh? I cannot believe it, what with that bright smile.'

'Don't be fooled,' Elenor said.

'Indeed. She's got the cheek of the devil, that one,' Aunt Maude teased. 'Ah, George.'

'Rose, don't be a nuisance to Mr St John, he has come to visit me for lunch. Go and fetch your mother, please. Do sit down, Jackson. Elenor, would you mind?'

George pointed to the drinks tray he'd set out that morning, and sat opposite Jackson, and in the chair her aunt had vacated in order to shake Jackson's hand.

Maude stared at him, and Elenor looked at him in disbelief.

At last you've shown your true colours in front of my aunt. Pompous ass!

'Aunt, do sit down. George, please let Aunt Maude sit in her chair. I know it is Christmas and things get altered around, but she needs to be near the fire. Sit next to Jackson, after you've fetched them both a drink. I'll go help Victoria with the meal.'

George turned and looked at her, but before he had a chance to move, Jackson was on his feet.

'Can I do anything to help? Mrs Matthews, please, take my seat,' he said, and ushered Maude into his chair.

'George?' Elenor said, raising her eyebrows.

She felt a tension in the room.

What is your game?

'Maybe you could offer our guest a drink, please? Jackson, sit on this chair, near my aunt.' Elenor pulled a chair close to her aunt's.

Elenor left the room and went to fetch Victoria.

'Is George unwell or merely extra ignorant today?' she asked as she entered the kitchen and leaned on both hands at the edge of the table where Victoria was plating up slices of cold meat.

Victoria looked at her with shock.

'He is playing lord of the manor over my aunt. Behaving as if I'm his servant. If it wasn't embarrassing enough, he has the cheek to sit in my aunt's chair.'

'Oh dear. He was in a strange mood this morning. I think he'd hoped to have his Canadian friend to himself. Are you ready for lunch? Maybe he'll settle down when he realises it isn't his place to play host. Although, to be fair, he did ask if Jackson could be his guest.'

Elenor stood upright.

'Yes, but it gives him no right to leave an elderly lady standing, and to order me to offer drinks. He should remember he has no position in this house. He is also a guest at our table. I'll take these through and tell them to take their seats.'

Victoria said nothing in reply and handed Elenor a tray filled with pickles and chutneys, and Elenor went to announce lunch.

She returned to the kitchen and, with the help of Rose, she and Victoria joined them.

When they entered the room, Elenor looked at the people seated at the table deep in conversation. George had altered them to keep him close to Jackson.

Annoyed, Elenor slid into her seat. She glanced to the end of the table across at Jackson who surprised her with a wink.

'Jackson. How's the flying going? Put in any more hours since we last met? The last letter I received from Samuel indicated a change afoot. Are you heading back home?'

Elenor looked at George, then to Jackson.

Jackson laid down his fork and wiped his mouth on a napkin. He gave a frown.

'You write to my grandfather? I didn't realise. When we bumped into each other you didn't say. Well, I'm not sure what is happening out there. I do know I'm only here for another six weeks. Shame. I'm enjoying the sights,' he said and stared over at Elenor.

'George mentioned flying hours. Do you have to achieve so many in a day, Mr St John?' her aunt asked.

'The hours vary, Mrs Matthews, depending on the plane. I'm flying a Blenheim next week. A much larger plane, and it has three in the crew.'

'Interesting. The Hawker Hind is retiring?' asked George.

'Not at all. It is a valuable training tool. I am grateful to the RAF for allowing me the opportunity to fly a more modern plane.'

'Modern? I thought the Blenheim was old-school,' said George.

'Let's just say it's had an overhaul,' said Jackson.

Elenor listened both with fascination and fear. She understood Jackson was a pilot but hadn't considered the dangers he might be in when flying.

'Will you fly if there is war, Jackson?' she asked.

'It depends upon our governments. The requirements at the time.'

'Surely the German Luftwaffe are more superior in the air. The British will need all the support it can gather,' George said, and sipped at a large glass of red wine. His cheeks were red, and his eyes had a glassy shimmer.

'I want to fly a plane, but I can't 'cos I am a girl,' Rose

chipped in and interrupted her father's question. Jackson turned to her and appeared to be grateful for her statement.

'Have you never heard of Amelia Earhart?' he asked. 'And Hanna Reitsch – both women pilots.'

'Really? Well, I want to be one when I grow up,' Rose declared.

'You will have better planes to fly by then, no doubt,' Elenor chipped in, delighted in the change of conversation. 'How wonderful, to be able to follow a dream.'

'Do you have a dream, Elenor?' Jackson asked.

'She needs to sing and be famous. My favourite thing is to hear Elenor sing, isn't it Mummy?' Rose said, looking at her mother.

Victoria gave a small smile. 'It is. Elenor has a fine voice.'

'My niece has the voice of an angel, Mr St John, and after our meal I insist she sings to us. Young Rose can play us a tune on the piano. A talented pair. Oh, and of course, George. He plays a note or two, don't you, George?'

All heads turned to George. His alcohol-flushed face tried to focus on one and then the other, eventually giving up and downing the remainder of his glass.

Victoria leaned across and it dawned on Elenor that Victoria had topped up his glass more than once during their conversation.

'Oh dear, I fear we've overfilled his glass. Victoria, feel free to take your husband for a walk this afternoon. We will entertain *his* guest. He won't remember much if he stays. Still, it is Christmas so who can blame him?' Elenor said, and gave an innocent smile to both her aunt and Jackson. Her aunt gave a wide grin back at her.

'Victoria, leave the dishes and take the afternoon off. We will worry about the kitchen this evening. Young Rose, come with me and we will choose two tunes for you to play.'

George gave a snort and rose from his seat. He tottered for a moment and everyone waited to see which way he would fall. He reached for a glass of water and drank it down in noisy slurps. Elenor and Rose giggled, but Maude banged the table.

'George. Enough. Take yourself out for some air with Victoria.' Her voice boomed around the room. 'My apologies, Mr St John. Come Rose. Victoria, your husband.' Maude pointed to the door. Victoria jumped from her seat and escorted her husband from the room.

CHAPTER 16

Elenor remained in her seat and watched the four leave. When they had closed the door, Jackson burst out laughing and she could not help but join him.

'I'm sorry you had to see that, Jackson. I think my aunt handled it well. She is so old-fashioned in her ways at times, she will be horrified by his behaviour.'

'If I am honest, Elenor, I am rather pleased. He's a bore. He has no humour. His wife is not the talkative type, either. But Rose, oh what a great kid she is, so entertaining with her questions.'

'She is, and she's a loving little thing. If only her parents could see it in her. Do you have any young children in your family?' Elenor asked.

Jackson smiled. 'I do. My sister has twins. Boys. They are a handful, but she's a good mother and copes well. I'm afraid I spoil them, as do most of our family. I miss the little guys. You? Do you have other family?'

Elenor watched Jackson lean back in his chair. He had an easy manner about him and it helped her relax. She knew her aunt had instigated the removal of Rose and her parents in order to give her some time alone with their visitor, and she was grateful. The longer she was in his company, the more she experienced new emotions. His voice soothed and calmed her with its friendly, soft accent. With reluctance she was reminded of her brothers with his question, and the comparisons stood out.

'I have twin brothers. Sadly, I am not considered their sister, more of a housekeeper.'

Jackson gave a frown.

'What do your parents think of their behaviour?'

With a slow shake of her head, Elenor looked at him and chewed at her bottom lip to prevent tears forming.

'My parents are dead. I was very fond of my mother but sadly she died when I was young. My father was of the same opinion as my brothers.'

Jackson reached out and touched her hand, and Elenor made no attempt to move hers away, it was another new experience to be savoured.

'I'm sorry, Elenor. That's dreadful to hear. Thank goodness for Mrs Matthews. She's very fond of you, it is clear in the way she looks at you. Mother to daughter affection.'

The gentle squeeze of her hand sent an explosion of feelings through Elenor. If this was what love did to a person, she wanted more. His kind nature and the way he looked at her made Jackson desirable in a way she could not describe. She was not sure she should feel such things, but the pleasure they gave was not to be ignored.

'Aunt Maude scared me when I arrived, but she's a gentle woman in many ways. I love her dearly and it saddens me to see her health deteriorating so rapidly. She reminds me of my own mother. They were sisters. She has no children, so I try and help where I can, and enjoy the time we have left.'

Another gentle squeeze sent her into a frenzy of internal turmoil, and Elenor slowly removed her hand from his. His eyes looked deep into hers and for a moment the world stood still. Her heart beat out a rhythm so fast she felt sure it would burst.

'I think my aunt has found the music for Rose now. Maybe we should join them.'

A playful smile flittered across Jackson's lips.

'Or maybe not,' he said.

'You really must hear Rose play, she is talented, and it is worth listening to her.'

Jackson stood up and walked to her chair. He leaned into her neck, close enough for her to feel his breath tease the hairs and send tingles across her shoulders.

'And I understand I will have the pleasure of listening to you sing. Such a treat cannot be missed.'

He eased her chair back from the table and Elenor stood upright trying hard not to get too close. She was convinced the effect he was having on her would not be deemed ladylike by her aunt.

'I think we should join them,' she said, and with reluctance walked to the door. She turned and gave him a soft smile.

'Thank you for caring about me,' she said and walked into the hall to join the others. She hoped she didn't look too flushed and her heart would settle into a natural rhythm by the time she reached the front room.

'Ah, there you are.'

Aunt Maude greeted them as they entered.

'Sit yourselves down. Oh, George, Victoria, you are joining us?'

Elenor turned to see George step into the room behind his wife, and both stood facing her aunt.

'I'd like to apologise for my bad manners over lunch, Mrs Matthews. The wine was stronger than I realised. Forgive me. I'd like to hear Rose play if you will allow us to stay.'

Elenor sat and watched her aunt ponder his words.

'Thank you for your apology. However, I think it is best directed to Mr St John, he is here at your invitation.'

Jackson waved away her words with a flip of his hand.

'No apology needed, Mrs Matthews. Wine has a way of embarrassing us when we least expect it.'

'Then let's all sit and enjoy ourselves.' Elenor's aunt sat in her chair and all attention focused upon the piano.

Rose climbed onto the piano stool and wiggled herself into a comfortable position. She turned to check her audience were seated and hit the first key. Her tiny fingers moved across the keys with accurate precision, and a haunting, solemn tune sounded out around the room. The deep, slow, and almost funereal notes sent shivers along Elenor's arm and neck. She looked at Rose's parents. George stood with his eyes closed, his hands behind his back and swayed on his heels. Victoria had her head drooped to her chest, and her hands were white across her knuckles as they sat in her lap. Elenor could see she'd dug her nails into the side of her left hand. The music had such an effect on Victoria, she'd also got a tear snaking its way down her cheek. Both parents did not look at their child. Nor did they look her way when the music sped into a higher crescendo and Rose's arms raced up and down with expert rhythm. Elenor was mesmerised and could see Maude and Jackson were drawn into the music in much the same way. When George moved his arm across to Rose to indicate it was time to finish, Elenor was disappointed, and almost exhausted with holding her breath in awe. With a final twiddle of the keys, Rose ran her finger along all the keys, slammed her hands down twice and it was over. With no hesitation, Elenor and Jackson jumped to their feet and clapped. Maude gave a polite clap, and Victoria sat staring at Rose. George went to the piano, picked up the music and put it into his case seated by a chair. Their lack of enthusiasm now annoyed Elenor. The child had excelled at something quite incredible and neither of them showed any joy. Rose clambered off her stool and took a bow. Elenor went to Rose, knelt down and gave her a hug when she noticed neither parent prepared to applaud the child's talent.

'Oh well done, Rose. My goodness, what an accomplished player you are. I have never heard you play like that before. Have you practised in secret when I've not been here?'

'Daddy has been giving me secret lessons.'

'Isn't it wonderful, Victoria? You must be very proud,' Elenor said.

Victoria stood up and walked towards the door. She turned around and looked across at George, then to Rose.

'We all have different tastes in music. You played it well and your father is a good teacher. I would rather hear you play something a little more light-hearted.'

Elenor didn't miss the dark stare between Rose's parents before Victoria left the room.

'What was it called, Rose? The music, what is it?' Jackson asked.

Rose thought for a moment.

'"Moonsinata."'

George corrected her, his voice more like a teacher than a father.

'It is "Moonlight Sonata" by the great composer, Beethoven, Rose. A song very dear to my heart, which is why I have encouraged you to practise so hard. You played well. A few mistakes, but well enough your audience would not have noticed.'

'Well, I think it was a splendid performance,' Maude said and patted the seat beside her. 'Come and sit here, I think you deserve a treat. Elenor, sing for us please.'

Rose wiggled into her seat. 'Yes please, sing please.'

'I've a feeling we are all in for a treat,' said Jackson and sat grinning at Elenor. Whenever asked to sing in the past, she'd had a few nervous twitches inside, but today she felt more nervous than ever.

'Forgive me. Not today . . .'

'There is no excuse. Keep an old lady happy and sing one song for me. A Christmas carol, anything.'

Elenor knew there was no arguing with her aunt. She had to overcome her nerves of performing in front of Jackson. She also knew the perfect song.

'Rose, we could do our song. We've practised it enough.'

'Yes, I love playing it for you. Elenor's going to sing "Heart and Soul."'

A bemused Aunt Maude looked at them both as they settled in their places.

'I don't recall this one. Don't keep us in suspense,' she said and gave a little clap.

After a first nervous faulty note, Elenor lost herself in the song, and Rose played along.

When they'd finished, Jackson and her aunt stood and applauded them both. Elenor giggled and grinned at Rose.

'Isn't she good, Jackson?' Rose said.

'Little lady, you were both a treat to listen too, and I agree, Elenor has a beautiful voice.'

Giving him a mock curtsey Elenor enjoyed the attention he gave her.

'It was beautiful. The words – perfect, Elenor,' her aunt said.

'Thank you. I'm parched after that, I'll pop down and make a cup of tea. Jackson, would you enjoy a cup, or something stronger. I think we have a beer.'

'And have me end up like George?' Jackson laughed, and shook his head. 'Tea is just fine, thank you. Let me help you.'

'No, thank you. I'll leave you to chat a while.'

Elenor needed to catch her breath. To step away from the man bringing her senses alive each time he looked her way.

In the kitchen she found Victoria washing dishes.

'I thought my aunt told you to leave them, Victoria. You should take some time for yourself.'

Victoria stopped rinsing plates and dried her hands.

'I enjoy the peace of the kitchen. I'll bring the tray, Elenor,' she said and lifted down the china from the cupboard. 'You bring the cake.'

Back in the company of Jackson, Elenor listened to the conversation he and her aunt were enjoying.

'Jackson was telling us of his great-great-grandmother. She was an Indian. Isn't that correct, Jackson?'

Elenor laid down the tray of tea cups, and Victoria followed through with her own laden tray. It amused Elenor to hear her aunt drop all formalities and call Jackson by his first name.

'How fascinating. Tell us more. Was she from India? I know that from the atlas,' she said.

Jackson accepted his cup of tea and slice of cake and placed them on the table beside him.

'No, she was Canadian Indian, of the Squamish people. Catori was her name, it means spirit. My great-great-grandfather found her after she'd fallen from rocks near his family farm. His mother took her in, and the rest is my history. I get my dark hair and eyes from her blood-line, I think.'

Rose sat cross-legged on the floor and rested her head in her cupped hands. Elenor saw the fascination flicker across her face and waited for the inevitable question waterfall. She didn't have to wait long.

'Did she have a bow and arrow? I saw a picture of

Indians dancing around a fire, did she dance? Did she live in a tent and carry her babies on her back?'

Jackson put up his hand to stem the flow and gave a loud infectious laugh.

'No. Maybe, possibly. Does that help? She lived on the farm after she married my great-great-grandfather, so maybe, before he found her, she lived in a tee-pee – a kind of tent.'

'What a wonderful family history to have run through your tree, Jackson,' Aunt Maude said.

'How romantic,' said Victoria, and everyone looked at her.

'See the effect your great-great-grandparents' story has had. Even Victoria enjoyed it. I can see my niece is also fascinated. Maybe you can add it to your Canadian project, Elenor. With Jackson's permission of course.'

Elenor nodded. 'I'd like that, could I, Jackson?'

'I'd be honoured. What is your project?'

Before she could answer her, her aunt spoke.

'Elenor has the urge to visit some of the countries she's found in her atlas. Canada was her first study after she met your grandfather. It keeps her occupied for hours.'

The heat rose up her neck and Elenor knew she was blushing. It happened a lot around Jackson.

'Well, I'll have to see this project, and maybe I can add to it when I return to Canada. I could write to you about my homeland, and its history.'

Rose jumped up with her arm in the air.

'Me, me. Would you write to me, Jackson and tell me about the Indians? Pleeease!'

Victoria stepped towards her daughter. Her face no longer wore a dream-like stare she'd worn when listening to Jackson. It was dark and thunderous.

'Sit down child. You have no manners. Better still, take

these into the kitchen. Thank Mrs Matthews for a lovely day and go find your father.' She turned to Maude and Jackson. 'Thank you for a pleasant day. Goodbye Mr St John, thank you for telling us about your family. Elenor.' Victoria picked up the trays, stacked the dishes and left the room with a disgruntled Rose.

Elenor's aunt rose to her feet. 'I think I'll take myself for a rest. I tire so easy nowadays. No, no. Stay and keep my niece company,' she said to Jackson as he went to stand up.

Elenor saw her aunt out and sat back down.

'Well, that was a visit to entertain you,' she said.

'It was entertaining for many reasons, Elenor. I thank my grandfather for one of them,' Jackson said, and to Elenor's surprise his cheeks flushed red.

'Your poor grandfather's foot. I'll never forget my attempt to enter that revolving door.'

'And I'll never forget your birthday tea.'

'Your ribs, your poor ribs.'

Jackson took a step towards her.

'They protect my heart.'

'Jackson. I . . .'

Before she could say any more, Elenor experienced her first kiss.

CHAPTER 17

A few days after Jackson's visit an envelope landed on the mat and for once, Elenor reached the post before George. It was addressed to her and her heart skipped a beat as she slid the letter opener along the sealed lip and pulled out the letter.

Jackson St John,
C/O RAF Hullavington,
Wiltshire,
England.

Dear Elenor,
   I hope this letter finds you and your aunt well. I am writing this sheltering from a flurry of snow. It is nothing to what I am used to in winter, but it is managing to make me nostalgic for skiing days of the past.
   I hope you have forgiven me for making such a bold move the day I visited. I left so soon after my embarrassing faux-pas as it seemed the right thing to do. It took me by as much surprise as it did you. You moved me with your song. Everything about you moves me.

*When I mentioned my great-great-grandmother's name,
and what it stood for, I thought of how like you she
might have been. A woman with spirit, strong, and yet
vulnerable. Kind and gentle. Beautiful. Knowing you
are probably blushing right now, I will stop writing
about you, and write about me.*

*I am writing to say I will be in Coventry in three
weeks' time and invite you to join me for afternoon
tea in the place we first met. I would like to call for
you around three in the afternoon, on Monday January
16th.*

*You will find enclosed beer labels bearing the
Canadian flag for your project.*

*It only leaves me to wish your household a Happy
New Year, and good fortune for 1939.*

Your friend,
Jackson St John

Elenor held the letter to her chest and stared out of the
window. The first flurry of snow had fallen in Coventry
and touched the city with its white embrace. She looked
down at the letter and skimmed through the words for a
second time.

'Oh Jackson. The kiss was perfect. I hated that you left
so suddenly, and how could I ever forget you? And yes, I
will join you for afternoon tea,' she whispered, placing the
letter back into its envelope. She took it to her room where
she slid it underneath her nightwear.

Downstairs, she ate breakfast alone and ventured into
the kitchen where Victoria and Rose were discussing the
reason why Rose would not be staying up until midnight.

'It's not fair, Elenor. Mummy and Daddy say I have to
go to bed,' Rose grumbled and pouted.

'Well then, you must do as you are told. And if I know

my aunt's and my own sleeping habits, we both will miss seeing in the New Year. How about we make a fuss over it in the morning. Anyway, I wanted to ask your mummy if you could spend some time with me today. My aunt is unwell, and I need to fetch her a few things from the pharmacy. But when I return maybe you'd like to join me in my study.'

Victoria clapped her hands together.

'A good idea. Keep you out of mischief and begging me to death.'

'Don't be long, Elenor. Hurry back. What shall we do to celebrate our New Year tomorrow, Bake a special cake for breakfast, Mummy?'

Elenor left Rose chatting ten to the dozen at her mother and headed into town. She spotted George in deep discussion with another man near one end of the high street, so took the entrance at the other. She had no desire to be introduced to a friend of George. He looked a spiv, and she'd come across a few of them when walking through town in the past.

She entered the chemist's shop and purchased items to aid her aunt's digestion, and headaches, both of which were not improving. In the newsagent's she purchased two scrapbooks, a box of crayons, a box of pencils, and a pot of glue.

En route home, she went into the department store and hunted down Mrs Green and Sally.

'Enjoy your New Year celebrations,' she said to them both as they stood near Mrs Green's desk.

'The same to you,' Mrs Green replied.

'Aren't you stepping out with your Canadian friend?' Sally teased.

'No, I am not, I am not stepping out with anyone.' Elenor gave her friend a light punch on the arm.

She whispered to Sally from behind a cupped hand. 'I did receive a letter from him though. He sent beer labels for my project.'

Mrs Green smiled and made her excuses to attend to a customer. Sally linked her arm though Elenor's and guided her into a vacant cubicle.

'Tell me what the letter said. Did he mention the kiss?'

'Why I confide in you Sally, I'll never know,' Elenor said and laughed.

'Quick, before Mrs Green comes back. Tell me,' Sally insisted.

'He apologised. Happy? Oh, and he is coming here in a couple of weeks and invited me to join him for afternoon tea.'

Sally clapped her hands. 'How exciting.'

'I must go, my aunt is really not well. I'm worried about her.'

'Oh, listen. There's a drama group setting up at the end of the month. Fancy joining with me? It will be fun,' Sally said.

'I'd like that, especially with you, it will be good to do something different. I'll speak soon. How exciting.'

Sally gave Elenor a swift hug and they left the cubicle in time to see Mrs Green back at her desk.

'What have you girls been up to? Chatting about Canadian air pilots no doubt – our Sally will lead you astray, Elenor. Give your aunt my regards, and a Happy New Year to you both.'

'I will, thank you.'

Elenor hurried from the store and outside, she glanced around to make sure George was not lingering and crossed the road. She heard him before she saw him.

'Miss Cardew, wait,' he called out.

Elenor pretended not to hear and didn't stop.

When she stepped into the kitchen Rose sat at the table alone.

'Elenor!'

'Hello Rose. What are you up to?' Elenor said as she unloaded her bags.

'I'm cleaning these things for Mummy.'

Elenor saw a pile of silver items in a heap, many tarnished and some she'd never seen before.

'She said it will give me something to do until you get home.'

'Well, I'm going to see my aunt, and then I'll be free. I'll come and fetch you.'

Elenor met Victoria at the top of the stairs.

'How's my aunt?'

'Still coughing. She's weak today and didn't want the curtains open.'

'I think I'll have the doctor to her. Would you ring him for me whilst I pay her a visit? I've got a few mixtures the chemist gave me. They might help.'

She tapped on the door and entered the dark room. It smelled of lavender oil.

Her aunt lay back in her bed and her pale face looked much thinner. She snored gently, but her chest rattled out a dreadful sound. Unwilling to disturb her, Elenor laid down her purchases and left the room. At the bottom of the stairs Victoria was talking to the doctor on the telephone, and Elenor left her to collect Rose.

'My aunt is quite unwell, so we will work quietly in my study until the doctor arrives. No running around the house, understand?'

'I'll be as quiet as a mouse,' Rose said and pressed a finger to her lips.

'Good girl.'

As they walked along the corridor, Elenor wanted to

laugh. Rose tiptoed to the study with large exaggerated steps, and when they met her mother she pointed to the study without a word.

'What on earth is the matter with her?' Victoria asked as they watched her daughter tiptoe into the study.

'I told her to be quiet due to Aunt Maude being unwell. She does make me giggle. Tell me when the doctor arrives, although I'll no doubt hear him.'

'He apologises; he's to check another patient first and will be about an hour.'

'It's not overly urgent, and she's sleeping.'

'You are giving her the best care. I know you sit beside her in the night. You must be exhausted, and yet it doesn't show.'

Elenor gave a wan smile. 'I nod off when I can during the day. I don't like the idea of her needing help and being unable to call out. Right, let's get this young lady working on her school project.'

'You spoil her, but I'm grateful she's not under my feet. I give her tasks.'

'The silver polishing didn't get finished. I don't recognise it, is it my aunt's?'

'Yes, she wanted it polished to give to you. It belonged to your mother's family.'

'Oh. I had no idea. Don't worry yourself over it, Victoria, I'll clean it another day.'

CHAPTER 18

Inside the study Rose was looking through an encyclopedia and turned to a page showing a large brown bear.

'Look. Jackson said he saw a bear once. I'd be so scared. He said you mustn't run from them, but I would. I'd run and run so fast the bear wouldn't be able to catch me.'

Elenor peered over her shoulder. 'My goodness, that is a big one. I think I'd run with you. I've a few things here which you might find useful. I thought we'd start with Canada as we know someone from there. Your friends at school won't have some of these things. Jackson has promised more.'

'Do you love him, Elenor?'

Rose's question threw Elenor into a quandary. She thought she did love him but was definitely not going to share it with the young girl.

'He's a friend, Rose. A pen-pal. Someone writing interesting things to me.'

'Will you put them in your scrapbook?' Rose asked and squeezed an overgenerous amount of glue onto the back of a beer label.

'Yes, anything he sends which will teach me more, I'll keep here.'

Sticking down her own labels Elenor tapped her scrapbook.

'This is fun. I think Jackson likes England, but Canada looks exciting. Great big Christmas trees everywhere, look at this picture.'

A knock at the door announced the doctor had arrived, and Elenor left Rose reading.

After checking over her aunt, he beckoned Elenor downstairs and once in the parlour he wasted no time.

'I'm afraid your aunt is dying, Elenor. I fear she has a disease which has taken a great toll on her body. There is no gentle way of telling you, and I know you want to hear the truth.'

Wringing her hands together, Elenor thought of the painful loss of her aunt.

'How long do you think she'll last? It is horrible hearing her fight for breath.'

'Not long. More days than weeks. Possibly hours. It will be a blessing. She's been fighting this for some time now, but her medication is of no use. Keep nursing her as you are. You have been good for her. She talks of you with deep affection.'

After seeing him out, Elenor checked in on Rose, then went to her aunt. Victoria was in the room helping Maude get more comfortable.

'You're awake,' Elenor said and gave a cheerful smile.

'For a few minutes, yes. Sit with me until I nod off again.'

'Rose is in the study, Victoria. She is happy enough. Please would you bring us tea, I'm sure my aunt would appreciate a cup.'

Victoria left the room and her aunt settled back into the plumped pillows.

'What is your news? What is the news about the threatening war?'

'The war news is quite depressing, Aunt. It scares me. I do believe it will happen. How did you cope during the last one?'

'I ran on hope. Each day I rose and thought of those fighting. I sent up a prayer, we all did, even those of us who didn't attend church made an effort. It was a dark time in our lives. In some ways I am fortunate.'

After waiting for a bout of coughing to finish, Elenor wiped her aunt's face. Sweat beaded upon her brow and across her lips. Her blue tinged lips.

'How are you fortunate, Aunt? You are unwell.'

'Precisely, I won't see the war arrive. Oh, don't look so shocked. I know I am near the end of my life. My concern is for you – and that little girl downstairs. With her parents, she will be evacuated away within a blink of your eye.'

'Not from here. London maybe. But enough talk of you not seeing it arrive. '

'Be realistic Elenor. I trust you to face the reality of what is happening around you. Enough of this gloom. Have you heard from the young pilot? Ah, I can see from your face that you have. I like him, he suits you.'

Another bout of coughing weakened her aunt into another sleep just as Victoria brought in the tray of tea.

She shook her head at Elenor and pulled a sad face.

'I'll sit with her, you go and get rest. George has come home and is now giving Rose a lesson in silver polishing. Everything comes with a lecture with him,' Victoria said.

The annoyance in her voice was not missed by Elenor.

'I'll go and have a nap. Call me if she worsens. I want to sit beside her tonight. She did the same for my mother and it is the last thing I can do for her.'

Back in her bedroom, Elenor pulled out Jackson's letter. It gave her comfort. Two hours later she woke from sleep still clutching it and read it again.

She looked at her watch. Five-thirty. Her stomach growled for food, but she had no desire to eat. She freshened her face with cool water and went downstairs. The house was silent. An eeriness fell around her, and she shivered.

Opting for a cheese sandwich and a cup of cocoa, she watched the milk bubble in a pan and contemplated her future. Without her Aunt Maude, she had no choice, she would have to return to Cornwall. Although it did run through her mind to ask Mrs Green if there was a vacancy in the store. She and her aunt had never discussed what would happen to Elenor after her death, but it was time for Elenor to make her own plans.

She took her food into the front room and sat beside the roaring fire. Either George or Victoria had banked it high, and she was grateful for its warmth. The previous day's newspaper was filled with articles about the pending war and statements from government ministers. A new enemy threatened her future and Elenor could not shake off the miserable mood which had struck her since leaving her aunt's room.

The door clicked open and Rose peered inside.

'There you are. Mummy said do you want to eat yet?' she said, her voice soft and low.

'Thank you Rose. Tell her I've eaten. I will go and sit with my aunt soon, so ask her if she could bring me a milky drink around eight o'clock?'

'I will.'

With a sudden bolt across the room, Rose threw herself into Elenor's lap.

'I'm sad,' she said with a sob in her voice.

'Darling, we all are, but we must be strong. We must also remember my aunt needs to be in a better place now. Her old body is too tired to stay here.'

Elenor put her arms around Rose who crawled onto her

lap and curled into a ball with her arms around Elenor's neck.

'I like her. She's my pretend grandmother.'

Elenor's heart went out to the girl. Aunt Maude had a role in Rose's life which none of them were really aware of.

'And she likes you, and probably pretends you are her granddaughter. Now, go and give Mummy my message and I'll see you in the morning.'

Placing a kiss on Rose's forehead, Elenor eased Rose onto the floor. She'd have loved to stay with the child snuggled on her lap, but her duty lay elsewhere.

She stood and stretched her legs, then climbed the stairs armed with writing materials and reading books.

She entered her aunt's room which now appeared dark and stuffy. Her aunt's breathing worsened throughout the evening, and when Victoria arrived with a hot drink at eight, they both knew there was limited time left for her. Elenor read poetry and from a prayer book her aunt kept beside her bed. Victoria sat and sewed until ten, and left Elenor for the night. Elenor curled up in the chair with an eiderdown around eleven o'clock. Sleep didn't come easy. The town clock boomed out midnight, and she fidgeted. The clock on the dresser ticked the minutes away, and Elenor caved into the moonlight filtering in through the curtains and went to the window. She pulled the eiderdown around her and stood watching out in the street. At the top of the road two men leaned against a wall, the glow from their cigarettes stood out against the dark brick. A third man joined them, and she recognised him as George. He handed over what appeared to be a large white envelope and stood talking for a moment. When he turned back towards the house, Elenor stepped back into the shadows of the room. What was he up to? George's recent behaviour could only be classed as out of character. Or was it? Was he a man with a past hiding behind the skirts of a woman he clearly had no affection for, and a child for whom he had no patience. Was he really a tutor?

So many questions ran through her mind and soon Elenor, tired of thinking about the man, allowed her thoughts to drift to another. What did Jackson want from her? Was she a passing fancy whilst he visited England, something she knew her aunt feared? Or did she mean more to him, much as he did to her?

A sudden noise from her aunt disturbed her thoughts and Elenor raced to her side. She lifted her hand and held it firm.

'I'm here, Aunt. Elenor's here. You are safe.'

Large tears dripped from Elenor's chin as they poured down her cheeks.

'My pilot wrote to me. I love him. You made me recognise love. Thank you. Rest now. I will be fine. Sleep now.'

For another hour she sat holding her aunt's hand until sleep took hold and she napped in the chair. The sound of a blackbird calling woke her, and she struggled round from her sleep. A deep sigh from her aunt caught her attention. Her aunt's skin was cooler, and her breathing had intermittent rasps. They held hands until only the clock made a sound in the room. Elenor noticed the covers did not rise and fall anymore.

This was it, the end of their time together. The day she had dreaded, possibly the end of her life in Coventry. She chided herself for the selfish thought.

She went to the door and called softly for Victoria. George came out of their room first.

'Please call the doctor, George.'

Victoria came into the room pulling on her dressing gown and went to her aunt's bedside. She nodded to Elenor.

The doctor arrived and signed papers to say his patient had died peacefully in her sleep.

When they were downstairs Elenor paced the room wringing her hands with worry.

'What happens now, Doctor?'

Elenor had so many new questions with the event of her aunt's death.

'Your aunt was not only a patient, but a friend. She confided in me and gave me instructions for this day. All will be taken care of and I am to ensure you are not troubled with the formalities which follow a death. Victoria will take care of you. Stay here until instructed otherwise, understand? These are your aunt's wishes.'

Numb with grief, Elenor slumped forward in her seat.

'She was too kind to die. We didn't have long enough together. I am frightened.'

A crystal glass with amber fluid was placed in her hand.

'Drink the brandy. It's medicinal. I will ask George to sit with you while I make arrangements for your aunt.'

Shaking her head, Elenor rose to her feet.

'It is kind of you – the brandy and help, but I only need the latter. As for George's company, no thank you. I will go and attend to my aunt with Victoria.'

The doctor stepped into her pathway as she went to leave the room.

'A young lady has no need to deal with such matters. Leave it to Victoria.'

'Young I might be, but I am her family, it is my duty.'

The doctor gave a soft smile.

'Maude said you have a caring heart. Go to your aunt, mourn and grieve her. I can see what she meant to you.'

As they entered the hallway, George stepped off the last stair. He walked towards the doctor with his hand out.

'Ah, Elenor. You are needed upstairs. Thank you for assisting us at such a sad time, Doctor. Let me see you out.'

The doctor placed his hat on his head, ignoring George's hand as if he hadn't noticed it, and opened the front door. He turned and faced Elenor.

'I will return this evening. In the meantime, take care, Miss Cardew and my condolences. Mr and Mrs Sherbourne will be on hand to see to your comfort. Now go attend your aunt if that is what you feel you need to do.'

Elenor resisted the urge to hug the doctor. He had blanked George and his pompous assumption he was head of the household.

When they'd finished attending to her aunt, Victoria left the room and Elenor sat for a moment allowing the peace and calm to wash over her. Eventually, Elenor was ready to let her aunt go. She leaned forward and kissed her brow.

'Goodbye Aunt Maude. Safe journey. I will never forget you.'

Her quiet moment was disturbed by the sound of raised voices from George and Victoria. Annoyed at the lack of respect for a house in mourning she closed the door on her aunt and went downstairs. When she pushed open the kitchen door she found Victoria and George facing each other and it was evident there was no love lost between them.

She glared at them, and Victoria had the decency to blush and hang her head in shame.

'How dare you? Please show respect. Whatever your problem is with each other, please sort it out. I am fed up with the tension between you two and need you to stop this constant arguing. Where is your daughter? She will be upset and need comforting. Did you know she looked to my aunt as a grandmother?'

Elenor noted the glance from George to Victoria and recognised his annoyance, but he kept quiet.

'I am going to write letters to those who need to hear of my aunt's death, and you two will both stay and help me through this, or you can leave. Either way I do not care. I am as unsure of my future as you both are, but I will not tolerate this nonsense whilst my aunt is still in her room.'

She turned on her heel and walked away. A new chapter in her life had started and she needed to take control.

CHAPTER 19

At her desk she sat and stared out of the window. The snow fell, and the fire gave her little comfort. After writing four formal letters she pulled out a sheet of paper and wrote to Jackson.

Elenor Cardew,
11 Stephenson Road,
Coventry.

Dear Jackson,
It is with deep sadness I write to you with news of my aunt. Early this morning before the dawn, she left us. It was a peaceful passing, but for me, a sad one.
There is much for me to consider but until I know of what is expected of me, I will remain here. The doctor informed me my aunt's solicitor will be visiting soon, and as the doctor is also an old friend of hers, she has asked him to organise her funeral, which I understand will be a week from today.
It is a lonely day, but I am sure Rose will help me through it with her child's view of life and death.
Your letter has given me great comfort during these

125

past few dark hours, and I accept your invitation to tea, providing I am still living here or free to do so. My future is uncertain, but I have plans to seek employment in Coventry. I have no intention of becoming dependent upon my brothers again.

Please fly with care, your friendship is valuable to me.

With affection, your friend,
Elenor.

Aunt Maude left her home at 4.32 in the afternoon. It was a dignified removal, and Elenor was grateful to all involved.

Doctor Blake returned in the early evening and brought along her aunt's solicitor. Victoria announced them to Elenor who sat in the front room.

'Elenor. Allow me to introduce Nigel Andrews.'

A middle-aged gentleman stood alongside the doctor, his face as sombre as his suit. He made Elenor nervous.

All three shook hands and Elenor invited them to sit. Victoria hovered in the doorway.

'It's all right, Victoria. I'll attend to my guests. You get some rest. Thank you for today.'

'My condolences, Miss Cardew. Under normal circumstances I would not be asked to carry out duties so soon after a client's death, but your aunt left strict instructions, and the doctor and I are honour bound to carry them out.'

Elenor sat back down, and the men followed suit. Although he gave her a polite smile, the solicitor still unnerved Elenor. She sipped at the cordial she'd poured earlier in the evening.

'Thank you, sir. Doctor, would you mind helping yourself and Mr Andrews to a drink? I am afraid my knowledge of what gentlemen drink is poor, and my hands have not stopped shaking since my aunt left us.'

'We understand. Mrs Matthews was quite frank about your background, and of what will happen when you return to your home.'

There it was. The 'when you return home' statement. Elenor took a mouthful of drink and screwed up her nose at the glass.

'Doctor, would it be wrong to ask for the medicinal brandy so long after the event?'

She looked to the man with kind eyes and they twinkled back at her, but they did nothing to lift the cloud which had settled over her head.

'Well, at least I know what my future holds, Mr Andrews, and it is more than Mr and Mrs Sherbourne. I assume the items my aunt gifted to me are mine to keep? I am not sure I will be able to transport the wireless set back to Cornwall, but I will be able to carry the rest.'

The solicitor drained the last of his glass and leaned over the arm of his chair and opened his briefcase. He held out a letter.

'This is from your aunt. Her instructions are you read it alone tonight, and I will return tomorrow to assist you with the formalities. Doctor Blake and I won't keep you any longer. Again, my condolences. I will call around eleven in the morning if that is suitable?'

Elenor rose to her feet and took the letter from him.

'Thank you. The time is perfect. Will you be here too, doctor?'

'No, my dear. My work is done here unless you become unwell. That said, should you need me for any advice or help, please do not hesitate to ask. As I said, your aunt was a friend.'

His smile warmed her heart, and she understood her aunt's fondness for the man.

'Thank you. I'll see you both out.'

She pulled open the door and was startled to see George standing in front of her, it displeased her to see he was just as startled. The man had been eavesdropping.

'Gentleman, Mr Sherbourne is keen to assist, so I will leave him to lock up behind you. Goodnight, and again, thank you.'

She did not wait for a response but took herself back into the front room and curled up on the sofa. She slit the envelope open and pulled out its contents. With a deep breath she unfolded the paper and looked down at the scrawled handwriting of her aunt.

My Dearest Elenor,

This letter is possibly easier for me to write than it is for you to read, in spite of my frail hands. I do hope you mourn me. Forgive my bluntness, for if you do not then I have misjudged you and our relationship.

Your life has not been an easy one and I blame my brother-in-law and your siblings. You are probably worrying about your future in Coventry and the truth is, I am too. I have moved in haste with my instructions so soon after my death because I fear you will pack and run back to Tre Lodhen before considering your options.

I have instructed my solicitor to write a formal will on my behalf, but for your benefit, I will lay out the basis of it here.

I leave everything I own to you. Sell what you want and bank it for the future. The house is rented but is paid for until the end of 1940. Victoria and Albert can stay until then, and I have organised a salary until the end of the tenancy. George Sherbourne is to be offered the position of your tutor. He is to instruct you on how to handle your household accounts in exchange for his bed and board. You will employ them both, never forget that, or to allow him to convince you otherwise. Should they decide differently, then Mr Andrews is instructed to give Victoria a small sum of money to see her over for a few months until re-employed. Mr Andrews will be your main point of contact for all things relating to the property.

My bank manager will contact you at a later date. You will not be rich, but most definitely not destitute. Do not fall for the flattery of young fools who will waste away your inheritance once your name is theirs. I will add, I trust our friend the pilot.

You are the daughter I longed for, and I begged your father to allow you to live with me after your mother died, but he would not hear of it. It saddens me we only had a short time together, but I want to thank you for bringing so much joy into my life. Elenor, I wish you every happiness for the future. I leave you with more than my material goods. I leave you with my love.

Aunt Maude.

Elenor reread the letter and slid it back inside the envelope. Her heart pounded behind her ribs and her breath came fast and heavy. She was to have money in a bank and she employed people. Her brothers would never see her again, and she could stay in Coventry. Overwhelmed and tired from the emotional events. Elenor took herself to bed and hoped her active thoughts would settle so she could get a good night's rest.

Noise outside her bedroom door alerted Elenor it was daytime. Sleep had come easier than she thought it might. Her aunt's letter nestled snug under her pillow, reminding her its contents were not a dream. Once again footsteps outside her room distracted her, and she climbed out of bed, pulled on her dressing gown and pulled the door open.

'George. Can I help you?'

Her voice held no politeness. The last thing she expected to see was him loitering outside of her bedroom door.

'Elenor. Good morning. We were wondering if you would be down for breakfast as usual.'

'I shall and please tell Victoria not to bring me tea upstairs. I'll have just toast for breakfast. Thank you.'

George made no move to leave.

'Something else, George?'

'It is rather delicate and needs to be addressed sooner rather than later, Elenor.'

'Well, as I am not yet ready to talk to you, and am in need of my breakfast, I will find you after I have finished.'

Without giving him the opportunity to respond, she closed the door.

She knew he wanted to find out about Victoria's position and was quite within his rights to be concerned, but Elenor had no desire to discuss such important matters on the landing in her nightclothes at seven in the morning. Today was going to be a long one with many decisions to make.

Entering the dining room flagged up one of her decisions to be made. George sat in her aunt's seat reading a letter. His disrespect, assumption, and arrogance stared Elenor in the face and her mind was made up. He had to go even if it meant losing a hardworking woman like Victoria.

He laid down the letter and looked up at her.

'Ah, you've arrived just in time. Victoria will be returning with poached eggs and kippers. You need to eat more than just toast. How are you this morning, Elenor?'

Not having made any move to sit at her seat, Elenor just

stared at him. He wore a black cravat and braces, but no jacket. His shirt sleeves were rolled to the elbow, and he looked comfortable in his environment. Too comfortable.

'Did Victoria cover the door knocker this morning, do you know?'

His question threw her, and she glanced around the room, then back at George.

'I beg your pardon?' she said.

'Mourning preparations. I forgot to ask Victoria if she had made a start. Ah, here she is now.'

Still standing, Elenor turned in a daze towards Victoria entering the room. She wore a black skirt and blouse. It reminded Elenor her navy clothes were not suitable. Victoria's outfit highlighted the dark rims under her eyes, and her complexion was paler than the previous day.

Victoria set the tray onto the table.

'Good morning, Elenor. George told me you have requested his company for breakfast. I understand you have things to talk about. I'll leave this here and he can tell me when you've finished.'

Elenor stared at George but he showed no sign of being caught out in a lie. The last man she would invite for breakfast would be George Sherbourne.

'Victoria, select food for yourself and sit with us. I have something to ask you and besides, you look worn out and I won't have you running around undernourished. Is Rose in school today?'

'Yes, she's just left. Thank you,' Victoria said and went towards a chair.

A movement from George caught Elenor's attention, she saw him make a slight move of his head from left to right, suggesting he warned Victoria off from joining them.

'George, are you not tutoring today? As you are not actually employed by the household, there is no reason for you to sit around here all day. I have the solicitor arriving at eleven, and a couple of things for Victoria to assist me with, other than that I won't need anyone else watching over me. Kind thought it is though, thank you.'

Elenor held back the barrage of abuse she wanted to hurtle at the snide male worming his way into her world.

'Victoria. Sit. Eat with me, please.'

Victoria looked at the spare seat next to her husband and then to him.

'Forgive me Elenor, I have eaten my breakfast already, and have things in the oven which need watching.'

'I understand.'

Elenor pulled out her seat and sat down.

'As I said, George, you can continue with your regular work, so please, do not feel you have to sit here and keep me company. I have the need for some time alone.'

The dismissive tone in her voice worked. George said nothing; he didn't need to, the redness from his neck and face told Elenor enough.

He snatched up his letter and left the room, following his wife into the kitchen. Within a short while, Elenor heard raised voices coming from the parlour. Puzzled, she followed the sound.

'Walking around as if she owns the place. She'll soon have her brothers to answer to, and we'll see how she likes that, three men to look after.'

George's voice filtered out into the hallway.

'They might not want us to work for them, George. We need to consider that possiblity.'

A thud told Elenor George had hit a piece of furniture.

'Having Rose was a big mistake. We must find a way to sort out this mess. Careless.'

'Careless? You forced yourself on me. I didn't have a choice, keeping her hidden . . .'

132

Elenor burst into the room, she'd heard enough. She'd been unwanted by her father but never her mother.

'Have you no respect?'

Victoria stood shell-shocked by her appearance. George stood open mouthed.

'How dare you enter into such a personal squabble in this house? Get out, the pair of you. Go to the kitchen, compose yourselves and then come and find me in my study in ten minutes. I have something to say about this whole wretched situation. And George, hold your tongue against Victoria, understand me?'

Elenor marched from the room without waiting for a response from either of them and back into the dining room. She poured herself a cup of tea and buttered two slices of toast. She heard the couple rush towards the kitchen and close the door. She bit into the toast, which was cold and tasteless but she ate it, nevertheless. The clock on the mantle ticked onto 8.45, and she sighed. Eleven couldn't come soon enough. The tea was stewed, but she gulped down several mouthfuls, then made her way to her study.

Picking up her pen she scribbled out a letter to Mrs Green informing her of her aunt's death, and that the solicitor would deal with the closing of her account. She asked for Sally to assist Victoria in choosing a mourning outfit similar to her navy, or whatever Mrs Green felt suitable. Victoria would be given a suitable sum to cover the cost. Elenor knew she had enough allowance money put away in her room.

Outside the window Elenor could see the world drifting past. A woman walked by holding a child's hand, an old man ambled along behind them. Across the road she could see a man polishing a car bonnet, and another cleaning windows. All unaware of the loss from inside her home, all going about their business unaffected by recent death, but she knew, if told, they would show more respect than George and Victoria.

A light tap at the door meant the pair were waiting for her to call them into the room. She left it a few seconds to compose herself.

'Come in.'

She turned around to face them. George strode in first.

'Our apologies.'

Elenor put up her hand to stop him talking. She pointed to a chair slightly to the right of her.

'Victoria, take a seat.'

Victoria did as she was told, and George looked about for one for himself.

'You won't be staying long, George,' Elenor said.

He straightened his shoulders and she could see he was put out by her comment. The longer he stood in front of her the more her temper rose, and she was not going to allow him to goad her into failure.

'As you were so vocal this morning, I could not help but overhear you. Thank goodness Rose did not do the same. Neither of you have a civil word to say to one another. It makes me uncomfortable in my own home.'

'We apologise, Elenor. We have placed you in an awkward position, and our behaviour is unforgivable. When your brothers arrive to take over, we will be gone. Please, find it in your heart to write a fair reference for me, I understand it is a lot to ask of you given the circumstances, but I did work hard for your aunt,' Victoria said.

George's head turned to her with such a speed Elenor feared he would break his neck.

'Thank you for your apology both of you. George, you need to get to work, your pupil will not gain a good education if his master is not in attendance.'

With her hands behind her back, Elenor smiled at him

and waited for him to speak. Instead it surprised her that he did as she said and left. Victoria watched him leave and turned back to Elenor.

'Elenor, I am heart sore with what you overheard this morning. Please, think kindly on what I ask about a reference. I will stay to help until after the funeral, and then we will leave.'

Elenor turned to her desk and picked up the letter for Mrs Green. She held it out to Victoria.

'I have listened to what you have to say, and whilst I consider your request, please take this to Mrs Green at the department store. Stay for her response. Mr Andrews will be here when you return, and I would appreciate privacy until he has gone. I think the fresh air will do you good, and it is best I do not see you or George for a few hours.'

Victoria took the letter and after a while Elenor saw her walk by the window accompanied by George. They parted ways at the bottom of the road, and she watched him drop a letter into the post box on the corner, then went back to her own letter writing. She was alone inside the house for the first time.

She went upstairs to her uncle's room and began clearing items she had no use for, then did the same in her aunt's. She kept a hand mirror and hairbrush she'd always admired for herself. She wanted to have a family heirloom, and Elenor knew it had once belonged to her grandmother. A walnut jewellery box sat on the left of the dressing table, and Elenor hesitated before opening it; somehow it seemed disrespectful. Inside she found various pretty pieces but nothing she would wish to keep for herself, except a strand of black jade beads. Once she had filled several bags she set them aside to be sold at the local auction house. Elenor also kept two of the small silver items Rose had polished.

She would give them to her when she came home from school. A gift from Aunt Maude.

The dull thud of the door knocker announced the arrival of the solicitor.

'Mr Andrews. Do come in.'

An hour of paper signing followed, with the end result overwhelming Elenor. She'd never owned so much money. It would rent a property for several years if she was careful.

The postman distracted her from reading formal papers the solicitor had left behind for her to read, and she watched the man amble along her front path. A solitary letter lay on the mat and it was addressed to George. What caught her attention was the postage stamp. It was two Angels hovering over the world, with an aeroplane between them. There was a number six and the word cent printed on the stamp, along with Canada. A letter from Samuel Fleming. If only it had been another from Jackson.

CHAPTER 20

Elenor moved around the house absorbing all that was hers. It seemed ruthless to consider such things so soon, but she needed to occupy herself.

Movement in the kitchen meant Victoria had returned.

'Elenor?'

Victoria's voice echoed in the hallway and Elenor went out to greet her.

'Mrs Green is here. She wanted to see you and offer her condolences.'

'Thank you, Victoria. Bring her in here.'

Mrs Green put her arms out to Elenor and embraced her as a friend.

'I am so sorry for your loss. Mrs Matthews was a fine woman.'

Releasing her hold, Mrs Green moved to a seat. Elenor sat opposite comforted by the woman's presence.

'Thank you. I will miss her.'

Mrs Green pointed to the packages on the table.

'I selected two dresses and a black cardigan. Sally sends her condolences. Will you return to Cornwall?'

Elenor shook her head.

'I want to see what Coventry offers without Aunt Maude

for a few months. My brothers don't need me to help on the farm, so I am a free agent and will look for a job here. I'd like to work in Owen's. Did I remember to ask you if you'd like tea?'

Mrs Green rose from her chair and crossed over to Elenor. She took her hands.

'My dear, I have to return to work. I know we are fully staffed at the moment but I will let you know as soon as a position is available. Look after yourself and when you are ready, come and see me.'

Elenor watched her walk towards the door.

'I'll see myself out. Look over the dresses and if they are not suitable we'll try again. Goodbye dear. Take heart in knowing your aunt was terribly fond of you.'

'Thank you again, Mrs Green.'

Elenor took the dresses upstairs and tried them on. They were a perfect fit and choice. Soft voices muttered from behind the kitchen door and she guessed George had returned home. The evening would be entertaining if all went to plan. She entered the kitchen and addressed Victoria unpacking shopping into a cupboard.

'I will eat my meal in the front room, Victoria, not the dining room, and please join me. You won't mind will you, George? It's just to keep me company during this sad time. I need to talk to another female, you do understand.'

She kept her voice soft and added a tired tone. Without fail, George pumped out his chest with importance.

'Not at all Elenor. My wife can keep you company after our meal, by all means.'

Adding a little tut, Elenor gave a smile.

'Silly me. I thought I'd said, she'll be eating with me, after she's attended to you and Rose. As I said, I am in need of female company.'

She held her head to one side emphasising sadness.

'Of course.'

George's sharp reply made Elenor want to laugh out loud. She knew it was wrong of her to taunt him, but she couldn't help herself.

She held up a book.

'Until then I am going to settle down to read. Enjoy your evening, George.'

She watched him shift from foot to foot and knew he wanted to speak. He would be curious about the solicitor's visit, but Elenor had no intention of telling him the outcome just yet.

'Actually, in hindsight, maybe you would like to join us around seven-thirty.'

George stroked his chin.

'I do have a few papers to mark, but I should be free by seven-thirty and happy to join you both. The bedrooms will need to be aired in anticipation of your brothers arriving for the funeral. I can oversee Victoria and ensure they are suitable for them.'

Oh, George. You have played right into my hands. Thank you.

Time spent with Victoria was quiet and both ate very little.

'This is cosy,' Elenor said.

'It is and thank you for inviting me to join you,' Victoria replied.

'I wanted to thank you for the care you've given my aunt over the years.'

'She gave me the position when I was pregnant with Rose. George arrived a year after. He'd been abroad teaching.'

'Really? I thought you came together.'

'No. We were, um, separated for a while. His work. My duties. I . . .'

A loud knock on the door interrupted the conversation, and George entered the room and Elenor ignored the way he helped himself to a generous brandy without asking.

'Do you think the snow will linger? It will hold up my aunt's funeral if it does,' she said and curled up on the sofa. 'Oh, by the way, did you find your letter, George? It has a very pretty stamp, and I see it is from Canada. Could I have it for my scrapbook please?

George gave a slight shrug of his right shoulder.

'Ah my friend, Samuel Fleming, I'll save it for Rose's project.'

Elenor ignored the slight.

'Of course. She'll be pleased.'

He took a large swig of the brandy and Elenor watched him swallow.

'I take it you understood the meeting with the solicitor or do you need me interpret his jargon? It must be quite daunting. When will we know the outcome?'

Another put down of her ability to understand things.

'On the contrary, I understood everything. My aunt was most explicit with her wishes, and Mr Andrews explained them well enough.'

George choked on his brandy and all eyes went to him.

'Are you all right, George? Gracious, it must have gone down the wrong way.'

He looked back at her with watering eyes and nodded.

When George had stopped coughing, she swung her legs around and stood up.

'You both must be worried about the future. I assume you do not earn enough as a tutor to provide a home for your family, George?'

George shifted in his seat and Victoria went pale. She faced them both with her hands behind her back.

'You will never know the outcome of the will as a whole,

it is not your business, but I can tell you I have two options for you.'

She looked to them both, first Victoria who sat with her hands in her lap and her brow creased with concern, and then George, who sat upright with his chest puffed out as usual.

'Two options? I don't understand what you mean?' he said.

'Oh, that part is easy, it means two choices George.'

Elenor got the distinct impression that George might have choked on his drink again had he taken a sip. She was enjoying the moment although she realised it was not fair to torment Victoria any longer.

'As Victoria is employed here, this is directed at her. Victoria, the new tenant of the house will be in need of someone to help run the place as you did with my aunt, and you are offered the position,' she said.

'George is also offered a job as a tutor. The offer only stands for both of you.'

George grunted. He went to stand but changed his mind.

'Ridiculous,' he muttered.

Elenor ignored him.

'The other alternative is a sum of money in Victoria's name to cover a month's wages and rent whilst she seeks a new position.'

An uncomfortable silence fell, and George looked at his wife.

On his feet once again, George crossed over to her. His neck was red and his voice menacing.

'I will not be told what to do or think by a farm girl from goodness knows where. One who has no idea of decent behaviour, or what her position is in life. Your return to the farm cannot come quick enough. Let the solicitor talk to us about our position in this house. Take your aunt's money and leave us be.'

'George!'

Victoria tugged at his arm.

'We need Elenor's reference.'

'You need her reference. I need nothing from her.'

'George, you have said your piece and I mine. Sit down, be quiet and listen.'

'I . . .'

'George. Do as Elenor asks, please. It is getting late.'

With a deep breath in and out, Elenor spoke in softer tones.

'The loss of my aunt has been an upset to the three of us, but I am her beneficiary. My brothers have inherited nothing. I'm the new tenant, and if Victoria wishes, her new employer. The job on offer, George is to teach me book-keeping. The choice is yours.'

George stared at her in disbelief. Elenor walked to the tray, picked up George's glass and held it out to him. He shook his head and waved it away. Victoria went to Elenor and held out her hand.

'Thank you for still considering us after my husband's outburst. George?'

He ran his hands down the front of his trouser legs and looked at Victoria.

'As my wife said. Apologies.'

He held out his hand and Elenor shook it.

'Thank you. Here's to a fresh start. I take it you have accepted my offer of employment?'

George nodded, and Victoria gave a small smile.

'We do have to consider Rose's needs. Can I ask we also be allowed to visit our families as before?' George asked.

'George, I understand. Family is important. And talking of family, you will never meet my brothers and I do not want them let into this house. They do not know, nor will they need to know of my aunt's death. Is that clear?'

Elenor directed the words to George.

George looked at her in surprise, and she knew she'd caught him considering making contact with them.

'They are not welcome here. Your jobs depend on it.' Elenor said and left the room with a sense he'd understood loud and clear.

CHAPTER 21

The morning of the funeral was a damp miserable one and Elenor was grateful for her warm coat. The funeral procession moved slowly away from the home and after an hour's service, the cars brought them back to Stephenson Road.

Victoria bustled about with cups of tea, but Elenor sat accepting condolences from a line of strangers. The day dragged on until three o'clock when she begged George to discourage more visitors. It was the loneliest day she'd ever experienced.

Each day that followed she rose expecting to see her aunt seated in her favourite chair and a deep sense of loss engulfed her from morning to night. Her excitement at seeing Jackson again helped her through the grieving process, yet at times she felt it was disrespectful to her aunt.

Victoria and George improved their efforts to get along, and tried to parent on a friendlier level, although Elenor noticed Victoria struggle. Rose walked through the house under a cloud of silence and black clothing, and it had a profound effect on Elenor each time she saw her.

On the morning of the fifteenth, a dream of life-changing challenges woke Elenor with a start. She'd dreamt of crying by raging waters, then the waves eased and Elenor moved along the coast to meet her mother and aunt for a picnic by the sea. They'd watched a bird wrapped in colourful ribbons flying behind it as it swooped through soft clouds tinged with yellow sunshine. Her mother told her to chase and catch the bird. Her aunt told her to catch a cloud. Laughing, and encouraged by the warmth of their love she ran along the soft sand and a gentle breeze lifted her until she soared high, and she captured both. Once she reached the two women back on the beach, they smiled, waved at her, then held hands and walked away.

She dressed quickly and ran downstairs.

'Victoria, Rose,' she called as she moved from room to room opening windows.

The kitchen door flung open and Victoria hurried along the hallway.

'What is it, Elenor? What's happened?'

Rose ran to Elenor when they found her in the parlour.

'Are you hurt?' she asked, her voice laden with worry.

Rose bent down and hugged her.

'No, darling girl. Today I feel alive. This house is gloomy, and my aunt would hate the sadness. Go and dress in your normal clothes. No more black. It is not disrespecting my aunt. I had a dream she and my mother were together. They were happy, and everything was so bright and beautiful. I think they were telling me it is time to move on with life. I'm meeting Jackson tomorrow, and will enjoy tea in pretty clothes, not a black mourning outfit.'

Elenor drew breath and both Victoria and Rose stared at her as she moved around the room pulling open curtains, and opening windows. The cold air rushed in and the door slammed shut.

'That scared me,' Rose declared.

'Me too. Are you sure you are feeling well enough to go out, Elenor?' Victoria asked.

'Yes. Yes. We need to air the rooms and brighten them with pretty things. My aunt loved me for being me.' She swept her arm around the room. 'This is not me! I cannot bear the gloom anymore. We will freshen up this home and live a better life. Sunshine on a gloomy day is the cure for sadness.'

Elenor flopped into a seat and beckoned Rose to her.

'What do you say young Rose? Doom and gloom or sunshine and happiness?'

Rose jumped up and down and clapped her hands.

'Sunshine and happiness,' she said.

With a loud laugh Elenor looked at Victoria.

'Don't be so shocked, Victoria. We have war knocking on our door. Gas masks in the hallway, and a future we are unsure of. It is time to step out of the darkness. We need joy in our lives again.'

'Well, if it is what you want, I'll help you work your way through your grief,' Victoria said and folded her arms.

'Don't look so grumpy. Come on Rose, I'll race you to my aunt's room.'

By the following morning a much happier Elenor had internal butterflies. Three o'clock could not come soon enough.

A hazy mist washed over the trees in the street and the snow now turned to grey slush, but Elenor found beauty in the thaw. She vowed nothing would overshadow her senses. Death could not be allowed to control life.

Dressed in her deep wine outfit with her hair loose and crowned by a wine beret, she sat at her desk. From there she watched Jackson stride along the pavement. Tall and straight-backed his physique could only be admired. Not wanting George or Victoria to break into the magic of the moment, she pulled on her coat and no sooner had he knocked on the door, she pulled it open.

'Elenor. Are you heading out or in a hurry to greet me?' Jackson said and stood with his cap in his hand.

'Both,' Elenor said. 'We'll come back here later, but I need to leave. To get outside of these four walls.'

'I'm so sorry about . . .'

Elenor placed her finger to his lips.

'Ssh, don't . . . save it for later. Happiness first.'

She pulled the door closed and looped her arm through a bemused Jackson's. Throughout their walk into town she chattered about many things related to the area, pointing out various buildings and their purpose. By the time they arrived at the tearooms, she'd covered each shop in the main street and realised Jackson had said nothing but yes or no, or interesting, at selected intervals.

As they sat at the table and placed their order, she smiled and boldly took his hand across the table.

'I've waited so long for this day. My aunt's death has suffocated me – did suffocate me, until today.'

Jackson made no attempt to remove his hand from under hers, even when the waitress brought their tea.

'I am sorry for your loss. I enjoyed your aunt's company.'

'Thank you. I'm sorry I've jabbered on today, but I've been stifled by it all, and my daily companions – Rose aside – are hard work.'

Jackson listened as he drank his tea and when she finished speaking she gave him an apologetic smile.

'I've talked too much again, haven't I?'

'Not at all. It is better than crying. Do you know where you go from here? Will you stay in Coventry?

Elenor nodded.

'I'm not going back to Cornwall, and I would like to find work locally. Tell me your news.'

'Hmm. It is not news I want to tell. Not seeing you so happy and wanting more of your delightful company.'

'Oh?'

'I'm waiting for papers to leave England. I have to return to Canada, and soon.'

Although Elenor always knew this moment was going to come, she didn't want to hear it today. She struggled to find words to express her disappointment but felt it wise to say nothing. Her eyes moistened with tears and in such a public place she didn't want to embarrass herself or Jackson.

'So, this is a farewell feast,' she said with jest.

'I will write to you if you don't mind. But don't look on this as farewell.'

'Everyone I . . .' Elenor felt it best to say no more. Her hand trembled as she lifted her cup and the warmth of the café no longer touched her body. A chill of loss overwhelmed her, much like the loss of her aunt.

'Tell me about your home, tell me something about where you live.'

Elenor needed to direct the conversation away from miserable thoughts.

'Ah, you have babbling brooks, we have raging waters. Crystal waters cascading over boulders, some the size of a motor car. Wide open spaces with pine trees so high they touch the clouds, and the smell they give off reminds us of Christmas trees every day. Totem poles, beautiful carved statues created out of cedar wood by the original inhabitants of the country. Each one has a different meaning for the First Nations, and their colours are vibrant and bright.'

'It sounds incredible,' Elenor said in awe.

'It is; my family run lumber mills – logs and timber – and I get to hike into the mountains to select the trees for felling. I never fail to fall in love with the mountains. They are vast and look magnificent even when covered in snow. Then we have the red-gold of the leaves of the maple trees when they turn the ground scarlet in the fall.'

'I've seen a few images of totem poles in my encyclopedia, but they are black and white. Everything sounds tall and large out there. What's the fall?'

'You call it autumn. Compared to Britain our countryside is enormous and has the most rugged, beautiful scenery but this country has a lot to offer in its own way, a quaintness. I discover something new each day. I'd be happy living here in England, providing I could visit my homeland each year.'

'You must write to me more about your town, village and city. I need to fill my scrapbook. It all sounds so wonderful,' Elenor said.

Jackson gave her a grin.

'I'll send anything I think you will enjoy.'

'Do you know when you will ever return to England?' Elenor said, her voice barely a whisper.

'I'll come back one day, Elenor.'

'Come and say goodbye to Rose, but please, she is fragile. It isn't easy for her in the house. I've had a spring-cleaning frenzy and tried to cheer us up with colour to fight off the gloom.'

'I'll do my best.'

On the walk home Jackson did the talking and Elenor listened in silence with a heavy heart.

Inside the house Jackson commented and complimented on the alterations. Rose played tour guide and Elenor followed behind, absorbing every movement Jackson made. She stored memories to remind her of a man she'd fallen in love with but who would walk away never knowing the depth of her feelings.

'Rose, Jackson has come to say goodbye to us. He has promised to write but it will be a very long time before we see him again.'

Rose looked at Jackson and then at Elenor.

'Are you not going to be friends with her anymore?'

'I will always be her friend – and yours. My job is important so I have to go. Besides, my mom wants to see me again.'

'Can I give you a hug for good luck?'

'I'd like that very much.'

'Rose, fetch your parents to come and say goodbye, please,' Elenor said and opened the door. She turned back to Jackson who stood looking at her and she could see his reluctance to leave.

'I'll shake your hand if you don't mind,' she said. 'I think a hug from Rose can never be beaten.'

She held out her hand and Jackson took it in his and stroked the back with his thumb.

'I'll return and claim one from you another time. In the meantime, I'll leave you with this.' He pulled her into his arms and for the second time in her life Elenor gave into the warmth of his lips. Only a discreet cough from Victoria broke them apart.

As she stood at the front door, he stopped at the end of the street and looked back and waved. Then he turned the corner and left her with a pain in her heart so deep Elenor could no longer see sunshine. The darkness had returned.

CHAPTER 22

February 1939

'Woo-hoo. Someone's got a Valentine.'

Rose's voice rang out around the hallway in a sing-song tease.

'Miss E Cardew. I think it is for yoo-hoo!'

Elenor laughed as she ventured downstairs. Rose ran up and down waving the letter in her hand.

'Stop your teasing and give me the post.'

Rose handed over the thick pile but refused to give her the one from the top.

Elenor flicked through the mixture of post and gave a giggle.

'Oh, see. I am not the only one to receive a love letter, Miss R Sherbourne,' she said and held another envelope high above her head. 'Swap?'

Rose gave up jumping high to try and reach her post and handed Elenor hers.

Elenor could smell cologne and engine oil and smiled. Jackson's familiar perfume always brought her a measure of hope.

Rose tore at her envelope and a card with cupids firing arrows fell to the floor.

'I wonder who it is from. Johnathon? That boy we met in the park?'

Elenor watched the girl run to show her parents. Dear Jackson had thought of Rose. Her envelope also smelled of him. She held hers close and went to the parlour to read it in peace.

Dear Elenor,

I know it is usual to hide the name of the sender of a Valentine's card, but I am making use of this one to write my latest update.

Since I last held you in my arms things have been busier with extra flying hours, so forgive me for not writing sooner. Thank you for your last letter, it is packed in my case ready to take home with me, to be put in a box of memories of my trip to England.

My commander-in-chief has signed off my British hours and I will be heading home by the time you receive this. War news is not looking favourable and if the forecast moves the way I think it might, it will be years before I can hold you in my arms again, and it is therefore my painful duty to let you go. The words read harsh on paper.

We are both young and our lives should not be put on hold – life is too short. You deserve to have a man with you on a more regular basis. Someone to take you to the movies, a lover to give you more than promises from afar.

I pray you will forgive my attempt at encouraging you to become more than a friend. It was unforgivable, and wrong of me to take advantage of your friendship.

Please, have a good life and should you find forgive-ness, please write to me.

With my deep friendship and respect,
Jackson St John.

Elenor watched the card and envelope flutter to the floor. It was all too much to bear. Another loss. She'd trusted Jackson with her heart and now he'd broken it, and with a Valentine's card of all things. She wanted to scream but held it inside. She stepped over the paper items on the floor and went into the hallway. Rose was reading the words of her card out loud to her parents, and Elenor couldn't bear to hear any more. She pulled on her coat and pushed her feet into her outdoor shoes. Nothing had prepared her for this new emotion. The front door clicked behind her and she focused on walking out of the street and towards the park.

For two hours she walked in the rain, barely noticing how drenched her coat and shoes were. As she walked she made plans to leave Coventry. London was a good distance away and offered a different kind of life. No one would know she had gone, that way she could never be hurt again. No bad news would touch her from those she loved. Leaving Rose would be hard, but it would be better than living in fear of losing her. And she would, one day. She would pack as soon as she could face going home again. She marched along the river bank, but her heartbreak overwhelmed her and she slid to the floor into darkness.

'She's coming round'

'Shhh.'

'Elenor. How do you feel?'

'My girl, you gave us quite a scare.'

Voices jabbered inside her head and Elenor tried to block them out. She wanted quiet to think.

Her body ached. She felt the warmth of a cloth on her face.

'Pack. I need to pack.'

'Hush now. You need to rest.'

'London.'

With effort Elenor tried to move. Her head pounded with pain and her joints burned.

'Well, she's out of the woods. Still delirious though. Keep her warm and try to get fluids down her. I'll check in tomorrow. I'll see myself out.'

Elenor made out the voice of the doctor. What was he doing in the park? Why was she lying down? She needed to get home to pack for London. She pulled at her coat, but it had wrapped itself around her body and she struggled to get free.

'Lie still, Elenor. Don't tire yourself.'

Victoria's voice was soft, and Elenor could smell fresh baking.

'I'll leave you to it and take Rose to school.'

George.

Why were they all in the park?

Too tired to think anymore, Elenor gave into her weariness and lay still. Her head pain eased.

'How is she today?'

Elenor roused herself to the sound of the doctor's voice and opened her eyes. The light of the room glared bright and she squinted.

'Hello, young lady.'

The doctor's face was a blur. She lifted her head from the pillow, but the pain increased and she fell back.

'Take it steady. You hit your head when you fell. Luckily the park-keeper found you in time. Goodness knows how long you'd been in the water.'

'Water?' Elenor tried to speak but a cough rasped from her lungs.

'We'll explain later. You've been out cold for the best part of a week.'

A week. She'd never packed for London. Why did she keep thinking about London?

A pain in her chest caught her breath again, and more coughing ensued.

'Listen to Victoria and do everything she says. Understand?'

Unable to nod without experiencing more pain, Elenor raised her head from the counterpane.

Darkness moved across her eyes and she fell under its spell once more.

Recovery from pneumonia and her head injury took its toll on Elenor. Victoria nursed her through the weeks of recovery with a tenderness Elenor had never experienced, and showed a side to Victoria that was unusual. George kept Rose from sitting beside her for too long and reassured her that everything was running smoothly downstairs. He and Victoria had moved a bed into the parlour in preparation for when she was ready to move around again.

Mrs Green visited and told her there would be a position vacant before the year was out, a member of staff was expecting a baby. She would put Elenor's name down as an applicant when the time came, but Elenor couldn't think that far into the future. She focused upon small daily tasks such as washing herself.

Each day Elenor tried to remember what had happened in the park but drew a blank. No-one could explain any more than that she'd been found bleeding from the head, hooked across a rock in the freezing river. The park-keeper found a wet receipt from Owen's in her pocket, made out her aunt's name and sent for help; from then on Mrs Green took charge.

One afternoon the sunshine broke through a chink in the curtains and Elenor struggled from the bed. Her lungs burned, and her legs felt like jelly, but she made it to the chair beside the window. Outside birds flitted from tree to tree, and Elenor could see spring nudging winter aside.

She sat going over in her head things she felt she needed to remember, and once satisfied she knew her name and address, and those of the people who'd attended to her needs whilst she'd been ill, she gave up trying to fathom out why she had intended to go to London. She'd once asked Victoria, but she couldn't give an answer.

'Can I come in?' Rose's voice called from behind the closed door.

'Come in, Rose.'

Her young friend stepped inside, and her face broke out into a wide grin.

'You're out of bed. You still look ill. You are skinny.'

'And you are still cheeky.'

Rose pulled the counterpane from the bed and dragged it across the floor. She pushed and poked it onto Elenor's lap.

'We have to keep you warm. Do you want a cup of tea? I'll go and tell Mummy. She's been ever so worried about you.'

'Everyone has been so kind. Yes please, ask Mummy for tea.'

She watched Rose scamper from the door, and slowly a memory returned of her jumping up and down in the hallway. Valentine's Day, and then Elenor remembered the reason she'd wanted to leave Coventry. A memory she'd forced to the back of her mind. A memory which appeared to have caused a burden on others. A memory no longer worthy of her time. She needed to concentrate on getting better.

The door opened, and Rose guided her mother inside the room. Victoria carried a tray laden with food, but Elenor could not face eating. She sipped at a cup of tea handed to her but felt only its warmth, she tasted nothing. She watched Victoria fuss around her bed plumping pillows, and Rose helping fold towels and bedclothes. Their lives had a purpose. To help her heal.

'Thank you,' she whispered, her body drained of all energy.

'I'll help you back to bed. The doctor said you mustn't tire yourself,' Victoria said, and helped Elenor across the room.

'How long has it been, Victoria? Since my accident?'

'Oh, we're talking a month today. The doctor did consider hospital for you at one point, but he decided moving you might do more harm than good. We've come through the worst, now we have to get you strong again.'

'You've had a lot to do, Victoria. I am truly grateful.'

'I have no doubt in my mind you'd have done the same for any of us. I saw how you tended your aunt.'

'But still, I am grateful. It was my own foolish fault. I remember now why I walked to the park. He let me down,' she said.

Victoria patted her arm.

'I found the card. It is in safe-keeping, but I think you are best off thinking about your future, not the past,' she said.

Elenor lay back and closed her eyes and drew a mental line under the last few weeks of the year. Victoria was right; it was time to look forward not backwards.

CHAPTER 23

'He's looking your way,' Sally whispered from behind the curtain.

'Will you stop it, Sally? He's the leading man and is checking we are ready. You are always trying to pair us off.'

Elenor adjusted the wig on her head and glared at her friend. She looked across at Prince Charming on the opposite side of the stage. He put up two thumbs in encouragement and she returned the gesture with a curtsey.

The local drama group had proven to be a good aid to her recovery and Elenor enjoyed Sally's company during practice, but only when she wasn't trying to marry her friend off to any male looking her way. Tonight's performance of Cinderella was full to capacity and Elenor could see her guests sitting in the front row. Rose sat in a pretty dress swinging her legs with impatience. George, Victoria and Mrs Green sat with programmes clasped in their hands.

The July heat was exacerbated by the layers of lace and the wig, and she kept her fingers crossed she would get through the evening without passing out. Nerves also added to the collection of issues Elenor tried to overcome. Now back in full health, it wouldn't do to faint.

After an hour it was time for her to sing the song for the finale, and Rose bounced in her seat in front. She knew each word and mouthed along with Elenor, and at the end of the performance stood with the rest of the audience. The noise of their applause rang through the hall and the performers ended the evening with pride.

'We did it,' Sally said and swung Elenor around.

'We did, and my princess did us proud,' Prince Charming said and kissed the back of Elenor's hand. 'Can I tempt you to join me for a drink when we've finished up backstage?' he asked.

Sally pulled faces behind Elenor's back and tried to encourage her to go. Elenor was aware the young man had feelings for her and had often hinted he'd like to walk out with her, but she had no intention of letting another man into her life. Her time at the drama club was freedom from her past, but if she allowed herself to become emotionally involved with a fellow member, it would not allow her to heal after Jackson's rejection. She needed to come to terms with her pain, not hide behind another relationship.

'Thank you, but no. I've enjoyed the evening but need to go home and rest. I have to work tomorrow.'

'Oh, go on. I'll come,' Sally said.

'You go. Enjoy yourselves. When I've finished removing this outfit and make-up I'm heading home with Rose. She'll never forgive me if I don't read her a bedtime story.'

Sally stepped forward and took Elenor's hand. 'You have to get over him.'

'I am. This is about Rose, not me. I'll see you at work tomorrow.' Elenor pulled her friend close and gave her a hug.

The following morning Elenor entered the store and stood behind the *Yardley* counter. She loved serving customers and had many returning customers. Her sales pleased Mrs Green and Elenor couldn't think of a better way of earning a living. She spotted Sally walking across the shop floor and beckoned her over.

'Did you go for a drink?'

'I did, and he was easily swayed, so I have a sneaking feeling you were right to head home. He was waiting for me outside my house this morning. Claims it's on his way to work. You will have to help me out at the new rehearsals. Take him off my hands.'

Sally put her hands together and begged. Elenor laughed. 'Your problem, not mine. I'm not taking anyone off your hands.' She giggled.

'I love you Elenor Cardew, but sometimes you push our friendship to the limits. It is *you* he wants. He'll hang round me until he gets you.'

'No amount of pleading will get me to take your castoffs. Now go and sell some undergarments and leave me to my hand cream. Meet for lunch?'

'Yes. And be prepared for more begging,' Sally said as she walked away with a dramatic swagger.

Morning customers kept Elenor busy and before she knew it, Sally was back at her counter and they headed to the staff room for their bags.

'Ready? Let's eat in the park. It's gorgeous outside.'

'Can't we eat somewhere else? I've not been back since . . .'

'No. We are going to face your demons. You cannot hide from the park, not on a sunny day. You are stronger now. Jackson let you down, but you will let yourself down if you hide from everything because of him.'

Elenor picked up her lunch.

'I will come but if I cry it will be your fault. A lot happened to me that day and I do not know how I'll cope.'

'If you cry Mrs Green will tell you off for black streaks of mascara,' Sally replied.

As they entered the park Elenor felt the hairs on her arms rise and tingle her skin. Sally chattered on about trivial things and they sat on the grass under the shade of a large oak.

'How are you feeling?' Sally asked and took a bite from her sandwich.

'Not as bad as I thought. I'm over Jackson, but it's the traumatic events after which hold me back. I'm afraid of water yet can't remember falling into the river. And the dark can sometimes trigger nightmares.'

'Understandable, I suppose. But now you've shaken off the fear of coming back here, that's a good thing, right?'

'Thanks Sally.'

'For what?'

'For being a bully with a heart.'

Once their lunch break was over they headed back to the store and Elenor felt as if a weight had been lifted from her shoulders.

That evening she kicked off her shoes in the hallway and scooped up two letters from the floor. Victoria and George were away, and Rose was having tea with a school friend. She was due home after six.

The letters were for George, and to Elenor's horror one bore the Canadian post mark. She stared at it and the pain of rejection threatened to reappear. She dropped the letters onto the sideboard in the hallway and walked away. Jackson's grandfather and George still communicated. It was something she had to accept.

Needing a distraction, she fetched the new script for a play from her desk, stepped into the kitchen and poured a glass of water, then sat in the garden to wait for Rose to come home. She did not have to wait long. A whirlwind of activity followed Rose's arrival. A barrage of what she'd done with her friend, what they'd eaten for tea, and what the girl's mother baked, all fell from Rose's lips faster than the speed of light. Elenor walked behind her picking up her coat and bag.

'Excuse me madam. When can I get a word in edge-ways? Just because your parents aren't here doesn't allow for laziness. I'm not your slave. Take these to your room, wash, clean your teeth and get your nightdress on and come and join me. We can sit in the garden where it is cooler. You can have an extra fifteen minutes after your bedtime but no more and bring down a book to read.'

'Thank you.' Rose's voice echoed down the stairs followed by a clattering of drawer banging.

Elenor shook her head and walked outside.

'Ooh, it's much better out here.' Rose's voice broke the silence.

'It is, and you can sit and calm down before bed.'

Rose climbed onto a chair beside Elenor.

'Why did Jackson write to Daddy and not you?'

Never shocked by Rose's ability to surprise her with a blunt question, Elenor found herself lost for words for this one. She'd forgotten the curiosity of a child and that Rose would have found the letters in the hall.

Composing herself, she took time to answer.

'I don't think it is from Jackson. I think it is his grand-father. Your father and he have written to each other for a long time.'

'Why did Jackson be so cruel? Mummy said he was cruel to you. I thought he was a nice man and loved you. He kissed you. Mummy told Daddy. So, if he kissed you he should have married you. Is that why he was cruel?'

Any strength Elenor thought she had left now drained

away. The words from a child's mouth managed to beat the breath from her lungs and she gulped for air.

'Jackson wasn't cruel. He had to go back to his own country.'

'But he hurt you and you had a poorly head. Mummy said he hurt you.'

Elenor looked at Rose. Her little face was creased with concern for Elenor and her innocence could not grasp the different meanings in the word 'hurt'.

'I was sad when he left. He was my friend. When Mummy said he hurt me she meant he made me sad. I hurt myself by falling over in the rain.'

'I don't like him anymore,' Rose said and her bottom lip dropped into a sulking pout.

'Please don't say that, Rose. Grown-ups make friends in different ways. Sometimes we have to let go of our friends, but we never forget them.'

Rose jumped from her chair onto the grass and put her hands on her hips. Elenor stared at her cherub-like image trying desperately to look fierce.

'He made you cry,' she said and stomped her foot.

Elenor swept her off her feet and sat her on her lap.

'I cried because I gave my heart over to him a bit too early. When you are a bit older you will understand we can love at the right time, but sometimes it is the wrong time. We have to learn by our mistakes. Jackson is a good man. One day I might meet someone like him, or I might not, but what I don't want to happen is that you think of him badly. Always remember him in a kind way.'

Rose leaned against Elenor's chest.

'I think your heart is working again. I can hear it. Mummy said he broke your heart.'

'Bless you, yes, my heart is working again. Now, I think it is time you climbed those stairs and into bed. I'm going to have an early night so won't be far behind you,' Elenor said and kissed Rose's cheek. 'And Rose, thank you for caring about me.'

Once she'd settled Rose into bed, Elenor walked through the house closing windows and shutting doors and wished it was that easy to switch off painful emotions. Victoria had been right. Jackson had broken her heart and she doubted she would ever find the right time to love another, no matter what she said to Rose.

CHAPTER 24

3rd September 1939, 11.25 am

'It's all hot air and pompous politicians sitting around a table,' George said. 'It means nothing. No different than what we are doing now. Sitting listening and talking.'

He picked up a cup and drank from it, then winced.

'Tea's cold,' he said and looked at Victoria. She remained seated beside the wireless and made no attempt to move.

'But we are at war. It is more than hot air,' Elenor replied. 'How can you say it means nothing? I think it is the most ridiculous thing anyone can say on a day like this. A war has been declared. What part of it do you consider means nothing?'

George lit a cigarette and puffed out a cloud of smoke.

'It will be over with by tomorrow. Talk. Talk and argue. Argue and talk. It has to be done. Hitler will get his way, and life in Britain will go back to waving flags at the King.'

'Have you been drinking George? Did you hear the Prime Minister's speech?' Elenor said and turned around. 'Victoria, did you hear war declared just now? A speech given by Mr Chamberlain – or was it only me?'

'I heard it,' Rose said. 'I heard the man. Oh, what is that? Has it started?'

The trill sound of a siren blasted through the mesh of the wireless grill.

'They're not wasting time, are they?' Victoria said.

Elenor watched Rose race around the room gathering items she said they might need inside the shelter.

'Calm down darling, it is a practice sound from London. You have given me an idea though. I think we should all pack a bag with useful things inside and leave them by the door. If a siren is sounded, we can grab them and go. Remember, it is three minutes walking fast with no stops to the nearest shelter.'

'I have to run. My legs are shorter,' Rose said.

George stood up and pressed the stub of his cigarette into an ashtray.

'I'd stay in the house. Safer. Any bombs dropped by Germany will be aimed at public places. Obvious targets, you get the majority that way. Look at the bombing of Broadgate last week. Nothing to do with Germany or Europe's war – allegedly Irish I think, but they targeted the general public in a main shopping area.'

'Don't remind me. The store shook. As if we've not got enough to contend with. Do you think they are allies with Germany?' Elenor said and gave an exaggerated shiver.

'Who knows? I do know, when Britain's enemies drop their devices more than the ground will shake. And the country is far from prepared,' George said and stood up.

'That's the sort of talk which no one wants to hear, George,' Elenor said and stared at the back of Rose's head to emphasise her point. 'Dangerous talk.'

'I think I'll make fresh tea,' Victoria said and gathered up the cups.

'I've a mind to go for a walk. Meet with a few chaps,' George said.

Elenor looked at the pair going about their business with little concern for the morning's announcement.

'The King is giving his speech at six,' she said, more for the sake of something to say. She didn't expect to sit beside the wireless for another seven hours.

'Ah, well that's it then. War will be over by teatime,' George said with heavy sarcasm.

'Really Daddy? Will it? I hope so. My mask stinks,' Rose said and stared up at her father.

Ruffling his daughter's hair George walked to the door.

'You won't need it for long,' he said and left the room.

'Tea, Elenor?' Victoria asked.

'Is it only me taking this seriously? Have you two taken something which calms the nerves – because if so, I want some please. My nerves are having a party inside my body, they are jangling so much. Come on Rose, let's pack.'

23rd November 1939

Dressed in preparation for several hours in the garden, Elenor gave thanks for the knitted items she'd made. The temperature had dropped overnight, and although the sun shone it provided little warmth.

'Good morning, George. Are you ready for a morning of digging? If only I had the plough.'

Elenor approached George outside the shed at the bottom of the garden.

'Morning. I think even the plough would struggle through this lot. It's run away with us and the ground is hard. We should have tackled it earlier,' he said and waved a trowel at the long grass and neglected flowerbeds.

'We'll appreciate the result. There are plenty of seeds here. Carrots, beet, cauliflower,' Elenor said and handed him a bag she'd bought in town.

'When we've finished, we've a treat waiting indoors. I also bought us smoked ham, and ham hock. If that isn't an incentive to dig fast and furious, I don't know what is.'

George laughed with her. He also held out a bag.

'Seed potatoes. Ah, here come the workers.'

Victoria and Rose joined them in the garden. Rose rushed up to her father.

'Daddy. Elenor brought home ham for my birthday tea. It smells wonderful. Mummy said if I work hard pulling out the dead flowers, and help you clean the tools, I can have some for lunch.'

Preparing the garden proved to be more fun with George than Elenor had anticipated. He joked with Rose, teasing her with worms, and moved from bed to bed in an orderly fashion pretending he was a sergeant major in the army, giving out instructions. Victoria worked in silence setting the seeds in trays and planting out the various plants ready for Rose's watering skills. Elenor dug up grass areas into squares and prepared the soil for the seed potatoes and inserted canes for peas and beans. By midday all were famished, and Victoria went inside to prepare a meal.

George turned over soil at a rapid pace and Elenor listened as he hummed whilst he worked.

'You really do enjoy gardening for a purpose, George. You've never put this much energy into flowers,' she said and laughed.

'Keeps the mind sharp and occupied,' he replied, tapping his head with his forefinger.

Skipping her way around the garden, Rose had lost concentration, and no longer pulled the dead marigolds from her allocated bed. Once again, Elenor envied her freedom and sent up a silent prayer for victory over their enemies. Life would be so very different if they were defeated.

Elenor saw Victoria wave from the back door.

'Rose, I think Mummy is calling you darling, go and wash your hands.'

Elenor patted Rose on the shoulder, then lifted her high and swung her around.

'Later I want to hear you play the 'Moonlight' tune. It will help me get into a serious mood for a scene in a new play we're rehearsing.'

Both George and Elenor watched Rose run inside and Elenor released a loud sigh. George looked at her.

'You're going back to Summercourt, aren't you? That's what the telegram was about. The one which you've not mentioned since it arrived yesterday,' he said.

Elenor rubbed the dirt from her spade.

'I'll have to go sometime, George. I'll put it off for as long as I can, but when the war is over my brothers will need a home. I can't have them live here, and if left in the hands of strangers I'm afraid Tre Lodhen will fall into neglect. From what I gather, they've both downed tools and joined the army. At least they've had the foresight to employ a manager to manage the land. He sent the message.'

She pulled out the telegram from her trouser pocket.

'No funds. Farm in ruins. Need advice and salary. My brothers must have given him my address and told him I'd pay his wages. They don't care about the family home but will want its income after someone else has done the hard work, that's for sure.'

'Have you considered handing it over to the government?' George asked.

'I can't do that, it's our family's heritage. I'd only do it if I couldn't cope, but it would be a last resort. I'll see how this man does first. But if I think about it, I'm not needed here. Not really,' Elenor said and sighed.

'You have work here,' George said. He stopped working and lit a cigarette. Elenor leaned against the wooden frame of the compost heap. She lifted her face to the thin stream of sunshine falling across the garden.

'My job is selling ladies face cream in a store. How can I do that knowing our family farm is going to rack and ruin? I spend evenings singing and practising for plays which, don't get me wrong, I love doing, but on the farm I can supply villagers with food, help them prepare gardens like we are today. Important work. When we gave our occupation details to the census woman last month, mine just felt trivial. Unlike Victoria who has a child to care for, and you teach and have mentioned joining a local cause. Me? I sell items of vanity.'

'Some women would argue and say selling them face cream is vital war work,' George said and gave a teasing laugh.

'See, even you are making fun of my job,' Elenor said and went back to planting seeds in the furrowed out rows.

'This is important work. Feeding ourselves,' George said, and poked the ground with a garden fork as he walked up and down the length of the garden.

'Yes, and I could do more at the farm. This is not my job, it is my duty to us in the home.' Elenor said. 'You are capable of doing it without me. So, I say again, I'm not needed here.'

She watched George and realised it was the most physical work she'd seen him carry out for years. He'd not been called up to fight due to problems with his feet and chest. Elenor had never known him to suffer with either, but apparently the army doctor turned him down and he took great pains to show off his stamped papers, so it was true enough.

'You and Victoria can stay here. I'll pay the rent for another year. My aunt left enough, and with my earnings I've not touched my inheritance. It will give me somewhere to come back to after the war is over. I won't be able to live with my brothers, and I am not slaving for them again. My intention is to come back to Coventry the day they return to Summercourt.'

Stretching his back and pushing his fork into the ground, George removed his flat cap and wiped the sweat from his forehead with a clean handkerchief from his pocket. He swept his hair back and replaced his cap.

'You must do what you think right for you. I'll do my bit and keep on top of the garden; keep us fed. When we fall to Germany, we will need to have food available. Look what happened to Holland back in May last year. Bombed until they were forced to surrender.' Annoyed by his assumption Britain was to be defeated, Elenor stopped what she was doing.

'When we fall? Germany won't take British soil, George, and the Germans won't starve us into surrender. There is no "when we fall" about it.'

'I'm not so sure. I've made arrangements for Victoria and me to go away for a couple of days soon. I think she mentioned having the time off. The older folk need a hand to prepare vegetable gardens. As usual we'll leave Rose with you, but if you have to go back to the farm we'll ask a friend to look after her.'

'Victoria did ask, and she is entitled to time off. Why don't you take Rose with you to your family and enjoy more than two days? She can help dig and plant for her family as well. Look how well she did this morning.'

Waving to Rose, who was beckoning them from the back door, George walked away without replying. It irked Elenor when he ignored her question about taking Rose with him

171

and Victoria. They were the oddest parents. She wished she could take Rose with her after Christmas, but it was a lot of responsibility running a farm and looking after someone else's child.

The day ended with Rose eating two large slices of birthday cake Elenor had purchased from the bakery in town.

'Make the most of it, Rose. From what I gather, the baker's delivery is suffering ingredient shortages already.'

'I'd better see what I can get and put aside for Christmas,' Victoria said.

George took a bite of a sandwich and waved it around in front of him while he chewed, getting ready to speak. He swallowed.

'I'd not bother. There will be a truce or an invasion. Either way Britain will not be at war on Christmas day.'

'Let's hope you are right George,' Elenor said and wiped her mouth on a napkin. 'About the truce, I mean.'

CHAPTER 25

The festive period of 1939 passed with Elenor holding onto memories of the previous year. As much as she wanted to let go of memories of Jackson, she couldn't. They were etched in her mind forever.

1940 slid in with a sharp shock. Freezing weather worked its way across the country and temperatures dropped on a daily basis.

A knock at the front door disturbed Elenor from writing out a list of numbers George had left her with that morning. What started off as a small task with fabricated figures had now become essential to the running of Tre Lodhen. The manager sent her paperwork each month, and Elenor created lists then transferred everything over to a large ledger.

Laying down her pen, she answered the door. Another package of papers from Cornwall and a letter for George bearing a London postmark.

'It's a cold one today, Miss Cardew,' the postman said as he handed her the mail and a pint of milk. 'Get this in before it's frozen. They say snow is falling heavy and heading this way.'

'Bye, stay warm,' Elenor said and gave him a grin.

She closed the door and turned over the letter for George. It was franked: *London E14*.

Chilled from the lingering outside air in the hallway, Elenor took herself off to the kitchen for a hot drink. A stew bubbled slowly on the stove and filled the room with its tempting aroma. Placing George's letter on the table, she filled the kettle and prepared the teapot.

A few potatoes sat near the sink and whilst she waited for the kettle to boil, Elenor scrubbed their outer skins. Turning the potatoes over in her hand brought about a pang of nostalgia for Cornwall. Going by the figures she'd written in the ledger that morning, the farm was ticking along and paid for itself, but showed no major growth since the brothers had left.

Outside the window the snow-laden skies blocked the light and midday appeared more like early evening it was so dull. And by the time Elenor poured hot water into her cup, snow fell. It gained speed and settled without melting. Back in the study she sat at her desk and sipped her hot drink. Her breath was white as she breathed in and out. She watched Victoria hurry past the window and round to the back path. Her head was covered with a woollen shawl, and Elenor guessed it was probably soaked with thawing flakes.

She went back into the kitchen and pulled down another cup just as Victoria backed her way indoors shaking off as much snow as possible.

'Get yourself inside, Victoria. You must be frozen.'

Victoria turned and Elenor saw nothing but a pale face with a red nose.

'Gracious, you are! Here, get this hot drink inside of you.'

'My toes are numb, my gloves feel like solid ice, but my shawl kept my head warm enough, although I'm convinced my nose will fall off if I touch it. I've never known it so cold out there. Rose will feel it when she comes home.'

Victoria stood near the stove and warmed her hands.

'That stew smells good,' Elenor said.

'We need to make the most of it while we can, there's word more rationing is heading our way,' replied Victoria, and she gave the pan a stir.

'I know. I'm trying to get used to my tea without sugar. I was tempted but your idea of having a bit on our porridge instead is a good idea. Oh, there's a letter for George. The postman looked as cold as you when he delivered it. Comes from London – the letter, not the postman,' Elenor said and laughed.

Victoria picked up the cream envelope and Elenor watched as her face paled.

'Are you all right? Is it bad news do you think?' she asked.

Victoria laid the letter back down and sat on a chair.

'It's from George's aunt I suspect,' she said.

Elenor looked to Victoria with a frown.

'I didn't realise he had an aunt in London. I thought his only family were his parents, and they live . . . actually, I don't know where your families live, Victoria. How odd after all these years, I've never thought to ask and never heard you say.'

With no response, a flushed faced Victoria tugged free Brussels sprouts from a stalk and sliced into the bases so hard Elenor felt sure she would cut herself.

'I can't recall a conversation, but now you know. George has an aunt in London. Do you want your bedroom fire banked up this afternoon? It is turning much colder as we stand here, even with the stove going.'

With conversation about family directed to lighting fires, Elenor marvelled at how adept Victoria was at changing subjects relating to her family – and George's. It had crossed her mind more than once whether they were married, and she hoped for Rose's sake there were no shocking secrets about the legitimacy of her birth.

'If it is all right with you, move Rose into my room and that way we'll save firewood. Just heat the parlour this evening. We'll play it by ear for the rest of the week.'

The shrill sound of the telephone from the hallway made them both jump. Elenor answered the call and returned to the kitchen.

'That was Sally. Our rehearsal has been cancelled this evening, there is a burst pipe in the hall. She's collecting her niece from school and will walk Rose to the end of our street to save us going out,' Elenor said.

'That's kind of Sally – thoughtful,' Victoria said.

'I'm back to the books,' said Elenor. 'Tell Rose she can come and see me in the study when she's home. We'll talk about snowflakes, I think. Brrr!'

The conversation about snow and snowflakes continued for several weeks. Every day they rose to another layer and by its last day, January had made it into the history books.

Today, fog greeted Elenor as she pulled back the curtains and the weather matched her mood. She tiptoed to the bathroom past Rose's bed but it was empty. When she opened her bedroom door the smell of fresh toast drifted from downstairs and her stomach rumbled.

'Oh, shut up you. Food is the last thing on my mind,' she muttered as she finished preparing herself for work.

Downstairs in the kitchen Victoria and George moved around each other, George with the newspaper under his arm, and Victoria with the teapot in her hand. Rose chewed on her breakfast and all three avoided making eye contact with Elenor.

'Morning,' she said and held out her cup to Victoria.

'Morning. Foggy out there today,' George said and flicked his paper open.

A strained atmosphere built between them with polite conversation, and Elenor couldn't wait to leave the house. She knew it was awkward for them, and it embarrassed her. The same happened on the anniversary of her aunt's passing, but that day they spoke about her and remembered her. This Valentine's Day held no excitement for her, it was more of an anniversary to be ignored, and yet, she'd been unable to push it away for a whole year. A year which had passed in a blur of emotional and physical recovery. Work would be her focus of the day, Sally, Mrs Green and strangers would help get her through this uphill climb.

Walking to work, the fog thickened and people huddled into their clothing. Everyone she met looked worn down and miserable. For the first time in a long time, Elenor wanted to leave Coventry. It was time to prepare for her return to Cornwall.

During her lunch break Elenor sent a telegram to the farm manager. She informed him she'd sent a cheque for his salary, and that she would return to live at Tre Lodhen again in the spring. Probably the middle of April.

She wrote out her notice and when back at the store, she handed it to Mrs Green.

'Are you sure you want that life again, Elenor? You are so well suited here.'

Elenor looked around the shop floor and pulled a face to express her disagreement.

'I'm grateful to you for finding me the work, but farming is important war work, and Tre Lodhen waits for me to turn it around. To feed the country. Please try to understand.'

Mrs Green gave a gentle nod.

'I do. I love my work here but have signed up for the Women's Voluntary Service. Like you, I want to do something more proactive within the community. I'm trying to persuade Sally, but she's not made up her mind what she wants to do yet. Apart from dancing of course,' Mrs Green said and gave a light laugh.

'She certainly enjoys life. I'll miss her,' Elenor said and gave a wan smile. 'I'll miss you both.'

'Oh, we'll come and stay in the summer. When the war is over. I fancy a visit outside of Coventry. Hark at me, inviting myself along.'

'You know you'll be most welcome. Right, I must get back to the counter and relieve Lilly. Thank you for understanding.'

'I do, and Elenor, I know you are trying to be brave today, too. The sun will shine again, it had better come soon. Our customers don't like the fog.'

Both looked to the door and the usual throng of people who kept it rotating were nowhere to be seen.

'Is there anything I can do in the stock room? I need to keep busy today,' Elenor asked.

'You go to the counter and polish it to a high shine. Don't run away. Fight the sadness.'

Elenor walked away and, with Mrs Green's words of encouragement, she set about using physical energy to disperse the mental sadness.

CHAPTER 26

April 1940

'I've booked the removal van for you, Elenor,' George said.

Lifting books down from the study shelf, Elenor turned to face him.

'Thank you, George. It will make the place feel cosier. The last time I visited I swear my brothers had used most of the furniture for fire wood. And what is left won't be worth salvaging. I'm ashamed of the pair of them sometimes.'

'You don't know where they are stationed yet? Strange they didn't write and tell you they were enlisting.'

'To be honest, it is typical of them. They won't have given me a thought apart from leaving me with their financial problems.'

'Did you hear the news? Denmark have surrendered. Won't be long before your brothers won't have an army to belong too. Surrender might be the best option for many countries.'

With astonishment, Elenor looked at him.

'That is a dreadful thing to say, George. How awful for Denmark to be in such a position.'

'It's fact, not dreadful news. That's the female vision of all disasters – dreadful. A stronger power will always overcome.'

'It's called bullying, George. We shouldn't tolerate it, and it is why we are at war. Let's say we fall to Germany, what will happen to you? You are not a strong man as your papers indicate. Will you be able to continue teaching English? Will I be allowed to return here, or will I be made to work my own farm under the rule of another? These are my fears George.'

George appeared to ignore her words and started to pack the books she handed him, but not before inspecting the spines of each one, and grunting.

'Fortunately, the books you are taking are ones I've already read,' he said when they'd filled two boxes.

'They are mine to take, George,' Elenor said in a sharp tone – she was still annoyed about his remarks about surrender. 'Everything in these rooms are mine, aside from your personal items, and I'd like to see everything in the same place when I return.'

George's face coloured and Elenor doubted it was with discomfort or embarrassment. She'd angered the man by reminding him of his position yet again.

George pulled out a cigarette from his case. She watched as he tapped the tip on the lid and put it to his lips.

'Oh, and that is something I meant to mention. I am not going to be here for you to earn your salary as my tutor. I can't think why we hadn't thought of it before, and suggest we come to an agreement. How about you do as you mentioned in the past, and maintain the garden, and upkeep of the property. Agreed?' Elenor said and held out her hand.

'I did mention to Victoria we needed to discuss the matter. Your proposal is satisfactory only due to the fact it will be a temporary one.'

'Ah, that depends. I might not need a tutor when I return, George. All done. Now I'm off to pack last minute things upstairs.'

She left him staring at her wide-eyed, still with the unlit cigarette hanging from his lip.

By the afternoon, Elenor had finished packing the majority of her things, and returned to the study with her tatty suitcase and filled it with paperwork. Without stopping to contemplate throwing anything out, she crammed everything into the case and clasped it shut. One day she would be brave enough to read through her projects and letters relating to Canada; they were part of her, a part which had opened her eyes to life. Before she had time to change her mind, Rose burst into the room.

'You're home. Good day at school?' Elenor asked.

Rose scooted herself onto Elenor's chair and sat on the desk.

'Is this going in the van?' she asked.

'It is.' Elenor smiled. 'Think of me sitting at it writing to you.'

'Think of me at the kitchen table writing to you,' Rose said. 'Are you taking your wireless? Daddy wants you to leave it behind.'

'I'll be taking it, Rose. It was a gift from my aunt – a very special gift.'

'Mummy said you won't come back.'

Elenor heard the sob in Rose's voice.

'I'm coming back, Rose. We'll see each other again, I promise. With my brothers away at war it is a difficult time for me. I want to be in two places at once.'

'Can't I come with you? Live with you?'

'We've had this conversation several times, Rose. You need to stay here with your parents and go to school. Everything will be back to normal in a few months, and we'll be at this desk working on a new project again.'

Rose slid down from the desk. She stomped her foot and burst into tears.

'It's just not fair. I want to see your farm. I want you to stay here. It's not fair!'

Elenor clenched her hands and raised her shoulders waiting for the door to slam shut as Rose ran from the room. It didn't matter what was said to reassure Rose, the child expressed her feelings in the only way she knew how – loudly.

Heading back upstairs, Elenor heard Victoria shout and reprimand Rose for crying. George instructed Rose to go outside and calm down.

It took all of Elenor's willpower not to unpack and cancel the trip back to Summercourt. Rose was George and Victoria's child, and she had no right to interfere in the way they brought her up.

Maybe time alone with Rose would help Victoria see how lucky she was. With the war in full flow, Elenor's future of becoming a wife and mother was even more uncertain.

The last day of April brought with it a mix of emotions. Rose had refused point blank to go to school and spent the time sulking or sobbing.

Sally and Mrs Green arrived to see Elenor off and promised Rose they would take her to the park after the van had left. Victoria and George looked relieved.

'We'd be grateful,' Victoria said. 'She's not taking Elenor leaving very well.'

'I hope the silly van doesn't work,' Rose said.

'Don't be so petulant child,' George said and handed her a small box. 'Go and give this to the removal man.'

Rose looked at Elenor with a puzzled frown.

'Cranky. Irritable,' Elenor said. 'Petulant. It's a big grown up word. I just think you are upset, so do as Daddy asks and then come and give me your biggest hug.'

Rose did as she was told, then returned to offer up her hug. After begging for room to breathe, Elenor and Rose parted.

'I can honestly say that was the biggest hug I've ever received. Thank you. It will last me until we get chance to have another one.' She wiped away Rose's tears. 'Don't cry. Be strong and look after Sally for me. And Mrs Green.'

Elenor moved to the adults waiting to say goodbye and holding back her tears for Rose's sake, she climbed into the passenger seat of the brown removal van. As they drove out of Coventry, Elenor remembered the day she'd arrived. The naïve girl with a battered suitcase left town a different person, and it amazed Elenor how much had happened in so few years. The tears she cried for those she'd left behind soon dried up, and her excitement mounted when Cornwall came into view.

Summercourt

Unpacking her things had taken Elenor the best part of three days, and over a period of three weeks she'd hired a mother and daughter to scrub and clean the farmhouse. The house had four large rooms and one small one which had once been hers.

The farmhands helped to move her brother's things into the small room at the back of the property. The view from the window was always her favourite when her parents were alive. Green hills and valleys rolled on for miles. Even in winter she would sit on the edge of their bed and watch as the hills turned white with frost, and sometimes snow.

Underneath the room was what she now considered her study and parlour of sorts, and she'd set up her desk in front of the window. She left the bedroom and ventured downstairs, the room called to her. She'd promised herself a half hour of relaxation before inspecting more of the farm.

The warmth of the room embraced her, and she smiled when she saw her wireless sat in pride of place on the sideboard. Elenor stroked the pale green curtains from the Coventry house which completed the cosy feel.

Outside the window she watched a rook settle onto a branch of a tree. The tree brought back a memory of when she was a child. One hot summer one of the farmhands had made a swing for her and had hooked it around the branch. She'd swung high and enjoyed what breeze it created. Elenor also recalled the day she fell off and her mother fussing around her, cheering her up with a slice of fresh-baked apple cake and relieving her of her few chores. So many happy memories needed to be encouraged to swamp out the bad, and with the country at war a positive mind was needed at all times.

She looked across to the yard where various pieces of farm equipment had been laid out in readiness for inspection. She noticed the old hen house had been expanded and rewired, and one barn was undergoing a roof repair. A few cattle chewed their way around the bottom meadow, and sheep grazed on the top pasture, all under the careful watch of three retired men from the village. The manager of Tre Lodhen had volunteered his services to the King and left the day after she'd arrived. Elenor knew she needed to consider her staffing options once she had the place running to full capacity.

An hour later she pulled on her outdoor clothing and strode around the farm with a notepad and pencil in her hand.

For two hours she trampled through unkempt land, making notes and enjoying the air. Her hair grew damp as the clouds dropped lower and formed a light mist.

Fashionable Coventry shopping and living no longer featured in her thoughts, instead she pondered what fields would grow what vegetables, and what seasons she had to consider. With excitement and deep concentration, she sketched out how she envisaged the various plots.

For a fleeting moment she thought of what would happen when her brothers returned. With a flick of her hair and taking a deep breath, Elenor reminded herself of their irresponsible handling of the place and if it wasn't for her taking control now, it would never have survived. When they did come home, she would fight her corner to stay but not as their skivvy. Coventry would always be her second home, this place had her heart.

'Hey Tre Lodhen,' she shouted at the top of her voice. 'I'm home and it's me and you against the world. Time to feed those who deserve our help.'

She marched down towards the farmhouse just as a young man on a bicycle headed up the entrance. He peddled with youthful energy and Elenor jotted down a reminder to purchase a new bicycle on her list.

'Miss Cardew?'

With a sick sensation in her gut she noticed his uniform, and he was holding something out to her.

'It's not a telegram. I offered to bring it for the postie, he's busy the other end of the village, and I was passing,' he said and handed her a white envelope.

The young boy peddled away, and Elenor stood and watched. She didn't envy his job, and her thoughts wandered to families who might well have received a telegram or were about to, and her heart went out to them. Her letter was from Coventry, and the scrawling handwriting of a child lit up her heart. Rose had sent her first letter.

Back indoors, Elenor removed her coat and hung it up for an airing in the corner of the room. She pulled off her boots and stood them by the door. She surveyed the tidy room, its neat appearance highlighting how bad it had looked when she'd last visited her brothers.

She placed the kettle on the range, cut herself a slice of cheese and bread, and went into the parlour. She couldn't wait to read Rose's news. Once she'd eaten at a small table beside her desk, she settled by the fire in a comfortable chair and slid her aunt's antique letter opener under the lip of the envelope. She lifted out two sheets of paper and smoothed them out in readiness to enjoy the world through a child's eyes.

June 1940
My house.

Deer Elenor
    Agnis helped me rite this to yoo. I tried hard to use my bestest handriting.
    Mummy is looking for daddy cause he is to long at his aunties house in lundun.
    Agnis helps a lot now. I am lonely when yoo and daddy and mummy are not heer. I play the music but I get sad.
    Have yoo got moor cows yet and chikens and a cat. We had a bomb near the park the ovver day. Have you got bombs. I saw a army man with Sally. When you get a army man I will be your bridesmade. Yoo will bee so pretty. I drawd yoo a cow.
    Love From
    Rose
    xxx

Elenor unfolded the other piece of paper and smiled at the cow with three legs smiling back at her. She reread the letter. George had gone on another trip and not returned to Coventry, and Victoria had gone to find him. Elenor went to her desk and wrote four letters, one to Rose telling her news of the farm, and one to Victoria enquiring after George. The other two were to Mrs Green, informing her of her safe arrival and asking her friend to pay a visit to Rose to cheer her up, and to Sally begging to hear more about the soldier Rose had seen her with, and of news about the drama group.

Not wanting to wait until the following day, she took a walk into the village to the post office. She smiled at a familiar group of women chattering at the corner of a street. Elenor was convinced they'd not moved from the day she left the village.

'Well if it isn't young Elenor from the farm. How are ee?' one woman called over to her.

'Yes, it is me. I'm well. You and yours?' Elenor asked.

'Well enough. The boys joined up with your brothers. All think they'll be the hero to bring 'itler down. You running that place alone?'

'I am. I've work up there if anyone wants it. I'm planting out soon.'

'I'll be up dreckly to 'ave a chat with you. Could do with a bit of work meself.'

'Tell five others. Oh, and the children can pitch in with a few chores for extra veg if you want to keep them close.'

After an hour of chatting to various shopkeepers and other residents happy to see her back in the village, Elenor walked home. She spent time reading through unopened letters from the onset of the war. Neither brother had read information from various war ministries with regard to future running of farms in England, and what was expected of farmers. Making notes, Elenor decided she could cope with the majority expected of her, but only with proper planning.

By the time evening came she'd milked cows, fed chickens, thrown swill to four loud sows, and chatted with her farmhands about jobs for the following day. In a lonely patch of soil she found carrots, a row of cabbages and onions. She pulled them up, scrubbed them and boiled them into a soup.

By seven in the evening she sat knitting socks with her wireless offering background noise, and before she knew it the clock on the kitchen mantle chimed out ten.

Elenor shut up the house for the night, climbed into bed and stretched out her tired limbs. It wasn't long before she gave into sleep, a sleep disturbed by the sounds of distance sirens screaming out their red alert in the early hours. She turned over and stuffed the pillow over her head. The sound was becoming more familiar as spring rolled into summer, but it was too far away to make her leave the house. She tossed and turned until sleep came her way again. The next sound she heard was the cockerel announcing the start of another day. A day she was handed two telegrams.

CHAPTER 27

Pulling her bike from the shed, Elenor peddled with a slight wind behind her to the village. It frustrated her she had to travel so far to use the telephone after the luxury of Coventry. She dialled the number and waited for someone to answer. It was Victoria.

'Victoria. You are back. Is George with you? Rose said you'd left to find him?'

'Elenor. How are you? I have no news of him yet. When I have I'll write, although as you know it has happened in the past. He has a tendency to move onto another relative without letting me know first.'

'True enough. Yes, write. How's Rose?'

A loud sigh travelled down the line.

'She's her usual self. I understand she wrote to you. I'll have to tell Agnes I want to read the letters before they are sent in future.'

Elenor laughed.

'She did well and all very innocent. I have a lovely picture of a cow.'

'But she obviously worried you by telling you about George, and about me going away to find him. I didn't realise she'd done that, sorry Elenor. She is a dreadful nuisance at times.

189

More so without her father here. You leaving didn't help, she really is too much.'

Victoria's voice and attitude towards Rose unsettled Elenor.

'Don't tell Rose off, she did the right thing. You should have sent word, Victoria.'

'Why? He's my husband and you are busy down there. You can do nothing for him. He'll return soon. You concentrate on the farm.'

Her dismissive tone was out of character and Elenor was taken aback.

'I am considering staying here for good, Victoria. The war has taken James and Walter. I own the farm now, and I'd forgotten how Cornish I am, but we can discuss it at a later date. You have a roof over your head and a wage for months so don't worry. Give my love to Rose. Oh, and say hello to George when he arrives. Bye Victoria.'

'Bye, Elenor. Sorry about your family.'

Cycling home, Elenor rolled the conversation around in her mind. Victoria had a standoffish attitude, and very obviously didn't want to talk. Elenor decided to take a trip to Coventry after the harvest.

Walking her bike along the dry cracked lane home, she saw the figure of a male leaning against the farm gate. A large black car was parked to one side. Expecting an official visit at some point, Elenor guessed it was today. She made no effort to hurry and called out to him.

'Can I help you?'

He turned and gave a wave.

'Miss Cardew? I'm from the Ministry of Agriculture.'

Elenor leaned upon the handles of her bike pushing it up the slight incline. Slow and steady. She was in no mood to talk to government officials.

'I take it you've come to help with the milking, and right on cue, Mr . . .?

'Stonnard. Graham Stonnard.' He held out his hand, but Elenor chose to ignore it and held onto her bike handles.

'Well, Mr Stonnard. Milking is carried out at four in the morning before the churns are collected. I take it you don't mind sleeping in with the animals; they are precious and sought after. It is most generous of the government to send me a helping hand, and such a strapping male. I have to make do with the elderly and am often fearful one will drop dead mid-tug. The cows can be tetchy at times.'

She kept her face straight as she teased. His face had the pallor of a snowflake – a definite city office worker.

Word had gone from farm to farm that the government were ordering cereals to be grown on spare grazing land, and Elenor had plenty of land, however, she didn't have the workforce to carry out a large harvest. Her brothers' neglect and her limited time had not produced a satisfactory volume on paper; she'd done her best, but it wouldn't be good enough for pen-pushers.

'I am not here to work. Well, I am but not physically. We need to discuss your options, and in the absence of your brothers—' he stopped to check his papers '—James and Walter Cardew, we have to discuss it with you as the third owner.'

Elenor huffed in disgust and walked away, this time wheeling her bike at a speed, and where slurry from the men washing out the barn had run down the path, mud splattered from her back wheel. She heard the man curse. After a few feet she turned around to find him still following and stepping from one dry area to another, avoiding the muddy puddles.

'We really do need to discuss this Miss Cardew. Maybe you'd like to write to a brother and ask advice, but it will take time.'

'More time than you can imagine. My brothers were

both killed in action in the Dunkirk evacuation last month. Their regiment remained to defend the rescue. Yesterday, a solicitor informed me I own the farm and I signed papers. I am the last member of my family, and you are looking at the woman who climbed from her bed at four o'clock, fed sheep, chickens and cattle, and then went on to milk the cows. I pulled buckets of vegetables for the villagers, and to meet my quota for your books, I'll pull more after my lunch. I peddled into town to use the telephone to contact a friend whose husband is missing, and to organise the slaughter of a cow to keep me legal,' Elenor said before she stopped to draw breath.

'Mr Stonnard, I, with respect, would like to know how you propose I bring in the next harvest. I've six women with their children working on my vegetable plots, and four men caring for the livestock. I suggest you turn around, tiptoe your way along the grassy banks of Cornwall and crawl back into your warm office in officialdom. Now, forgive me but I am late to relieve Daisy of her swollen udders. Unless you would like to try your hand?'

The anger she'd held back from voicing at Victoria down the telephone fell from Elenor's lips and the man stood flabbergasted as she ranted her way through her speech. Then, to her surprise, his moustache twitched, and he gave the loudest laugh.

'You, young lady, have more fire in your belly than I have ever seen in any man. The German army needs to run scared. Forgive me,' he said and held up a hand. 'I am truly sorry for your loss, and had I been given such important information, believe me I would not be standing here today. However, I would be standing here at a future date.'

'Oh, I've no doubt. You and several other officials with clipboards. It's brawn I need, not brain.'

'I'll mark you as a priority and add your name to our

Land Army listing. I warn you though, it won't be until mid to late August.'

He placed his paperwork into his briefcase and gave a smile as he clasped it shut.

'I'll be in touch, and now, as much as I'd like to learn how to milk a cow, I must be off to upset another farmer in another village. Good afternoon, and again, my condolences. I ask your forgiveness.'

With a grin, and then a sheepish look as she watched him brush away specks of mud from his suit, she held out her hand.

'You are forgiven. My apologies, it is trying times for us all, and I should not have taken it out on you.'

As the shadows fell around the barn that evening, and the cows shuffled their way into the stalls, Elenor wondered when help would arrive. It would be most welcome.

CHAPTER 28

A fox had pulled wire from the henhouse during the night, and Elenor's first task of the day was to shore it up. As she stood back to double check her handiwork the postman waved and called her name from the bottom gate. Elenor raced to meet him. Her new dog Seth, a gift from a farmer in Redruth, was better at rounding up humans than sheep. Elenor loved his company, but he lacked manners when it came to greeting visitors.

'I'm sorry about him. All noise and no brains.'

'You are more popular than me it seems,' said the postman and handed her several envelopes.

'I heard your niece, Susie, is looking for a job? I need someone to look after the house. I liked her work when she cleaned up for my move home.'

'I'll let her know. She's a good sort and I can see why you'd want her around.'

After ushering Shep into the kitchen and persuading him to sit for more than five minutes, Elenor sorted the post into official and pleasure. She read her name on the front of a small white envelope. She didn't recognise the neat handwriting and tearing it open she was thrilled to see it was from Sally.

July 1940
Coventry

Dearest Elenor,

I miss you. Life on stage is just not the same. I've got the leading role in a soppy romance, and your Prince Charming is the lead. He's not too bad, but his hands are over-friendly.

Mrs Green sends her best wishes. How are you? How's the farm? Any handsome young men with muscles lending a hand yet? I suppose they're all at war, the same as those here.

The shop looks bleak without some of the stock on the shelves. Oh, and Lilly ran off with a soldier. Her mother is furious. I run the counter now. I've bumped into Rose and taken her to feed the ducks a couple of times. Her parents are a strange pair. I sent my dad round to yours last week as Rose said she'd tried to pull up some of the vegetables. I didn't know George wasn't at home anymore. It was overgrown out the back, so Dad did his bit. He took a pail full in payment. They were tasty.

Isn't it horrible trying to write a letter? If we were together we'd be chatting nonstop for days. Mrs G said she's saving for a holiday if you are still there next summer. I'll save for a ticket and come too, but don't get me touching animals and stuff like that, you know me, I'm the fussy one.

Off to the flicks soon, you take care
Much love, your dear friend,
Sally
x

Elenor folded the letter and set it to one side. George was still not around. Poor Rose with just her mother for company. She fetched her pen and paper and wrote back to Sally.

July 1940
Tre Lodhen
Summercourt
Cornwall.

My dear friend,
How wonderful to hear from you! I did giggle about Prince Charming, he is a handy man. Ha ha. Enjoy the show. I miss the stage but have made my choices for the duration of war.

Naughty Lilly! She's a sly thing. I bet her mother tore down the walls looking for her.

Thank your father for me. I had no idea. Victoria keeps these things from me. I should have realised she couldn't cope with the house, Rose, and the garden. Please, ask your father to continue until George comes back, and take his pickings home as payment. I am grateful to him.

My life has had a major turnaround due to the death of my brothers. Both were hailed as heroes at Dunkirk, and I find comfort that in their deaths they did some good. It isn't easy as I still remember two drunks. I haven't mourned them in the way the village expects, but they were virtual strangers to me. I have agreed to sing at a church service in the memory of our village recruits. We lost so many. Generations wiped out.

This is hard for me to say, but I don't think I'll return to live in Coventry. I have inherited the farm as the last member of my family. It is hard work but worth the effort. I am about to employ a shepherd and buy more sheep. A bit different to ordering new cream for a pretty counter!

I'd love to have you both here for a holiday. You can feed the chickens, that's not so dirty and my girls are gentle souls, they will only flap if you do.

Take care Sally and enjoy the cinema. It's a long time since I took time off, but I'm happy enough.

Much love,

Elenor.

X

Elenor took Sally's letter to her case and pulled out a box of letters she'd tried to ignore. Her aunt's and Jackson's. When she lifted the lid, she was shocked to see the Valentine's card from Jackson staring up at her and her breath filled her lungs until they were painful. Victoria must have slipped it into her case. Underneath there were two letters she didn't recognise that were addressed to George. Puzzled, she pulled them out and read the first. It was from Jackson. He spoke vaguely about his grandfather, and appeared to answer questions George had asked, but not in any depth. Elenor got the impression he wrote out of politeness. His words at the end of the page stood out and she sunk into a seat.

Thank you for informing us of Elenor's illness. We wish her a speedy recovery. If I venture into Coventry I wonder if she would receive me as a friend visiting a sick one. Please let my grandfather know when you write next.

With things happening around us I am not certain I'll be returning to Canada, and it is to be decided whether I remain here to train the new recruits.

My regards to your wife and Rose. You are a lucky man.
Jackson St John.

George had said nothing to her of Jackson's good wishes, or his grandfather's. Elenor opened the other envelope. She skimmed through words relating to war chatter, none of which held anything of interest, merely a polite response to another letter from George. Again, the contents at the bottom of the page caught her eye.

The news of Elenor's recovery is heartening. Tell her I understand her not wanting to see me again. She was quite right to dismiss my request. At times I act rashly and asking to see her when she was so ill was wrong of me. Mourning her aunt in such a way – to try and take her life, how sad. I thank God she's survived. Elenor has a special place in my heart but I had to release her for fear we'd never meet again.

Due to my commitments here, I will not write again, but my grandfather enjoys your letters, and will write back, but I am not sure how long the post takes to reach England, so be patient.

Give my regards to all.
J. St John

A bubble of anger rose from deep inside. Elenor screamed. Loud and feral, it reverberated around the room. George had told her nothing of Jackson's request to visit. She would probably have refused him, but it had not been George's decision to make. She dropped to her knees with the letters scrunched in her hands, and the card lay face up with its pretty picture taunting her. Her love for Jackson was not a love of the past, and Elenor cried a river of tears before hauling herself to her desk and put the letters away.

Staring at the Valentine's card, she read through the painful rejection of her love once again, and then fed it to the flames of the fire and her pain of the past spiralled away with the smoke.

CHAPTER 29

Weeks of toil proved worth the effort. Elenor, in an attempt to cast aside her feelings for Jackson threw herself into her daily tasks with renewed vigour and hoped a better harvest was her reward.

Susie was a good worker and made life much easier for Elenor.

Today, she stood on a stool washing down the kitchen window.

'The Germans meant business last night. I don't think I've ever been so scared,' Susie said.

Pulling on her coat and picking up her boots, Elenor sighed. 'It is scary, last night was loud and noisy. Mind you, Seth was noisier. The sirens drive him crazy,' Elenor said and pushed her feet into her boots. 'Right, I'm off muck spreading. See you later.'

Susie climbed down from the stool and leaned on the handle of her broom.

'I reckon it's the dark. We're used to darkness round here, but not the German boogieman.'

With a stab in the air with her finger, Susie shouted to the ceiling.

'In my Gran's words, "we'll get the bettermost of 'ee', that we will".'

Elenor burst out laughing, and pulled her hair into a ponytail, then wound her blue scarf into a turban over her head.

'That we will, Susie. Talking of grandmothers, I learned my few words of the old tongue from mine, and I recall her telling my father off for cursing in Cornish. She threw a shoe at him, she said if the language is to die out with only his translation left, she'd rather not hear it again,' Elenor said and gave a sigh. 'I have a feeling she would use the word herself nowadays, each day is a bad day in any language.'

Outside, the wind blew into Elenor's face from the direction of the previous night's target and she caught a whiff of rubber or chemical substance. War was on their doorstep and showed no sign of leaving.

'Come on ladies, this smell won't kill us, but starving will.'

Elenor looked at the rows of steaming pails of manure she'd collected that morning and snatched up her rake.

She and the women she employed to help plant out the vegetable plots raked and hoed the manure around the plants. Sore back and hands were soon forgotten when Elenor stood back and looked at her handiwork. Her four helpers, and their nine children of various ages, did the same.

Straight rows of newly watered vegetable plants displayed their fresh green shoots. Carrots, lettuce, radishes and beetroot were piled high in wooden crates, and newly erected canes tied wigwam style gave pea and bean plants something to cling onto.

'There's something about planting out and reaping the

reward,' Elenor said. 'And reap you will. I've never known such hard workers.'

She was fond of this small group; each woman understood Elenor's position and vowed to stand by her during the hard days ahead. She offered them a small wage with a bucket of vegetables, a pail of milk per week, and a rabbit once a month. The rabbits were a nuisance on the fields and two men were given the status of official rabbit catchers. They shared their catch with her and then sold their own. The women also collected large acorns and the pigs were more than well catered for thanks to the enthusiasm of the children.

A little boy made his way through the women and children and placed three large potatoes into an empty bucket beside Elenor. She looked down, puzzled.

'Where did you find those beauties? We've not got a crop yet.'

All faces looked to the little face that wore a cheeky grin, and Elenor's heart went out to him. His life was in turmoil with the war and he still managed a sweet smile. A willing child, he always turned up with his mother without complaint.

'There's more, lots. Behind the tithe barn that's fallin' down. Over there,' he said and pointed to a dilapidated building on the far side of the farm.

'I never knew my brothers had planted out that area before they left, maybe it was the manager. I've been too busy over this way to have noticed anything growing. It's early, too. Clever man,' she said and patted the boy's head.

Bending over the bucket, she looked at the potatoes. There was no sign of any blight. She turned to the women.

Armed with extra pails, wooden crates and forks, the group walked to where the young boy jumped up and down with excitement, pointing to his find. To Elenor's amazement a small field sat sporting its treasures in row after row. She put down her equipment and stood with her hands on her hips.

'How on earth had I not seen this before?'

'Well they'd not grown before,' the lad said.

The group laughed at his cheeky reply. His mother planted a kiss on his cheek which he swiftly wiped away with a 'yuk' and drew more laughter from his audience.

'Extra oggy for you, my prince.'

'I think there'll be many an extra pasty made this week. There's so many potatoes here, you can have two pails per household,' Elenor said.

Cheers went up, and they all moved in to gather the find, with the little lad giving out instructions to his siblings and friends. She marvelled at their luck. The extra crop would bring in a small profit. She rewarded the boy with a few coins. He would have received more but his mother pointed out that by playing over near the potato plot, he had not fully pulled his weight with the rest of them in planting out the rest of the vegetables.

Back out on the fields, Elenor checked the sheep and chatted with the newly appointed shepherd, Tom. He'd offered his services when his previous boss closed his farm after his son was killed. Elenor purchased a ram and four ewes from him, and two heifers whose paperwork showed a milk volume proved to be worth what she'd paid for all seven animals. It gave her a thrill when she'd travelled over to collect them. What surprised her was the attitude of the farmer. He would not accept she was capable of running a farm, let alone owning one. His argument ended in the fact he considered she would fail without a good man behind her. Someone with farming savvy, not emotional dreams. He was however, happy to negotiate a hard bargain with her and take her money.

A tired Elenor greeted Susie inside the house that evening and placed a pail of potatoes by her feet.

'There's more for your mother outside in the barn. I can't believe I didn't see them growing. What a useless farmer I am,' she said and kicked off her boots.

'Useful, I'd say. My mum will make good use of those beauties. Thanks. I'll take the small cart and bring it back tomorrow,' said Susie. 'Did I see you unloading new livestock?'

'Yes, with Tom. By the way, I said you'd help clean his cottage instead of here for a week. It needs a good turnout. Is that all right with you?'

'Yes, fine. I boiled a bit of gammon today. I'll cut him a slice and take it over tomorrow morning and make a start.'

With heavy eyes, Elenor struggled through her meal. Susie left for home and the last of the evening chores were finished. Aside from Seth's snores there was silence. With little energy left, Elenor climbed the stairs and into bed. The drone of planes overhead and Seth's barking alerted her she was to lose another night of sleep. Her back ached and blisters on her hands tingled with the hours of hoeing.

'Settle down, Seth. Good boy,' she called downstairs.

She fumbled around in the dark to find her lamp but a glow from the side of her curtain caught her eye. Not wanting to breach the no-light law, she remained in darkness and teased back the two sets of curtains at the window. A bright orange sky in the distance had joined the full moon and between them lit the land and sky as far as Elenor could see.

The orange, Elenor realised, were flames from the bombs burning out whatever town had been hit. She estimated it was the Plymouth area. Wild in their movement, the flames licked high and flickered their warning around the Cornish countryside. The noise droned on until she could bear it no longer.

'Oh Seth! No. Those poor people. What a dreadful two days we've had.'

Elenor settled back the blackout blind and her pretty curtains, double-checked they were sealed from the outside world, and lit her bedside lamp.

Boom after boom echoed out another announcement of either a bomb strike or of a building demolished by gas explosions. On and on the enemy moved across the skies.

'Enough,' Elenor said and put her hands over her ears.

'Come on Seth. It's cold up here and I don't know about you, but sleep has gone walkabout. Hot milk for me I think.'

Wrapped in her dressing gown, she gathered up an eiderdown from her bed, and carrying the oil lamp, she followed the dog downstairs. Seth wagged his tail in excitement and gave a yip at the back door.

'You go out and be clean. Come straight back,' Elenor said.

She turned off her lamp and opened the door.

The dog raced out into the night and barked his way up into the top pasture. Flecks of his white fur moved from one side to another, and Elenor watched from the darkness of her kitchen. Shadows from trees flashed a dance across the yard each time an orange flame flicked high across the skyline, or the moon moved behind a rare, soft cloud. Her heart pounded in her chest. She heard the rat-tat of returning fire and Seth's barks becoming more and more frantic.

'Seth. Come. Home boy!' she called and added a beckoning whistle.

His huffing and puffing came before his physical presence, and when he saw her at the door, he barked and skittered around her ankles.

'You wouldn't be so excited if you understood what was happening my friend.'

Elenor tickled him behind the ears and he rolled over onto his back.

'No, no. Indoors.'

She pulled him inside and as she pushed the door to, she was startled by a shadow running across the field Seth had just raced through. The dog tried to squeeze his way back outside, but she grabbed his collar.

'No lad, inside with me,' she whispered.

Elenor closed the door and made her way to the kitchen window. A gunshot made her jump, and she grabbed onto the sink to stop her falling backwards.

Another shadow followed the other, a much taller figure. They wove their way around the field. Another shot rang out, and both figures scurried into the trees.

Then it dawned on her and she stepped away from the window.

'The lads are making the most of the background noise tonight, Seth. You'd best stay inside. Rabbits, dogs and gun-crazy hunters are not always a good mix in the dark. Thank goodness for that, I thought we'd got the enemy on our hands.'

Boiling milk on the stove hissed and distracted Elenor from thinking too much about being alone at night. Until she'd seen the shadowy figures scurrying around in her fields, she'd given it no real thought, other than to how lonely it could feel sometimes.

She poured the milk into her mug and was tempted to pour a nip of brandy in the hope it would settle her nerves and help her sleep. She'd found several bottles stashed away; her brothers had not managed to drink them all. Thinking back to the state the two men were in the last time she'd seen them, she refrained from opening a bottle and took herself into the parlour.

At the insistence of Susie, her father had pulled a large, heavy table into one corner, and converted it into a shelter of sorts. Its intention was to protect Elenor from a bomb attack, but Seth had other ideas and used it as a cosy kennel, and the moment they entered the parlour, he raced into his den. Elenor placed another log onto the fire and allowed her bones to absorb their warmth. She looked to the dog already curled up asleep and was half tempted to join him. Instead she dragged her chair to the opposite side of the fire, away from the window, and pulled the eiderdown over her. As she sipped her milk, she noted the planes were no longer active, and soon the snores of the dog were the only sound she heard.

Still unable to sleep, Elenor sat curled up on the seat thinking of days gone by, of friends she'd made, especially Jackson St John. No matter how hard she tried to blank him from her mind, her thoughts always drifted to the kisses they'd shared.

'Fanciful thoughts are going to get us nowhere, eh Seth?'

A snore from the dog brought more envy of his ability to sleep, and Elenor draped the eiderdown around her shoulders, got out of her seat and shuffled to the window. White spiralling smoke replaced the orange glow, and silence had smothered the booms from the distance. An eeriness had cloaked its way around Tre Lodhen and Elenor shivered despite the warmth of the cover. Daylight couldn't come soon enough.

Spitfire the cockerel, named by Susie when he attacked her, called in the dawn chorus as usual. Elenor uncurled her body and stretched her legs to the best of her ability. When she'd climbed into the shelter three hours before, with the intention of shaking off the loneliness sitting heavy inside her, she'd drawn comfort from Seth when he'd settled back down across her legs.

Numb limbs, a dry mouth and grumbling stomach were followed by the assault on her face by an overexcited dog.

'The longest night I can ever recall, Seth. Get off, you daft mutt.'

She crawled out from under the table and enjoyed another stretching session. She pulled back the curtains. No longer orange or white, the grey sky summed up her emotion as she looked over the fields. Sadness. What had the world come to?

With a heavy heart she shuffled into the kitchen with Seth hitching a ride on the bottom of the eiderdown.

Full from a hearty breakfast of eggs and toast, Elenor fed Seth his own scraps and went back upstairs to get dressed whilst he ate.

'Hello, anybody home?'

Susie's voice drifted upstairs and Elenor could hear her making a fuss of the dog.

'Up here, be down in a minute,' Elenor called out.

Susie was a welcome visitor after the dreadful night Elenor had experienced. Glad to see the back of the eerie shadows, Elenor threw open her bedroom window and allowed the bracing chill of the air to circulate around her room. It felt like a ritual, a releasing of bad spirits – and thoughts.

Entering the kitchen Elenor let Seth outside just as Susie re-entered with a basket of eggs. The girl never wasted time.

'Good morning, Elenor. Not a good one for some though. Dreadful night again.'

Taking the egg basket from Susie, Elenor nodded her agreement.

'I've not slept a wink. Plymouth way again, those poor people,' she said.

Susie grabbed her brush and swept her way around the room with such a fierceness, Elenor feared the tiled floor would wear thin.

'Oh, by the way, my uncle asked me to bring your post. It's on the table.'

Elenor picked up the smaller of the two letters. It was from Victoria.

31st July 1940
Wales

Elenor,
   Just to inform you I am not in Coventry for a month. Rose is being cared for by my friend Agnes. She is fine. Your friend's father is keeping watch on the garden and the hens are laying well.
   George sends his regards. He is joining me in Wales soon.
   Victoria.

'Good news?' Susie asked.

Elenor stuffed the letter back into the envelope.

'Mixed. Short and sweet, no real news, except it appears George is no longer missing. He's joining Victoria in Wales.'

'Ah, that will be nice for their little girl,' Susie said.

'She's farmed out to a friend. For a month! They never take her anywhere with them. I miss her so much. I hope to have her here for a holiday when the war is over. Not now though, the amount of hits on Cornwall means she's better off where she is.'

Elenor slit open the second letter and sighed.

'At last. We are to have a girl from the Land Army,' she said and waved the paper in the air.

'Good news. You could do with the help out there.'

'Oh, and another will arrive in time for the September harvest.'

'Two. Even better,' Susie said.

'Yes, but do I sound ungrateful if I say I'd wish they'd both come at the same time?'

'Well, I'm glad they haven't. We will have to prepare their rooms.'

'You're right. My brothers' things are still sitting in them. I'll make a start on clearing out,' Elenor said.

'I'm off to Tom's place. Good luck, I think I'll have the more pleasant task,' Susie said and gave a laugh.

CHAPTER 30

Susie wasn't wrong. Apple crates stood floor to ceiling in the smallest bedroom. Each crate held something her brothers had kept for one reason or another, but by the end of sorting through, Elenor couldn't fathom why. Every piece of clothing was not worth repair, and the boots and shoes had seen better days. Their personal items consisted more of posters and picture cards of scantily clad women than toiletries, and Elenor dragged everything outside, piled it high and set fire to it all.

By the time she'd watched the last flame die away, Elenor felt a pang of sadness. How could two young men who'd had the best start in life throw it all away? And for the first time she gave thanks for the war; at least their names were on a register proving they'd fallen with pride. The Cardew name stood for something.

She looked around the medium spare room and began a morning of cleaning. No date of arrival for the young woman had been given, but as August had already arrived, she had to be prepared. To have a companion in the evenings would be a novelty, but a welcome break from the lonely ones.

The 21st of August started with an argument between

Susie and her mother and Susie arriving on Elenor's doorstep in tears.

'She's taking it out on me 'cos my sister is leaving to be a nurse.' Susie sobbed into her pinafore. 'I was only half an hour late home. I'm nearly seventeen, I can look after myself.'

'But not during a war, Susie. You are her baby and she's protecting you. She's upset and worried. She has a business to run, and more responsibility than ever before, and it has all blown out in her telling you off. She's scared. Bound to be,' Elenor said and guided Susie to a chair.

'Sit there and calm down. It will blow itself out during the day. I'd be the same as your mother,' Elenor said and handed Susie a fresh handkerchief from the pile she'd just ironed.

'You wouldn't. You'd understand I need to be with my friends after work. I work hard and pay my way,' Susie said and more nose-blowing ensued.

'I can't say. I've never had children, but your mother is a kind woman and she won't be mad at you for long. Take her a box of veggies, sweeten her mood.'

A rat-tat on the back door was followed by high-pitched voice.

'Coo-wee.'

'Come in,' Elenor said and looked to Susie with a frown.

'Who is it?' Susie whispered to Elenor as the door swung open.

'Dorothy Saunders. Call me Dottie,' said a short, stout girl as she dropped a suitcase to the floor.

'I think your uniform gives it away. You must be my Land Army help. Welcome to Tre Lodhen,' Elenor said and took the girl by the hand.

'Thanks. Didn't think I'd make it, darn Jerries dropped a few on the train station I needed. Grabbed me a lift with a chappie billeted in town. You must be Miss Cardew.'

'Elenor. Please, call me Elenor.'

'Well Elenor, would it be rude of me to ask for a glass of water? Parched. Not walked so far in years. Bit out of the way here, aren't you? Lovely, that's how I like it. Any horses?'

Susie burst out laughing and shook her head to a bemused Elenor.

'I'm sorry. Silly emotions,' she said to Dottie and waved her hand in front of her face. She pointed to the end of the kitchen. 'Bathroom if you need it. I'll fetch you a drink.' Her giggles grew louder and Elenor feared she was on the point of hysteria.

'Susie?' She questioned her friend with a raised brow.

'Ah, I could do with a pee, thanks ever so,' Dottie said and disappeared into bathroom. By which time Susie was bent double and gasping for air.

'What's got into you?' Elenor whispered to Susie.

'Well, just as she said about us having horses I'd thought to myself she was like a little Shetland pony: all belly, hair and little legs,' Susie said in a low voice choking with giggles.

Elenor pinched her lips together and held back tears of laughter. She shook her head, moved Susie aside and poured a glass of water from the jug on the draining board.

'Perfect description. A green Shetland pony with a squeaky voice,' she whispered back.

'At least it isn't a bucket in the corner. Daddy warned me there might be – that or an outside lav.' Dorothy's voice sounded out from the end of the room.

Susie looked at Elenor and both turned away from each other.

'Yes, it is handy,' Elenor said, as Dorothy came back into the room. 'Your water. Susie will cut you bread and cheese, and then we'll show you your room. Oh, and we don't have any horses here – we did, but the Great War took our last.'

'I love horses, but I'll cope with the rest of your animals. You have agriculture and livestock, so I'm told. I'm for the cattle shed according to my training, but don't be fooled, I can turn my hand to anything.'

'What ho,' Susie said and immediately clamped her hand over her mouth. Elenor simply pointed to the hallway and kept her lips clamped to stop the laughter. Susie grabbed the freshly ironed bedlinen and ran upstairs. From the kitchen both Elenor and Dottie could hear great gasps of laughter.

'She had a row with her mother this morning. It's played havoc with her emotions today,' Elenor said and hoped Dottie accepted the weak explanation.

Dottie munched on her sandwich and gave a nod.

Elenor smiled. 'I am pleased you are here. I'm worn out. My workers are the best, and another is most welcome. You have your own private room. There's only me here, so it gets quiet and lonely at times. I have a wireless in the parlour, through the hallway,' she said and pointed out of the kitchen door to where Susie had just left. 'I will move another comfortable chair in there for you. Mine is the green one and I've worn the springs just as I like them. No touching my desk please as I have a strict order in how I deal with things. Feel free to have a bath once a week, just choose an evening other than a Saturday, that's my treat night. We have electricity but no gas. The stove is wood burning. Hot water runs from the new boiler in the old scullery opposite the bathroom. Susie takes care of it for me, so don't worry about not having any for the bath, it is always ready and waiting. Any questions?'

'Who makes the cheese? It's a good strong one,' Dottie said.

Amused by the question, Elenor cut another slice and placed it onto her guest's plate.

'I do. We are fortunate, but I have to be careful about sending my fair share into the village. Where do you come from, Dottie?' she asked.

Wiping crumbs from her mouth, Dorothy swallowed her mouthful. 'Oxford.'

'Oxford. I've heard of it but never been. What did you do before the Land Army?'

Elenor sat down. Before she pushed the girl into a hard day's work she felt it only fair she knew something of her background.

'Nothing. Straight out of boarding school and into a life of social vetting for a rich husband. Mummy is probably still screaming at Daddy for letting me sign up. She wanted me to stay home and wind bandages. I said I'd drive an ambulance, but as Daddy pointed out, my legs are far too short to touch the pedals. And then there's the lifting of stretchers. Short arms, see.' Dorothy waggled her arms around and gave a laugh resembling the call of a donkey.

Dear God, why me? Elenor sent out a silent plea and once again bit onto her now sore lips.

'Ah, I see,' she said and wondered of what use Dottie was going to be milking a cow. Even a hoe handle was taller than the girl still waving her arms and legs around whilst balanced on the chair.

Elenor wondered if this was Graham Stonnard's revenge from the day she splattered him in mud.

'Will farm work suit you? I take it you went through training or you wouldn't be here. I'd hate for you to injure yourself,' she said.

'Oh, don't worry about what I can or can't do. I achieve most things. I've ridden a pig's back guiding it into a sty before now.'

At that moment Elenor froze. She waited, and the donkey laugh followed just as Susie walked into the room. They couldn't look at each other and Susie spun on her heel, went into the front room and closed the door. Elenor had little doubt her friend had stifled a laugh, and she struggled to control her own.

'Well, that conjures up a multitude of images, Dottie. Ready to see your room?' she said and allowed a laugh to follow before she exploded.

As they walked past the front room door she tapped on it and called out to Susie.

'Remind me to consider a horse for the farm again, Susie.'

The muffled reply was incomprehensible.

A week later, Elenor and Dottie were out on the farm together. 'Let's go and meet Tom, my shepherd. He's been away for a week helping another farmer. I rarely lend him out, but the farmer was in need of help after a stray bomb hit,' Elenor said to Dottie and pointed to the man in the top pasture.

'She'll scare the sheep,' Tom said as he watched Dottie bustle around the field with his sheepdog Bessie.

'Susie can't look at her without crying when the girl laughs and I'm afraid I'm the same. She's lovely though. Plum in her mouth but you'd never know she's from money. I think she'll fit in well with the others. She's not stopped working since she arrived.'

'Is it true you said she looked like a Shetland pony?' Tom asked and grinned at her.

She whipped the length of grass he chewed on away from his mouth.

'I did not. Susie, said it first. I said Dottie reminded me of a green one. Oh Tom, she's been a source of amusement for a week now, and I can't imagine life without her round here. She's tidy, too.'

'Ai, and she's a dab hand with the milking so I'm told. Look, Bessie likes her. Probably 'cos her new friend is the same height.'

Elenor gave him a gentle punch on the arm. 'Stop it. What if she hears us joking about her? It's not right. We must stop.'

'I'll stop laughing if you will,' said Tom and he whistled for Bessie to come to his side.

'Tom. Tom!' Dottie called out and waved her arms above her head.

'Can barely see her above the grass,' he muttered as they walked across the meadow.

'Stop it,' Elenor said under her breath and held back her laughter as best she could.

All thoughts of laughter vanished when she saw one of the ewes lying panting on her side.

'Tom?' She looked at her shepherd.

'She's in labour. Earlier than I expected. Look, she's not bagged up yet,' he said as he knelt down and pointed to the ewe's teats.

'We'll get her down to the barn. You go and ready the stall, and I'll follow on.'

'Come on Dottie, we'll need hay and grab a lantern in case we're there through the night,' Elenor called as she ran across the field.

When Elenor had finished her preparations, Dottie reached her side with a lantern. 'Susie said she's ready with hot water. What do you want me to do?'

'Stay here and help Tom. I've pulled a bale apart and spread it in that stall.' Elenor pointed to her right. 'Listen and do as he asks. I'll go with Bessie and watch over the others. Thanks, Dottie.'

'Rather excited. Never seen an animal give birth before.'

'Just keep your voice to a soft level and remain calm. Tom is an expert and I've every faith we'll have two little ones running around by morning.'

Elenor left Dottie bustling around Tom as he arrived with the ewe. Dottie was as short as Tom was tall; their silhouettes amused Elenor.

Before she headed to the top pasture she called in on Susie.

'It's going well in the barn. I've left Tom under the care of Dottie and all we can do is pray she doesn't laugh or the lambs will run away the moment they've arrived.'

Susie giggled. 'And you tell me off for saying things. I'm heading home early tonight. My sister leaves in the morning. Two more girls in the village have signed up for nurse training. Good luck to them, it is not for me. I do have to decide my place though. Housekeeping for you isn't exactly war work, and Dad is keen I do something more useful. Mum is scared of us all leaving and never coming home again. Her nerves are bad.'

Elenor filled a flask with tea for Susie to give to Tom.

'I understand what you mean, but you are valuable here. What do you think of me registering you as a live-in farm hand? That way you are secured a place here and keep both parents happy. You can continue looking after the house and no one will be any the wiser,' Elenor said and handed her the flask.

Susie packed her bag and placed it on the table.

'I'd love to live here but Dad will have the last word. The job would win him over, though – and Mum. Fingers crossed.'

Bessie rounded up a stray ewe, and Elenor watched over them for four hours. She could never understand the fascination of becoming a shepherd. Her sheep were precious to her but unless they were new-born lambs, they bored her. Not that she'd ever dare share the sentiment with Tom. Whilst she walked around her land she pondered new ideas and decided that although it might be nice to have a horse, she needed to think with her head and not her heart.

'Coo-ee!'

Dottie's voice echoed across the farm and a startled Elenor almost lost her footing.

'Come back,' Elenor commanded Bessie.

The sunlight had given way to the stars, and it promised to be a clear night. On such evenings Tom liked the sheep closer to home. The dog moved with expertise and soon had the sheep under control. Elenor walked towards the young woman marching her way through the fields. It did Elenor's heart good to see she wore a beaming smile.

'You were right. Two. A boy and a girl. It was incredible. Tom was fascinating to watch. He's so calm,' Dottie said in breathless excitement.

'Thank goodness. And Mum?'

Dottie took two steps to every one of Elenor's and bounced her way back to the barn.

'Oh, she's fine. Apparently, she's a good mother. I must say she looked awfully proud of herself. Mummy would have had a fainting fit if she'd seen me feeling my way around a sheep's nether regions. Tom taught me so much today.'

By the time they reached the barn, two small lambs wobbled their way around their mother and nudged at her teats.

Elenor gave Tom a smile and handed him his crook. 'Clever man, thank you,' she said.

'Nothing to do with me. She's a good mum.'

'What will you call them?' Dottie asked.

'Beg pardon?' Tom said.

'The lambs, what are their names?'

With a small laugh Elenor shook her head. 'We tend not to name them as it isn't easy to let them go if you do.'

She noticed Dottie's crestfallen face and gave Tom a wink.

'However, this time around I will be keeping these beauties, so how about Tom and Dottie?'

The laugh rang out around the barn and the lambs staggered at the sound.

'Sshh, for goodness' sake woman, you bray louder than a donkey. Their poor ears,' Tom said and grinned at Dottie.

Elenor stood and watched the pair in amazement. She waited for Dottie to get upset or angry, but she pulled her shoulders to her ears and pinched her lips together in apology.

'Sorry 'bout that. Inherited from Mummy, I'm afraid. I'll try and keep it under control,' she whispered.

'Outside is fine. It does me heart good to hear you enjoy the farm, but in here, we'll have rules. No laughing,' Tom said and gave both women another grin. 'Unless it is quiet – or smothered.'

Elenor and Tom watched Dottie run from the barn and heard the girl giggle.

'She'll do,' Tom said and turned back to the latest edition to his flock. Elenor walked away and headed inside to record the delivery. Dottie joined her.

'He's a good sort, that Tom. Says what he thinks.'

'I think I am lucky to have both of you at my side. I've asked Susie to join us at the house as a permanent resident. I've a feeling Tre Lodhen received a blessing this year.'

'You love this place, don't you? I can see why,' Dottie said.

'I do, Dottie. It has helped me heal.'

'Heal?'

'I lost people close to me and it made me ill. I'm recovered now, and ready to bring this place alive once again. Ready for supper?'

'Always,' said Dottie.

CHAPTER 31

September 1940

'Doesn't bear thinking about,' Dottie said and shifted in her seat.

'Makes you shiver at just the thought,' said Susie pulling her dressing gown tighter around her waist.

Elenor switched off the wireless and looked at her friends. Both had tears in their eyes.

'It must be the most heartbreaking thing to happen. I can't imagine this place raised to the ground. Poor London.'

'We've taken a bashing, and now London. When will it end? I just want my life back,' Susie said.

'I'll telephone Mummy later. She's got family on the outside of the city. We have work to do until then, and I'm ready for a cuppa,' Dottie said and filled the kettle. Placing it on the stove, she turned to Elenor.

'I'll dig a ditch to run off from the top pasture. When the rain comes it will flood the bottom plots. If we dig out it won't be such a deluge.'

Elenor looked at her and had so much admiration for the girl with such a privileged background. She had no airs or graces and her ideas were always actioned by Dottie herself. She doubted Dottie knew what the word shirk meant. All three looked forward to the arrival of another girl from the Land Army due that month, but for now the news of heavy bombing and deaths in London occupied their thoughts.

She stretched and yawned. Planes had disturbed their sleep and they'd sat inside the shelter. It was cramped now all three of them used it, and Elenor had ordered an Anderson one to be set up beside the chicken coop.

It took two days to dig out Dottie's ditch and she proved to be a hard taskmaster. Elenor had handed over the project to Dottie and bore the blisters to prove she'd done her bit. Each day the news reported more about the enemy targeting the country, and she found it hard to find cheer in daily duties, but Dottie's enthusiasm chivvied her along. The girl never showed signs of wear and tear, nor did she let the war dampen her love of life.

A tap on the parlour window one morning distracted her from her book-keeping. Elenor opened the window to Susie's uncle.

'Telegram. And one from the Ag ministry. Sorry,' he said.

'Thanks Jim.'

'Hope the news isn't too dreadful.'

'At least the telegram is from you and not the lad with the "we regret to inform" ones,' Elenor said. 'This one from the agricultural lot will be worse. More rules and regs, for sure.'

Opening the buff envelope Elenor read the few words from Victoria.

George killed. London. No funeral to attend. Rose coping well. Will write soon. Victoria.

Shocked, Elenor read the words again. She'd often wished George out of her life but never dead. Poor Victoria. Poor Rose.

'Well, if that's the good news . . .' Elenor muttered as she tore open the brown envelope. She was relieved to see it was notification telling her that the second Land Army girl would not join them until the New Year. However, Dorothy Saunders would remain at Tre Lodhen indefinitely and the department would review the situation in January.

'Pah, she's ten girls rolled into one. You'd have to fight me for my Dottie,' Elenor said out loud and Seth's ears perked up. He lifted one eye.

'And you can go back to sleep,' she snapped at him.

Elenor scribbled a note alongside the telegram on the kitchen table informing Susie she'd gone to call Victoria and offer her condolences. Ruffling Seth's ears Elenor felt mean for snapping at him.

'Sorry lad. It's not your fault.'

The moment she pulled on her coat, Seth jumped and yelped his way around the kitchen.

'Calm down, you can come, but no pulling me off my bike.'

The peddling down to the village took longer than normal. Seth had a tendency to pull to the hedge each time he heard a rustle. Elenor let him off the lead for a short run and once bored with chasing the bike, he chased a rabbit. By the time she'd reached the telephone box she'd decided he was best left on the farm and to never put herself through the trauma again. She tied him to the bicycle frame and left him to battle out his escape while she rang Coventry.

Agnes answered, and Elenor could hear music in the background.

'Is that Rose playing, Agnes?'

'Yes, her mother has told her to play it every day in her father's memory. It's bloomin' morbid I can tell you.'

Elenor tutted her disapproval.

'Is Victoria there, Agnes?'

'She's not back until tomorrow. Muttered something about family calling and left first thing.'

'Again? Is she ever home? Agnes, is she coping? Rose is not suffering too much?' Elenor asked.

Distracted by the dog barking outside, Elenor missed something Agnes said.

'Sorry, repeat that.'

'The child is happier when she's alone with her music. Can't say I blame her, that Victoria is a cold fish.'

'Right, yes, well I am sure under the circumstances, Agnes,' Elenor said.

She had heard the undertone of disapproval in Agnes' voice, and her concerns for Rose deepened.

'Tell Victoria when she's home that I'm going to come back for Rose's birthday in November as a surprise. I'll ring again next week. Thank you for helping, Agnes, it is appreciated.'

The last few notes of a piano tune tinkled out as Agnes replaced the handset. Rose spent too many days alone with Agnes, and Elenor needed to speak about it to Victoria.

Seth expressed his joy that she'd joined him once again, and she untied him from the frame. With one sharp tug he managed to release himself from her grip and headed off in the wrong direction.

'Come back you rascal. Seth!'

Elenor peddled as fast as she could along the bumpy lane. She could hear Seth barking in the distance accompanied by several male voices. A soldier marched ahead of a group of men flanked by more soldiers either side and at the rear. Seth wove his way amongst their marching legs and one man gave him a swift kick with his boot and the dog yelped.

'Hey, there's no need to kick him.' Elenor dismounted and rushed to Seth whining in the ditch.

'Apologies ma'am. They've got no manners.' The soldier at the rear marched by and called out his apology. Elenor watched them head the way she'd just ridden.

'Well, Seth. You managed to upset a group of absconders by the looks of things and got a shock for your efforts. Maybe now you'll stay to heel.'

Not wanting to risk him running after the men again, she tied him to the handlebars and wheeled the bike home. When she opened her gate, she was about to release him when one of her men finishing for the day walked towards her.

'You seen them cheeky beggars? Marched right over the top field towards White Cross. Good job I haven't turned it over yet.' He pointed to the trail of men she'd encountered.

'Who, Jack? The soldiers?'

'Yeah, them and their prisoners. Germans.'

Elenor forgave him for his indelicate spit on the ground.

'Prisoners of war already? Near Summercourt, how worrying.'

'You'll be safe, Miss. They are well secured. Only out to help dig a ditch at the bottom of the village. Making them work for their keep while our lads fight for us.'

'Seth here tried to take the shoe from one of them. I thought they were ours. Scared runaways,' she said.

Jack bent down and stroked Seth's back.

'Well done lad. Next time take a chunk for my Jimmy.'

Elenor pulled her lips tight. The man had lost his son at the same time James and Walter had been killed.

She touched his shoulder, words were unnecessary. They walked their separate ways, and Elenor had no doubt they both carried the same thought. Roll on the end of the war. She was due to turn twenty at the end of the month, and some days wondered she whether her mind and body realised she was still a young woman.

CHAPTER 32

'I'm sorry but keeping quiet about your birthday has annoyed me,' Susie said as she stood with her hands on her hips. 'Goodness knows how many more any of us will *ever* have, and you want to hush up the ones you *can* have?'

Ignoring her friend's rant, Elenor continued to pat the butter into equal slabs. Susie had started her barrage of ticking off when her uncle had dropped off the post. A late card from Rose had arrived and without thinking, Elenor stood it on the mantelpiece.

'I am busy and don't celebrate birthdays, Susie. It was last week and is now in the past.'

'But it is . . .'

Elenor put her finger to her lips and leaned over to Susie. 'Shhh. No more.'

'But you are not twenty every day of the week,' Susie said, her words rushed before Elenor could shush her again.

'I am. Every day for another year,' Elenor said and went back to the butter.

'Oh, very clever.'

'Who's clever?' Dottie said with a yawn as she walked into the kitchen.

'Did you know it was Elenor's birthday last week?' Susie demanded.

'Tea?' said Elenor to Dottie and held out the teapot.

'Belated wishes,' Dottie said and smothered another yawn before pouring herself a drink from the pot.

'Belated wishes? Is that all you can say? The woman was twenty and told no one,' Susie said, her voice raised a notch louder.

'Shh, my head hurts. How much crab-apple cider did you give me last night?' Dottie said and looked accusingly at Elenor.

'Half a glass. You poured the rest,' Elenor said and laughed. 'It helped you sleep, didn't it?'

'Yes, yes. You proved a point. I can't stay awake after a drink.'

'Every time you have more than a quarter of a glass you snore for England,' Elenor said.

Dottie gave a playful scoff and put her hands to her head. 'Ouch. Still, it was a good drop of cider.'

Susie stomped around the room.

'I need a *brandy* with you two as housemates. Well, don't say I didn't try and give you a happy birthday,' she said and stared at the other two who now sat watching her over the lips of their teacups.

'Finished?' Elenor asked. 'We didn't forget yours, so that's the most important thing. Can we please move onto something more proactive, such as who is going to drive the tractor now it is fixed?'

Dottie jumped from her seat and knocked her cup flying across the table.

'Sorry. Sorry,' she said as she grabbed a cloth and mopped up the spillage. 'It's fixed?'

'Yippee dee,' said Susie with sarcasm.

'All done. Ron, the soldier from the POW camp, worked

on it on his day off. Trundles around a treat. Plough is cleaned and fixed. Providing the weather is on our side, we will get another field turned over ready for the fertiliser. Next year's harvest will be easier and cheaper,' Elenor said.

'Do I exist? Am I in the room?' Susie said and waved her arms around like a bird.

Elenor made a great play of looking around.

'Did somebody speak?'

The instant the words fell from her mouth she knew what would follow. True to her style, Dottie hee-hawed her two-toned bray, and both Elenor and Susie burst out laughing.

'Is it really only six-thirty?' Susie said as she looked to the clock on the mantle.

'Yes. And I've had to listen to you since five. Your punishment is when you've finished around here, at eight o'clock you can take the butter into the village, and fetch back flour and sugar. Use my ration book. I'll let you make me a birthday cake. Happy? Oh, and post a letter for me, please,' Elenor said. 'I'll bring it through when I've written it.'

'It's something, I suppose,' Susie said.

'Oh, Susie, don't sulk. Come and ride on the tractor later,' Dottie said.

'With you at the wheel? Thanks, I'll pass.'

Elenor left the pair throwing each other cheerful banter. Each morning was much brighter with them in her home.

At the desk she looked out over the hills as she composed her words. A soft drizzle fell from a scattering of clouds. She watched them roll by as she made up her mind whether to write the letter she'd composed inside her head during breakfast. She'd decided to write to Jackson's grandfather. His address was on the letters to George, and she doubted Victoria would have informed him of George's death. She also needed to face the past. There were days when it slid into her world without notice and caught her unawares. Today she wanted to take a step forward with her connection with Jackson's grandfather. His kindness shown to her had given her courage and once again she'd draw on that courage with him in mind.

Miss Elenor Ruth Cardew,
Tre Lodhen,
Summercourt,
Cornwall,
England.
7th October 1940

Dear Squadron Leader Fleming,

I hope this letter finds you and your family in good health. A lot has happened since we last met, and sadly, one of those is the death of your pen-friend George Sherbourne.

I am reassured both his wife Victoria, and daughter Rose, are well and coping with the sad news. As I understand it, he was caught in the London Blitz. I will return to see them in late November, for Rose's birthday. They will remain in the Coventry house until Victoria decides otherwise, due to the fact I no longer live there as you will notice from my address on this letter.

My brothers were killed abroad, and I am now the sole survivor of my family and have inherited the farm. My brothers left it in a dreadful state. My life is different to the new one I'd formed in Coventry. A special place in my heart is set for that city, and I can still recall the day we entered the department store together, but I can never recall it without a giggle or a smile.

It is time for me to start my busy day as Farmer Cardew and don my country bumpkin clothing. No selecting fine clothes for me nowadays.

Food rationing is hard for many, but we are blessed here on the farm. I've cultivated two acres of apple and pear trees and four acres of various crops. Flax and wheat yields have increased since I took over, something of which I am rather proud. Nothing is wasted. The pigs have never been happier. We had a good feast on strawberries, but sadly, they only last a couple of weeks. I have strict regulations to follow and pride myself in helping to keep people fed. My workforce is mainly made up of women, but we gathered the harvest well enough. Sadly, we've experienced heavy bombing here too, and several farms have experienced hayrick fires which spread to precious crops. I live in fear of such an event here on my home, but to date, am one of the lucky ones. Enough about me. I am sorry to be the bearer of bad news.

My very best wishes,
E R Cardew.

Elenor licked the envelope and pondered over sending the letter. Finally, convinced Victoria would not have written to him she handed the letter to Susie before she changed her mind.

'Canada?' Susie said looking at the address.

'Yes, it is a friend of the family. I realised he might not have heard about George – they were pen-pals. Time to head out. Ready Dottie? See you teatime, Susie,' Elenor called out before closing the door to start another day of land clearing.

*

'. . . and that's how I came to understand the study of . . .' Elenor stopped talking to Dottie when she pushed open the back door and saw Susie, her mother, Tom and the rest of the staff waving and smiling at her.

'Surprise!'

'What is going on?' Elenor said and looked back at Dottie.

'No point in asking me, but I do see cake, so it's nothing dreadful.'

'It's your birthday treat. Go and wash, change then come down to eat,' Susie said and guided Elenor to the far end of the room by her shoulders.

'You couldn't resist it, could you?' Elenor laughed.

As she washed she could hear the chink of crockery and laughter. After a hard day on the field she wanted to rest, but the kindness of her friends gave her energy to last a few more hours. She scuttled past the table which was laden with food and returned dressed in a skirt and blouse.

'Twit twoo,' Susie said, and the rest of the guests followed suit.

'Stop it. I just thought if you'd made an effort, so would I. What's for tea? I'm starving.'

'Have a cuppa on Tom. He gave over an extra spoonful for the pot. You get the first of the strong brew.' Susie handed Elenor a cup of dark brown tea.

'Ooh, I'd almost forgotten what colour a good cup carried. Thank you, Tom. It's generous of you.'

'Mum made the cake and it has a rose flavouring. The rest of us pitched in for the rest. Happy birthday!' Susie said.

'It is appreciated, Susie. Very kind of you all, thank you.'

'You spoil everyone else, it is about time we returned the gift. Tuck in.'

Elenor enjoyed a plate of sandwiches, and encouraged to cut her cake, took a bite of the first slice.

'Oh my. This is the best sponge I've eaten in years.'

Elenor took another bite and chewed it for a while, then licked her lips.

She turned to her friends in the room.

'Thank you all. I didn't think I'd enjoy celebrating a birthday again, but I have, thanks to you. Dottie, I have brandy and cider for those who'd enjoy a drop.'

'Really? You are doing that to me after last night?'

'Just don't have more than a sip and we might be able to enjoy your company for a while longer.'

Laughter rang around and Elenor counted her blessings as she helped herself to another slice of cake.

The evening moved onto a singalong to Tom's harmonica and ended with Dottie falling asleep snoring louder than the music.

Elenor and Susie tiptoed around her as they cleared up after the last of the guests had left. As Elenor climbed the step-stool to put away the best of the dishes the ground vibrated.

'What on earth?' she said and climbed down.

'Jerry planes. Flying low,' Susie said and continued to wash the dishes.

'How can you tell they're the enemy planes?' Elenor asked and climbed back onto the steps.

'They drone and whine in a different way. A bit like Dottie asleep,' Susie said and giggled.

'She's a laugh a minute that one. Pass me the last,' Elenor said and leaned down for the plates. Just as she did another group of planes threatened to vibrate her from the steps.

'That's it for the night – for us anyway. I hope Dottie isn't the only one to get sleep. See you in the morning, and thanks again Susie.'

CHAPTER 33

Exciting changes on the farm kept everyone busy and each day new ideas were formed and carried out. Tom or the postman alerted Elenor to auctions and her livestock and machinery collection grew. Every day was different, but time flew by and before Elenor knew it she was marking off the sixth day into November.

Night after night for weeks they'd endured the drone of planes, or sirens echoing around the county. Sometimes it was not a false alarm, and they listened to explosions in the distance. Each time they moved from bed to shelter and back again.

Tiredness was fought by the determination that the country would not be defeated. Elenor often amazed herself by finding inner strength. She ensured all her workers had an hour's nap each day, which they took inside the farmhouse in stages.

Their resilience was commendable. Rarely did they work in silence. A song or laughter rallied round the yard or on the fields, and only when bad news came for a family did they have moments of quiet.

Dottie and Tom had formed such a strong friendship it made Elenor envious. Sally wrote and told her of another new boyfriend, and Susie had several offers to escort her to the cinema week in and week out. Today she moaned about having to choose which of the young men she should go out with, as if she turned down one she might have chosen the wrong one.

'Why not ask one for tomorrow and the other the day after?' Elenor said and her tone was not light-hearted.

'But what if I like the one tonight *and* the one tomorrow?'

'Oh, for goodness' sake, choose one and be grateful. Some of us . . .'

Not wanting to say more, Elenor walked out of the door and into the yard. She took great gulps of air, brushed away the raindrops falling onto her cheeks and walked back inside.

'Some of us what?' Susie said and stood with her feet astride, her hands on her hips.

'Forget it. Just choose the one you think would stand by you no matter what happened. The one you'd trust to hold your heart forever. Just choose one. Be thankful someone thinks enough of you to want you in their life.'

'So that's it. Jealousy,' Susie said and walked out into the hall. 'Jealousy can make some people ugly, you know.'

'Grow up,' Elenor shouted after her.

Ramming her fist into her mouth, Elenor bit back the bitterness building inside.

The chugging sound of the tractor engine distracted her, and she looked out of the window to see Dottie perched on the seat. Women followed on planting out and their children followed on behind covering the seed.

From the top of the hill the silhouette of a plane appeared against a patch of grey sky. Silver flecks glinted inside the small white clouds dotted about as it disappeared through them. Elenor's first reaction was to warn the workers but no sirens sounded which meant the plane had a right to fly. The plane dipped and dived over the treetops like a graceful bird. There was something mesmerising about the way it glided and swooped, and it fascinated Elenor. She willed the pilot to fly their way, so the children could wave as they often did when they spotted them in the sky. Unsure as to why this plane stood out like no others, she continued to admire the graceful swirls and turns the pilot created with expertise. It flew closer to the farm and she snatched up her coat. She rammed her feet into her boots as she shuffled out of the door, not wanting to miss a moment of the performance.

Elenor ran to the right side of the farm to get a closer look, and although she had never been to the ballet, she imagined the plane to be as graceful as a performer as it made smooth turns in and out of the cotton clouds. Drizzling rain made no difference, she'd fallen for the beauty above her. For once she did not have to run or hide. For the first time she could appreciate the skills of the man flying. She held her breath as it rolled, up-righted itself and rolled again. No words could explain the disappointment she felt when it turned and flew back to where it came from, and in her mind she replayed the scene. Her thoughts wandered to Jackson and of his ability to perform such a magnificent act. It unnerved her to think he'd fly like that with the enemy on his tail.

'It was brilliant, wasn't it?' a small boy said as he joined her, his voice loaded with admiration.

'Marvellous,' Elenor said quashing thoughts of Jackson. 'I wondered what sort of plane it was, but they don't have labels.'

'A Defiant,' the boy said.

'You know plane names? How clever.'

'My uncle fixes 'em. He took me to a base at St Eval. One flew in for a repair. I saw lots of planes and my uncle helped me identify them. I hope the war lasts a long time. I want to be a fighter pilot,' the boy said as he ran off impersonating the sound of gunfire with his arms open wide like the wings of a plane.

'I truly hope it never happens little one,' Elenor whispered after him.

Across the field she spotted Tom and went to join him. The ewes were ready to be taken for tupping and needed to have their rear-ends clipped and cleaned. This year would be the first time Elenor had helped, and the first year they would use their own ram. It amused Elenor to think she used to get excited over cream for her hands, and nowadays it was the mating efforts of her flock.

'He gave a good display. Liked how he didn't scare the flock neither. Kept his distance. Hope you've built up your muscles. Got a couple of maiden ewes and they're going to put up a struggle.'

Elenor laughed. 'I'm stronger than I look, but this is my maiden journey with clipping the backsides of my ewes.'

'Have a bit of faith in yourself woman. Time to go. Bess!'

Scraping the mud from her boots at the end of her day, Elenor hoped Susie had made up her mind and gone out with the boy of her choice. She was in no mood for confront-ation, and although she'd worked hard all day, she still couldn't shake the imagery of the plane and yet again, thoughts of Jackson. It troubled her the way she couldn't live a day without thinking of him. Simple things would conjure up a memory of how he had held her and kissed her, and resentment ate away inside.

'Anybody home?' she called. The house was quiet. Tom had hinted Dottie was eating at his cottage that evening, and it also appeared Susie had made a choice and gone out. The silence seemed strange after having company for so long, and a bout of sadness crept in for Elenor. If she never married it worried her this was the life she had to look forward to: a life of silence and loneliness.

By ten that evening it was obvious Dottie was not coming home and Elenor was too tired to listen to Susie's tales of her eventful or uneventful night, so took herself to bed. Within what seemed like minutes of her putting her head on the pillow, the sirens were wailing. She pulled on a newly acquired siren suit and raced downstairs. The temptation to stay and use the smaller shelter might have brought Dottie or Tom looking for her. She grabbed her bag and case of papers and ran out into the night. Search lights danced across the sky and in complete contrast to the beauty of the morning display, the planes rolled in like black beasts dropping dark shapes onto the horizon. A nightmare come to life. Elenor ran to the shelter and opened the door.

'Evening,' Tom said, and a flushed Dottie raised a tin mug to her arrival.

'Thank goodness you are both here. I'm assuming Susie is at her mother's.'

'I put in extra blankets today. It's getting colder at night and I've a feeling this will not be the end of our visits,' Dottie said.

'Thanks, good thinking Dottie. Busy day?'

'We did all right. Old Tor is a good one.'

'Tor?' A puzzled Elenor looked at Dottie.

'Tractor. Tor. I've named her. She's my metal horse.'

Tom looked to Elenor and both braced themselves for the friend's abuse of their eardrums.

A bang in the distance stopped their chatter, and the noise above deepened.

'More than I've heard in a while,' said Tom.

'Let me in. Let me in.' Susie's voice rang out as she

pummelled at the door from outside. Elenor opened the door and a sobbing Susie threw herself into her arms.

'Susie, you're damp through. I thought you'd gone to your mother's,' Elenor said. 'Dottie, pass me a blanket please. Thanks.'

'No. David's brother left his gas mask at home, so we walked to The Blue Anchor at Fraddon to give it to him. We missed the bus home and were only halfway when the planes flew over. I've never been so scared. David ran off and left me when we got to the outskirts.'

Elenor rubbed Susie warm with the blanket, and Tom handed her a tea from the flask. Dottie took Susie's hand until her sobs subsided to sniffles.

'I chose the wrong one,' she said and looked to Elenor with a sad smile.

'Some of us do, and some of us are lucky first time,' Elenor said and gave Tom a smile. He gave an embarrassed grin and looked at Dottie whose shadowed colour deepened, and Elenor knew if the lamp had been brighter she would have seen a blush.

'Ah, here we go,' Tom said and stretched his legs.

'I love the sound of the all clear,' said Dottie. 'Two hours' sleep and we are off again. See you later, Tom.'

Elenor felt sorry for Tom whose dampened romantic evenings were becoming more regular thanks to enemy planes.

'I'm aiming for more than two hours. My feet are sore and my legs tired,' Susie said and rubbed her calves.

Trying to ignore the smoke and orange glow in the distance, they all focused upon Seth bouncing around in front of them and headed indoors. Inside no longer held the lonely feel Elenor had experienced earlier, and she knew she'd never live alone again. She wouldn't wait until after the war, she'd write to Victoria and offer her and Rose a home at Tre Lodhen. She'd speak with her when she visited them on the 20th.

'I'm thinking of asking Victoria and Rose to come live with us in December. It will mean you'd have to share with the other girl when she arrives, Dottie, but the room is big enough,' Elenor said as she removed her outdoor clothes.

Susie clambered onto the couch and pulled the blanket around her body.

'I can move back home,' she said.

'You will not – unless you want to of course, but this is your home now. We won't be cramped.'

'Dottie can always kip over with Tom if we do,' Susie said and added a cheeky wink.

'We don't have that sort of a relationship if you don't mind,' said Dottie and gave Susie a frown.

'Oh, listen to you miss la-di-da. I bet you aren't as innocent as you make out,' Susie said and the spiteful tone shocked Elenor.

'Susie. Apologise. Dottie and Tom's business is none of ours,' she said.

'Sorry. I'm fed up and shouldn't take it out on you.'

'You're young and speak before you think. You're forgiven. Right, I'm off to bed. See you both in the morning, if not before,' Dottie said.

Each woman gave a groan and followed Dottie upstairs.

CHAPTER 34

November 1940

Fleming Mill,
Lynn Valley,
North Vancouver,
Canada
British Columbia.
November 1940

My dear Miss Cardew – Farmer Cardew,
   How touched I was to receive your letter. This is short as I have the opportunity to send my reply with a colleague.
   Thank you for letting me know about George Sherbourne. My condolences to his wife and daughter. I also send you condolences over the death of your brothers.
   I take my hat off to you ladies over there, it can't be easy. I am not sure how long this letter will take to reach you, so I will also send good wishes for Christmas and the New Year. We pray for the hostilities to cease any day.

You Brits are known for your stiff upper lip and I've seen it with my own eyes. May you all find peace soon.

With my best wishes,
Samuel Fleming.

Elenor folded the letter and placed it into her case. Another hurdle overcome.

Picking up her stock control papers, she spotted a woman in Women's Voluntary Service uniform by the gate.

'Not another military official here to tell me what to plant,' she muttered to the empty room.

Seth was in his outdoor pen to stop him chasing the POW gang. She'd granted permission for them to walk through the top of the farm twice a day. At times she was tempted to leave Seth to run and greet visitors, especially when an official from the Agricultural Office called, but a woman from the WVS didn't deserve to be slobbered over. Elenor guessed she was after support for a local family and headed out to meet the woman.

He yapped and barked and Elenor waved at the woman carrying a small suitcase and valise, who approached the yard with caution.

'It's safe, he's in his . . . Mrs Green, how lovely to see you!' Elenor said. 'Come for a holiday? Welcome to Tre Lodhen.'

She rushed towards her friend then stopped in her tracks. From behind Alice Green stepped Rose. She was pale-faced, with dark rings around her eyes, a gash across her forehead, bandaged hands and Elenor could see large bruises on her legs. Rose stared up at Elenor with tears in her eyes.

'Rose! Oh, baby girl, what has happened to you?'

Elenor knelt beside the child and gently pulled her close. 'What happened, Mrs Green?'

'Call me Alice. We'd best go inside, Elenor. She's exhausted.'

Elenor settled the child onto the comfy sofa, and Alice took off her coat.

Elenor busied herself with the kettle on the range.

'Sit down. Rest. I'll make tea.'

Elenor indicated to a comfortable chair for Alice. Rose had fallen asleep and Alice shook her head and pointed to the hallway.

'What is going on? Where's Victoria?' Elenor asked, keeping her voice low as she guided Alice into the parlour.

With her hands clasped, a weary Alice sighed.

'She's gone, Elenor.'

Elenor stared at her friend in disbelief.

'Gone where? Did she abandon Rose? What's going on?

Alice shuffled in her seat. Elenor saw the tiredness in her face, her eyes were dull and aged.

'Coventry was hit badly the night of the fourteenth. The town, nigh on gone. The cathedral, destroyed. Everything turned to rubble and dust.'

Large tears fell down her face and Alice did nothing to stop them. Her body gave into loud sobs, and Elenor rushed to the door and checked on Rose.

'Victoria is dead, Elenor. Killed when the house was hit. It's gone, all gone, Elenor. So many dead. Sally, Victoria, Agnes, all dead.'

'Sally's gone?' Elenor whispered.

'Yes. I'm sorry to bring such terrible news. Rose is my greatest concern. All the child has left is you and a photograph of her parents, poor lamb. I've collected clothes from the donation box. There was a note inside her gasmask box which has named you as her next of kin, along with the name Argyle, a solicitor. I went to find him, to get help, but he's gone too. It's exhausting, so sad, Elenor.'

Alice pulled the wooden framed photograph she'd mentioned out of her bag. Elenor had never seen it before, and it looked as if it was taken not long before George died. Not one parent smiled. Elenor placed it on her desk.

'And you, Alice, she has you. Thank you for bringing her here. Are your family safe? What about you, do you need a home here too?' Elenor asked.

She looked at the woman who'd given her guidance into womanhood. There was a grey tinge to her skin which highlighted dark bags beneath her eyes.

Elenor pulled Alice into her arms and hugged her tight. 'When did you last sleep?'

'My family are safe, I am one of the lucky ones. I need to return tomorrow, the city needs everyone who can help the poor souls left homeless, it's dreadful.'

Elenor put her hands over her face, and fought back the tears for a city she'd once known as home. She needed to be the strong one.

'Victoria's funeral. I assume her family will need to be informed.'

Alice gave a slight cough.

'After they rescued Rose, what she doesn't know is there was a gas explosion. Victoria has already been buried, as has Sally. A communal burial, Elenor. You understand what I am telling you? I attended on Rose's behalf.'

Elenor let her shoulders slump.

'How dreadful. Thank you. Thank you for caring.'

A shout and scream from the kitchen sent both women running to Rose's side. The child flailed about under the covers, screaming at the top of her lungs. Her little body shook despite the warmth from the fire. Elenor swooped her into her arms and held her tight.

'Don't cry Rose, Elenor's here. I'm here, you're safe now.'

Two little arms snaked their way around her neck and

Elenor let her own tears fall. Fate had brought them both together, two lonely people in need of love and company.

'You're home, my darling girl. You are home.'

Alice removed the bandages from the child's hands. They were red, but Rose shook her head when asked if they were sore.

'Not now. Mrs Green nursed them better,' she said and burst into tears.

Elenor tugged a handkerchief from her cardigan pocket and dried Rose's eyes.

'She can leave the bandages off if she wears gloves and keeps them clean,' Alice said. 'If you are worried at any time, your doctor will know what to do, but the burns and cuts were superficial. It's love and comfort she needs now.'

'I can give her that, but what about the rest? I've never had a child, I'm not a mother.'

'You've been more of one than her own. It's a big responsibility, but you are more than capable, Elenor. Please write if you need advice. Time and patience, Elenor.'

Both Susie and Dottie arrived home and immediately reorganised their sleeping arrangements to accommodate the guests. Rose and Alice barely ate the food in front of them, and Elenor worried about Alice as much as she did about Rose.

'Just let us know what we can do,' Susie said.

'Watch over Rose when I can't. That's all I ask,' Elenor said.

'She's a lucky girl having you in her life.'

'Thanks Dottie, but it's early days. Goodness knows how I'll cope,' Elenor said.

'We're here for you. You are not alone,' said Susie.

'But one day, when the war is over, I will be. This is such a shock. Next of kin. She has family, they were visited by George and Victoria often enough.'

Elenor ran her fingers through her hair and paced the floor.

'Listen, you have friends in the village. No one will see you struggle. We'll help you get through this.'

CHAPTER 35

The following morning brought with it a sense of loss. An exhausted Rose had slept in Elenor's bed, clinging onto her for the best part of an hour until sleep came to them both. No bombs fell that night and Elenor was grateful for more than five hours' rest.

She and Alice rose early and Elenor was touched to find a note saying the girls had gone to organise the staff and she was to concentrate on Rose. Whilst Alice sat down to breakfast, both waited for the moment Rose would wake and need comfort.

'You have a train home, Alice? Can I pay for the ticket, it's the least I can do.'

'Thank you, but the WVS have arranged a lift home for me. I'm to join a support convoy heading to Coventry at ten. A truck will pick me up. I am grateful for the rest and food.'

'Don't be grateful to me. I will never forget what you've done for both Rose and me, now and in the past. Eat up, and I'll prepare you a lunch pail for the journey. I'll just let Seth off for a run.'

Seth had been kept outside for fear of upsetting Rose as

neither women were sure she'd ever met a dog. He greeted Elenor with his usual enthusiasm and gave a bark.

'You shush. There's a little girl who needs sleep inside. It is time for you to be calm.'

She released him off into the fields where he ran carefree. Elenor looked on with envy. She turned to head back into the house and saw a tousle-haired Rose standing in the doorway.

'Good morning sleepyhead. I'm just coming to see if you are ready to eat something.'

Alice had hinted she'd refused food since the bombings. Today would be the fifth day.

'We need to feed you up. You will turn seven in a few days. Seven? Can you believe it, I certainly can't. Now where is Mrs Green, I've something for her.'

Elenor kept her tone upbeat. It broke her heart to see the little girl so scared. A loud bark echoed out from the top meadow and Rose jumped.

'Ah, that's Seth. He keeps me company. I'll introduce you later.'

She ushered Rose inside just as Alice entered the kitchen.

'I've packed my bag. Ah, Rose, come and give an old lady a hug for her journey.'

Alice sat on an armchair and Rose rushed over to her and Alice read to Rose until her lift arrived.

'I've food for you outside, meat, veg and fruit, and a sack of potatoes, I'll get the lads to load them for you. I've also put money in an envelope, use it as you see fit. It's not a lot, but hopefully it will help.'

'It is kind of you, Elenor. My family will appreciate the food, and I'll take the money to our local treasurer. Thank you.'

A honk of a horn and several male voices in the yard were followed by Susie's laughter. Seth had found Alice's escort home. Alice dropped a kiss on the top of Rose's head and eased her onto her feet and turned her around to face her.

'You are in good hands, little one. Write to me, Elenor has my address. I'll visit when I can, when I've helped fix Coventry. This is your home now, and you know you are safe.'

No words came from Rose's lips, nor did she offer a smile. She grabbed Alice's hand and then went to Elenor's side.

'That's a good girl. You take care of Elenor for me.'

Rose nodded her head and buried it into the side of Elenor's hip.

'You take care, Alice. I'll just pop out to instruct the lads to load you up, and then we'll wave you off.'

Walking to the door it was obvious she would have to either drag Rose with her or carry her. 'It's cold outside darling. Stay with Alice.' But Rose clung onto her and had no intention of letting Elenor out of her sight.

As Elenor stepped outside one of the soldiers swore loudly, and Elenor gave him a withering look – an instinctive reaction to protect the child in her arms.

'Sorry missus, didn't think.'

'No harm done. Seth, inside,' Elenor said and pointed to the pen.

The dog obeyed, and Susie shut the clasp tight. All the while, Elenor was aware of Rose watching the dog.

Following a tearful farewell with Alice, they stood watching until the back of the transport had left the lane.

'Do you need help, Elenor?' Susie asked.

'No, I think we'll be just fine. Missy here is going to have a late breakfast and we'll take it from there. Thank you, Susie.'

'Well, as you can probably hear, Dottie is with her team

and Tom up in the top pastures. I'll be around here mucking out and milking with the girls. Shout if you need us for anything. See you later Rose.'

Rose gave a shy wave as Elenor carried her inside and sat her at the large pine table. She looked so tiny, so vulnerable and barely reached the plate on the surface.

'I think you need a cushion to sit on, Rose. I'm going to make us some scrambled eggs. My chickens laid them especially for you, so please make them happy and eat up.'

Rose sat staring out of the window. Elenor knew at her level she would only be watching the clouds scud over the treetops.

She plated up their breakfast and placed Rose's in front of her. Rose looked at it and with slow movements picked up her spoon and took a mouthful. Without being asked, when the plate was empty, Elenor refilled it, and again, Rose ate. She drank her milk and cuffed away the cream from her top lip. Elenor watched as she clambered down from her seat and put both dish and cup onto the drainer.

'We have a small bathroom downstairs, Rose. Over there. Your wash bag is waiting for you.'

Rose padded in her unlaced shoes to the bathroom. Minutes later she returned, her face still serious. Elenor selected Rose a tan-coloured woollen dress and cardigan, and a pair of white woollen socks.

'Get yourself dressed. I have to feed some of my animals, and maybe you'd like to meet them. I have cows, pigs and sheep, not just chickens and a crazy dog. And we'll pull some carrots for dinner. Would you like to have a walk around the farm for a while?'

From under the neck of her dress Rose popped up her head. She nodded.

'I have lots of people come from the village, and most have children you can play with. Tom is our shepherd and lives in the cottage on the farm. Don't be shy, they are kind people, and will always help you.'

Back out in the yard, Seth gave loud bursts of excited barking at Rose, and she gave him a wide berth. She clutched Elenor's hand as they walked to the milking shed where three women sat on their stools and worked in a continuous rhythm against each cow. Elenor felt Rose tense and grip her hand harder. She took a step back when one of the heifers gave a soft moo.

'They're no threat, Rose. One day, maybe you can learn how to milk them, but just say hello to them for now and then we'll meet the sheep, and Tom. Once we have got through all the introductions, we will go back inside and I'll show you around the house.'

Skipping and jumping around the field, the sheep and the shepherd's own sheepdog, Bess, entertained Rose. Elenor noticed her face soften as she watched them from the fence. Pink cheeks lifted into a partial smile and Elenor let out a sigh of relief. It would take time, but Rose would heal and hopefully, love the farm as she did. Another woof from Seth reminded her she had to try to get him on the calm side when he met Rose. An impossible task on the best of days.

'Let's head back Rose. Seth wants to meet you, and he's missing me.'

With slow movements, Rose moved towards the pen and Seth yapped with excitement.

'Quiet, Seth. Quiet,' Elenor said.

The dog sat wagging his tail, but Rose made no move to approach him.

With her hand taking all the licks Seth could offer, Elenor smiled at Rose.

'He'll lick the life out of me if he can. Never be afraid of him, and if he jumps up, push him away. He's only a young dog and we have to train him. He was supposed to go with the shepherd, but he's more of a house dog now. Bess puts him right. Both dogs are gentle, trust me.'

Inside the house she could hear singing.

'Ah, Susie's doing her own chores now. She keeps house for us.'

Susie looked at Elenor with tears in her eyes after they'd left Rose wandering from room to room upstairs and shown her her new bedroom. Elenor shared all she knew about Rose's experience.

'That poor little thing. Once she's down from her room, I'll open the window, air it out before we start with the decorating. It will be fun for us and the little tot.'

Rose peered around the door leading from the hallway.

'Do you like your room?' Elenor asked. 'Susie is going to fix it up for you. You will have the same view as me, over the back of the farm.'

They entered the bedroom, and both went to the window.

'We will make it a pretty room, Rose. It will be yours. You understand this is your new home now, don't you?' Elenor said. Rose nodded.

'Let's go look for paint and curtains in my storeroom near the bathroom.'

Rose ran ahead of Elenor down the stairs, and Susie looked up from her ironing in surprise at the pair of them giggling.

'Well, what do we have here, a smiling face? I take it madam is ready to fix her room?'

Looking up at Elenor and then back at Susie, Rose smiled.

'Yes, I want it painted yellow. Just like Elenor painted the one in our old house. She told Mummy it reminded her of sunshine and green fields. Mummy said it was a silly idea,' Rose said.

'I did, I painted my room after my aunt died. Fancy you remembering why I chose yellow.'

Rose twisted at the sleeve of her dress and looked at Susie.

'My mummy is dead, so is my daddy. Elenor is going to look after me, and she is not silly, she is sunshine, and outside are the green fields.'

Both Elenor and Susie exchanged stunned glances as Rose headed towards the storeroom.

'Like my little brothers, all or nothing with them at times, and they come out with the oddest things. That's kids for you. She's a survivor and loves the bones of you. Even a blind man would see it well enough.'

Following Rose skipping around much like an over-excited Seth, Elenor put her hands in the air in wonderment, then dropped them to her side. It was time to decorate and rebuild lives.

CHAPTER 36

23rd November 1940

Putting the finishing touches to a cake for Rose's birthday, Elenor knew she had to prepare herself for all eventualities. Rose had woken with nightmares twice in the night, and Elenor had been tempted to cancel the tea party she'd arranged to encourage Rose to make friends. Susie deposited plates of sandwiches and cakes onto the table; her promised gift to Rose.

'It is very generous of you and your family, Susie.' Elenor said.

Susie bustled around the kitchen pulling together a birthday tea table before Elenor's eyes.

'When I told them about her there was no stopping them. They all contributed a bit from their rations.'

Elenor marvelled at their generosity, but remembered her mother saying she'd helped feed people during World War One. Now her community pulled together for a little girl to help stop the nightmares.

Footsteps on the stairs alerted them Rose was on her way down. Elenor picked up the cake and hid it in the larder on the top shelf.

'Happy birthday, Miss Seven-Years-Old,' she called out as Rose hurtled into the kitchen.

Even a few days of fresh air had brought the colour back in her cheeks, and a sparkle in her eye.

'I've just seen a snowflake falling. Just a little one,' Rose said. She dragged a chair to the window and stood on it. 'Look, there's more. See?'

Elenor and Susie looked outside and watched as a few flakes fell melting within seconds.

'Thank goodness the ground isn't too cold, I don't think we'll get much, but how lovely it fell for your birthday,' Susie said.

'But I want more. Why can't we have more?' Rose asked.

'Ah, well we can't all have what we want, even on our birthday. Now climb down, there's a good girl,' Elenor said.

With everything in place the table contents waited to be demolished by nine noisy little visitors and Rose.

'It is my birthday,' was her favourite quip each time she tried to sneak something from a plate.

At two o'clock the kitchen filled with laughter and Rose stood to one side of Elenor as she was introduced to each person through the door.

By three o'clock, Elenor knew she had no need to worry about Rose finding friends. A happy girl accepted simple gifts with glee and looked relaxed in their company.

Her face lit up with sheer delight when presented with her cake, and before they knew it, it was over and a contented Rose waved her new friends goodbye.

'You wouldn't have known there was a war on this afternoon,' Susie said.

'Really? I thought it . . .'

Elenor had been about to make a joke about the place looking like an explosion had taken place, but bit back her words just in time.

Aside from the stack of empty plates, a pile of unwrapped presents sat on the table.

'Have you shown Susie your gifts, Rose?'

With great gusto, Rose held out a pair of knitted socks in green, a beret in blue and grey, a white vest with an embroidered rosebud on one strap, a lollipop, a dog carved from wood, and two pink ribbons.

'Aren't I lucky, Susie? All these things, and they are mine to keep.'

'I think you are the luckiest girl in the world,' Susie said.

'Ah wait, I've not given you mine yet,' Elenor said.

She handed Rose a parcel and watched as the little girl tugged away the ribbon, and unwrapped the paper. Her face lit up as she pulled out a blue ragdoll. She hugged the doll close, then inspected the wonky eyes, nose and face.

'She's beautiful. The man who found my photograph tried to find Annie, but he couldn't.'

She ran to Elenor and kissed her cheek.

'Thank you, Elenor, and I will call her Annie-two.'

Elenor put her hand to where Rose's lips had touched her face. She'd made the doll from one of her mother's old skirts, and the kiss made up for the frantic sewing when Rose was asleep in bed.

'Annie-two, welcome to Tre Lodhen. Now Rose, you run along and put your new things upstairs. The paint is dry in your own room, so why don't you put them in there,' Elenor said.

She winked at Susie. Whilst the children played at the party, Susie and another mum had put the room together.

Rose raced upstairs. Elenor and Susie tiptoed behind and stood by the door. Elenor frowned at Susie. Both expected a loud squeal, some kind of reaction, but there was none. Elenor stepped inside.

'Rose, do you like it?'

She beckoned Susie inside, and both stood watching the little girl move around the room kissing each piece of furniture she came to, and eventually she looked up at them with tears dribbling from her chin.

'S'beautiful, all sunshine and green fields, just like I wanted.'

'You keep it clean, miss. I will inspect it every day,' Susie said, then picked her up and placed a large kiss on her cheek. 'We'll be all right, me 'n' ee.'

Susie, Dottie and Tom took the remainder of the food to his cottage, and left Elenor to have some quiet time with Rose before bedtime.

In her bedroom, they sat and watched the shadows of the farmhands move around the land from the window. Elenor wanted her to become familiar with the dark country nights now she was to spend them in her own room. Seth gave a bark, and Elenor sat Rose on the bed.

'Rose, before you came to live here, Seth took care of me at night. He made sure I heard if a fox was after the chickens, but he did it from inside. He slept in the kitchen. The outside pen is only meant for a few hours in the daytime. He belongs inside as much as Susie and Dottie, do you understand?'

Rose listened with deep concentration. Elenor continued in a soft reassuring tone.

'I know you are nervous of him, but he won't hurt you. It makes me sad for him to sleep in the cold. We will have to get you both to make friends soon, understand?'

With a nod of her head, Rose clambered down from the bed and went to the window. She turned around and placed Annie-two on the pillow, then took Elenor by the hand.

'We can try tonight, Elenor. He might like a piece of my cake. Can dogs eat cake?'

With a chuckle, Elenor stood up, pulled the blackout shade down, and drew the curtains.

'Seth will eat anything, and a piece of your cake will be gone in seconds.'

With relief, Elenor settled Rose into a seat downstairs whilst she fetched Seth.

'Brace yourself. I'll bring him to you, just stay still and let him sniff your feet. Don't scream or shout.'

Rose did as Elenor said and sat watching Seth get closer. At one point, Elenor saw her close her eyes.

'Brave girl, well done. He's at your feet now, look.'

Opening her eyes, Rose looked at the dog inhaling all he could about her from her toes to her heel.

'It tickles,' she said.

'If you are feeling brave, you could put out your hand for him to sniff, or you could stroke his head.'

As Rose moved her hand to his head, Seth sat still, sensing his need for calm. Elenor watched on in amazement; she'd never seen him sit still for so long. Rose touched the top of his head with her finger, then the palm of her hand.

'He's soft,' she whispered.

'Soft in the head,' Elenor said and laughed.

Seth laid down on the floor by the fire and beside Rose's chair, and Elenor took the opportunity to unclip his lead. Before she had time to blink the dog had bounced onto the seat and gave Rose's face lick upon face lick.

'Argh, he's got smelly breath,' she said but made no effort to move. 'Sit down, and then I'll stroke you, you crazy animal.'

Elenor relaxed and sat on the sofa.

'Hey you, you know you are not allowed on there. Off.'

Seth slunk onto the rug and Rose knelt beside him.

'I'm going to stroke you. Don't make me jump.'

Sitting back in her seat, Elenor watched the bonding of

dog and child. By the time it came around for Rose to go to bed the pair lay stretched out on the mat. She gave herself a virtual pat on the back for leaping another hurdle. Another goodness knows how many years of hurdles were to be overcome, but for the moment Elenor was happy to settle for the ones she'd jumped so far.

CHAPTER 37

December whizzed by with nightmares, excited dog-and-child days, and tantrums, all of which Elenor learned to handle by luck more than judgement.

By Christmas Eve, Christmas Day preparations were well underway and the house was filled with many creative activities. Rose, Dottie and Susie made paper chains from newspaper and Elenor prepared the vegetables.

Old decorations were found in a tin trunk stored in one of the spare rooms. Threadbare tinsel gained new paper dolls hanging by cotton threads and Elenor found six wooden stars made by her grandfather when she was ten. They'd lost their colours over time and the wood had a sheen to it, but Rose insisted they should be repainted, and within an hour Elenor had six yellow star-shaped baubles drying on the window ledge. Susie was a godsend when it came to entertaining Rose. She had patience and sensed a wobble in the child's emotions before they had time to erupt into heartbreaking sobs. Dottie had a no-nonsense approach and the balance worked well.

Seth had been relegated to the pen because of his inability to stop tugging at the Christmas decorations, and Tom felled a small Christmas tree from a field Elenor's father had planted several years before she was born, and it sat in a bucket of soil in the corner.

'Righteo, that's the cocoa fudge set well enough, and before you ask, no, you cannot have any, young Rose. It is for tomorrow. I gave up sugar in my tea for this, so I intend to eat at least one piece,' Dottie said, and giggling, flipped away Rose's hand.

Christmas morning passed with several visitors dropping by to wish them a happy event, and Rose insisted on a new poem or verse from her children's poetry book, a gift from Elenor, every hour. It was hard to say no to her pleading eyes.

Elenor had invited Tom and a widower from the village to join them for Christmas dinner, and all doted upon the little orphan girl who'd melted their hearts with her Christmas prayer for peace. She'd learned the words from a wireless programme and lisped her way with only a few hesitations.

Applause went out for the Christmas pudding as it sat with its brandy flame bringing warmth of friendship to the room.

'To friendship,' Elenor said and raised her glass of mulled cider.

She looked to the faces around the table and wondered about their lives, their Christmases before her attempt to entertain them. Many in the village enjoyed rabbit instead of chicken or turkey, her table enjoyed the pleasures of beef, pork and rabbit. Carved with care she ensured there would be a generous portion for her guests to take home for the next day. Elenor knew she was one of the lucky ones, but she also knew she had responsibilities, and as a naïve twenty-year-old, felt her burdens were plenty enough for her to carry into the New Year.

She'd moved the wireless into the front room ready to

listen to King George's speech, and Elenor watched Rose play with Annie-two in her new doll's cot. Memories of the previous Christmas with her generous aunt, and Rose's parents sitting listening to the King's first message came flooding back. What would her aunt make of Elenor now, back to her country bumpkin ways with a child on her hands?

Then she remembered how they'd sung carols around the piano, and of the first time she'd heard Rose play the 'Moonlight Sonata' with such perfection it brought chills to her bones. She decided to find a piano for Rose, she had too much talent to go to waste. She also needed to consider getting her into school, applying for new papers and registering her as a local resident with her own ration book. Alice told her when the solicitor had been killed in his office his papers were lost in the fires which followed. Today though, she took time out to relax.

A brandy and cider steeped shepherd and her housemates roused themselves from their comfortable seats around four o'clock as a tired Rose curled up on the sofa. Seth, forgiven for his attempts to destroy the tree, enjoyed a plate of leftovers by the backdoor. Once done he snuck himself beside Rose. With the last of the dishes dried and away, Elenor slumped into her own chair. She handed Rose the precious orange from her Christmas stocking, now peeled and segmented on a plate.

'Elenor. Do you think Mummy and Daddy had Christmas Day in Heaven?'

Unprepared for such a question, Elenor took time to encourage Rose to eat a segment or two before answering. She knew each answer would be stored away as a fact, and she had to get it right.

'I think they probably did, Rose. Along with my Aunt Maude, and I bet they are all watching over us and glad we had a good day too, that's what I think.'

Rose chewed on her orange deep in thought.

'Do you think they were happy Elenor? I mean, laughing happy. I try to remember their faces, but they never have smiles on them. I can't remember if they laughed like we laugh.'

The little girl's serious voice with its hint of worry stirred something inside of Elenor. Her three friends looked her way and for a second, Elenor floundered. Dottie gave an encouraging smile and Elenor chose her words with care.

'It's funny what tricks our memories play on us, Rose. I often wondered the same about my aunt. I came to the conclusion that it must be something to do with being a responsible grown up,' Elenor said.

'But you are a responsibubble grown up and you laugh.'

Elenor watched Dottie and Susie smother their mouths, and Tom turned his head away.

'Well, I'm a rare kind of responsibubble grown up my darling girl, and you coming into my life has made me very happy,' Elenor said and had no choice but to give into the giggles brewing up inside. Rose joined in, losing her serious face, and Elenor felt relief her answer had satisfied. Dottie released her bray, and more laughter rang around the room.

All chores done, Elenor persuaded a sleepy Rose to remain on the couch with Seth watching over her whilst the adults saw to the last jobs of the day outside. Elenor checked on the cowshed and welcomed the soft sounds from her animals. The laughter of children was a wonderful thing, but the pressures of enforced parenthood brought about headaches. A cow gave a soft moo, and thoughts of the Christmas carol 'Away in a Manger' came to her and she started to hum the tune. Peace couldn't come soon enough.

1941

CHAPTER 38

Seth alerted the household that their much-awaited visitor had arrived. Rose rushed outside and called him into his pen. The two were rarely separated. Rose adored the dog and he had abandoned Elenor for his new mistress.

'This is it girls, extra hands, great start to the New Year. Let's give her a warm Tre Lodhen welcome,' Elenor said to Dottie and Susie.

'Jeepers, I'll need a ladder to speak with her!' Dottie said and pointed out of the window to an exceptionally tall young woman standing by the gate waving to the back of a truck driving off down the lane.

'Behave, and no laughing. We don't want to scare her away,' Susie said and waggled her finger at Dottie. 'It's enough she has to share a room with you and your snoring.'

'Both of you behave. Ah, Rose come on, let's go and meet her.'

The woman leaned over the gate and unhitched the lock when she saw Elenor approaching.

'Where's the guvna luv? Gotta check meself in. Not what I was expectin', pokey hole ain't it? You been 'ere long?'

'You must be Victoria Lewis. I'm Elenor Cardew, the owner of this pokey hole, and this is Rose Sherbourne my ward. Dottie, as you can see, is LA, and Susie is in charge of farm welfare. Welcome to Tre Lodhen.'

'Is that dog safe?' the woman said and pointed to Seth. 'I ain't really been round many you see. I don't 'ate em, just ain't seen many in me time.'

Rose interjected with loud enthusiasm.

'My mummy's name was Victoria, but she's dead. Seth won't hurt you, just don't let him be the boss. I don't think you'll fit in your bed, you're very tall.'

Her matter-of-fact speech took Elenor by surprise and she raised her eyebrows at Victoria as an apology and gave Dottie a warning glance. Susie rushed inside declaring she'd left something on the stove.

'I can't add to that, except I'm sure you will fit into your bed, Victoria. And yes, sadly Rose lost both her parents. Her father, so I'm informed, was in London when he lost his life, your neck of the woods I understand.'

Dottie took Victoria's bags inside and joined Susie. Elenor had no doubts they were giggling behind the curtains.

'Well, me real name's Victoria but most folk call me Titch, 'cos of me bein' so tall, see. Call me Titch, I ain't used to the other name, and it feels a bit sad 'cos of the kid's ma,' Titch said, pointing to Rose.

Both Rose and Elenor looked at Titch, and then to each other.

'I think I know what you said. My daddy told me not to drop my 'aiches, but you can't help it 'cos of being from London. They do round here, too. He told me once you all sound like that in London. He could talk like you sometimes. I think Titch is a silly name for a tall person,' Rose said and kicked at a stone.

'Rose, don't be rude,' Elenor chided.

'Kid's not rude, she's tellin' the truth. We Londoners are well known for our cockney accent. True Londoners that is, not these poncy fellas who run the country. And it is daft callin' me Titch, but blame me old man, he was a laugh a minute.'

Titch reached down and touched Rose's head.

'Sorry 'bout yer pa. Clever if he could talk like me, it's a born gift to be a Bow Bells kid.'

'Don't be sad, I've got Elenor. She's got a different accent, and so have I, so we are a real muddle of English.'

Elenor smiled. She liked Titch, and felt she'd come in handy during the hay harvest – she wouldn't need to use ladders.

'Right, cuppa first then a tour of the farm. Susie and Dottie won't go to work until they've settled you in and found out all about you. I will warn you, Dottie has a very unique laugh. She's aware of it, but it can catch you out when you least expect it.'

'She sounds like a donkey with hiccups. Your room faces the front, where you've just come from. Dottie sleeps in there too. She snores like a donkey, too,' Rose said and ran ahead to open the door.

'Rose Sherbourne, you cheeky monkey, I heard you,' Dottie said and gave a snigger. 'I'm in training to tone the laugh down. Come on, we're parched.'

'A cuppa is just the ticket, and I look forward to gettin' me 'ands grubby. I ain't no shirker, Elenor. I ain't outta line by callin' you Elenor, am I? Only I know some folk get a bit arsey when it comes ta bein' a boss.' Titch gave a grin.

'Elenor is fine,' Elenor said. 'But I won't have bad language around Rose. Understand?'

'Lordy, me 'n' me big gob. I forget meself sometimes. I'm sorry, so used to bein' around brothers who cuss. Ma was always cuffin' me for me bad mouth.'

Over the following weeks leading into February, it became obvious to all that Titch was not cut out for working the land. No amount of training she'd already had could be improved upon as the girl disliked hard work. She became a hindrance, and Dottie complained about unfinished jobs.

Harsh words didn't seem to bother her, and her bad language became a major problem. Rose had been heard telling Seth off in unsavoury terms on more than one occasion.

Today, Titch was found sleeping behind the barn and Elenor was called from skinning a rabbit to have a word with her.

'Not surprising with all the bloody work I 'ave to do round 'ere,' Titch grumbled.

'Have you been drinking?'

'Nah, 'course I 'ain't.' She stood and staggered.

'This won't do, Titch. I don't want to report you as a slacker. Take Rose and do something useful in the bean field. This is your last warning.'

As she turned to head back to the potato field, Elenor spotted the POW gang walking through the fields.

'Hello there,' she called out to the soldier heading the group. 'Could I have a word?'

With instructions shouted down the line, the men stood still and all watched Elenor heading their way.

'I heard you take the men to help with community work and wondered who I need to approach for a barn repair. Granted, it isn't a bombed barn, so I am willing to pay into a food fund or whatever is required.'

Elenor puffed out her words as she walked beside the soldier pacing up and down smoking his cigarette. He glared at a couple of the men and they dropped their heads to their chests. Elenor noticed how well fed they looked, and their clothes were suited to the season. She hoped the captured British soldiers were treated in much the same way.

'I'll have a word with the captain. This lot are workers, I'll grant them. Couple could do with a hiding, but to be fair, they're no different from my brothers back home.'

'Thank you. I appreciate you taking the time.'

She shook the soldier's hand.

'You're lucky, they're clean for once.'

Both laughed, and Elenor laughed louder when a wolf whistle rang out as she walked away, and a soldier barked a respect order at one of his charges.

'If you've got a job for them today, I could do with keeping them occupied,' he said.

'I've got a stone wall needing repair over on the far side,' Elenor said and pointed to the left of the field. 'Two fields over.'

'Consider it done. Name's Ron, by the way.'

'Elenor, Elenor Cardew. I own the place. Thanks. I'll catch you later.'

Halfway down the field she met Titch sitting on the fence of the carrot plot.

'Cor, there's a few lookers in that bunch.'

'They are out of bounds. Do you understand? They are prisoners of war and you are not to go anywhere near them.'

Elenor stood with her hands on her hips. Elenor looked around but could see no sign of Rose or Seth.

'And where's Rose? I gave you instructions to start planting out the broad beans and look after her.'

'Keep yer drawers on. She's playing with that darn dog. Me back ached, and I went to stretch me legs. I ain't her bleedin' babysitter.'

Titch had the decency to blush over her blatant lie, and Elenor's temper exploded.

'You left my girl on her own while you went sniffing around Tom like a bitch in heat. You know he's Dottie's man and he's not interested. Get back to the field and do some work.'

Elenor marched off down the field followed by a torrent of abuse.

'I ain't no bitch, so take it back. You're the dried up prune. Frigid cow. I'll go pack my bags now.'

'You'll do no such thing. If you want to eat, you work. You are here for a reason, now go. I have to look for Rose.'

The farmhands worked a field at the right side of the farm on a top pasture repairing fencing, and she headed off with speed in the hope Rose had joined them.

As she ran towards Tom's cottage, a bark alerted her to behind the dilapidated barn, and she ran towards the sound.

'Seth, where are you boy?'

More barks rang out, sharp and excited yaps.

As she turned the corner Elenor spotted Rose lying on the ground, and Seth laid out beside her.

'Rose, Rose!'

The child lay still on her front. Elenor lifted her with care and two little blue eyes stared back at her as she cradled Rose in her lap.

'Hello you. I can see you've bumped your head. Do you feel all right?' She spoke softly, the relief flooding through her body.

'Go find him, Seth. Fetch Tom. Tom! Tom!' Elenor kept up her continuous calling for him, and Seth barked each time he heard Tom's name.

After what seemed a lifetime, but was really only minutes, Tom and Bess ran to her side.

'Please, go and fetch the doctor. Take my bicycle. Rose is awake, but she's had a fall and a bump. I want her checked over.'

When the doctor arrived, Susie, Dottie and a humbled

Titch rushed around preparing a makeshift bed on the kitchen table for the doctor to examine Rose.

'She's fine. A bit shocked but no broken bones. Keep an eye on her and rest her up for the day. No more climbing young lady,' the doctor said and tapped Rose's arm.

'Yes doctor.' Rose said.

'Thanks doc, I'll see you out,' Dottie said and guided the man out of the door.

'Titch, you go and finish your job. We'll speak later,' Elenor said.

She went to Rose and stroked her forehead. Lifting her down onto the sofa, she made a fuss of kissing away her bruise.

'Yuk. Stop it, you're worse than Seth.'

'You gave me a scare. What on earth were you doing on the old barn? You never disobey me, ever, so why go there? I take it you climbed too high.'

Rose's lip trembled, and her face paled.

'Don't be angry with me, Elenor. It was my fault. Titch said I was a scaredy-cat when I said I didn't like to climb high. She got to the top.'

Elenor sunk back on her heels. She was tempted to call for Titch's blood, but she controlled herself.

'I'll never be angry with you, and Titch is wrong, you are the bravest little girl I know. We'll say no more about it, and you rest up.'

'That Titch is hard work. She's upsetting Dottie and Tom. He's flattered but really not interested,' Susie said.

'I know, she's trouble. I'm not sure how much longer I can cope with her. I'll speak to the Crops Officer on the next visit.'

Around the supper table Dottie asked Rose why she'd climbed so high. Elenor had forgotten she wasn't in on the earlier conversation.

'It was a mishap, Dottie. Rose tried to . . .'

Titch slammed down her fork and made the rest around the table jump.

'The kid copied me. I climbed to the top and dared her. I was wrong. I was bored growing veggies, and I 'ate animals, so let's stop going on about it. Bleedin' rabbitin' on about it all the darn time.'

Before Elenor could say a word, Dottie responded and not in a quiet voice.

'Hold your tongue. You wear a uniform and work for your government. We have a duty to our country. You disrespect someone who has given you billeted quarters which would make others green with envy. Elenor doesn't deserve this kind of stupidity. Rose is part of the farm, we care for her when asked. There is nothing boring about this place. And you will leave my man alone, or be bored somewhere else.'

Her face was red and Elenor sensed the anger towards Titch would heighten if not calmed sooner rather than later.

Elenor looked over at Rose whose mouth was wide open in amazement and looked at the angry faces of the others before standing up.

'I'm going to say this once. We live under the same roof and work as a family. Families have upsets and arguments. This is one of them. Rose did wrong copying Titch, and Titch did wrong leading her astray. Titch, you need to heed Dottie's words. We had a scare today, and I need to trust you with Rose, so please Titch, make an effort or leave. Apple pie anyone?'

Elenor's hand shook as she cut the pie but when Susie gave her a thumbs up, she calmed down. February was not her favourite month.

CHAPTER 39

Life wasn't any easier by springtime with enemy air raids causing chaos and sleepless nights, but everyone rose each day, thankful they still had the gift of another.

April showers had fallen for a week, and so had the temperatures, but slowly something changed. The blackbirds sang louder and blue-tits dotted from shrub to tree. Each day the sun grew stronger.

The first stage of working on the tithe barn had begun and a group of ten POW residents worked diligently removing the stonework. With school finished for the Easter holidays, Rose checked upon the pregnant ewes with Tom every day and relayed their progress to the household, impatient for the lambs to arrive. Today was no different, and Elenor felt it time she spoke about the lambs' future and duty to become food for the British people. Through sobbing tears, Rose declared she understood, but once peace came she wanted a pet lamb, just like Mary in her nursery rhyme book. Elenor made no promises.

'We cannot predict our future, Rose, nor those of the lambs. In the meantime, we have cheese and butter to make.'

Whenever her bones ached, and the pressures of running

the farm and caring for Rose got her down, Elenor reminded herself she would not be able to provide so much for Rose in Coventry.

'Are you coming to the dance on Saturday, Elenor? Dottie and Tom are going. I'll be surprised if Titch doesn't,' Susie asked as she squeezed the liquid from rennet.

'I don't go to dances anymore, and besides, how can I?' Elenor said and lifted her chin towards Rose.

'She can sleep at ours, Mum suggested it. She gets on with our Brian's girl, and she's sleeping over. Let your hair down for once, goodness knows you deserve it, and I know you love music.'

Rose stopped beating the cream in her bowl.

'Sleep at your house? Can I Elenor, please, can I?' she pleaded.

Susie stood with her hands on her hips and stared at Elenor.

'I give in. Goodness, you two are an army to deal with. Yes, you can, and yes, I'd like to go to the dance with you Susie. It will make a change, thank you.'

Elenor was grateful to Susie, there was no age difference when it came to their likes and dislikes, and Susie behaved like a blood relative rather than paid help. The more Rose chattered on about it, the more excited about Saturday evening Elenor became. It would be her first dance since leaving Coventry.

'All done,' Elenor declared and looked at the filled bowls set aside on the dresser. 'I'm off to do my fence checks, and then join the others with the muck spreading, Rose. You have the choice of joining me or helping Susie with clearing up here. You can peel potatoes and help her feed the pigs. What's it to be?' Elenor said and placed her hands on Rose's shoulders.

'Yuk, I'll help Susie.'

Elenor pulled a light cardigan across her shoulders and tied it at the front. The shady areas in the woods still held a chill. She pulled on her boots, stepped outside into the sunshine and lifted her face to the sky to let the warmth of the sun touch her skin. Seth ran to her side, and they tugged and pulled on a piece of rope until they reached the edge of the woods.

Turning around, Elenor looked over at a neglected piece of arable land and pulled out her notepad, making a note to turn it over to clover crops for more cattle feed.

'Writing to me?'

A male voice startled her, but without lifting her head she licked the end of the pencil and carried on writing. Just those few words stirred a storm inside her, his silky tone stroked every fibre in her body, the hairs on her neck tingled, and behind her breastbone her heart beat so fast she feared for her life.

'Why on earth would I want to write to you about clover fields?' she said without raising her head from her writing.

'Fair point.'

As she wrote, Elenor's hand shook. Jackson was here, in front of her and she dared not look for fear he would disappear if she did. When she could resist it no longer, she gave a coy smile. With his jacket slung over his left shoulder, and his sleeves rolled up showing off his muscular arms he looked every bit the film star she'd admired on the cinema screen. Her eyes strayed to his chest, a broad platform screaming out for her to touch the firm flesh beneath.

Control Elenor. Control.

'Why, if it isn't Jackson St John from Canada. Passing by, are you?' she joked.

Her mind fired up with so many thoughts. Why was he here? What on earth did she look like? Why did he come here with her looking the way she did?

'Yeah, took a stroll from Canada to Cornwall, and dropped by Summercourt for a cup of British tea.'

Elenor raised her eyes higher and looked straight at him and knew it was her downfall. His deep brown eyes stared back at her, and his white teeth offered such a smile she could not help but smile back. Smart in his uniform, he was certain to have turned heads when he walked through the village. He'd matured since she met him last, he'd gone from boy to man. He was more than handsome, more than a good looker, to Elenor he was a fine specimen of a man. He was her temptation.

'I assume you're lost then, Airman St John. Ever thought of investing in a decent compass?' she teased.

'I don't need one,' he said.

'Really? You could have fooled me, you are a long way from home.'

'Oh, I knew where I was headed Miss, and my internal compass got me here.'

With a nervous giggle, and completely floored by his sudden appearance and the effect it was having on her, Elenor made a pretend note in her pad.

'Forgive me, I was just busy with planning the farm for next season. Not all of us have the luxury of wandering the countryside on a whim. Some of us have to cultivate it to stop starvation, it's our fight against the enemy, especially when we are given the freedom to do so,' she said and regretted the sarcasm in her voice. Although she delighted in the fact he stood in front of her, she could not forget he'd let her down.

'Can you ever forgive me, Elenor?' he asked. 'I was wrong to let you go. I handled it badly.'

'A Valentine's card of all things,' Elenor whispered.

'Forgive me. Please forgive me.'

Elenor looked up at him again. His eyes smiled into hers,

and her feelings confused her; she wanted the world to stop and the moment to never end. She wanted him to say he loved her and to run with her through the fields, to stroke her hair during the bombing raids and to hold her hands on a dark night under the stars. All the things she'd read in the romance novels Susie lent her. She wanted Jackson to give her those things. She wanted to forgive him, and yet, something held her back.

Seth interrupted her thoughts when he raced back from inside the woods. He yipped at Jackson and received a scratch behind the ears in return.

'So, you'll not refuse a cup of tea then?' she said, all thoughts of muck spreading gone from her mind.

'Lead the way, Farmer Cardew, lead the way.'

When they reached the yard, Rose greeted Seth, and looked to Elenor and Jackson walking through the bottom vegetable plots. She shielded her eyes from the sun.

'Oh, you found a pilot in the woods, Elenor. Where's your aeroplane?'

Her question brought about a burst of laughter from the two adults.

'In a way, yes, I did Rose, and he left his plane at home. You remember Jackson, the man your daddy and I wrote to in Canada?'

Jackson knelt down in front of Rose. 'You sent me a picture once, it was inside your daddy's letter. Apparently, you asked about the type of plane I wanted to fly, and it was a lovely drawing.'

Elenor saw the frown flit across Rose's face. Then she thought of George.

'Sadly, George is no longer with us, Jackson. I'm so sorry, I wrote to your grandfather to let him know, but he obviously hasn't told you.'

'Post takes weeks to get here, and often gets sent to the

wrong base. I move around a lot, he'd let me know for sure.'

Jackson stooped down and took one of Rose's hands and held it in his, Elenor was touched by the gesture.

'Rose, I am sorry for your loss. It is a dreadful thing for you to have to live through. Are you on your Easter holidays with Elenor?'

Shaking her head and pulling away her hand, Rose picked up the rope and threw it for Seth who'd taken to jumping around them both.

'No, I live here. My family are dead. No one else wants me. I'm a norphan. That's right isn't it, Elenor?'

Elenor smiled at her, 'Orphan, darling. *An* orphan. Anyway, it is rude to keep our visitor waiting, run on and let Susie know we've a guest.'

She waited until Rose had gone inside before she spoke.

'I'm afraid Victoria was killed, too. All traces of her family have disappeared. Any paperwork on her or her parents have been destroyed in a fire. I try to give her hope, but alas, I think she is stuck with me as her guardian.'

Turning his hat round and round in his hands, Jackson stood quiet. When he spoke she heard the concern in his voice.

'You have a lot on your shoulders, Elenor. My goodness, most girls would have run a mile at the thought of running a farm alone, without taking on the added responsibility of an orphaned child. You have a lifetime obligation.'

Shrugging her shoulders Elenor made a move towards the house. For some reason his words niggled her. Maybe it was because they flagged up her future. One she'd once dreamed might have been with Jackson. When she saw him in her field today, it gave her hope, but the realisation of her present life reared up in her face with his statement.

'What was I to do, leave her alone and bereaved?

I'm her named next of kin. What was I supposed to say, thanks but no thanks, I have my own life to lead?'

'Calm down, I didn't mean what you think. I simply said you have taken on a lot, and I'm sure you'll cope. You're one heck of a girl. It's just sad your life has been mapped out this way. Fate didn't deal a kind hand.'

Brushing away his hand from her shoulder, Elenor tugged her turbaned scarf from her head and shook down her hair. She'd grown hot and irritated and her temper flared. Her emotions raged through her body like a storm at sea, swirling everything around. Any thoughts of life with Jackson were farcical, it was never going to happen. What made her think they ever would? He was right, she was a girl trapped in a woman's world. But what irked her more, was the fact he could not understand why she took on Rose. Anyone entering her life had to understand, had to accept, Rose and Elenor came as a pair.

'No, I'm not a heck of a girl, I'm me. Fate hasn't dealt me an unkind hand, it's given me a child to care for thanks to an enemy bomb. I'm someone whose life is as it is meant to be. Rose is like my daughter and we will get through this together.'

Her throat constricted with fighting off tears and she gulped down her disappointment.

'I'm afraid I need to go inside, please, don't follow. Your words have reminded me of my priorities. Our pen-pal days have been over for some time now, and *you* made that choice Jackson. I think it is best you leave.'

Fighting back tears of sadness, Elenor gave Jackson no time to respond. She couldn't cope with having her heart-broken again. They had a different future.

'I don't confess to understand what just happened, Elenor, but I will do as you ask. I've not come here to cause you distress. Take care of yourself.'

She heard his metal tipped boots clip across the yard but did not to look his way for fear of changing her mind. Once inside she explained to Rose and Susie that Jackson had to leave for duty. She pleaded a headache and went to her room and sobbed silently into her pillow. After an hour she composed herself and went downstairs. Giving into the demands of Susie, she told her their story and why she'd sent Jackson away. They debated romance and duty during wartime, and concluded Elenor had done the right thing in putting Rose first. Something confirmed when Rose placed a damp kiss on Elenor's cheek.

'This is to make you happy again,' she said.

Elenor scooped her into her arms and swung her around.

'Right young Rose, about Saturday, I need a few things before I show my face at a dance. I suggest tomorrow we take a trip into St Austell. It is time we had a day out together.'

Her reward was a squealed response from Rose.

Snuggled on the sofa that evening, they made plans for their trip the following day. When instructed to go to bed, Rose stood in front of Elenor and put her hands on her hips. She looked comical but Elenor had learned never to laugh when Rose was in her serious mode.

'Jackson was silly,' she said, her voice indignant and matched her stance.

'Pardon me?' Elenor said.

'He said I drew him a picture, I didn't. I can't draw planes. I didn't ask about his silly plane. He's a muddle brain.'

'Maybe it was another little girl whose daddy wrote to him. Now off to bed.'

Elenor sat back and wondered how many other young females had fallen for Jackson St John's charms.

CHAPTER 40

Saturday morning arrived and Elenor raced through her farming chores. With her hair in pin curls under her turban, Elenor pounded the ground with her hoe and fork. Each time her mind drifted to thoughts of Jackson, she plunged into a bout of soil turning and sweated them away. She'd thought over his brief visit and wondered if she had handled the situation badly, but when she recalled him saying fate had given her a rough deal the ground received another bashing.

After they'd eaten their evening meal, Rose was sent to pack her overnight bag whilst Elenor got ready.

The sun had bleached a few layers and her chestnut curls shone. They sat around a neat plaited roll swept to one side. She teased a few rogue strands into place and stood back to see the end result and was relieved the no-fringe style suited her heart-shaped face.

In St Austell she'd found a pretty flame-red short-sleeved dress with pearl buttons. When she'd stepped out from the changing room, it gained instant approval of Rose and the shop assistant.

Upon arrival at Susie's house, an excited Rose ran off with her nine-year-old hostess, sharing her excitement by showing off a new nightdress. Elenor accepted and gave compliments. More friends of Susie's arrived and a happy group of females linked arms and chatted their way to the village hall.

Once they'd arrived Elenor heard the music and laughter coming from inside.

'Oh Susie, I've missed this, thank you for asking me along.'

Susie squeezed her arm in affection.

'You've dedicated your life to others, but you deserve a bit of happiness yourself, my lovely. Come on, let's see who's got two left feet.'

A group of people moved around the room, all in a clockwise path and enjoying a cheerful waltz together. Elenor and Susie fetched a lemonade and joined Dottie, Tom and Titch at a table near the stage.

Service men and women mingled around the room, and Elenor accepted offers of a dance once in a while, but always only one dance with each man. Some needed to be reminded where their hands sat during the dance, and others politely reprimanded when manoeuvring for a kiss. It was during one of those moments when Elenor swiftly moved her head to one side and saw a group of uniformed men walk through the door. She recognised their blue serge uniforms as that of the Canadian Air Force, and her heart skipped a beat; they wore the same as Jackson.

Her dance partner moved her around the room with the grace of a donkey hauling a load, and after treading on her toes for the third time, he staggered off to join his friends at the bar. As she went to walk away, she spotted Jackson talking to a colleague. Not wanting him to see her she moved into the crowd and headed back to her table.

Susie and Titch joined her when the dance finished.

'How did you last another dance? They're a ham-fisted

lot, no idea of how to treat a lady. I see you ditched yours pretty quickly at the end, Susie,' she said.

Titch laughed. 'She did. Mine was not a bad dancer,' she said and pointed across the room. 'Oh, isn't that your visitor from the other afternoon? The chappie I saw you walking with on the farm? If you don't, I will.'

Susie giggled. 'It is. It's your man, Elenor.' She stood up and staggered. Elenor grabbed her arm.

'Are you drunk, Susie? Put that glass down. I thought it was lemonade?' Elenor said and picked up Susie's glass. She sniffed at the contents. Titch grinned.

'Did you put something in her drink Titch?'

'So what? Lighten up a bit and enjoy the night.'

Susie gave a horrified look at her glass and then to Elenor. 'I never knew, I swear.'

Elenor turned to say something to Titch but she'd disappeared, and Elenor felt it just as well.

Furious, Elenor watched Dottie call the band leader to the edge of the stage. The band leader clapped his hands and called for attention and all eyes turned his way.

'It appears we have a local singer in our midst whom, and I quote, "sings like an angel to her cows". Now I've not heard this for myself, but I also understand she has been in a few shows in Coventry before the war. I'd like to invite our very own Elenor Cardew to the stage.'

Whistles and applause thudded around the room and an embarrassed Elenor glared at Dottie.

'What did you do that for? I'm in no mood for goodness' sake.'

Dottie grabbed her by the hand and tugged her to her feet.

'Lose the mood. We get to hear you sing all the time, give these guys something to take with them when they go back to barracks. A happy memory.'

Cheers rang out as Susie and Dottie pushed her forward. The clarinettist helped her up the steps and onto the stage. She felt her face burn with embarrassment, but she also tingled with excitement. It had been years since she'd stepped onto a stage and sung to an audience, but now she looked out at the eager faces, she wanted nothing more. Then she remembered Jackson was in the room and her nerve left her. She went to walk away but the bandleader thought she was about to suggest a song and moved closer. There was no way off the stage without embarrassing herself even more. She whispered her song choice when a man called out from the audience.

'What about the one about a sparrow in a square?'

Laughter rang out and Elenor giggled. She nodded to the band and the first few notes of 'A Nightingale Sang in Berkley Square' shushed the room and slowly people moved with the tune around the dance floor. It gladdened her heart to see such love and affection under one roof. Although her hands trembled as she held onto the microphone, her voice was steady and clear. At the end of the song the roar of approval and calls for more deafened her. She went to walk away but soon realised she had to satisfy her audience with another song. Three songs later, and after a joint rendition of 'Roll out the Barrel', she relented to one last song. Susie offered her up a glass of water and she took a sip.

'Sing your favourite, the way you sing it is beautiful,' Susie said.

As Elenor handed back her glass, she risked a glance in the direction of where she'd seen Jackson standing with his friends. To her disappointment in his place stood another pilot with his arm around Titch. The clapping audience urged her to sing an encore, and she moved to the band leader, explained she liked to sing 'All the Things You Are', with a slow, soft rhythm and he picked up on her key.

A hush fell around the room within the first few lines, and Elenor allowed her voice to soar with emotion. She sang her message to Jackson loud and clear. He was her promised kiss, someone to warm her in winter, and he reminded her of her most precious things. She wanted him to hold her and be hers in one divine moment. The haunting notes of the soft clarinet bled into her soul and Elenor allowed the words of the song to fall from her lips with a passion she had never experienced. She let it express her love for the man who'd relit a flame which burned deep inside. Elenor became aware all childlike feelings had fled, and Jackson had drawn out the woman she suppressed.

When the last note dwindled away she received the applause, drew a breath and re-joined her friends.

'You were brilliant, Elenor. That last song made the hairs on my arms stand to attention. They love you, look at 'em trying to get a chance to speak with you. Did you see your man?' Susie said and jumped around with great excitement.

'Stand still, you're worse than Rose at Christmas,' Elenor said and laughed at her friend.

'Bleedin' 'ell. You sang that for someone. Made me tear up,' Titch said.

'It was beautiful,' Dottie said and moved closer to Tom. 'The words were lovely.'

'Shame your man isn't here,' said Susie. 'He missed a treat.'

'I have no man, and so long as you all enjoyed the song, I'm happy,' Elenor said and placed a restraining hand on Susie's shoulder to stop her jumping up each time she saw a Canadian airman walk into the room.

She spent most of the remaining time dodging waist grabbers and cheek kissers who declared their love for her in loud, slurred voices. By the end of the evening, the thrill of singing on stage was still with her, but there was also a stab of sadness. She could not see one Canadian uniform in the hall and it meant only one thing: they'd been called back to their camp taking with them her opportunity to apologise to Jackson.

Spilling out of the hall with the crowd, Susie and Elenor took a slow walk to Susie's home, where she was informed Rose was sound asleep and no bother. Susie stayed home with her sister and said she'd bring Rose home after breakfast.

Elenor walked on for the next five minutes to the farm with Dottie and Tom.

'You're all right about it, Elenor? I'll stay home if not,' Dottie said.

'Yes, go. Be together. Goodness knows we need time to enjoy ourselves. Night, and Dottie, take your time tomorrow. Have the morning off.'

She watched them walk hand in hand towards the cottage and a stab of envy hit her.

Seth heard her approach the door and barked from inside the house.

'Hello you,' she said, and let him out into the fields, where he ran from one side to the other sniffing out rabbits. He returned every minute or so to check upon her. A drop in temperature made her shiver and while Seth still raced around on the top field she slipped inside for her cardigan. For once she wasn't tired and decided to look at the stars for a while. She climbed onto the fence and perched on the top watching the dog chase a rabbit. The tune of her last song came to her and knowing she was alone she gave into the urge to sing it once more. With no one within earshot she didn't hold back. Seth raced to the fence and gave an excited bark, jumping up at the fence.

'Calm down lad, it's only me.' She climbed down and went to the gate to let him back into the yard.

'I think it's me he's barking at. You were busy singing and didn't hear me arrive.'

From behind her, Elenor heard Jackson's unmistakable accent and deep gravelled voice. Hardly daring to move, she clung to her cardigan and pulled it tight around her. Inhaling and catching the scent of his sandalwood soap, she closed her eyes, then swung around to face him. She took in his masculinity. He had a power over her she couldn't explain and she trembled.

Fight, Elenor, don't cave in, he's an untouchable, and he's a pilot from another country. He'll die and let you down.

Her mind rampaged with words of defensive encouragement. When she opened her mouth, she'd pulled up a drawbridge of emotional protection.

'What on earth are you doing here at this time of night?' she demanded and immediately chided herself for sounding such an old maid.

Jackson took a step backwards and Elenor's heartbeat troubled her. It gained speed at the thought he was about to walk away, but the innocent girl in her didn't know what to do. She was about to barrage him with another set of questions when he interrupted her thoughts.

'I heard you sing in the hall and couldn't bear not to tell you how your words of that last song touched me. I was outside and about to leave . . .'

Jackson stood tall and to attention, his relaxed body language of his previous visit carefully hidden. Elenor realised if he walked away now he would never return and the chance to let him into her life, even for one night, was dwindling. Seeing him stand there, she knew there was no time to waste on starchy comments and taking yet another swipe at him with a spiteful tongue. He deserved better.

'At ease Airman. I won't bite.'

'Are you alone? I should leave,' he said and turned to look at the house in darkness.

Walking towards him, Elenor smiled.

'I am but will invite you in for a nightcap just the same.'

She gave a half turn and held out her hand. He took it and Elenor shook off all thoughts of the future. She wanted to embrace the present and bathe in its promise of a pleasant few hours.

CHAPTER 41

June 1941

Sweetheart. Honey. My girl. The words once alien to Elenor now changed her life – her identity. At nearly twenty-one, Elenor had embraced the love of a man who had returned the love, allowing her to trust him throughout their lovemaking.

Jackson had confessed his nerves but proved to be a gentle lover. A fleeting pang of a guilty conscience filtered away with each kiss or a stroke of his hand.

With coffee-scented breath he'd kissed her with such passion she could still feel the pressure after he'd gone. With concern for her reputation he'd slipped away before Rose returned home. And now, two months later, Elenor's busy days on the farm filled the hours but not her desires. She wanted the comfort of her man, to be held in his reassuring arms, and to listen to the beat of his heart as she laid her head across his chest. She wanted their last few precious hours repeated time after time, but his duty prevented him from visiting Tre Lodhen. She'd received one hastily scribbled note following their night together, and she kept it close, reading it each day before she slept. He'd simply written, *I have your song in my heart*, and she understood his message. It was a lifetime of letters if he never made it back on British soil.

Each time she heard the thud of a bomb or the distinctive sound of enemy planes, she braced herself for the day a message would come her way. Jackson had promised to make sure word got to her if anything happened to him.

Every night she leaned against the tree she'd once swung on as a child and would lift her head skyward wondering which aeroplane took her lover overseas. She was glad she never knew, and she rarely counted them out, for when she did, she dared not count them back home. The nights were the worst, they were her lonely times. Not like the loneliness of her past, but the loneliness of the new future promised to Elenor. Her nights were her burden as May gave way to June.

During the day she had people to talk with and it helped the days feel less drawn out.

The German POW workers gave her no trouble and their captors watched over them ensuring they gave no cause to fear their presence. Every day they called hello, but she only gave a simple nod. She could not shake off the nagging truth; they were the enemy. Their compatriots were a threat to Jackson's life. She needed a project to take her mind off hatred, and get used to the idea the men were around until the end of war.

Elenor approached the sergeant in charge of the prisoners to ask for assistance with the whitewashing of the walls of the front room, and help moving the furniture. Two prisoners were selected and Ron watched over them, although Elenor often found him with one eye on Susie when the girl took them sustenance, and the POWs were entertained by Titch more often than Elenor liked.

Once the front room was given an overhaul, Elenor's

next project was Susie's room, and she had her bed moved in with Rose.

She'd invested in a piano for Rose to complete the front room, and arranged for it to be delivered whilst Rose was at school. The day had arrived, and the POWs pushed it around the room until she was satisfied of where she wanted it to stay. Elenor couldn't wait to see Rose's face.

Seth announced her arrival, and Elenor closed the front room door just as the back door burst open.

'I'm home,' Rose called out and slammed the door shut.

'So I hear. Have a good day?' Elenor said and stepped into the kitchen.

She prepared a glass of milk and an apple and placed the plate onto the table. Rose washed her hands at the sink and sat at the table swinging her legs. Elenor could see something worried her and with her arms folded, waited patiently for Rose to confide in her. She never had to wait long.

'Sort of. Not really. We had to write about our parents today. I wrote down Mummy and Daddy were dead, but Mr Drake said that it wasn't enough.'

She took a sip of milk.

'I told him, it's all I've got. I think you might hear from him. Sorry. I tried not to be rude, but he said I was.'

Rose looked so forlorn, and at seven years old, she should never have been subjected to such a question. Especially when the master was fully aware of her orphan status. Elenor pushed her snack towards her.

'I'll explain you were telling the truth. Don't fret darling. When you've finished, I need you to help run the duster over the front room furniture. The work upstairs is creating dust everywhere. We can't expect Susie to do it all.'

'Mm, mm, yes,' Rose said and chomped into her apple. Elenor marvelled at how well-behaved Rose was; she rarely had to speak to her about her behaviour. Listening to people in the village who'd taken in evacuees, Elenor knew how lucky she was to have an obedient child under her roof. Clambering down from her chair, Rose tossed the apple core into the pigswill bucket, and snatched up a duster. Elenor watched her push open the front room door and waited.

'For me?'

Rose peered from around the door, and her grin spread from ear to ear. Elenor shook her head.

'No, for me,' she said.

'You fibber, you can't play a tune,' Rose said and giggled.

'Yes, it is for you. Go, practise. It's been too long since you played.'

A hush from upstairs fell when the first notes of a practice tune sounded, a tune Elenor recognised from when Rose first learned to play. Susie called down from the top of the stairs.

'Is that her? She's a little star.'

'You haven't heard anything yet. You wait,' Elenor replied.

CHAPTER 42

Papers piled high on her desk, each one read and studied time and time again. Elenor sighed. Finding Rose's identity papers or any form of paperwork acknowledging her existence had reached a dead end. Elenor's next quest was to decide whether to register Rose as her adopted daughter.

She'd not spoken to Rose about formally adopting her and decided to wait until told it was possible. She glanced at her watch; it was time to leave for her appointment with her new solicitor in St Columb Major. There were so many things she needed to attend to in order to secure Rose's future at Tre Lodhen.

As she headed to her bedroom, a loud bang rang out from Rose's room. Male voices growled out what she could only assume were German curses. Ron also swore, and his words she recognised loud and clear. She marched into the room.

'What they said is neither here nor there, but I'd ask you not to use language like that in my house, thank you,' she reprimanded him, and he had the courtesy to blush and apologise.

'What happened?' She looked at a photograph frame lying on the floor and stooped to pick it up.

'Pair of clumsy ars . . . idiots, knocked into the cabinet when shiftin' this wardrobe,' Ron said, hitching his shoulder towards the POWs.

'Accidents happen. It's not broken. I'll keep it safe in my room. It's Rose's parents, and it's all she has left of them. She looks like her mother,' she said. Ron nodded.

One of the POWs leaned in for a closer look and frowned.

'Pleaze, me?' he said and took it from Elenor's hand.

'The glass is not broken, look,' Elenor said, slowly and in the hope he understood as she watched him stare at the photograph.

He nodded, looked back at the photograph and frowned again, then gave a smile.

'Gut,' he said and handed it back.

Back in her room Elenor looked over the frame for damage and noticed a small splintered section. She slid her nail across it and made a note to smooth it over. As she did, she spotted a small white fleck inside the hollow frame. She eased it to the surface with her fingernail and saw it was a piece of paper. Another glance at her watch told her it was time to leave and once downstairs she placed the photograph on her desk for when she returned.

The appointment with the solicitor was a favourable one. He told her that under the circumstances with Rose, he could move things forward with regard to getting her official papers reinstated and would begin the adoption process.

Hooking her coat on the hanger, Elenor walked to the front room when she noticed a movement on the stairs. The POW who'd asked to see the photograph that morning, sat motionless on the top stair, listening to the music coming from the front room. His face had a pained expression, almost a haunted look. Elenor gave a gentle smile – she wondered if he'd got a daughter who'd played the piano back in Germany. It was easy to forget they were no different from the men who'd left her village, leaving behind families to fight the enemy.

'Good?' she whispered.

He stared down at her with a surly expression, stood up and walked back to continue with his work.

She shrugged and pushed open the door allowing the music to fill their home. The noise from upstairs stopped, and when Rose hit the last note applause rang out from everyone upstairs.

Rose came out from the room and with a cheeky grin gave a curtsey. The men laughed.

The German who'd ignored Elenor earlier took a step forward, but Ron prevented him with an outstretched arm.

'Stay there, sunshine,' he commanded.

With a smart salute, Ron addressed Rose.

'Well little lady, you are one clever little girl. I wouldn't know where to start when it comes to reading music.'

Rose giggled.

'I find the beginning is the best place, it flows better.'

'Rose Sherbourne, don't be so cheeky,' Elenor said.

'Nah, she's all right. Like my nephew. Same age I reckon.'

'I'm seven,' Rose said and held up her fingers to show off the number.

'Yeah, seven going on seventy, I bet. Wise and witty. Anyways, best get these two back. Thanks for the grub, never knew carrot soup could taste so good.'

Elenor and Rose followed them out into the yard. Ron and one of the men walked over to Seth and threw a stick for him. He loved to race after them through the fields whenever they left the farm.

The sullen man hung back slightly and looked at Rose, Elenor took her by her hand. Although they were under her roof and she felt no threat from them, she still ensured the POWs never got close to Rose. The man gave Rose a broad smile.

'Sie spielen das Klavier sehr gut,' he said.

Rose looked up at him, her eyes shining bright.

'Danke, mein Vater hat es mir beigebracht.'

Elenor stared at the child then back at the man who'd now crouched down on one knee. She glanced over at Ron but he still played with the dog.

'What did he say to you Rose? How did you know what he said?' Elenor asked with urgency.

'He said I played the piano very well. And I told him Daddy taught me.'

'I didn't know you could speak German.'

'He and Mummy spoke it in their rooms, but we weren't allowed to speak it outside. I told Daddy it was silly, but he got angry and shook me. Mummy scolded me. But they are dead now and can't tell me off,' Rose said with a note of importance.

'I didn't know you all spoke another language. How on earth didn't I know? We need to talk about this. I think it is time we went inside.'

Elenor became nervous, but before she could usher Rose inside, the man spoke fast but soft and quiet.

'Ich sah sein Foto und deine Mutter.'

'Sie sind tot. Du hast sie umgebracht. Ihre Bomben,' Rose said.

'Ich mochte die Musik, die du gespielt hast.' he said.

Elenor pulled at Rose's hand.

'What are you both saying?' she demanded.

'He said he saw the photograph of mummy and daddy. I told him his bombs killed them. He said he liked my music.'

'Enough now. Come on inside.'

She tugged at Rose's hand but the girl twisted it from her and spoke to the German who now stood up.

'Es ist die Mondscheinsonate von Beethoven'.

'Ja, ich kenne den Namen sehr gut.'

Elenor kept one eye on Ron now smoking and chatting with Susie, while the other POW threw a stick for Seth.

'What did you say to each other, Rose? Tell me! '

With a sigh, Rose translated.

'I told him the name of the song and he said he knew the name very well. Why are you looking so worried Elenor? It is lovely to hear him speak Daddy's secret language.'

With a look of innocence, Rose gave Elenor a sad smile. Elenor called Ron over.

'Please take the men back and thank you for your help. I understand the room is ready, so they won't be needed anymore. Am I allowed to give them a gift of food?'

'All dandy, not allowed gifts I'm afraid. They're a pair of workers, I'll grant them that. Mind, the one there is trying to learn English, and I told him, try smiling first. He's a miserable b at times.'

'Yes, well I think he tried to get Rose to learn a few words of German, but she couldn't understand him. Isn't that right, Rose?'

Offering up a puzzled look and receiving a severe frown from Elenor, Rose nodded.

'It sounded funny,' she said.

To Elenor's relief the German stood quiet, but he unnerved her with his stare. Something bugged her about the way he watched Rose.

'I'd better get cracking. Again, thank you and no doubt we'll see you again on the tithe barn project. Susie, do me a favour and help with the milking for a while. I've got to talk with Rose. I'll take over soon. Thanks.'

Elenor called out to her friend watching Ron walk away.

Once inside she wasted no time sitting Rose down in the parlour and set about seeking answers from her.

'Rose darling, when did Daddy teach you German? And why did he call it a secret language?'

'He said because of the Great War some people didn't like to hear foreign languages. He taught me a little French, too. He said it made people suspicious 'cos they're jealous of clever people.'

Elenor leaned forward with her hands in her lap, her fingers entwined together so tight they ached. She feared for Rose now the German knew she spoke his language.

'Darling girl, Daddy was right to keep it a secret. I want you to never speak it again, especially now we are at war with Germany. Have you spoken it to anyone else?' Elenor said and gripped her hands tighter.

Rose shook her head.

'It's the first time since Daddy left, since before he was killed. I never heard the men speak it before, and when that man spoke to me I wanted to see if I could remember. And I did, didn't I?'

Releasing her fingers and stretching them out, Elenor sat upright.

'You did, and you are very clever. You are also wise enough to understand the words "grave danger". Which is what you'll be in if you speak it again, darling. Those suspicious people Daddy spoke about will not be kind to either of us. Please, promise me with all of your heart you will never speak it again,' Elenor pleaded.

'Ever?' Rose asked, her eyes wide.

Understanding her horror of being deprived of such a skill, Elenor compromised.

'When the war is over, perhaps, but please, right now, never again. Pretend you didn't understand the man even if he tries to tell them you did speak it. They'll believe you over him. I'm sorry sweetheart but I have to keep you safe. I truly didn't know Daddy had given you those lessons, he

300

certainly was a sly fox,' Elenor said and gave a laugh to lighten the tense atmosphere she'd created.

'I promise. Pinky promise.' Rose said and held out her hand whilst wiggling her little finger.

With relief, Elenor hooked her little finger around Rose's and they sealed the promise. Her next task was to ensure Rose never came into contact with the POWs again.

301

CHAPTER 43

Sirens blared their high-pitched warning around the village, and the sound above their heads was lower and more menacing than on previous nights. The windows of the farmhouse rattled and Elenor leapt from her bed.

'Elenor, I'm scared,' Rose called out to her.

'I'm coming Rose. Get ready for the shelter.'

She felt her way in the dark to her dresser and lit her lamp as a loud boom made her hand tremble. Taking one deep breath, she composed herself and ran into Rose's room.

Lights flashed outside and flickered shades of white through gaps on either side of the blackout blinds. A familiar rumble sent shivers down her spine as the planes dropped bombs and the ground shuddered. Fear gripped Elenor's gut as the threat drew closer. As she crossed the landing a sudden boom told her the enemy was not too far away.

'I'm here. I'm here.'

Rose screamed and Elenor grabbed her hand. Her thoughts went out to Susie and family who were celebrating a visit home from Susie's sister.

Please let them be safe.

'It's all right darling. Hold my hand and move fast. We'll be safe soon.'

'Dottie! Titch!' She banged on their door.

'We're on our way,' Titch replied. 'Get Rose to safety, we'll grab the bags.'

The minute they reached the shelter, Elenor pulled open its door and Rose dropped to her knees. She crawled into the shelter alongside Seth, her sobs coming fast and furious.

'Try to breathe slowly, Rose. We're all here now. Wiggle down to let Dottie sit, that's it, curl up with Seth.'

Elenor started towards the door but Rose gave another scream.

'Hush now,' Elenor said and wrapped her arms around Rose's trembling body. Her hysterics intensified. It was the worst night they'd experienced since Rose's arrival, and demons returned to haunt the child.

'Hush, hush. I'm here,' Elenor whispered.

'My things, I've left them in my room. I want Annie-two. My photograph, I want my things,' Rose wailed.

'Anyone home?' Tom said as he rushed inside. 'Flock's not happy. Bleating their heads off, but I'm not keeping them in the barn, could lose them all that way.'

'Nooo!' screamed Rose.

'Hush now. Settle down. Tom's got his harmonica, he'll play for us and drown out the noise when the others get here.'

'All cosy inside?' Dottie called through the doorway.

'Get in, ya bleedin' idiot.'

'Titch has arrived I hear,' Tom said.

'Tom,' Dottie said.

'All right, gal?' Tom said and patted the seat beside him. 'Scoot up here and Rose can snuggle close.'

'We left my photograph. My things,' Rose whimpered.

'They'll still be there in the 'ouse when we get back. Things ain't important right now.'

Rose's call for her photograph disturbed Elenor. She'd sanded smooth the rough splintered area in the frame and picked at the white fleck. It was a small piece of paper. The words on the paper made her skin crawl and heightened her fears for Rose. Now she faced the dilemma of who to trust with her findings.

After two hours the all-clear siren rang out and everyone heaved a sigh of relief.

Rose had drifted into a light sleep and woke when they moved around the shelter gathering their things.

'I'll check outside first,' said Tom.

'I'll take Rose indoors. Poor little tyke,' Dottie said. 'It must be hard on her and bring back horrible memories. I'll make you a hot milk when we're inside, my lovely.'

Rose's sobs continued and she clung onto Elenor.

'It's over, Rose. Go with Dottie. I need to check there are no fires in the fields.'

Rose grabbed at Elenor's arm and clutched tight.

'No, don't leave me,' she cried.

With tender care Elenor eased Rose's fingers from her arm and stroked her cheek.

'I'll be back in no time. Be brave for me darling.'

She handed her over to Dottie and ran to check the cattle.

She could see flames leaping high around the borders of a nearby farm about six large fields away. She knew a farmer and family who lived there, and she sent up a silent prayer for their safety. The clang of the local fire-engine rallied out, and she was grateful she didn't need it on Tre Lodhen.

She heard the grinding crunch of tyres racing up the lane. A truck pulled up outside the gate and a figure rushed into the farmyard shining a torch in her direction.

'Elenor. Elenor,' a male voice called out.

Willing her feet to move, Elenor staggered towards him.

'Jackson. You're here. You're safe,' she whispered, her voice cracked with emotion.

She clung onto him as he pulled her close.

'Just landed. I heard a farm had been hit near Summercourt and begged the loan of the truck. I had to see you, and here you are honey, safe in my arms.'

'Oh Jackson, I was so scared. It was close.'

His lips found hers and Elenor let herself bathe in the warmth of his embrace. She returned his kiss with equal passion. As they parted for air, she remembered Rose.

'Rose. My goodness, the girl is petrified indoors. Dottie and Titch are with her, but it's me she wants Jackson, she's scared witless. I must go to her.'

In the darkness of the kitchen, Jackson pulled her in for one more kiss, but she placed her finger on his lips.

'Wait, we must wait.'

She ran into the kitchen and turned back to him with a wink.

'Rose, it's safe darling, and guess what, I found a hero in the yard.'

Seth scampered across the room and greeted Jackson with boundless energy. Elenor pointed to the door and he let the dog outside.

'Where's Rose?'

'Upstairs packin' 'er important stuff,' Titch said with sarcasm.

Elenor grabbed Titch's arm. 'Rose's things are important to her. Never forget she lost everything in Coventry.'

'Keep ya 'air on.'

'Oh, go away.'

'Ooh. Yes miss.'

Elenor glared at her as she left in a huff.

'Hello, you must be Elenor's friend Jackson, I'm Dottie,' said Dottie.

'I sure am. Nice to meet you, Dottie. Bit of a night, hey? Is that hot milk?' he said and pointed to the pan she held in her hand.

'It is, grab some.'

Dottie drained her own glass and retired to her bed. Elenor went to Jackson and gave him kiss on the cheek.

'Brandy in your milk? I'm having one. I need it after tonight.'

'Sounds good,' he said.

Movement on the stairs told them Rose was on her way, and Elenor waved Jackson back into the shadows. Elenor went to the doorway of the hall where Rose sat on the bottom step clutching her photograph, a bag and Annie-Two. Elenor's hand went automatically to the pocket of her shirt where she'd placed the paper for safe keeping.

'Come on darling. It's safe now, and we have company. Come and meet a hero,' Elenor said.

Rose stood up and peered through the doorway.

'I can't see anyone. Where's the hero?'

Jackson stepped out of the shadows. He stood to attention.

'Flying Officer Jackson St John at your service, ma'am,' he said, and gave a smart salute

'He's very tired but landed his plane and came to check we were both safe,' Elenor said.

'Why are you a hero?' she asked and looked over at Elenor. 'Elenor said you were a hero.'

Jackson walked to her and knelt down. Elenor watched as he gently placed his hands on Rose's shoulders.

'I'm no hero, Rose. You and Elenor are the heroes of this war. You keep us focused on what we fight for, and besides, you work hard feeding the country. I'm just doing my job – protecting you both.'

Jackson stood up and saluted her again.

With care Rose placed her things onto the kitchen table and ran back to him flinging her arms around his waist.

'Thank you,' she whispered, her voice heavy with emotion.

Elenor looked on and made no attempt to stem her tears. Jackson looked at her over Rose's head and she saw a tear roll down his cheek.

'You are welcome, Rose,' he said and scooped her up into his arms.

Rose gave him a shy peck of a kiss on his cheek and nestled her head into his neck.

Seth broke the thick emotional atmosphere by scratching to be let back inside. Rose wriggled herself free from Jackson's arms and went to the door. She looked to Elenor for confirmation.

'Is it safe?'

'It is. We've checked. Let Mr Trouble in, and we'll get you snuggled back into your own bed. And yes, he can sleep in your room tonight.'

Once she'd settled Rose upstairs, Elenor re-joined Jackson in the kitchen.

'Let's go into my cosy room, the seats are comfier,' she said, and beckoned Jackson to follow.

'Yes ma'am,' Jackson replied in a jovial tone.

Settling into their seats and sipping their drinks, Elenor thought of how easy Jackson's company was to enjoy. He – and the brandy – had her relaxed and unwound in under five minutes. What she'd found in Rose's photo frame was something she'd consider sharing with him later. She loved Jackson, but this kind of information was dangerous, and she needed to ensure she could trust him for Rose's sake.

'Was it a bad night?' Elenor asked.

'We lost a few but they lost more.'

'I don't know how you do it. I watched a plane fly over

the top fields once. It was beautiful to watch. I've never appreciated the skills you must have to do those manoeuvres, and with the enemy to contend with, well, it must be one of the most frightening jobs.'

'I love flying. I can't imagine doing anything else, but it is exhausting. The thing that keeps us going is downing one of theirs. Keeping our loved ones safe.'

Elenor went to him and sat on his lap. She placed her head on his shoulder and they stayed locked together in the silence, both drawing comfort from one another.

A dawn chorus from the chickens and cockerel, followed by a blackbird chirruping outside the window, made Jackson jump. Elenor unfurled her body from his and stood up. Jackson leapt to his feet.

'I must go. I've a report to fill and there will be hell to pay if I don't get the jeep back. If we're lucky, I'll get an hour tonight. I call in and see you when I can. I can't promise times. I can't promise to come, it all depends on our nightly visitors.'

Elenor went to him as he held open his arms.

'Anytime, day or night. Be safe, my love.'

Once again, she lost herself in his kisses. Both knew they wanted more from each other and Jackson made the first move to pull away.

'Let me go woman,' he teased, and walked to the door. 'I have to go. Wait for me. If I can't get away tonight, say you'll wait for me.'

Elenor blew him a kiss.

'Forever,' she said and watched him walk away before she burst into tears.

When she settled in her chair with a blanket to grab a short nap, Elenor pulled out the paper from her pocket. She looked to the fire, then back at the paper. Torn over whether to burn it, she hesitated, then refolded it and placed it back into her pocket. She would trust Jackson to know what to do, she'd ask for his advice when she saw him again. She clung onto the word when, never allowing herself to think – if.

A note from Jackson sending his love and apologies arrived the following afternoon. He had to move onto another camp and was unsure when he would return. By the time August was through, he'd sent two more letters filled with his love for her, but Elenor craved more than his words on paper.

CHAPTER 44

September 1941

The chug from the threshing machine vibrated the ground, and the sun burned the back of her arms, but Elenor battled on, thankful for the equipment she'd inherited from a bombed-out farm in a nearby village.

September kept her busy with the harvest and their crops gave a higher yield than the previous year. Elenor had promised to hold a small party on the Saturday.

She pulled the machine to a halt.

'Are you done up there?' Dottie called to her.

'Yes. Your turn. Where's Titch?'

'No idea. Last I saw of her was over there,' Dottie said and pointed towards the tithe barn.

'Right. Time to go find the lazy madam. Have fun!'

Elenor marched towards where the POWs were finishing the last of the barn repairs. She could see Titch flirting on the edge of the group, bending over with her shirt exposing her cleavage and generally tormenting the men in direct view. To the far side of the farm she caught site of Rose playing with the other children in and out of the woods, and once Elenor was satisfied she was safe, she strode towards Titch.

'I'd appreciate it if you would go and fetch the food baskets from the house and bring them here.'

'I'm watchin' this lot for ya.'

'It's thoughtful of you, but I'll do the watching, thanks.'

'Do this, do that.'

'Titch,' Elenor said with warning in her voice.

When Titch returned they handed the baskets over to Ron.

'I've brought a thank you lunch,' Elenor said. 'Titch will help hand it out.'

The main group mingled around the food basket and the flighty Titch, but the man who'd exchanged words with Rose stood away from them and lit a cigarette.

'For you,' Elenor said and handed out a slice of cake.

He took it and nodded his thanks.

With a good view of the soldiers looking the other way, she took out the piece of paper and pointed to the word.

'Dinkelsbühl,' he said and took a drag of his cigarette.

'Dinkelsbull?' Elenor repeated.

'Jah. Dinkelsbühl,' he said and went to walk away but changed his mind.

'Rose. Mother and Father. Dinkelsbühl. Germany.'

Elenor felt the cold of fear tingle on the surface of her skin when he gave a sly grin.

'Rose is German. I recognised her parents.' His voice was low with a hint of menace.

Bile rose in her gullet and Elenor thought she was going to be sick or faint. He spoke clear English.

'You know them?' She whispered.

'Jah. I like the cake. I like cigarettes, too,' he said, and ground the butt of his cigarette into the floor, before flicking his head towards the rest of the group. The soldiers were rounding everyone up.

Elenor understood his message loud and clear. Her heart pounded in her chest.

Ron wandered over.

'That was grand, thank you. Did ol' misery guts give you a hard time? We rarely have trouble from that one, but he's a bit of a loner and I wonder about him at times. He makes no effort to speak to us, whereas the others will try a bit of English for a fag or writing paper.'

'I think he said thank you in German, and I tried to get him to say apple cake, but like you say, he's not bothered. Oh, there is one thing, could you ask if I could have the use of him – or another – but preferably him as Rose knows him . . .'

Stopping for breath and giving her mind time to find a reason, she walked to the POW group to collect her baskets.

'Only the bathroom needs a whitewash, there's mould on the wall. My workers are too busy with the harvest.' Elenor hoped her voice sounded calm and casual.

'Don't see why not. They need to keep busy or they'll be plotting to escape. I'll ask, and I'll see if they can't all come and lend a hand with the stacks. It gets me out in the fresh air, and they don't give me grief.'

'Thanks. I'll owe you a cake of your own,' Elenor said and gave a forced grin.

The following morning Titch ran towards Elenor through the vegetable plots and into the hayfield waving a towel.

'The Germans 'ave arrived,' she yelled at Elenor.

Not a sound could be heard after her last word was out and she bent to catch her breath. Bodies stood pale faced, and all stared at Elenor.

'Where?' Elenor asked. 'Where have they landed?'

'In the yard. That nice officer 'as brought them to 'elp. 'E said old misery guts is 'ere to paint,' Titch said and stared at everyone looking at her open-mouthed.

Everyone burst out laughing leaving Titch with a puzzled look on her face.

'Think about what you just did and said, Titch. Scared the living daylights out of us all. The Germans have arrived – where? In the yard.' Elenor could hardly speak for laughing.

Susie came running towards them.

'Your painter has arrived. I haven't got to stay home with him, have I? He gives me the willies,' she said to Elenor.

'You take over the barn from me, and I'll do my accounts while he whitewashes the bathroom, that black mould, you know,' Elenor said.

'I'll stay with him if you have things to do,' Titch volunteered.

'You just stay with Dottie and get on with today's work,' Elenor said. 'If I need you, I'll call.

Susie and Elenor linked arms as they strode through the fields and back to the yard. Elenor greeted Ron heading the group.

'Morning. Titch said the Germans had arrived and gave that lot up there the scare of their lives, poor things,' she said and pointed to her helpers.

'She frightened the heck out of me. We're used to these fellas being called POWs, not Germans,' Susie said and giggled.

'Na, Susie, us Brits will take care of ya, gal,' Ron said and gave Susie a wink.

'I think you are in more danger from this one than that lot put together,' Elenor quipped.

The prisoner responsible for her sleepless night stared over at her, and Elenor's stomach churned.

'Is my painter to be watched by one of you, or are you happy enough for me to watch over him?' she asked Ron.

'Old misery has been allocated for the job, like you say, he's been in your house, if you're happy enough, I'll be out here. Keep a shovel 'andy just in case,' Ron said and laughed at what he considered was a joke. What he didn't know was Elenor and the girls had secreted a few pieces of wood around the home in case they ever needed to defend themselves.

Once inside the house, Elenor wasted no time. 'Sit,' she said in a firm voice and pointed to a chair.

She handed him a cup of tea and pulled out a chair for herself.

He obliged and stared out of the window, then back at her.

'Where is the German child?' he asked and took a sip of his tea.

Preparing herself that morning, she decided not to play into his hands and be intimidated by him. She had to be in control.

'She's English. Her parents are English – were English.'

'You have proof?' he asked.

'I do, and it is not your business. She learned your language through her father and made the mistake of using it during a dangerous time in our lives. And you are sly, pretending not to speak English.'

'It is war. War is not always about guns and bombs,' he said. 'She is the child of the people in the photograph which means she is German blood.'

He took another sip. Elenor pushed a slice of carrot cake his way.

'She is the daughter of George and Victoria Sherbourne. Of England,' Elenor said.

'Nein. She is the daughter of Ernst Huber, and Frieda Meier. I know this because I have worked with them. They are spies for Germany.'

Elenor knew she'd gone pale. She felt the blood rush from her face and body when dizziness took over. She gripped onto the edge of the table. He'd said the two names written on the white paper, the names she'd suspected were the true ones of Victoria and George. With no English papers and with someone able to prove they were German, Rose would almost certainly be taken from her and sent to Germany.

'The name I showed you yesterday, what is that?'

'Dinkelsbühl? That is the village they probably come from, we never know where our spies live. They might have been born here. We just help them move around. Protect them during missions. The child must be a complication for them.'

'A complication for me; they are dead. If what you say is true, she is illegitimate *and* German. What would happen to her in Germany if she was sent back?' Elenor asked.

'She is of good stock, but without family, who knows? Maybe she will be given to one of the Gestapo families and brought up a pure blood. Maybe she will not be so lucky.'

'She is a child, and I love her. Do you have children – a daughter?' Elenor asked.

Leaning back in his chair he stared at her, but not in an unkind way and Elenor knew she'd hit a nerve.

'Could your daughter be in the same position? Are your family still alive?' She persisted, and when he sat upright, she knew she'd broken through a hostile barrier.

'I like cake and cigarettes,' he said.

'I have cake, I'll get you some. Cigarettes will have to wait. But don't think you can bribe me. Rose needs protection, it should come from both sides. Did you know her parents well? I lived with them for many years and they never loved her. I didn't know he taught her languages. It occurs to me now, he was probably grooming her to become a spy,' Elenor said.

She slapped her hands on the table with temper and made the German jump. He was as nervous as she was, and it gave her a bit more strength.

'Listen, I'll cut more cake. You go and paint a bit on the wall, so they can smell you've been working, and we'll talk this through. We cannot be enemies over children. Your child would be cared for by a British soldier, I can assure you,' she said with a firm voice, willing him to understand her dilemma. 'If, as you say, Rose is of German blood, we must keep quiet and protect her.'

He rose to his feet and said nothing.

'My name is Elenor. What is your name?' Elenor asked. She felt if she could ease the tension between them she might defuse the situation.

CHAPTER 45

Fritz? Really, his name was Fritz?

Elenor had heard bawdy jokes from some of the soldiers, and ninety per cent of the time the butt of the joke was always a German named Fritz.

A hand slam knock on the back door summoned the POW to re-join his gang. Their conversation during the day had moved around the topic of Rose smoother than a pair of professional dancers performing a waltz. It frustrated Elenor that he would not accept Rose could hide under her care as an English child, and she curbed her temper on more than one occasion. She learned he had one child, and she was the image of her mother –whatever that might be – and she was the same age as Rose.

'We'll discuss this more tomorrow,' she said through gritted teeth.

'I like the cake and cigarettes,' he replied and threw her one of his sly grins.

The hairs on her neck rose. Was he playing games, or did he want to help?

'He's all yours. Mind, he'd best return to clear up his mess tomorrow, lazy swine. What's got into him?' she said to Ron.

'Unusual, he's normally tidy. We'll be back, got a three-day allocation for Tre Lodhen.' Ron winked, and Elenor knew he'd pushed for the job so he could see Susie.

'Thanks. It helps take the pressure off my team. See you tomorrow.'

Elenor waved off the group just as Rose ran through the gate. She ran straight into Elenor's arms.

'I missed you,' she said and then ran off to say the same to Seth.

Bemused, and with a heart full of love for Rose, Elenor watched her run free and happy around the yard. Her throat constricted with emotion at the thought of the child being taken from her and shipped off to Germany or held in a camp for illegals. She thought back to Victoria's attitude in Coventry and wondered if George had raped her. Two spies trapped into parenthood.

'Well, good riddance to you both,' she said and stomped into the kitchen. She thought about the solicitor and her adoption request. All seemed hopeless – she needed to get away, to run from her problems, to have the life of a young woman and not be burdened with the troubles brought to her door.

But you love the girl. Protect her as I should have protected you. Don't go to your grave with regrets like me.

Her aunt's voice couldn't have been any clearer in her head than if she stood in front of Elenor.

You're hearing voices now, Elenor Cardew. Crazy woman.

A commotion at the back door gained her attention, and Rose dragged Seth into the kitchen.

'He tried to get in the chicken run and cut his paw,' she cried.

Elenor looked at the blood dripping from the dog's foot.

'Serves him ruddy well right,' she snapped, and in an instant regretted her words. It was neither the dog's nor Rose's fault she was in such a bad mood.

'I'm teasing.' She ruffled Rose's hair and felt guilty when she looked at her crestfallen face.

'He's a dummkopf,' Rose said, and Elenor knew she was taking advantage of the curse word she'd used in her grumpy response. However, the word Rose used shook Elenor to the core, and she could not allow it to go unnoticed.

With one movement Elenor turned and knelt down in front of Rose.

'Never. *Never* say that,' she whispered with urgency in her voice.

'Do you know what it means then?' Rose challenged but had a cockiness to her tone.

'I don't care. It is not English. What have I told you about speaking nothing but English? It is too dangerous for people to speak German in public. Please tell me you haven't spoken it at school,' Elenor said and felt the familiar rise of bile rise into her gullet.

'Of course not. They wouldn't understand what I said,' Rose said with indignation. 'Besides, you told me never to speak it again. It just slipped out 'cos Daddy called me it once, and I liked the sound of it, and Seth is one.'

'I take it he is a silly billy,' Elenor said, trying to steer Rose away from the German version.

'Yes, a silly billy. That's what you are, Seth,' Rose ruffled the dog's ears.

Once Seth had his paw bathed, Elenor and Rose took a walk to the refurbished tithe barn.

'What will we keep in there?' Rose asked.

It touched Elenor how she'd used the word 'we'.

'I'm thinking the tractor. It will free up the main barn for the thresher and the other equipment we've inherited.'

Rose kicked at a stone and wandered inside the barn; Elenor followed.

'Before we do that, can we hold the harvest party in here? Make it a bigger party where we can run and dance.'

Rose ran around the barn waving her arms and skipping. Laughing, Elenor joined in with her and they spent two or three minutes playing the fool, all thoughts of war forgotten.

Stopping for breath, Elenor stopped and watched Rose enjoying herself and decided the barn party would be a good idea. During the renovations she'd had an electricity supply run through and also upgraded Tom's cottage.

'We could use a few hay bales for seats,' Rose said and clapped her hands. 'It will need sweeping out, but I'll help.'

Elenor chuckled.

'It will be clean in no time with your help. I think it will need all hands on deck but what fun we'll have.'

Rose's enthusiasm rubbed off onto Susie, Dottie and Titch during their evening meal, and Elenor left them making plans for the party whilst she went to her desk to complete government forms for the month. The last of the evening sun dropped over the hills and filtered into the room – winter was only a few days away. Late summer could say it gave a good fight until the end. Elenor pulled off her headscarf and shook her hair free. She rolled up the sleeves of her cardigan, grateful she could make the most of the warmth. It would make the logs last longer. Never shirking from chopping her fair share, her hands suffered. They showed signs of hard work. Blistered and splintered, they were no longer the soft ones of Coventry, and with her creams long gone Elenor accepted they were the hands of a farmer and not of a young socialite. Humming the song she considered hers and Jackson's, she pulled out a sheet of paper.

The Secret Orphan

Tre Lodhen
September 1941

My dearest Jackson,
    I hope this finds you well and not too tired. I miss you. Days pass us by but each one carries a prayer for your safety. We've had quiet times when I've wondered if the war has ended, but then along comes an incendiary or gunfire to remind us we are still knee deep.
    Harvest is making headway. Dottie is a dream, but I despair with Titch. Still, another pair of hands is better than none, even if I have to hunt her out from sleeping on the job each day.
    Rose is organising the harvest supper and combining it with a birthday celebration for me. She's doing well, and I cannot imagine life without her. On dark days she is my sunlight. She has drawn you a picture of the sheep, Tom and Dottie. I think you can guess who is who.
    I look forward to seeing you again and enjoying a moment in your arms.
    Take care,
    With love,
    Elenor.
    x

She licked the envelope and sealed it, just as she heard giggling from the kitchen.

'Are you up to no good out there?' she called out and stood to pull the blinds closed. 'Time to turn out the lights.'

'Really? A little forward don't you think ma'am?'

Laughter from her friends, Rose, and Jackson filled the room. Elenor turned around in amazement. She stared at the smiling faces. With her arms open wide she went to

321

Jackson, and the girls ushered a giggling Rose upstairs to bed with promises of hot cocoa and bedtime stories.

Elenor flung her arms around Jackson's neck and he held her tight in his.

'How long have you been here? I must have summoned you with the letter I've just written you,' she said, breathless with excitement.

'I snuck in without Seth hearing me, and Susie saw me at the window. I stood here and watched you write,' he said as he ran his fingers through her hair. 'When you shook your hair loose I wanted to do this, but I couldn't disturb the memory I want to take with me. You fly with me, Elenor.'

'I've missed you so much,' Elenor whispered into his neck as she planted kiss after kiss.

'I'm here now and have a forty-eight-hour pass. Can I stay or would you rather I holed up in the village for Rose's sake?'

Elenor released her arms and stood back to look at him. Jackson had lost weight, and he looked exhausted. There was no way she was going to let him walk away from her until he had to, he needed her comfort and care. She replied with a kiss loaded with enough passion that he understood her meaning.

A tap on the door from Susie reminded them they weren't alone in the house and they stepped away from one another.

'Elenor, Rose wants to say goodnight. She's upstairs waiting. Dottie has gone to Tom's, and Titch is already asleep, I swear it's a hobby with her, and I'm heading up now, it's been a busy night. Night both.'

Susie gave an exaggerated yawn and Elenor burst out laughing. She pulled open the door.

'Don't let us chase you off, Susie. Sit and keep Jackson company until I come back down. I won't be long.'

When she'd finished saying goodnight to Rose, Susie slipped into the room.

'Your man is asleep. I bored him that much,' she whispered and giggled.

'Silly goose. Poor man is worn out. I'll see to him, you take yourself off. Night.'

'Night. And Elenor, I'm glad he made it home to you. It's a precious thing, love. Especially nowadays. Ron says . . .'

'Ron?' Elenor ushered Susie out of the room and pulled the door closed. 'Ron who's got the eye for you?'

'You know who I mean, and yes, we're a couple. He had a cuppa at Mum's. She approved. Life's too short to waste.'

'It is, Susie, I'm pleased for you. Night,' Elenor said and gave Susie a hug goodnight.

She tiptoed downstairs ready to give herself freely to the man she loved. It amused her to think she had shed all guilt and wondered how many other couples were making the most of their time together that night. And although she knew Jackson was exhausted, she also knew he would want her to wake him and not waste a precious second of their time together. Tomorrow she would approach him about the situation with Fritz and Rose. Tomorrow she'd face her fears.

CHAPTER 46

Elenor padded around the kitchen mulling over what to say to Jackson. She had an inkling Fritz would arrive to push boundaries and she needed to be prepared. Today was her only hope of preventing him from telling someone about what she found – and what she now hid from the authorities. She'd broken the law and as much as it scared her, losing Rose frightened her more.

'Morning,' Jackson said and disturbed her train of thought.

Tousle-haired he walked through to the bathroom.

'I put your things in there, and the hot water is ready for you. I've a POW painting in there later, he made a start but has to finish off today. Coffee is waiting for you. Oh, and thank you for the goodies. I found them on the table. You spoil us, and we'll let you, it's been a long time since we've had soap and creams.'

Jackson stood in the bathroom doorway and it took all her effort not to go to him and drag him back to bed.

'I can't have you smelling like a farmyard animal every day, now can I?' he said and grinned at her when she threw a dishcloth his way.

'Cheeky. Hurry now or the coffee will evaporate.'

Chatter over breakfast felt natural. Titch had set out early to work with Dottie, and Susie prepared Rose for school.

'If we get a microphone for the party, you can sing Elenor. With electricity we can do so much more,' Susie said, and Elenor gave her a shy smile.

'We'll see,' she said.

'We could put my piano in there.'

Elenor put her arms around Rose's shoulders and gave her a hug.

'I don't think so, darling.'

Jackson wiped his mouth free from the egg and bacon he'd just enjoyed and looked at Rose.

'You have a piano?' he asked.

'I have, do you want to hear me play? Can I, Elenor?'

'The whole world needs to hear you play,' Susie said and collected up the plates.

'I'll let you off your pre-school chores if you play me my favourite piece,' Elenor said.

Rose tugged at Jackson's hand.

'Come on, it's in the front room. You can sit next to me.'

The first few notes of the 'Moonlight Sonata' drifted around the cottage.

'That girl's got talent,' Susie said to Elenor as they washed and dried the dishes.

'She's played since she was two, it's a natural talent. Classical pieces are her speciality, but this one is my absolute favourite. You must be bored of hearing it by now.'

'Not at all. It has a haunting sound, but I don't know, does something to my insides, soul maybe. Whatever it is, the tune is powerful.'

A rat-tat on the back door announced the arrival of a damp group of POWs, and Susie dashed to open the door before Elenor had a chance to dry her hands.

'Ron,' she said as she pulled it open. 'Oh, it's you.'

She pulled the door wide and Fritz walked inside. Susie peered out into the yard.

'Where's the rest?' she asked, but Fritz ignored her. He stood with his head cocked to one side, listening to the piano music now in full flow.

'Go and find him, Susie. I'll get nothing from you until I do. He can't be far now can he, Fritz didn't come on his own.'

Susie wasted no time and ran through the yard.

'Sit,' instructed Elenor. She was determined to maintain the upper hand.

Cocking his head to emphasise he was listening to the music, Fritz remained standing.

'Gut,' he said.

'Yes, but you are not here to do nothing, and I have a friend sitting with her, so our conversation will have to wait.'

'You know the music is Coventry?' he said.

Shocked by the mention of the city where Rose was born, Elenor stared at him.

'What do you mean, is Coventry?'

'Spies. Codes. Bombs. Coventry. I know these words very well,' he said and sneered into her face.

'Do not speak English. My friend is Canadian, he will hear you and report you. I don't understand what you mean. Go and do the painting.' Panicked by his words, Elenor pointed to the bathroom, and then changed her mind.

'No, instead, come with me. I'll do the bathroom myself.' She opened the back door.

'Outside.'

Fritz stepped out and leaned into her ear.

'Bomb. Coventry. Music. Code. See, I understand English

very well,' he whispered and laughed a deep ugly laugh. 'Her song was a code.'

'Why are you like this? Yesterday, you were friendly enough, so why so hostile today? I never want to see you again. If you tell on Rose I'll say you attacked me, understand?' Elenor said, and hoped the anger overrode the fear in her voice.

'Sergeant,' she called out to Ron who was standing talking with Susie. They both turned and saw her pushing the POW along with her hand in the small of his back.

'Move. And remember, say nothing,' she said.

'He's finished. It took less time than we thought. I heard Joe the farrier needs a hand with heavy lifting. Fritz here will help. I got that he likes cake and cigarettes, and his name is Fritz. You're right, he doesn't care to learn English. I'll get cake and cigarettes for him as a thank you. Will I have to bring them to the camp?' Elenor said and looked at the POW to show him she'd protected him. She tried to communicate she'd found him another job he'd enjoy, and for him to keep quiet.

'I'll make sure 'e gets 'em,' Ron said, and held up his hand. 'Scouts 'onour.'

'Thank you. I can trust you Ron, after all, I trust you with Susie.' Elenor gave a laugh, then turned to Fritz.

'Cake and cigarettes. For you. Ron give,' she said in stilted English and pointed to Ron.

'Danke. Coventry. Music,' he replied and gave a half smile.

Tempted to wipe it from his face with the back of her hand, Elenor turned away from him and spoke to Ron and Susie.

'Oh, and he learned a couple of new words. Bye Fritz,' she said and walked away.

Each step she took made her heart beat faster. She'd put

Rose's future into the hands of the enemy, but would he see Rose as a fellow countryman and keep quiet? Trust. Was it a word he lived by? She could only hope.

By the time she reached the back door, Jackson was waiting for her.

'Not painting today?' he said and pointed up to the group in the field.

'I asked if he can come another day. It's the tall guy with the black hair, he stands out from the group, see.'

Elenor wanted Jackson to know who she was talking about when she told him her secret, but she hadn't wanted the two men to meet.

'We need to talk, Jackson. I have something to tell you. It's to do with Rose. Susie is going to walk her to school and do some shopping for me, it will give us more time together.' She called for Rose.

'Say goodbye to Jackson. He might not be here when you get home. Susie is going to walk you to school today and see what's available in the shops for the party.'

Elenor looked at Jackson who gave her a puzzled glance.

'I'm on a forty-eight-hour pass, don't forget honey,' he said.

Elenor didn't respond. She called Susie away from Ron and explained what she needed in the village.

When they'd left Jackson snuggled into her neck from behind. 'Why wouldn't I be here, Elenor? Are you done with me, have I overstayed my welcome, or shall we . . .?'

The warmth of his breath sent shivers down her spine and Elenor had to pull away before courage failed her and she gave into his suggestions.

'We need to talk, Jackson. I'm going to pray I know you well enough to trust you with a secret. When I've finished I need you to walk away, I can't have you implicated in any way. Can I trust you with something which could affect Rose's life and alter mine forever?'

Elenor twisted her hands and fingers with anxiety. Telling Jackson he had to leave broke her heart, but she felt he deserved to know the reason why.

Jackson took her hands in his.

'Listen sweet girl, if you are going to tell me Rose is your child, I do not care. You do not have to tell me your secret, or who the father is, but please, do not tell me to walk away from our love.'

Jackson put his arms around her and held her close. Elenor allowed herself a minute of his comfort then moved to the seats by the fireplace. She pointed to the seat opposite and beckoned him to sit.

'My concerns for you are due to the correspondence between you and George Sherbourne. Telling you what I know could put you in danger as I am not certain of your relationship with him, but I know you, the man, and feel you were duped like me, and are not part of his, and Victoria's world.'

Leaning forward in his seat, Jackson's body language indicated intrigue and Elenor continued and told him all she knew.

When she'd finished she sat in silence with her hands in her lap. Jackson raked his fingers through his hair and rose to his feet. Her jaw ached where she'd jammed her mouth shut and fought against screaming and crying. Jackson was leaving. Whatever happened now was down to him and Fritz. Elenor had exposed herself and Rose to the truth.

'Jeez, sweetheart. You knew all this and held it close? Do you know the danger you are in? You love her that much?' Jackson said as he eased himself beside her on the small sofa.

'You know I do. What would you have done? My mistake

was asking Fritz about the village name, a nightmare of a coincidence. How was I to know he was connected to them? Rose is my world, and I'll do anything to save her, but I can't do it alone. I am about to adopt her, but what if the authorities find out who she really is? As I said, you must walk away, but I wanted you to know why I have to let you go. There'll be no one else in my life, you know that, don't you?' Elenor continued to twist her fingers and dug her nails into her palms. Her lungs burned inside and the dam she'd built broke down. Tears fell, and her resolve crumpled.

'Just go, Jackson. I'll go to the police about this, but I won't say George and you were pen-pals, it's not fair. I have to face the consequences of what I've done. Fritz wins. Him and his Coventry, bombs and codes. I hate him!'

Elenor felt hysterics rising within her, but could not restrain them. Jackson ran to the door, and she heard him pull the bolt across. The next thing she knew he pulled her to her feet and held her tight.

'I'm going nowhere. We can deal with this together. You've trusted me, and I will repay that trust. Let me deal with the German. That man has won nothing, you keep it together for Rose. Promise?'

He said and kissed the top of her head. 'I'll get my pass extended. I'll go to the doc, he'll sign me off with exhaustion.'

Elenor went to protest but he put up his hand to stop her. 'I'll sort this for our sakes. I love you both and will not lose you. What we have is special, real. Trust me. I'll be back on Saturday to hear you sing.'

Moans of fear and sadness released themselves from her body, and Elenor, drained of all energy, sank into the seat. Jackson went to her and lifted her to her feet. He smothered her face in kisses.

'Trust me, Elenor.'

'I do,' she whispered.

'You concentrate on Rose. Tell her I've had to go back to work and I'll see her on Saturday. She's got to dance with me. It will be fine honey, Jackson's here for you, don't be scared.'

With no fight left, Elenor allowed his lips to seek out hers and they sealed a pact of trust and love, but deep inside Elenor feared the enemy would destroy them with words over bombs.

CHAPTER 47

For two days Elenor walked around in a daze. Each time she anticipated the reaction of the residents of Summercourt against Rose she clenched her fists, digging her nails into her palms until they were sore. Elenor had been born in this village, a village which considered Rose as her child, but if the truth came out, their hatred of the enemy would override their feelings. All she could do was wait for the knock on the door which would bring her world crashing down around her.

She snapped more than once at the girls and Rose. One morning she overheard Susie comforting Rose, saying Elenor was out of sorts because of Jackson, and she knew she had to stop living in fear.

'I'm sorry you two,' she said and gave them both a hug. 'With Jackson being recalled like that, I'm a bit of a grump. We have a party to organise. The barn looks fabulous. Bunting and hay bales makes it look so pretty. Thank your mum for me, Susie.'

'She's a dab hand with the needle is Mum, always happy to teach someone,' said Susie with pride in her voice.

'She can make your wedding dress when you marry Jackson,' Rose said and attempted to sneak away before

Elenor could chase her, but she was too late and squealed for help when tickled.

'Now there's a dress waiting to be made if you ask me,' Susie said.

Elenor did not respond. Instead, she started scrubbing the endless pile of potatoes in readiness for the evening. The party would not be a lavish one owing to the ration situation, but Tom's cloam oven would be hosting endless baked potatoes. Scrubbing another potato, she thanked goodness the guest list wasn't a large one. True to her word, Susie had tracked down a microphone, and rounded up five musicians not on civilian duties for the night. A heavy mist rolled across the fields and it more than hinted a thickening fog was promised for the evening. As it thickened it became the focus of conversation when people arrived. A fog might prevent Jackson arriving. Elenor thought it ironic he could fly a plane in fog but driving on the ground could prove to be far more dangerous.

Although the party was in full swing, Elenor couldn't relax. Susie told Elenor Rose was going to sleep at Tom's with Dottie once she'd heard Elenor sing.

'I'm going to stay up late tonight. Dottie is camping at Tom's house,' Rose said.

She looked angelic in a pretty lemon dress.

'You lucky thing. Don't keep Dottie awake all night with your chatter though,' Elenor said.

Caving into the demands of the room, Elenor sang a medley of songs and enjoyed a dance or two, but all the time her eye was on the door.

After the last song, she spotted Joe in the corner and took him a drink.

'Cheers Joe. How's the POW I sent down to you working out?'

The old man raised his glass.

'Cheers. Many happy returns. POW? No one came my way. Nice of you to think of me though, thanks.'

Chinking her glass against his, Elenor moved on to speak with Ron.

'Joe said Fritz never arrived. Any reason? I'll send Tom to help him out tomorrow. I owe him a favour.'

''E's gone. Moved off somewhere in the middle of the night. I think he'd brewed trouble for himself. I said, didn't I, he was acting a bit odd,' Ron slurred his words.

'Ah, there's my answer,' she said and moved away.

Now what? Where had he gone? What had he said? Her thoughts ran rampant.

By the time the eating had finished, and the drinking was well under way, Jackson appeared, flanked by three friends. Titch declared she was in heaven and moved in for the kill. Elenor danced with Rose, then Jackson stepped up to claim his dance. Rose hugged him. She'd never seen Rose react with her own father like she did with Jackson, a virtual stranger. She despised Victoria for conning her into believing she was a timid woman, when all along she was a spy, and in all probability, a trained killer. Her anger deepened at how they'd deceived her aunt. A call for her to sing was declined with the excuse that she needed some air, and she left Jackson dancing. When she heard the music stop, she stepped back inside.

'Rose darling, I think it is time for bed. Dottie's over there.'

'Will I see you in the morning, Jackson?' Rose asked and smothered a yawn.

Elenor looked to Jackson who gave a nod.

The evening livened up and soon Elenor found herself free to enjoy a dance with Jackson.

'How have you been?' he asked.

'Nervous, tetchy. Grumpy. You?'

'Busy. Fritz will give us no bother. I had him removed.'

Elenor stopped dancing and stared at him.

'I heard he went in the night. It was you?'

Moving her around the floor again, Jackson gave her a gentle smile.

'Not me personally.'

'Where is he, can I ask?'

'You can ask but I can't tell. No matter what that man says about you, Rose or anyone in this country, no one will believe him. Let's just say he's fond of the drink.'

Elenor clasped her hand over her mouth. She stood statue still and stared at him. A ripple of voices around them faded into the distance and the room spun.

'You look as if you could do with a drink, sweet girl.'

'I'm fine. Really. You gave me a shock. He's a drunk?' she said and handed him back the glass.

'We plied him with so much alcohol he can't remember his own name.'

'We?' Elenor said. 'You involved others? Ron, the POW guard?'

Jackson led her to the dance floor again, and they moved to the slow music.

'I told them he'd made a threat to you and Rose, and spoke of escape plans, that's all. That was all I needed to say. They've put him in solitary and he's on his way to an isolation camp. I did it to help you. He needs to be kept quiet.'

'You've helped get a man drunk but when he's sober what will happen? You can't keep him locked away forever. Oh Jackson, have you made things worse for yourself?'

'I'll be fine. Ron will be fine. Fritz will find himself in trouble on more than one occasion, and his stories will be ignored. Rumours will follow him around. We have our ways. He'll be unharmed, but no longer a danger to you,' he said and tapped the side of his nose.

Unconvinced, Elenor tried to enjoy the rest of the evening but couldn't relax. Even Jackson's gentle lovemaking didn't sooth her nerves.

Jackson's attempt to hush Fritz against talking about Rose was not as tight as she'd hoped. The German still had power over her no matter what Jackson said to reassure her.

Dottie arrived home with Rose the following morning, and a bedraggled Titch followed an hour later.

'Them Canadian guys are fun,' Titch said as she made her way to the bathroom. 'Jackson gone?

'Yes, his leave is up. I hope you didn't wear them all out, Titch.'

Dottie gave a laugh and bustled her way around the kitchen.

'Rose was a good girl. Tom said if we ever have a girl he'd like one just like her.'

'Really? You two are serious then?' Elenor said.

A flush-faced Dottie looked back at her.

'He proposed last night, and I've said yes.'

'About bleedin' time,' Titch yelled from the doorway.

'Titch!' Elenor said. 'Congratulations. I couldn't have wished for happier news. Susie will be thrilled. She loves wedding talk. When are you thinking?'

'Soon. No point in leaving it too late,' Dottie said. 'Where is Susie? It's unusual for her to be late back from her mother's, even with Ron to distract her.'

'Dottie said I can be her bridesmaid,' Rose said with excitement.

'Ah, that's wonderful. How lovely. I hate to say it though, even brides and bridesmaids have work to do. We need to get a wiggle on.'

By the end of the day Elenor had found Titch asleep twice and Rose practising walking down the aisle. Susie had not returned to the farm and Elenor accepted she was having a rare Sunday at home with her family. She'd worked hard enough the previous day. By Tuesday, Susie had still not arrived back to Tre Lodhen, and Elenor walked Rose to school with the intention of dropping by to find out why.

Walking away from the school she spotted Ron and Susie talking at the end of the lane leading back to White Cross. Elenor hesitated beside a hedge. She watched them link arms and walk her way. Stepping out further into the lane, Elenor called out to them.

'Morning stranger,' she teased Susie.

Susie looked to Ron and then to the floor, but both continued walking towards her.

'Are you all right, Susie? I was a little worried,' Elenor said.

Susie shook her head then burst into tears. Ron's protective arm went around her shoulders.

'I can't do nuthin' with her, Elenor. She's refusin' to come back to you on the farm, and she don't want to speak to her ma.' Ron looked to Elenor with grave concern.

'So where have you been, Susie? Come home, I'll look after you. Are you ill?'

And a thought hit home after Elenor said the words.

'Are you in the family way?' she asked with gentle encouragement.

Ron's head looked to both women with a rapid movement. His face paled, and he pulled Susie around to face him.

'Are you?' he asked. 'Are you pregnant?' His words were barely a whisper.

A scared Susie looked back at them and burst into tears.

'Oh my god,' Ron said.

'Ron. Go back to work. I'll look after her. When you've

finished, come and see us. It will be all right if you do the honourable thing. Understand?'

'I mean, I um, I . . .' Ron stammered out his words, his neck flushed with embarrassment.

'Ron. Do as I say. I'll deal with this. Just as you and Jackson have helped me out,' Elenor said and hinted she knew his involvement with Fritz.

Ron pulled Susie to his side.

'I'll come back. I'll stand by you. I promise.'

Susie gave him a smile and Elenor guided her back to the farm.

'It will be fine, Susie. I'm here for you, and Ron is a good man. He'll be true to his word. We'll speak with your parents together. Don't be afraid.'

'I wanted to keep it a secret, but I can't do it alone,' Susie whispered.

'Secrets make heavy burdens, Susie. We'll let this one out. You can stay living here if you want.'

Elenor's head was spinning with the events of the past three weeks. A wedding and a baby might be just the distraction she needed. One thing she was sure of, life was never boring at Tre Lodhen.

CHAPTER 48

'A double wedding?' What a wonderful idea,' Elenor said.

Dottie and Susie stood holding hands in front of her and both looked radiant. Tom and Ron stood to one side discussing an unexploded bomb on one of the beaches.

Telling Susie's parents about the baby wasn't as hard as Ron and Susie had first thought, and after a few tears and a ticking off for Ron, another engagement was announced.

Although she was excited by the happy news from both couples, Elenor still felt vulnerable. A paranoia had set in and no matter which way she turned she couldn't shake it off, and every day she wondered if it was the end for her and Rose. Susie behaved oddly around her since she and Ron announced their marriage, and she wondered if Ron had found out something about Fritz and told her.

Subtle questions posed to Rose gave no clue that anything had changed for her. According to Rose school was a happy place, and all children treated her well – except for Freddie. Freddie poked his tongue out at her for being a girl, but he did it to all the girls.

Elenor went to the calendar and realised it was 20th October, her mother's birthday. She wrote 'Dottie and Susie wedding' in the box marked the 30th. She stood a moment and watched rain drizzle down the windowpane. The bad weather had set in for the day. She saw the cows trudge their way into the barn followed by farmhands encouraging them to walk faster as the weather worsened. The sky darkened as if it was evening.

Looking to the top of the fields Elenor saw a movement followed by the flare of a match. She continued to watch the figure from the kitchen window when a crash of thunder made her jump.

'Thanks for that, as if my nerves aren't bad enough,' she yelled as she stumbled against the scraps pail and dropped her scissors.

When she returned to the window, the figure had gone. Another crash of thunder was followed by a fine fork of lightning and Elenor noticed one or two sheep wandering towards the vegetable plots.

'Now what?' she muttered as she pulled on her wellington boots and raincoat.

Squelching her way through the muddy path Elenor shouted to the workers in the barn to check for more wandering sheep.

'Where the heck is Tom?' she asked Titch who'd wandered out from behind the tithe barn.

'Kissin' the donkey no doubt,' Titch called back.

'Don't be cruel, Titch. Help with the sheep.'

Voices echoed across the fields, all calling for Tom above the wind. Bess hunkered down in one corner and Elenor guided her to round up the sheep.

'Head them into the small pen beside the cottage, we'll gather them up and count heads after we've tracked down Tom,' she called to Titch and three others.

Another movement in the trees caught her attention, and she pointed to them.

'Anyone know who that is? They were there earlier on.'

'I can't see anyone,' said Titch.

Elenor moved closer to the wooded area, but the figure disappeared before her arm was at her side.

'I'm seeing things. Anyone seen Tom yet?'

'Here, Elenor. I'm here.'

Breathless, Tom called down from the right-hand side of the farm, moving five sheep forward.

'Sorry, the boundary fence is broken. Can't think how but it is a right mess. Did you get the others? These wandered into the woods.'

'Yes, in the pen, you'd best go count them and I'll see to the fencing. Send Titch up with equipment to repair the damage.'

After four hours of repair work the fencing was stronger than before. Dottie decided a bull must have trampled through, while Titch reckoned it was an enemy tank. Torrential rain pelted them halfway through the repairs but only Titch complained. One of the mothers offered to collect Rose from school and would walk her back to the farm once the worst of the weather had blown over.

Once home Elenor noticed a small brown envelope sitting on the worktop. There was no name on the front and the only way she was to find out the owner was to open it. She pulled out a scruffy piece of paper with the word LONDON in wonky capital letters scrawled in pencil. She put it to one side in case it belonged to Rose.

Tom gave his three-rap knock on the door and stepped inside.

'All present and correct, Elenor. I take it the fence is ready?'

'It is and thank goodness the sheep are unharmed,' said Elenor.

'Bloody rabbit hunters, I bet they took a shortcut and climbed the fence. I've had to repair after them once before,' said Tom.

'Thanks Tom. Oh, and keep an eye on the top woods, I've a feeling I've got a veggie thief on the prowl.'

By five o'clock the rain had eased to a drizzle and when Elenor had finished mucking out the cattle shed, she decided to fetch Rose for herself. After a few yards of avoiding potholes and large puddles, Elenor saw Susie walking hand in hand with Rose.

'Hello, you two.'

'Susie came to fetch me,' Rose called back, and dropped her hand from Susie's, splashing and skipping to Elenor for a cuddle. The child smelled of fresh air and home baking, and Elenor took a moment to register the smell for the future. She shook off the thought 'just in case.'

'You missed the excitement. We had escaped sheep and had to fetch them home through the mud, then fix the fence. It's been a messy day. You feeling better, Susie?'

Morning sickness weakened Susie, and Elenor did the best she could to cover for her. Dottie knew about the baby, but they dared not mention anything to Titch. She'd a reputation as a village gossip.

'I'm coping,' Susie said.

Rose jumped and skipped ahead, unable to resist puddles, and Elenor blessed the creator of wellington boots.

As they ventured near the door of the farmhouse, Elenor turned to them both.

'Keep a watch from your windows when you can, we have someone after the vegetables,' Elenor said and kicked off her boots, then she noticed their faces frown with concern. 'Nothing to worry about, just shout if you see someone you don't know helping themselves.'

Once inside Susie suggested Rose played 'Here Comes the Bride' on the piano.

'Are you moving back home, Susie?' Elenor asked seeing Susie's bags packed in the corner.

'I think of this as home, but I can't stay,' Susie said and slumped onto the sofa.

'Why? Are you unhappy here?'

Elenor busied herself at the table through the silence of Susie, dreading her reply.

'If you want to go back to your true home, please go. Don't live here if you are homesick, Susie. Gracious, you are only young, we forget that at times.'

'I love this place. I love you both.'

'I feel a *but* coming on, Susie. Please tell me.' Elenor's heart pounded in her chest.

'It's Jackson,' she said.

Elenor stared at her. This was it, the truth was about to come out.

'What do you mean?' asked Elenor, dreading the rest of the conversation.

'He'll have you, Rose, and the farm in his life forever. When the war is over, you will start your own lives here. I've seen the way he looks at you, there's no way that man is going back to Canada,' she said, and Elenor's heart went out to her. She could see by Susie's face that this was the full cause of her anxieties and upset. It had nothing to do with Rose being a German, and she let out a loud sigh of relief.

'Ah, Susie. As I've said, I am in no hurry to marry anyone because of the commitment to the farm. Even if we did marry, you, Ron and the baby would live here with us.'

Susie looked up at her and gave a shy smile.

'No more talk of leaving. Tomorrow I'm going to my mother's grave, would you mind watching over Rose for me, please? Or if it's too much with the sickness wearing you down, I'll wait. Only it will be too muddy for her to work the plots. Plus, I've a feeling she's going to be clinging to your pinny now she's to be your bridesmaid as well as Dottie's.'

Rising to her feet, Susie went to Elenor and kissed her cheek.

'Thank you. You go, I'll be all right. I feel so much better now we've talked.'

Neither of them saw the shadow of Titch on the stairs.

CHAPTER 49

The night had been a quiet one with the weather standing firm against the enemy. All the residents of Tre Lodhen got plenty of sleep and woke in good spirits.

Elenor entered the cemetery and bypassed her father's grave to attend her mother's, clearing her previous offerings.

'Sorry I didn't make it yesterday, Mum. The rains fell heavy. Things are ticking along on the farm, but this war makes life difficult. I have to account for every slice of bacon, and each pint of milk. I've met a man, Mum. You'd like him. He's from Canada, thousands of miles away,' Elenor said and sighed. 'But the war is not in our favour. I've a little girl now, well, not my own, but I'm going to adopt her. She's the dearest little . . .'

Standing and stretching her legs, Elenor looked to the corner of the cemetery wall where she'd spotted a shadow flicker and move behind a tree. Elenor had the feeling she was being watched. She turned back to the grave.

'I have to go now, Mum. I miss you.' Elenor kissed the tips of her fingers and placed her hand onto the headstone, then turned to leave. As she did so, the shadow remained on show. It was a tall male. A spiral of smoke from a cigarette wafted her way, and she upped her pace as she walked the path out of the cemetery. When she reached the exit Elenor kept one eye on the shadow beside a tree on the boundary wall, but it still made no attempt to move.

As she left the entrance, which was formed of two large brick walls, she gave a swift glance along the street and to her surprise, could see nobody there.

'You're seeing things, Elenor Cardew. This has to stop,' she muttered to herself and headed back to the farm. Walking past the green on the edge of the lane she was taken by surprise by a pair of hands which gripped her by the shoulders. With no force her attacker spun her around, but before Elenor had time to scream a pair soft lips smothered any sounds she tried to make. Jackson had come home to her, he was the lurking shadow.

Breathless, she pushed him away.

'You scared me half to death you fool. Have you followed me from the cemetery? I saw someone lingering. I never guessed it was you, it was a creepy shadow,' she said and laughed.

Jackson put his hands in his pocket and bowed his head. He pulled a sorrowful, yet playful face.

'Susie told me you were there. I wanted to surprise you.'

'Come here, you big oaf.'

The walk back to the farm was filled with chatter about the escaped sheep, and Jackson's friend who'd managed to break his arm by sliding from the side of his plane when adding his new wife's initials for good luck. Once inside the gates, Elenor knew Susie must have kept an eye out for them to arrive when they were greeted by an overexcited Rose.

'Jackson!' she yelled and raced into his arms, with Seth yapping around his ankles.

Elenor and Susie watched on with amusement.

'Now that's a fine greeting for a hero,' he said and swung her high.

'You said you weren't a hero,' Rose said.

Jackson put her down on the ground and pulled out a chocolate bar.

'Will this make me one?' he said and gave her a wink.

'Yes. Yes. Can I have a piece now, Elenor? Can I, please?' Rose begged with her hands as if in prayer.

'Make it last more than a day and give Susie a piece,' Elenor said.

'No need,' said Jackson. 'I've brought you all one, even Tom.'

'That's so kind of you, Jackson, thank you,' Susie said, and gave him a kiss on the cheek.

'Don't go making Elenor jealous now,' Jackson said and touched his cheek.

'As if that will happen,' Elenor teased back. 'She's to be a married woman at the end of the month.'

'Ron told me when I saw him the other day. Congratulations. Wonderful news. Tom and Dottie too, so I hear.'

Susie nudged Elenor and inclined her head towards the top of the farm. 'Sorry, don't look now, but I think our vegetable friend is in the woods.'

With a slow movement, Elenor manoeuvred her body for a better view. Sure enough, the figure leaned against a tree.

'Let's go inside, I'll explain there, Jackson,' she said, responding to Jackson's querying frown, and headed to the house.

'We think we have a vegetable thief, taking for the black market or their own gain. It's the second day we know of, they might have been there longer. Tom's not sure whether they might be involved with the escaped sheep business, but we're watching like hawks at the moment.'

Jackson bent and peered through the window.

'Let's leave these two here, Elenor, and take a walk. Show them the area is not for lingering around. Maybe they'll move on if you do it often enough.'

'Good idea. I'll keep Rose here,' Susie said.

'We can fetch the last of the chestnuts and apples, too. Grab a couple of pails, Jackson,' said Elenor.

Bending down picking up windfalls, Elenor and Jackson moved their way slowly across the field. The figure had disappeared and had left no obvious signs of ever being by the trees.

'I think it is a case of us being vigilant. It annoys me when my workers put so much effort into our crops and someone just waltzes in and helps themselves,' Elenor said.

Back at the house, they offloaded their pails to Susie and checked the potato patch. To their horror the crop had been trampled and crushed.

'This must have happened during the lunch break. Someone knows our routine. I hate this feeling of being watched,' Elenor said.

Jackson put his arm around her and gave her a comforting squeeze.

'How can I let Rose roam freely? I'm running out of excuses for keeping her occupied indoors or close to my heels. First it was Fritz, and now this devil.'

'I'll have a word with Ron while I'm here. See if he can do a couple of patrols through the woods. Put off the thief once and for all. We need to get this plot back in order,' Jackson said.

'Oh, Jackson, I don't expect you to spend your time off doing my farm work. The others will be back soon.'

When they returned to the farmhouse, Susie and Rose had left a note saying they'd gone back to Susie's mother's house to collect a few things. Snuggled together after a frantic bout of lovemaking, Elenor broached the subject of Fritz.

'I've heard nothing of him since he was taken. My friend reassured me he would make life a living hell for the man, and I have no reason to doubt him. It's been a while now, and I think you need to move onto adopting Rose. Fritz made a wrong move, and they'll see he makes all the right ones from now on,' Jackson said, and smothered her with kisses until her giggles made her body ache.

'Stop. Stop. I surrender,' she said and climbed from the bed.

Reluctant to leave the comfort of his arms, she pulled her clothes back on, and brushed her hair into a ponytail. His warm breath kissed her neck as he tried to persuade her back under the blankets.

'We must go downstairs. Rose will be back soon, she'll question why we are in bed during the afternoon,' Elenor giggled.

She watched him through the mirror as he walked back to pick up his abandoned clothes. His body was firm and tight, and a tanned upper body hinted at outdoor activities.

How she longed to climb back into the security of his arms, to allow life to drift by in a haze of passion day after day. Snatching at the odd hour once in a while no longer satisfied her, and Elenor became disturbed by her thoughts of the future.

Jackson clasped the buckle of his belt and turned around. His handsome face beamed back at her, and the next thing she knew he was down on one knee. He held out his hand and in the palm nestled a small gold ring.

'Marry me?' he asked. His wide smile reached his eyes and Elenor could do nothing more than smile back. Then the smile dwindled away, and she felt the sinking feeling of how impossible it all was.

Elenor's breath caught in her throat. The day she'd dreamed of had arrived but no excitement gripped her. Her body tensed and she stretched back her shoulders. A heavy ache inside trapped the joy she wanted to feel. Here was the man she loved down on one knee but her stronger self knew she could not accept his proposal.

'I can't marry you, Jackson. I have the farm to run, and Rose to care for. You will return to Canada when the war ends. As much as I'd give anything to be your wife, I cannot burden you with another man's child, and one which is not even my own. It's not fair on you – or your family. You would be hundreds of miles away from them and it would be cruel of me to say yes.'

She kept her voice soft and tried hard to portray her love through her words. The last thing Elenor wanted was to hurt Jackson. Tears teetered on the edge of her lids and she squeezed them back. When she opened her eyes Jackson stood in front of her still holding out the ring.

'We will work this place together. It will give me a purpose in life, Elenor. And as for Rose, we will adopt her, make her ours. I love that kid, she deserves a family life. I ask you again, marry me?'

Elenor reached up and touched his face, she stroked his cheek and he stared into her eyes. She could see hope.

'If I say yes, it comes with conditions.'

'Fire away ma'am.'

Reaching out for his hand she held it in hers.

'I cannot marry you until this war is over. I hate to say the words, but I would not cope as a war widow. Put the ring away, keep it safe and I'll wear it the day they declare peace, that is a promise. Yes, I'll marry you, but not until then. When it is over, we will marry and adopt Rose. We'll make a life for her here. Please say you understand.'

Jackson dropped his hand away and put the ring back into its box. He gave a slow nod of his head.

'I think I understand, although the others have managed to see past the war and become husband and wife. I respect your reasons but understand on the day this war ends I'll ask you again. In the meantime, I'll take a kiss as a consolation prize, Miss Cardew.'

Outside in the yard Seth barked his way to the door, and Rose bowled through armed with a large bag closely followed by Susie also loaded down with bags.

'I've lots of new clothes Elenor. Heaps of them. Susie's mum had a clearout,' Rose said and offloaded her bags onto a seat. She pulled out dresses and cardigans, all the time declaring how she loved each item.

'That's generous of her, Susie,' Elenor said and watched Rose entertain Jackson with a fashion show of sorts.

'I will have a new dress to wear for the wedding, and my birthday, *and* a different one for Christmas,' Rose said and clapped her hands.

'Hey little lady, what will you wear for *my* birthday?' Jackson asked.

'When is your birthday, is it near mine? We can have tea together.' Rose ran to the calendar. 'I'll write it on here, then we'll remember. How old will you be?' she said.

'It's the 19th of December, and I'll be a year older than Elenor. I hope they declare peace for my birthday treat,' he said and winked at Elenor.

CHAPTER 50

'White? You're wearing a white dress?' Titch said with a sneer and pointed at Susie standing in her wedding dress.

'And why shouldn't she?' Dottie asked. 'I'm older and wearing the same colour.'

'Yeh, well, you ain't preggers, are ya?' Titch said.

Susie gasped and put her hand to her mouth. Dottie went to her and put her arm around Susie's waist.

'No, I am not, and you've guessed Susie is and it would be kind of you to keep your unpleasant mouth shut,' Dottie said. 'Your jealousy will not ruin our day.'

'Jealous? What, of a stupid girl caught by a boy with no brain, and a strumped up madam with a bean pole of a fiancé? Na, I'm not jealous – lucky. Lucky 'cos my man is a man.'

Elenor moved from the front room holding Rose's dress in her arms into the kitchen. The dress rehearsal was not going to plan, and yet again, it was thanks to Titch.

'What is going on? Susie, Dottie you look beautiful. Don't they look beautiful, Titch?'

'They look bleedin' ridiculous if you ask me.'

'Titch!' Elenor said and rushed to Susie's side as her lip trembled and tears threatened.

'We are both going to give our friends the best day tomorrow. You will help me get them dressed and help with their hair. I don't know why you are being so mean.'

'Nor me. She says she's got a man but not sure how long he'll hang around,' Dottie said as she tugged her dress over her head.

'A man? I'm sure the girls would love to invite him along tomorrow,' Elenor said and went to help the struggling Dottie.

'Nah, he's away tonight. I'll come and watch the show, though. Need a laugh in this 'ell 'ole.'

'Titch. Rose is upstairs and bless her, she is so excited about the weddings, so please be civil. Girls, I'll take your dresses into my room while Titch apologises.'

As Elenor climbed the stairs she heard a weak apology and a slam of the door. Rose came from her room.

'I don't like her. She's always horrid to me. She asked me to spy on you and Jackson once, and on Ron and Susie. I told her no, but she pulled my hair.'

'Well, she won't be around much longer. I can't have her treating people like she does. She's unhappy here and it's wrong of us to force her to stay. Come along, let's show the girls how pretty their bridesmaid is going to be tomorrow.'

'Keep still, Susie,' her sister said as she put the veil in place.

'Still no sign of Titch?' Dottie asked.

'No, it will be me doing your hair, and I'll try to make a decent job of it,' Elenor said.

'I'd rather it be you, Titch would singe it on purpose.'

Rose scampered out of the bathroom and ran with her hands in the air, twirling in circles around the furniture.

'Someone's excited,' Dottie said.

'I don't think she's bothered,' Elenor said and gave a laugh.

'Shall I put my dress on yet? Is it time?' Rose asked.

'Not yet darling, sit quiet while we get the brides ready.'

By the time Ron's van and Susie's father's car arrived, Elenor was worn out. She pulled her wine outfit on and thought back to the last time she'd worn it – tea with Jackson in Coventry.

They waited a while for Titch, but she was nowhere to be seen and they left without her. Elenor felt it was probably for the best. The girl couldn't keep her jealousy in check and Elenor was in no mood for her spiteful tongue. She'd received a disappointing message from Jackson. He'd sent word he could not make the wedding as his unit were on the move. It frustrated her she did not know where he was going and lived in hope it wasn't back to Canada.

The wedding celebrations went well and helped bring a smile to her face. Dottie and Tom made an odd couple visually, but it was obvious they adored each other. Ron and Susie were nervous but got through their vows leaving Elenor feeling emotional.

By early evening the reception was in full swing in the tithe barn. Elenor told them to make full use of it and those members of their families who were able to attend put on a fine spread. Dottie's parents were everything she expected them to be, and her father was generous with his financial donation towards their honeymoon. Elenor had told Tom to take a week away, and they chose to visit Penzance. No amount of persuading them to leave the county worked. Both insisted on not wanting to travel far. Ron had to return to barracks the following morning, so Susie's parents gave over their house for the wedding night. Susie said they would do without a honeymoon due to the expense. Unlike Titch, she showed no sign of jealousy.

Rose was disappointed the beautiful cake sitting centrepiece on the table was made from cardboard with fake icing. She did forgive the brides when they each gave her a slice of their un-iced boiled fruit cakes made by Elenor.

'They have brandy in, so don't get tiddly,' Elenor said as Rose ate her second slice.

'Titch is tiddly,' Rose said as she chewed.

'She's here?'

Rose pointed across the room to where Titch teetered her way around a group of males. Unsure whether to interrupt, Elenor kept a close eye to ensure Titch did nothing to embarrass Dottie or Susie and upset their day.

When she saw Titch place her hand on the backside of Susie's uncle, Elenor knew it was time to step in and calm her down.

'Titch. You made it. Did you get to see the service?' Elenor said and manoeuvred Titch's arm from its offending position. Not that the uncle appeared to mind or notice.

'Nah. Not one for weddins, just receptions. They're more my style.'

'Did your man make it? What's his name?'

'None of your bizzy,' Titch said and tapped the end of Elenor's nose. Elenor noticed her glassy bloodshot eyes. Titch was more than tiddly.

'I'm heading back with Rose. I take it you will be coming home tonight. We missed you last night.'

'It depends,' Titch said and walked away.

Not wanting to cause a scene, Elenor left Titch, persuaded Rose to say goodnight and headed back to the house.

With the weddings out of the way she could now concentrate on Titch. It was time to lay down stricter ground rules.

'Titch. Titch, are you home?'

Elenor called out and tapped on Titch's bedroom door.

When she didn't get a reply she opened the door and noticed the bed was still made.

'Rose, time to rise and shine, the chickens won't feed themselves. I've got to tend the sheep for Tom.'

A tousle-haired Rose ventured out of her room.

'Ready to eat?'

When they'd finished eating breakfast they set about their outdoor tasks. Rose was joined by several friends and moved onto the coop. Elenor set about the farm delegating jobs and keeping a watch out for Titch. She saw people clearing the tithe barn but Titch was not one of them.

She found one of her farmhands hoeing the plot nearest Tom's cottage and called out to him.

'Do me a favour and watch the flock today. I'm missing Tom, Dottie, and Susie. On top of that, Titch is not around. You haven't seen her, have you?'

'Last I saw of her was staggering over to Tom's place late last night. Bess is waiting by the bottom pasture,' he said.

Elenor pulled a puzzled face and gave him a nod. Someone had let Bess out of her kennel. She walked to Tom's cottage and went to knock on the door. She withdrew her hand and chose to go inside without knocking. If Titch was skiving and sleeping off a hangover she wanted to catch her out.

Once inside she noticed two glasses unwashed by the sink, and a plate of unfinished food.

She ventured to the bottom of the stairs.

'Hello,' she called and stood back waiting for a response.

She didn't have to wait long to know someone was upstairs. The thud of feet moving around also told her there was more than one person.

'Titch. If that is you, you have fifteen minutes to ready yourself for work. Tell your friend to leave now.'

She turned around and went to the door when a male's cough from upstairs stopped her in her tracks. It was followed by muffled whispers.

'Titch. Work. Cattle shed. Now,' Elenor shouted and stormed out of the cottage.

She went to the cattle shed and joined two of the milk-maids. After about forty minutes, Titch arrived.

'I understand you've been lookin' for me,' she said and stood with her hands in her jodhpur pockets.

'I have,' Elenor said and carried on brushing mud from a cow's tail.

'Well I'm here. What d'ya want?'

'A private word. In the house please,' Elenor said and put down her brush. She walked past Titch and out of the barn. 'Now, please.'

Inside the house she stood with her arms folded in front of her and stared at Titch.

'You look a mess. What's got into you? Where were you last night and this morning?'

Titch pulled out a chair and sat down.

'We both know where I've been, and I tell you now. Things are going to change around here.'

Elenor stared at her wide-eyed and unfolded her arms. She stood with her fists clenched not wanting her temper to get the better of her.

'I'm sorry, did I hear you just say what I was about to say? Things *are* going to change around here, Titch. We cannot have this behaviour on the farm.'

'Oh, and what sort of behaviour is that – keeping secrets? Telling lies? Making life hard for others?' Titch said, and her words held a hint of menace.

'What on earth are you talking about?'

'S'for me to know and you to find out, but I tell you now, walls are thin. Right, I'm off for an hour's kip and then I'll finish up outside. See ya.' Titch kicked back the chair and it hit the floor. Elenor stared at it and then at Titch's back as she headed into the hallway. And then paranoia returned. Titch knew something about Fritz and Rose. She'd no doubt slept with one of Ron's wedding guests who'd helped him remove Fritz from the camp. Drink and the promise of a good time had probably loosened his tongue.

Before she could rush after Titch or react in any way, Susie entered the kitchen.

'Well, if it isn't Mrs Susie Braithwaite,' Elenor said gaining control of her nerves.

'Sounds weird hearing you say it out loud,' Susie said.

'Ron's gone back to White Cross I take it?'

'Yes, left an hour ago. It was a lovely day, but I'm happy to get back to normal.'

'Whatever normal might be here at Tre Lodhen,' Elenor said and added a laugh.

Throughout the rest of the day she and Titch danced around each other on the farm. Elenor did not want to have Titch removed without finding out what she knew but was nervous of the outcome of the conversation. Susie kept Rose entertained and by mid-afternoon, Elenor decided to try and visit Ron and rode over to White Cross.

Armed with a story about needing more help on the farm, Elenor was granted permission to speak with him. They stood inside the barrack grounds and Elenor could see POWs tending their own vegetable gardens.

'We keep them busy, even here,' said Ron.

'I don't want to hold you up, but Titch has hinted she knows something about Fritz. I'm sure it's what she meant.' Elenor said and relayed Titch's words to him.

'Sounds like it. But how would she know?'

'I've a feeling someone from the wedding stayed overnight with her in Tom's place.'

'Bloomin' 'eck. One of my lot you mean? It will be one of two. I'll check it out. How's the wife?' he said with a grin.

'She's fine. I'll look after her, don't worry. Thanks for checking, Ron. Titch is trouble and spiteful, I don't trust her. If she can make trouble for us all, she will.'

'She's probably just messin' to get 'erself out of bother. A sly bitch, that's what I think.'

'True enough. See you soon, Ron. Take care.'

The evening finished and once Rose had settled down to a bedtime story, Susie sat knitting a baby cardigan, and Elenor settled down to a basket of darning. 'How does that girl wear so many holes in her socks?' Elenor sighed.

'Titch was quiet tonight. Couldn't wait to get out. Can't say I'm fussed,' said Susie.

Titch had left the farm the moment her meal was finished, and Elenor was grateful she didn't have to sit in her company for too long.

'It's calmer without her around,' Elenor said.

A noise outside the door disturbed Seth, and he gave a low growl.

'The fox is back,' Elenor said and jumped to her feet. She knocked a tin of darning needles to the floor. 'Drat.'

'I'll pick them up, you see to the fox. Or it might just be Titch fooling around. You know how silly she gets at times,' Susie said, and scrabbled around on the floor picking up the needles.

Seth sniffed under the back door, his heckles raised and his teeth bared.

'He knows Titch and wouldn't show his teeth. What on earth has upset you boy? What's going on?' Elenor shoved her feet into her boots as she held his collar. Seth scratched at the door to be let out. 'Wait. What on earth's got into you?'

'I'll come with you,' said Susie, and she pulled on her jacket.

Outside they held onto each other and felt their way across to the hen house. Seth headed off across the fields.

'Strange, he's not interested in the coop. They are very quiet inside, so I don't think there are problems there. It's so dark, there's no moon, and it doesn't make life easy without a lamp.'

A rustle in the trees made Susie jump, and she gripped onto Elenor's arm.

'Owl,' Elenor said just as the white outline scooted from one tree to another.

It gave a hoot and settled down. Silence hit the farm once more.

When they reached the coop, one or two chickens objected to their presence, but there was no sign of the fox, or an attempt to get inside.

'That darn dog is a pest. He hears something and tricks us all into believing him it's worth investigating,' Elenor said as she checked the outer door. 'You head back inside and I'll check the barn. Seth can come with me and I'll leave him out in case our veggie thief is back. Best get back to Rose.'

When she reached the barn, Elenor took a quick look inside and once satisfied all was well, she headed back to the house. She checked on the chickens, and as she left the coop Elenor thought she heard a cough, a deep rasp smothered by a muffled one. The same cough she'd heard in the cottage.

'Ron?' She called out. 'Tom?'

Her stomach flipped. She'd been caught out before.

'Jackson?' His name came as a whisper.

'Jackson, is that you?'

Nothing. Silence. An owl hoot. Then nothing. Elenor stood straining to hear a sound, the hint of another human.

'Elenor. Elenor. Are you out there?' Susie's voice interrupted the silence and Elenor tutted. Straight away she told herself off for her impatience with her caring friend.

'I'm fine, Susie,' she said and walked back to the house. 'I think our vegetable thief is still loitering. I've left Seth outside for the night. Is Rose asleep?'

'Yes, she snuggled down with no argument.'

'Right, well we'd best get some sleep. Tomorrow I want to barbwire the plots. I'll not have folk sneaking around here in the dark. I like to know who my visitors are.'

As she slid inside her bedclothes, Elenor heard Titch come home. She banged around inside the house with no consideration for others. A few minutes later she heard a man's voice. As she thought about going downstairs and telling Titch off for breaking house rules, she heard whispers and the back door click shut. A few seconds later she heard Titch climb the stairs.

CHAPTER 51

Rose's eighth birthday came and went with rationing limiting the celebratory tea. A card arrived with only Coventry written inside, and Elenor put it with the London note. She had a feeling Fritz was still able to communicate his threat. Unsure what to do, she set them aside and kept quiet. They were a reminder of their vulnerability.

November slipped away and December brought cold frosts lasting most of the day, and the ground hardened, making life difficult. Elenor and her workers had pulled the last of the crops for storage and selling. They laboured hard, layering fertilizer and straw from the barns across the soil in readiness for the start of spring.

'With the wire and the manure, our thief will not get a pleasant surprise in the night,' Elenor said.

'If a bomb dropped and destroyed them I'd be annoyed, but to have someone steal them makes me angrier,' Susie said.

Titch blew on her fingers. 'Too bleedin' cold to be doing outside work.'

Elenor and Susie looked at each other and shook their heads.

They walked from the plots to the barn to fetch down storage crates from the rafters.

'Oh look, we have visitors,' Susie said with excitement and ran towards Ron and Jackson striding across the yard.

'Hello you two. Heard Susie baked scones earlier, did you?' Elenor teased, but neither man smiled.

Titch kicked at a stone. 'Well, that's me on me tod for the night then.'

'Not at all, Titch. Stay with us and eat. You keep slipping off alone and you really don't have to, this is your home.'

'Ruddy prison if you ask me,' Titch said and stomped off indoors.

Elenor ignored her and turned her attention to the two men.

'You both look exhausted. Go inside with Susie, I'll be in just as soon as I've fetch a few more of these.' Elenor said and pointed to the crates. She gave Jackson a smile but noticed his was not forthcoming.

'Right you two. What's going on? You've both got faces which carry bad news,' she said and nudged Jackson's arm. 'Inside, this can wait.'

Neither man objected – or spoke. Poker-faced, Ron looked from his wife to Elenor.

'We're the bearers of bad news I'm afraid, Elenor,' he said.

Jackson went to her and took her hands.

'Where's Rose?' he asked.

'At school. She's another hour. Why, what's wrong Jackson? You are worrying me, both of you. What's the bad news?'

Ron looked to Jackson and came to what appeared to be a silent agreement that Jackson would do the talking.

'It's Fritz. He's escaped from the camp.' Jackson held up his hands as if in surrender. 'I know, I own up, I thought he'd never be able to get away. White Cross were informed in case he returned to assist a breakout here. Ron got the

363

news and contacted me straight away. I'm here to warn you and then I have to get back to my unit.'

'The POW who threatened you, Elenor? Ron told me about what he did,' Susie said.

Ron stood, nodding his head with a scowl on his face.

'Ron, take Susie for a walk. I'll fill Elenor in with what we know, and what she needs to do,' Jackson said and opened the back door. Ron wasted no time.

'Come on, we'll patrol the woods,' he said and gave Susie a wink.

'Be'ave, my lover,' Susie said, exaggerating her accent, and gave him a playful tap on the shoulder and pulled on her coat.

'Escaped POW? Now there's a worry for ya,' Titch's voice interrupted their conversation. Elenor bit her lip, she'd forgotten Titch was upstairs.

'Yes. He attacked Elenor, so we must be careful. You be careful, all that wandering around at night alone,' Susie said.

Titch threw up her hands in a sarcastic swoop and waved them around.

'Cor blimey, married for five minutes and she's treatin' me like 'er kid. If it's all right with you, *Ma*, I'm goin' for a gander to the village. Bit cramped here for me.'

Jackson waited for the three of them to leave before he spoke again.

'Fritz told anyone who'd listen about Rose. It appears he boasted about working with spies, and he knows of their child, a German hidden by an English woman,' Jackson took a deep breath. 'Most told him he was a fool, a dreamer, but a couple of guards started to ask questions.'

Elenor gasped and allowed Jackson to take her in his arms.

'It won't be long before they start taking things seriously.

Oh Jackson, what shall I do? They can't take her from me, they can't. And Fritz, do you think he's here? I wonder if he's the one we think is our thief. Someone was here last night. I think Titch has something to do with it as well.' Elenor started to pace around the floor. 'I must think. Maybe get away, take Rose somewhere else. Back to Coventry? No, no, there's nothing there for us. Maybe Mrs Green, perhaps I could . . .'

'Stop. Slow down, Elenor. We don't know who believes him, and now he's on the run they'll probably brush what he said aside. Keep calm. I'll find out what I can and get back to you with news. Ron felt you should know, I wasn't sure at first, but honey, we must keep the secret to protect Rose, so stay strong for her. Titch is all hot air. Trust me.'

'Oh, I do Jackson, with my life,' Elenor said and kissed his lips with such fierceness, he pulled back. 'But someone has sent notes, only with London and Coventry written on them, but I'm sure they are from Fritz.'

'I'll look into it but I have to go, Elenor. Remain calm and give this to Rose for Christmas. It's my version of a totem pole. Tell her about them, this is my story. It has a rose and a heart, along with a maple leaf. She's my English Rose, the leaf is native to my country, and you are my heart, you are all part of my story Elenor. We will get through this together. '

'I'm afraid I'll lose you,' Elenor said with throaty emotion. Her tears flowed freely, and an overwhelming darkness gripped her thoughts.

With a gentle easing of her fingers from his arm, Jackson released her hold and Elenor stepped to one side. Jackson walked to the door but stopped and took a step back to her. He pulled her turban scarf away from her head and raked his fingers through her hair. It tugged but

Elenor never complained, she felt his love in the way he held her. He cupped her face in his hands and kissed her again. His final gesture was a gentle stroke of his thumb across her cheek. Neither spoke as he walked away. Elenor heard him call for Ron, and the click of their boots as they walked across the yard. She listened for the gate to click shut, and for Susie to come back indoors.

Christmas and New Year held no excitement for her, but she had to pretend for the sake of the others. She was grateful to Jackson for telling her about the German, but she wondered if she'd been better off not knowing he now wandered the English countryside posing a threat to all she held dear. Word in the village was that a brother and sister in their late sixties were reporting people for minor rule-breaking acts. Elenor often shivered when she walked past their home knowing they would relish the opportunity to be the ones ousting out protectors of the enemy. If ever they heard of Rose's bloodline they would waste little time telling all who came into contact with them.

Susie banged around the kitchen, in an obviously lovesick mood. With Rose due home from school the atmosphere in the home needed lifting.

'Well, at least we can assume we know who is sneaking around at night. He'll get more than he bargained for soon. I've a new bull arriving and am going to convert the top field into his grazing ground. Let's see old Fritz get by the master of the farm when he arrives.' Elenor gave a forced laugh.

CHAPTER 52

Rose came home from school and announced she was to be an angel in the school Christmas play. Everyone was astounded when Titch arrived home with a contribution, but no one dared ask how she'd come by them. Rose's joy on seeing the parachute material with white feathers from an old feather boa brought smiles to everyone in the room. Tom and Dottie were dragged from the pasture to see her model it on the kitchen table, and Elenor insisted Tom stir the Christmas pudding and make a wish.

'The wishes must all be the same in puddings around the country – the world, now,' he said.

'He's right. I bet our wishes are all similar to each other's,' Susie said through a mouthful of pins.

December had nudged its way into the end of the year with America mourning the attack on Pearl Harbour.

'This will mean the Americans will be at war with them, then,' Susie said when it was first announced.

'No doubt. I wonder if it will affect us in any way,' Elenor said. Her words were more of a statement than a question. 'Thank goodness for our Commonwealth companions'.

'You would say that, bein' in love with a Canadian.

I 'ope to see a bit of action when the boys from the USA arrive. 'Eard they're loaded,' Titch said as she stitched feathers onto wire wings.

Although wary of Titch's sudden interest in Rose's outfit and the way she was now working harder than ever, Elenor was grateful for her help and tried to be friendly.

'What will your man say if you run off with one? You can't leave him heartbroken, Titch.'

''Ere she goes, lookin' at life through rosy specs,' Titch said and gave a laugh.

'I'll shut up. You find your rich American, and the world will be perfect,' Elenor said with jovial banter. She had no reason to believe Titch wouldn't get her rich American, she appeared to have the knack of getting her own way.

Jackson's birthday came and went, only marked by Hitler taking command of his army, and a few days later the postman delivered the Christmas mail.

Elenor held the small pile of post in her hands and placed them into orderly piles. Official letters and Christmas cards addressed to her and Rose, and cards for the others.

One official envelope was from her solicitor. He informed her Rose was now registered as an orphan with no traceable immediate family. A second paper declared Elenor as the official guardian of Rose Sherbourne, parents deceased. If all went their way it would be formal by the summer. Elenor was confident the only barrier was Fritz. The summer could not come soon enough. Once the papers were signed and Rose was her child, he would have no grounds for spreading rumours or creating problems.

She tore open more letters from various ministries and then made a start on a few Christmas cards.

'Rose, your turn, open these,' Elenor said and handed an excited Rose a small pile of cards.

'Ooh, this is a pretty one. Look, a robin in the snow.'

'Very pretty. It's from Mrs Green. See if you can read the next one yourself,' said Elenor.

'Ah, a pretty angel, look Elenor. Oh, there's just three words inside. Music, London, Coventry. How silly.'

'Silly. A joke from someone. Could you fetch my cardigan please?'

Once Rose was out of the room, Elenor pulled Susie to one side.

'I think it is from Fritz.'

Susie stared at her. 'Why on earth would you think that? How could he send a card?'

Elenor gave a small smile. 'You're right, of course. I'm letting my mind run away with me.'

'I've found it.' Rose sang out as she rushed back into the room.

'Thank you. I think the card is from Sally's dad. You keep opening them while I write to Jackson.'

Elenor walked to the parlour and hid the card on the desk.

She pulled out a sheet of writing paper and penned a letter to Jackson.

Dearest J,

I hope this letter finds you well. Rose is counting days until we see you again.

All went well with the solicitor and I intend to speak with Rose once Christmas is over. It has occurred to me she might not want to be my daughter. She's had parents and may feel it disrespectful to their memory. I have so much to consider about our future together. I also spoke with Tom and Dottie, and they have agreed to become her guardians if anything should happen to me. If it does Jackson, know I love you and please watch over my girl.

She is to be an angel in the school nativity play on Christmas Eve. Even Titch has got involved with making the outfit. She gave us the material. Very cooperative nowadays but I don't trust her.

So far, and I am touching wood, there has been no sighting of our friend, Fred. I can only assume he no longer needs vegetables. He did send us a Christmas card though.

Stay safe my darling. I miss you so very much.

E x

Sealing the envelope with a kiss, she went through into the kitchen.

'All done. Now I've brawn to prepare, and tongue to press for Christmas.'

'I'm off out. I ain't 'angin' around to watch that, got betta things to do. Catcha later,' Titch said and pulled on her outside clothing.

'Be careful, remember,' Elenor said as the door clicked shut.

'I bet she's seeing a married man. She's so secretive about him,' Susie said.

'Wouldn't surprise me in the least,' replied Elenor.

1942

CHAPTER 53

Elenor battled through the rain and wind into the village with her arm looped through Jackson's. Christmas was long forgotten but today was his opportunity to celebrate with them, albeit seven weeks late. They went to collect Rose from school together.

'She'll be so happy to see you, Jackson.'

Sure enough, Rose ran into his arms with such excitement Elenor had to calm her down.

'Let's get him home and dry, Rose. Jackson's tired and needs quiet, so we are going to enjoy a family feast. We have a lot to celebrate.'

When they got back to the farm Elenor pushed open the back door and Susie stood staring at them, her eyes wide.

'Are you feeling all right, Susie? The baby. You look pale,' Elenor said and went to go to her side.

Susie flicked her eyes towards the bathroom and in the shadows of the kitchen Elenor could see Fritz. She shuffled backwards out of view and turned around to face Jackson making a play of pulling off Rose's boots.

'Take Rose to Tom and Dottie. Say nothing, get help. He's here. I'll keep him occupied, go!' she whispered, while pushing him backwards out of the door. She held her finger to her lips.

'I'm not feeling well, Elenor. Maybe a cold,' Susie said to cover the sounds of Jackson and Rose shuffling out of the doorway.

Jackson nodded to Elenor, told Rose to be quiet as Susie was sick, and stepped away as quietly as his boots would allow. Elenor made a great pretence of banging mud from her own boots to cover the sound.

'I'm sorry to hear that. We can't have you ill. Maybe you should return to your mother for a bit of home comfort. I can manage here,' Elenor chattered on and made a fuss of hanging up her coat, all the time trying to judge when Fritz would make his appearance.

'I'm starving. Bread and cheese will go down nicely. Want some?'

Susie shook her head.

'Sit down and rest,' Elenor said.

When she clicked the door shut Fritz moved fast from his hiding corner.

'You are alone. Where is the child?' he asked.

Making no surprise sounds or movements, Elenor walked to the table.

'Fritz. You look tired and hungry. Join us,' she said, gripping her hands against her hips to stop them trembling.

'I've come for the child.' he said, his voice low.

'What do you want with her? What's he on about, Elenor? And how long has he spoken English?' Susie looked from one to the other.

Elenor shook her head. 'I've no idea,' she said and pointed to the food. 'Eat. We know you've run away, Fritz. And you've been hiding in the woods. I could have reported it to the authorities, but I know you mean us no harm. Rose is due home later, so rest up and you can hear her play the piano before she goes to bed.'

She glared at him, trying to communicate with her eyes that Susie had no idea about their secret. His shone back with realisation.

'I am here to take her back to Germany.'

His words hung in the air and felt heavier and more threatening than any bomb.

Swivelling around to face him, Susie held out the bread knife. 'Over my dead body,' she shouted.

Elenor saw Fritz make a move forward, and she held up her hand.

'Susie. Calm down, put the knife down and let's eat. Fritz, sit.'

She rushed to the dresser and pulled down plates, then grabbed the food. To her relief, he sat down. She pushed food in front of him and he snatched it up and crammed it in his mouth.

Nudging a frightened Susie to the end of the table, away from him, Elenor pushed a sandwich towards her.

'Eat up, Susie,' she said in an over the top cheery voice. 'I'm famished. It's hard work running the farm. What did you used to do before the war, Fritz?'

He continued to eat and said nothing. His eyes flicked around the kitchen in nervous anticipation.

'Do you have a child? It is important children are protected during times of war. After all, not everyone believes in fighting it out,' Elenor chattered nonstop whilst he ate. 'I'm sure you must worry. It would worry you if someone broke into your home and threatened to take your child to another country. You say take Rose back, yet she has never been. Just because you miss your child doesn't mean you can take mine.'

Fritz stopped eating. His face twisted into a raged

expression. Elenor could see his temper rise and her heart pounded against her ribcage.

'She is not yours. She is a daughter of Deutschland.'

'He's crazy, Elenor. Call the guards.' Susie's voice raised a few octaves.

Worried about Susie, Elenor spoke to Fritz.

'Susie's going to sit in the parlour. She is pregnant. Food makes her sick.'

'She stays here,' Fritz said.

Taking a sneak glance at her watch Elenor knew it would not be long before help arrived.

'How about she sits in the parlour? She can listen to the wireless.'

Susie pushed back her chair.

'Go. We will hear Germany has defeated you, then I will choose my room,' Fritz cackled out a laugh before cramming more food into his mouth. Elenor shuddered and put her hand into her overall pocket. She checked the small knife she'd hidden away was still there.

For the longest ten minutes she'd ever known, Elenor sat making small talk whilst Fritz ate their week's rations. She gave him a half bottle of brandy and he gulped it down.

'Seems to be a lot of activity on the front lines, Elenor,' Susie called out, and then entered the kitchen. 'All in our favour at the moment,' she said and moved to the sink in the pretence of washing her hands.

'That's good. Oh, hear Seth, the chickens are teasing him again. Let him in, Susie – have more cheese, Fritz.' Elenor pushed a plate of meat and cheese towards Fritz distracting him from Susie running to the door. She pulled it open and stepped outside. With what appeared to be one movement, Jackson and five soldiers entered the room and rushed to Fritz. He gave a shout and tried to push the table over but the heavy pine proved too much of a barrier for him.

'The child is a German. Her parents are spies. German blood.' He ranted and raved out the words as the soldiers tackled him to the ground and bound him.

'Why is he so obsessed with Rose and saying she's German?' Susie asked.

She stood with her hands on her hips while she watched him being manhandled away to a truck.

'He seems convinced she is German, and what was he on about, her parents are spies? Elenor, is there something I should know? What is going on?' Susie's voice became louder as she demanded a response from Elenor.

Jackson went to her. 'The man is drunk,' he said.

'No. I am sorry Jackson, but you weren't here. Elenor's hiding something.'

Both Elenor and Jackson stared at her. Susie had never shown any sign of having a temper, but she gave off a mood which gave Elenor great concern. Suspicion had set in, and it would take a lot of skill to distract her away from the truth.

'It's all very confusing, Susie. The man's clearly homesick and missing his child. Look how he said he wanted to take Rose back to Germany when she's never been,' Elenor said, keeping her voice calm and soft.

'Ah, but how do I know that? We are told to keep our ears and eyes open, and that man seemed clear enough in what he said. His English is perfect. You didn't blink an eye when he spoke it, Elenor. You are not telling me the truth. Something's not right.'

Susie continued to stare and kept her hands on her hips. Elenor's nerves jarred as she tried to keep control.

'Did the soldiers look concerned? Are there any out there waiting to take Rose – or me – away? No. They didn't take his rantings as fact or serious. Just calm down, Susie. We're both shaken up by what has happened,' Elenor said and went to her friend. She put out her hand, but Susie pushed hers into her overall pockets.

'Maybe you're right, I'm being hysterical. But I do find it a bit odd he's become obsessed. When he broke in, he said he'd come to return property belonging to the rich or something.'

'Reich,' said Jackson. He stood by the door, and Elenor wondered if it was to prevent Susie from running before she'd calmed down. 'It's a word like an empire.'

'Rose belongs to an empire?' Susie said with a frown. 'What, she's a princess? A German princess?'

Jackson gave a loud sigh of impatience and Elenor held her breath. Susie glared at him.

'What was that for, you think I'm ignorant or silly? I tell you that German seemed pretty convincing to me. I think you need to explain yourself, Elenor. Who is Rose? Where are her parents? The Canadian's in on this too?'

'Right! That's it,' Elenor shouted and banged the table.

Susie flinched, and Jackson stood upright with shock.

'If the Germans haven't won the war yet, they soon will if this is how we are to behave. We'll be at each other's throats with them sowing seeds of suspicion. We are not spies, Rose is not the daughter of spies, and any doubt you've had is propaganda tosh brought through the door by a violent criminal. Jeepers, Susie, you've known us long enough. Why are you more convinced by him – a stranger – than by us your closest friends?'

A loud sob burst from Susie and Jackson turned to comfort her. Elenor let him guide the girl across the room and then she put her arms around her.

'It's going to be fine, Susie. You were brave and scared. I'm sorry I shouted. Now we must get back under control before Rose returns. We are her rock, all she has in life. We cannot crumble.'

Susie stepped away from Elenor.

'I'm fine. You're right, we have to stop bickering and being suspicious. It's the shock.'

'I'll go and fetch Rose from Tom's, and then we'll settle down a bit more. We're all in shock, but I think Tom might be more so with Rose landing on his doorstep,' Elenor said and added a light laugh to lift the tense atmosphere.

CHAPTER 54

Tension in the home was something Elenor disliked and that evening Titch brought more when she heard about Fritz. Dottie tried to lighten the atmosphere, but in the end she went back to the cottage. Titch continued to pester and badger Elenor.

'Why did 'e want Rose? Is she 'is? What's so special about 'er?' she asked Elenor. With Rose playing in the front room, Elenor didn't want to continue the conversation.

'It is all a misunderstanding,' she said.

'Strange that, 'cos I think I understand well enuff.'

'What do you mean, Titch?' Susie asked.

'I mean, there is something dodgy goin' on. Are you German?' Titch said and turned to Elenor.

Elenor burst out laughing. 'Really? You think I'm German and am hiding a German POW's daughter. Give me strength. I'm a Cornish farmer with more on my shoulders than I'd like.'

'Nah. There's something. I'll find out, trust me.'

'I'll try,' said Elenor with sarcasm. 'But trust *me*, there is nothing dodgy about me or Rose.'

'So you say,' Titch muttered. 'I'm off out. Not sure I want to be around a Jerry lover.'

'Take that back!' Elenor shouted.

'Ah, now there's a guilty answer if ever I heard one.'

'I think it's time you left Tre Lodhen. I'll make a call and you won't have to live in fear any longer,' Elenor said with angry passion.

'Suits me. But don't think I'm done 'ere. I know there's more than you're lettin' on.'

Elenor turned and left the room. She sat on her bed trying to calm down. Titch's mean streak was back and Elenor had a feeling bribery would follow.

Jackson sent word he'd managed to get a forty-eight-hour pass, and tickets for the local Valentine's dance. Elenor was excited but at the same time her nerves failed her. She'd convinced herself that Titch was spreading rumours. Susie said her mother had mentioned something about Rose's parentage after Titch had planted the seed that Rose might be Elenor's, and her father a German teacher from Coventry. Susie had quashed the story as a jealous fantasy and explained about Fritz hiding on the farm. She hinted that Titch had also accused Elenor of hiding his child. Susie's mother had scoffed at the accusations and things settled down, but the situation made Elenor uncomfortable.

Jackson offered his and his sister's help. He convinced Elenor his sister was more than capable of giving Rose a good life in Canada, if they needed to get her to safety. It worried Elenor she should have to think along those lines but agreed it would be ideal and they'd discuss it before his leave was finished.

'Elenor, are you there?' Rose called through Elenor's bedroom door.

'Yes darling, I am. Come in. Let me see your dress.'

Jackson and Elenor promised Rose she could join them at the dance. They agreed two hours' dancing and home by nine. If Elenor hadn't felt the need to keep things relatively normal, she'd have stayed at home. However, they wanted tonight to be special. All papers were prepared and ready to be signed for Rose's adoption, and she wanted to talk with her about it after the dance. Elenor had signed so many papers that day, her head was in a spin.

'Oh my word. You will be the prettiest girl in the room.' Elenor clapped her hands and made Rose give a twirl in a pretty pink dress with daisies around the neck.

Her own dress was the one she'd worn for many of the village dances, and Jackson always said it brought out the colour in her cheeks. She considered it her favourite dress as when she wore it she always shared special moments with him.

Susie had chosen to dress at her mother's house, and Elenor suspected it was down to Titch tiring them both out with her sly comments.

A beep of a horn alerted them Jackson was waiting and Rose whooped with glee.

'Hurry Elenor, come on. Are you going to sing tonight?'

'No, not tonight. Remember, two hours and we are home.'

Once they were through the village hall door, Rose raced to meet with her friends.

Elenor and Jackson joined Susie and Ron across the opposite side of the hall. Ron encouraged them closer as he spoke above the music.

'Watch out for Titch. Dottie and Tom are with her now. She's drunk and blabbin' on about Fritz, and Rose being 'is daughter. Most folk are laughing it off, but you know what some of them are like round 'ere. Susie's worryin' herself silly.'

Jackson squeezed Elenor's hand.

'We'll ignore it and as you say, she's drunk.'

'I'll go out and see what's happening. You stay here,'

382

Ron said. Elenor and Jackson kept Susie company, re-assuring her all was well. Ron returned a few minutes later.

'Tom and Dottie have taken her back to theirs. She's in no fit state to be out and about.'

'Oh, no. What a shame. They'll miss the dance,' Elenor said.

'Dottie's instructions are you should stay here and enjoy the evening. She won't take no for an answer.'

'In which case I will look for a girl to dance with,' Jackson said and made a pretence of looking around the room.

'Oh, here's a girl for you. Your Valentine for the evening,' Elenor said as Rose skipped towards them.

'Freddie said he's my Valentine, but I told him to go away 'cos he's a silly boy,' Rose said.

'Come on my sweet Valentine girl, come dance with me,' Jackson said and scooped Rose into his arms.

As Susie and Ron took to the floor, Elenor looked around the room and noticed a small cluster of women looking her way. They whispered behind their hands. The gossip had spread. She headed over to the group.

'It's a good turn out, and the fundraising for the troops is such a good idea,' she said.

'For *our* troops, yes,' one woman said, and her insinuation was not lost on Elenor.

'You need to be careful keeping those POW sorts on your farm. It doesn't pay to be friends with the enemy.'

Shocked by their words Elenor gained control and smiled.

'Ah, but our lads keep a close eye on them for me. We have nothing to worry about other than a gossiping drunk who can't find a husband. She's a handful and loves to spread rumours. She talks about local women having affairs when their husbands are away fighting, but we all know it's fabrication.'

Elenor held onto hope the small snippet of gossip she'd heard in the post office about the woman who'd challenged her was true and going by her face, Elenor had struck lucky.

'Oh, I do understand, Elenor. But we can't be too careful nowadays. Your farm has a wonderful reputation, but you are open to gossip and we can't control who has already heard it.' The woman glanced at the brother and sister who'd report their own family. They'd call the authorities and rally up a lynch mob.

At that moment, Elenor knew her days in Summercourt were numbered. For Rose's safety it was time to leave Tre Lodhen.

CHAPTER 55

Back at the farm they called in to see Dottie and Tom. Titch was asleep in their spare room.

'She's gunning for you two. I'm convinced she's had a nervous breakdown,' said Dottie. 'She was rambling on about her and Fritz being lovers. She's dangerous with that tongue. Anyone who'd listen got told her bit of gossip.'

'We'll keep her here overnight and sort it tomorrow. Did you enjoy the dance, Rose?' said Tom.

Rose relayed her evening and entertained everyone with stories of boys chasing her for a Valentine's kiss. She ended her story with 'all boys are silly'.

When they got back to the house they settled in the parlour. The fire glowed and a sense of peace washed over Elenor. She and Jackson curled up on the couch with Rose performing dance moves she'd learned that evening.

'Am I silly, Rose?' Jackson asked in a serious voice.

Rose stopped skipping around and looked at him with her head to one side. Her rosebud mouth pursed in thought.

'No, you can't be silly. You fly a plane and say big words. You only kiss Elenor, not all the girls like Freddy.'

Elenor fought to hold back her laughter.

'Rose. How would you feel about having Jackson as your daddy?' she asked.

'Really? Like a proper daddy?' Rose said and rocked the toe of her foot back and forth, deep in thought.

'That's right little lady, like a proper daddy,' Jackson said.

With a slow deliberate movement, Rose approached him and clambered onto his knee.

'I can't 'cos we haven't got a mummy,' she said in a loud whisper.

'Ah, that's not entirely true, Rose. I'll let you into a secret only Dottie and Tom know. Elenor and I got married this morning. We wanted to surprise you. Elenor is Mrs St John. Would you like to become Rose St John? Would you like to live in Canada with us and be a proper family?'

Struggling free from his arms, Rose stood in front of Elenor and looked her up and down. 'Did you get married in that dress?' she demanded, and Elenor tried not to smile at her serious face.

'She sure did, and doesn't she look very much the bride?' Jackson said.

Rose gave an exaggerated swipe of her hand across her brow.

'Phew, at least she didn't wear her overalls and that turban. Where's your ring?'

Elenor could no longer hold back the laughter, and let Jackson slip on her hidden rings and held out her arms to Rose.

'Darling girl, you are my world. Please, can I be your mummy? Can we sail away on a big ship with a new daddy and live in a big new country? All we have to do is sign a paper to make it official. We'd be honoured if you did. It would be the most wonderful thing in our lives, Rose,' Elenor said and Jackson nodded in agreement. She saw the teardrops glistening on his dark lashes.

'Yes please,' Rose's voice was so soft, and her eyes so full of wonderment, Elenor's heart swelled with love.

'You said yes, you'll be our daughter? Well, I think that is better than getting married to Elenor,' Jackson said and lifted her high. He kissed her cheeks, and she squealed for him to stop being so soppy.

Once her feet were back on the ground, she went to Elenor and the two embraced until Rose fell asleep in her arms.

From the moment Rose said yes things moved fast for Elenor and Jackson. He arranged for papers to allow Elenor and Rose to enter Canada and telephoned his family with the news.

Elenor asked Dottie and Tom to move into the farmhouse and run Tre Lodhen, and Susie and Ron were given the cottage. Tom was approached by Joe, who was concerned farm goods were being sold by one of the rabbit catchers. It appeared he – and others – received them from Titch in exchange for money. Elenor reported Titch for theft. All protests of Rose being a German were ignored as the rantings of a guilty woman.

Their friends insisted on holding a farewell party and invited what seemed like the whole village. Only a few accepted, confirming that not everyone thought Elenor innocent.

Leaving day arrived and before Elenor knew it, the three of them were on a train heading for the port. Elenor held her nerves together, but as they stood on the dockside, she floundered.

Jackson's arms reassured her, and his kisses burned a fire in her belly so fierce she ached with love for him.

Rose's hand felt tiny in hers as they walked the gangway onto the ship. Leaving England was a hard decision, but one Elenor knew would keep Rose safe.

The man who'd taken them on as a couple stood beside them and Elenor's heart swelled with pride. She wanted to tell the world of a Canadian hero who'd saved an orphan, her hero and the man she had fallen deeply in love with. But Elenor knew she never would. Some things were best left a secret.

ACKNOWLEDGEMENTS

My thanks to Charlotte Ledger, Editorial Director of HarperImpulse, for having faith in me, and for co-ordinating the best team ever to guide me through to publication.

To my wonderful family and friends, thanks for reminding me how much I can achieve with you at my side.

To my readers, without you I am nothing. Thank you for your support.

Special thanks go to authors: Talli Roland, Terri Nixon, Esther Chilton, Debbie (Jonty) Johnston, and David Evans. Also to Kate Nash of the Kate Nash Literary Agency, and Lucie Wheeler for inviting me along to her book launch in September 2017, and unknowingly setting the wheels in motion for Charlotte and I to fall into fate's plans and bring this book into the world.

Last, but by no means least, to the Poppy Sellers of Vancouver. Thank you for reminding me about the allies who'd fought alongside Britain during WW2. When I visited the city in 2017, you inspired a fictional Canadian pilot, and he features in this novel.

LOVE BOOKS?

So do we! And we love nothing more than chatting about our books with you lovely readers.

If you'd like to find out about our latest titles, as well as exclusive competitions, author interviews, offers and lots more, join us on our Facebook page! Why not leave a note on our wall to tell us what you thought of this book or what you'd like to see us publish more of?

f /HarperImpulse

You can also tweet us 🐦@harperimpulse and see exclusively behind the scenes on our Instagram page www.instagram.com/harperimpulse

To be the first to know about upcoming books and events, sign up to our newsletter at: http://www.harperimpulseromance.com/

HELP US SHARE THE LOVE!

If you love this wonderful book as much as we do then please share your reviews online.

Leaving reviews makes a huge difference and helps our books reach even more readers.

So get reviewing and sharing, we want to hear what you think!

Love, HarperImpulse x

Please leave your reviews online!

amazon.co.uk   kobo   goodreads   Lovereading   iBooks

And on social!

f/HarperImpulse   y@harperimpulse
@HarperImpulse